9. 00

The
Tempest

Also by James Lilliefors

The Psalmist
The Leviathan Effect
Viral

The Tempest

A Bowers and Hunter Mystery

JAMES LILLIEFORS

WITNESS

An Imprint of HarperCollins*Publishers*

HarperCollins books may be purchased for educational, business, or sales promotional use. For information, please e-mail the Special Markets Department at SPSales@harpercollins.com.

FIRST EDITION

Designed by Diahann Sturge

ISBN 978-0-06-234972-9

15 16 17 18 19   OV/RRD   10 9 8 7 6 5 4 3 2 1

For Janet

And the wind ceased and there was a great calm.
—MARK 4:39

Prologue

Spring

Miracles. What can I tell you? In a skeptical world, if a real miracle occurred, it wouldn't even make the evening news. Who would believe it? This one, though, will be different. This one, the skeptics won't be able to explain. People will want to see for themselves; they'll line up around the block to have a look. That's what we need to talk about."

Walter Kepler watched his attorney's own skepticism harden slightly as he waited on the details of Kepler's plan. Jacob Weber was used to this, to Kepler's Barnum-like enthusiasm as he introduced a new idea. Weber had precise, dark eyes, a narrow face, bristly white hair cut close to the scalp. Seen from behind, he could appear as small and fragile as a child. But he also possessed that rarest of human qualities—consistent good judgment: unerringly good, in Kepler's estimation.

As presented, Kepler's plan consisted of three parts: A sells a painting to B; B sells the painting to C; and C (who was Kepler) uses the painting to bring about a "miracle." The first two parts of the plan he would handle himself, with the assistance of Nicholas Champlain and, of course, Belasco. It was for the third part that he needed Jacob Weber's help—needed his judgment, and, ultimately, his skills as a negotiator.

Kepler had been formulating versions of this plan in his head since he was a boy, trailing his father through the great art museums of the Northeast and Europe, stopping to stare at some painting or sculpture that, his father insisted, was not only an important work but also a masterpiece. With time, Kepler had learned to tell the difference, to understand why certain paintings—like certain people, and ideas—held greater intrinsic value than others. He had spent much of his adult life refining that understanding, through the storms of sudden wealth, divorce, and the more mundane trials of daily living.

When he finished telling Weber his plan, Kepler turned the conversation to the painting. He watched Weber's face flush with a new interest as he described the masterpiece that had dominated his thoughts for the past three weeks, ever since he'd ascertained that it was the real thing. *The Tempest.* Fourteen men trapped on a boat. Each responds differently to a life-threatening storm: one trying valiantly to fix the main sail, another cowering in terror from the waves, one calmly steering the rudder. Fourteen men, fourteen reactions. Kepler imagined how his attorney would react once the waters began to churn in another several months.

Then Kepler sat back and let Jacob Weber voice his concerns. They were much as he had expected—candid, well-reasoned, occasionally surprising. Kepler managed to fend off most; those he couldn't, he stored away.

"So what are we looking at?" his attorney asked. "When would it need to happen?"

Kepler glanced at Weber's right hand, absently tracing the stem of the coffee cup. It was a pleasant April morning, the Bay shivering with whitecaps.

"Late summer," he said. "August, I'm thinking."

His attorney thought about that, showing no expression. Calculating how the plan would interrupt and impact his own life, no doubt. Jacob Weber finally closed and opened his eyes. He nodded. "It's doable," he said. After a thoughtful pause, he added, "Actually, I kind of like it."

Weber's response would have sounded lukewarm to an outsider. To Kepler, it was a hearty endorsement. In fact, he had never known Jacob Weber to be quite so enthusiastic about one of his ideas. All in all, it was a very good start.

PART 1

Deadly Bluff

A painting is complete when it has the shadows of a god.

—Rembrandt van Rijn

Summer is only the unfulfilled promise of spring, a charlatan in place of the warm balmy nights I dream of in April.

—F. Scott Fitzgerald, *This Side of Paradise*

Chapter One

Not all mysteries are meant to be solved, and Susan Champlain, it seemed, would be one of those that wasn't—an unknowable visitor who came in like the heat of summer, left impressions as tangible as sunburns, and then slipped away into the cooler air of September.

That was how Luke Bowers figured it, anyway.

But on the afternoon of July 30, the fifth Tuesday of the year's warmest month, the mystery of Susan Champlain became more complicated. And the next day, it turned deadly.

Susan Champlain was one of the summer people, who came to Tidewater County for its informality, for the boating, the steamed crabs, the long breezy evenings. The summer people were part of the transformation that Tidewater went through every June, when the quieter instruments of its nature—the wash of wind through the marsh grasses, the clangs of harbor buoys, the honks of Canada geese—gave way to the cacophony of tourism. Summer people tended to come in two varieties—the regulars, who owned vacation homes or condos, and the short-termers, who visited for a week or a weekend, some just for the day.

But Susan Champlain, who had arrived with her husband in early June, didn't fit neatly into either category. The Champlains were renting the old Victorian place at Cooper's Point for the summer, and were so private that no one knew who they were or what their connection, if any, was to Tidewater County. Uneasy with such a dearth of information, some locals did what people do in that situation: they invented stories. One that Luke had heard told several times now was that Nicholas Champlain, a construction contractor whose business was based in the Philadelphia area, had been relocated to Tidewater under the federal witness protection program. As near as Luke could tell, the only basis for this tale was the fact that Champlain vaguely looked the part—he was big and swarthy, with a self-assured smile and a matching walk; on the two occasions that Luke had seen him, he'd been wearing a gold neck chain.

The only time either of the Champlains was spotted with any regularity was on Sunday mornings, when Susan showed up, alone, at Luke's church, Tidewater Methodist, where he served as head pastor. The sixty-year-old wooden church, which sat prominently on a bluff high above the Chesapeake Bay, was largely immune to the summer transformation that went on elsewhere in the county. The congregation grew a little larger in July and August, but only a little; summer people tended to sleep in on Sundays. When visitors did show up, some of the congregation tried to make them feel at home, and some didn't. Despite the spirit of fellowship the church fostered, congregants tended to hold fast to their own social orbits. And a few were, by nature, wary of outsiders.

This divide seemed particularly evident when Susan Champlain began attending in early June. Several congregants (a few of the men, in particular) went out of their way at first to make her acquaintance, while others seemed to ignore her. She cut a striking appearance—tall and long-legged with full, shoulder-length blond hair that bounced as she walked. There was a compelling downward twist to her mouth as she smiled that made her seem like someone people knew—although she wasn't quite as friendly, it turned out, as the smile suggested. There was also a self-sufficient, detached quality about her, which created the impression that she was concealing herself out in the open.

Luke had long been a student of the whims and mysteries of human nature, and something about Susan Champlain's elusiveness aroused his curiosity. Whoever she was, she was a loner at heart, he had decided, and Luke felt a small kinship with her because of it.

His astute wife, Charlotte, had told him early on that Susan seemed troubled. As the summer unwound, and he spoke with her briefly after each Sunday's service, Luke began to suspect that Susan was coming to church to get away from some unpleasantness at home. About a month earlier, he had said to her, "You know, my door's always open if you ever want to come by and talk."

But she didn't. And by late July, when the cornfields were taller than most of the people in Tidewater County, the heat so intense that locals spent their afternoons indoors, Luke had stopped thinking she might. Susan Champlain, he'd decided, would be one of that summer's small mysteries that remained unsolved.

So Luke was surprised on the afternoon of July 30 when he looked up from his desk and saw a BMW braking across from his window, raising a cloud of gravel dust as it skidded to a stop beside his Explorer. It was Susan Champlain who emerged, dressed in white cotton slacks and a sleeveless blouse, a large handbag slung over her right shoulder. Luke watched through the Venetian blinds as she strode toward the church offices as if heading to a business appointment.

There were various facets to Luke's job as head pastor, many of them administrative and not terribly interesting. He prepared the annual budget and was also the final arbiter on such matters as how many church bulletins to print each week and whether to set the thermostat at 72 or 74 degrees in summer. He presided at weddings and funerals, performed baptisms (sometimes in the Bay) and gave a sermon every Sunday. But the most rewarding parts of his job were the one-on-one interactions with church members. Luke liked to think that he was in the good and evil business; his job was to help people find greater meaning in the ordinary march of their days, to bring light into the darker corners of their lives.

He kept his door open and encouraged congregants to stop by anytime—although not a lot of people did. This week, he'd been visited by Tim Blake, a film school student who was trying to convince Luke and the staff parish committee to let him shoot a zombie movie at the church (he'd offered Luke a "prominent" role); J. Michael Bunting, the irrepressible new reporter for the *Tidewater Times*, who was writing about the church's off-season "pet worship" proposal as if it were a local controversy (even though he hadn't yet found anyone opposed); and Delores Crowley, who wanted to leave a chunk of her fortune to the church on the condition that the Activities Room be renamed for her late husband and, more problematic, that his name be mentioned at the start of each Sunday service ad infinitum.

Yesterday, a large family with cameras had stopped by simply to gawk at the imposing building, with its tall, narrow stained windows and skyward-pointing spire. When Luke looked up from his desk at one point, three of them had been at the window peering in, waving, surprised to find that someone actually worked here.

He looked up now and saw Agnes Collins, his efficient and protective office manager, standing diminutively in the doorway.

"There's a Susan Champlain to see you," she announced in her slightly breathy voice.

"*A* Susan Champlain, or *the* Susan Champlain?" he almost said but decided against it. Aggie was a delicate soul who'd lost her husband to suicide five years earlier. She'd emerged from mourning as a refreshingly different person, more talkative and open to surprising new interests, including, for a while, singing in the church choir. The only unattractive trait she'd acquired was a proclivity to gossip. It was from Aggie that Luke had first heard that Nick Champlain was in witness protection. She'd also mentioned to him at least twice over the summer how people were starting to talk about Susan Champlain always being the last to arrive for Sunday service.

Susan was lurking just behind her now, three or four inches taller than Aggie, jockeying to establish eye contact with him through the crack in the doorway.

"Sorry," she said as soon as Luke waved her through, angling sideways past Aggie. "I hope I'm not interrupting anything."

"No," he said. "Please."

Her eyes did a quick scan of Luke's office. Then she eagerly reached to shake his hand, bending at the waist and exaggerating the effort, not seeming to notice that Luke's left arm was in a sling this afternoon.

"Susan Champlain," she said. "I thought I ought to finally stop by and say hello properly. It's always so hectic on Sunday."

"I'm glad you did." Luke nodded for her to sit; they both sat before he realized that Aggie was still in the room.

"Would either of you like some coffee or water?"

"No, thank you." Susan turned slightly to face her.

"We're fine," Luke said.

"Hot tea?" she said, to Susan.

"No. Thank you." Susan showed Aggie a pleasant smile, which disappeared as soon as she closed the door.

"I appreciate this," Susan said, and her eyes suddenly widened, looking at his sling. "What *happened*?"

"I fell," Luke said, feeling a little embarrassed. "Cleaning the drains on our house yesterday, nothing serious."

"Ouch." She winced. "I hope you're right-handed."

"Fortunately, yes."

Preliminaries over, Susan scooted forward. She moved his stapler one way and his desk calendar the other, claiming the new space for her arms. And then she began to tell Luke about herself and her husband, answering many of the questions that people had been asking all summer, without Luke having to say anything.

Susan and Nicholas Champlain had come to Tidewater from Philadelphia, she said, to escape the city for a few months. Nicholas, a contractor and land developer, had brought down his boat, a thirty-footer called *Carlotta*, named after his grown daughter. But he was in the midst of a big shopping-center deal that required travel back and forth to Philadelphia, so they rarely got out on the water. Sometimes, he'd leave her in Tidewater for two or three days at a time, she said. "Which is okay for me, I'm pretty good at being alone, but not always great for our marriage."

Susan described herself as an artist, a "primitive photographer," originally from Iowa, although she had lived more recently in New York City, Greenwich Village, before meeting Nicholas and moving to Philadelphia four and a half years ago. She spoke with a surprising facility, revealing rounded Midwestern inflections that Luke hadn't noticed before. Her skin was tanned and lightly freckled, which brought out the blue of her eyes, and her hands couldn't seem to keep still; Luke took note of her multi-carat diamond wedding ring as she gestured.

It soon became apparent that she was working her way, in a very roundabout fashion, toward a point, and that, whatever the point was, it was the real purpose of her visit. Luke was a good listener, and he waited for it, nodding and smiling appropriately as she talked.

Finally, after telling him of her summer exercise regimen—a combination of free weights, jogging and bike riding—Susan leaned back, looked at the ceiling and blew a long stream of breath from her mouth.

"Actually," she said, "I really kind of need to talk to someone."
She licked her lips once, her eyes going to Luke's.

"Can I tell you a story?"

Chapter Two

Ihis has to be in strict confidence," Susan Champlain said,
moving Luke's paper-clip holder several inches to one side.

"Sure," he said, wondering for a moment what the difference
was between "strict" confidence and regular confidence.

"Because I could be in trouble if it ever came out that we were
doing this."

Her eyes checked with his before she went on. Luke gave her
a reassuring nod.

At first, the story Susan told struck Luke as sadly predictable.
Champlain and her husband—"an older man," she called him—
had been having problems in recent weeks—months, really. Part
of it was just the stress of his being away so much, she said. "We
never seem to be able to get into a rhythm, so to speak." But at
the same time, he'd begun keeping tabs on her, watching where
she went when he was in town. It had gotten to the point where
there were only a few places she felt she could go anymore—
the Old Shore Inn, the public library, the wildlife sanctuary, the
Humane Society, and the church.

"Not to alarm you," she said, "but—he knows I'm here right now. And I think the only reason he's okay with me coming to church is he assumes I won't get into any trouble here. I told him I was going to see you about volunteering." Her blue eyes seemed to widen slightly, as if letting in light. "You do have volunteers, right?"

"Sure."

Five nights ago, she said, her voice thickening for a moment, Nicholas had returned from Philadelphia and they'd gotten into it "big-time."

"It's reached the point where it's starting to scare me a little. I'm just afraid something's going to happen, someone's going to get hurt. Have you met my husband?"

"Not yet, no. I've seen him in town."

"Well." Her eyes turned briefly to the window. "I mean, you see him in public, he's very personable. Always sounds perfectly reasonable. He used to be a politician, and in a way, he still is. He's a very clever man. But, I mean—I hate to have to put it this way but, basically, he's been threatening me."

That was when Susan Champlain's story stopped being predictable.

"He hasn't hit me, if that's what you're thinking. But the other night—" She leaned back and took a long, deliberate breath. "The other night, he said to me—he was kind of jacked up, and he said, 'You know, I could make you disappear if I had to, and no one would ever find you.'"

She stared at Luke and he watched her eyes moisten. "No one would believe that, of course. And he always tries to turn it around after the fact. Make it seem, oh, I was only joking, or

I was just trying to make a point. He has a very sneaky style of arguing."

Susan lowered her head and seemed to clear her throat; moments later, Luke realized that she was crying. He rushed around the desk and plucked a box of tissues from Aggie's office. Aggie kept her eyes on her computer screen, pretending not to notice. People came to Luke for all sorts of reasons. Often it was just the idea that he represented some sort of higher authority, which had somehow gone missing in their lives.

"Sorry. Thank you," Susan said, dabbing her eyes. "I guess I'm kind of a mess right now."

"No, take your time."

Aggie, whose own inquisitiveness knew no bounds, knocked softly on the door. "Is there anything I can get for you?" she said, peering in. "Water?"

"We're fine," Luke said.

Her eyes made a quick assessment of Susan Champlain before she closed the door.

"What was this argument about the other night?" Luke asked once she had regained her composure. "If you don't mind my asking."

"It was over *noth*ing. Well, I mean it was over *some*thing, of course." She touched the tissue to each eye. "It was basically over a picture I had."

"A picture."

"Yes. Just a *photo* I'd taken, last year, with my iPhone. I take candids, it's part of what I do.

"For my art," she added, reading his frown. "I create photographic art, incorporating images of real life. You know, like Irving Herzberg?" Luke raised his eyebrows inquiringly. "He secretly photographed people on the New York City subway, back in the sixties. Or, like, Weegee, who'd go out in the middle of the night and do candids of people on the streets. In that tradition." She blinked, her eyes nearly dry again. "I mean, I'm not trying to be a *spy*, but I've even taken a couple of shots surreptitiously during your Sunday service. I hope you don't mind."

Luke shook his head, although he couldn't imagine that members of the congregation would be pleased to hear she'd been taking "candids" during Sunday service.

"But he saw this one *particular* picture . . ." She straightened her back. ". . . and went ballistic. Absolutely ballistic. He didn't hit me, but he grabbed my arm. And that was it—that's when he said he could make me disappear."

"What was this photo of, that it would have caused such a reaction?"

"Well—that's the funny part. It was nothing, really. Just someone's house. But I guess . . . In fairness, he did make a point of saying, 'Don't even think about taking pictures here,' and I did, anyway. So in a sense, it was my own fault. I mean, I know Nicholas is involved in some things that are sensitive, that he's legally prohibited from talking about."

"Oh? What might those be?" Luke asked.

"Government contracts?" She lifted her shoulders in an exaggerated shrug. "I don't even go there. We don't talk about his business."

"Okay."

It was clear by now that Susan hadn't come to Luke seeking advice. She'd come seeking help. And he didn't know that he could provide the kind of help that she needed.

"Have you told anyone else about this? Sometimes talking about something—"

Susan was shaking her head. "If he knew I was telling you this, he'd have a fit. I mean, I've mentioned a few things in the past to my sister. She's in Iowa, though; there's not much she's going to do."

She reached into her purse, rooting around for something, maybe another tissue, Luke thought.

"Do you want to see it?"

"See it?"

"The picture."

"You mean you still have it?"

"A copy, yeah."

She smiled quickly and Luke saw something unexpected in the way the muscles of her face aligned—a determined recklessness, it seemed. Briefly, he wondered if he *should* look, if doing so would make him complicit.

But Susan had rounded the desk by then and was holding the phone in front of his face.

"There," she said, not quite letting him touch it.

The picture was of two men, standing in a large, empty room that appeared old and once-elegant. It might have been a palace in Italy: polished wooden floor, ornate wallpaper, a large French-style gilded mirror reflecting another room. The men were turned from the camera, one slender, wearing a dark suit, the other stockier, African-American, in jeans, a light green jacket and running shoes, gesturing with his right hand.

"What was the issue he had with this photo?"

"See? You don't get it, either." Susan studied the photo herself before turning it off. "I guess the gentleman, his client, just had an issue with pictures."

"But he didn't know you were taking it, right?"

"No," she said. "He didn't. Nicholas was the only one who knew I had this. He took away my phone as soon as he found out. But I have it on iCloud." She allowed a thin smile. "He's not especially computer literate. But he was looking through my cell photos the other night—on the pretense that he needed to find something to send his daughter—and he discovered that I still had this, which I'd more or less forgotten. And that's when he went ballistic. Telling me, 'I can't believe you still have this. People could get killed, you wave this thing around.' I thought he was absolutely nuts."

"And you don't have any idea why he was so upset? Or what sort of client this is?"

"No, it's— That isn't my business, like I say. We were, um, on our way to the airport at the time. And this man called, he asked Nicholas to stop by, pick up some papers or something." She was moving her hands again. "Normally, he wouldn't have taken me, of course, but it was all sort of impromptu. He told me, 'Wait in the car.' But then it dragged on. After a while, I needed a bathroom. There was a side door open, like a servants' entrance, so I walked down the hallway, and saw this empty ballroom. I decided I'd take a quick picture as I walked past."

"It looks like it's Europe."

"Yes, I know. It's actually Philadelphia. The suburbs. Main Line."

"Who else knows about this?"

"The picture?" Her eyes went a little funny then. "No one, really." She took a breath, leaned back and crossed her arms. Luke realized after a moment that she was waiting for him, as if he might be able to wave a wand and make her problem disappear.

"Well, I'd like to help," Luke said. "I do think it's important sometimes that we step back and look at things in a larger context. And understand that our problems are better dealt with on God's terms rather than our own. Sometimes we only make things worse when we try to fix them on our own."

Realizing that this might not be the most practical advice for the situation, Luke added, with a quick throat-clearing, "I also think, if he's threatening you, and you feel you're in danger, as you say, you probably ought to talk with the police." Susan leaned forward and her eyes dropped to his desk, her blond hair falling forward. "I could recommend someone," Luke said, "who would talk with you in confidence." Her right index finger began to trace a triangle shape on his desk. "Also, there are counselors with county health services, trained for this sort of thing. No charge involved. We have people here, too—why are you shaking your head?"

"I couldn't do that," she said. "Any of what you said."

"Why not?"

"I'm afraid what would happen if he found out. Also, I think he may have some sort of connection with the sheriff and state's attorney here. I'm not sure. He becomes friendly with people quite easily when he wants to, wherever we go. I know he's given a lot of money to the local Fraternal Order of Police." She was still tracing the triangle on his desk.

"Does your husband ever come to church? It might be helpful if you—"

"No," she said. She raised her eyes to his. "No interest. If you ask him, he'll tell you he believes in God, but that religion's a *personal* matter. He has a whole speech about it." She made a surprising snort, most of it unintended. "I can count on one finger the number of times I've seen him pray."

"One finger?" Luke said. "Or one hand?"

"Finger."

Luke closed his eyes for a moment, deciding what to do. "How about if we pray," he said.

She shrugged. "All right." Susan Champlain squeezed her eyes tightly, as if doing so would make the prayer more effective. And Luke prayed, asking for guidance to help her through this difficult passage, citing St. Paul's admonition that we keep our faith in times of tribulation and quoting Psalm 37, the psalm of patience. After he said "Amen," Susan opened her eyes again, blinking at the room as if expecting to have been transported somewhere else.

Before she stood, they exchanged phone numbers and agreed to talk again, in another day or two.

"And maybe you could think about what I've suggested," Luke told her, standing in the gravel parking lot out front. It was a hot afternoon, but the breeze from the Bay was pleasant. Susan raised her eyebrows. Luke clarified: "About the police or county services, I mean."

"Oh."

"And please—again—feel free to call me at any time."

"I will."

Luke extended his right hand again to shake. She smiled, nodding at the sling. "You take care of that."

"I will."

As Luke came back in, Aggie asked, "Is she all right?"

Her eyes asked the real question: *What did she tell you?*

"I think so," Luke said. "Just having a little rough patch."

Luke went in his office and closed the door. He watched Susan getting into her BMW with the Pennsylvania plates and pulling out, admiring the spark of courage that had prompted her to come see him.

Luke had a feeling he'd be hearing a lot more from Susan Champlain in the coming days.

But he was wrong about that.

THREE AND A half hours later, Belasco watched the front porch light go on at the sprawling Victorian house on Cooper's Point. It was beginning to drizzle, the sky darkening early. Meaning there would be no sunset tonight; Susan Champlain would not be coming out again. How ironic that a storm had given her this reprieve.

Belasco watched through binoculars as she moved sleekly in and out of view, barefoot, wearing an oversized T-shirt. Safe on the other side of the glass. A self-assured woman, at least when she was alone. Bouncing a little, probably listening to some music. Belasco sighed, and turned away. They'd have to wait for her, then. One more day.

Chapter Three

L ouis Nicholas Champlain."

"That's him."

Charlotte Bowers's face glowed in computer light. She was seated at the worktable in her tiny study, searching for information about Susan and Nicholas Champlain. Sneakers, their mixed yellow Lab, was curled contentedly on the floor beneath her, his favorite after-supper spot. The house smelled of cream-of-crab soup.

This was the night that they had planned to talk about their "future," although it was a subject they'd been flirting with for weeks, always managing—artfully, for the most part—to put it off. Tonight, the excuse would be Susan Champlain, Luke could see, and he'd have to take the blame for that. He had called Charlotte from work to ask if she wanted him to pick up a bottle of wine and ended up telling her all about their conversation. Charlotte's curiosity was legendary.

"What do you see?" he asked her.

"Not a lot."

"Sorry." Luke realized that he was blocking her light. "I'm hovering, aren't I?"

"No, please hover. Although if you wanted to hover in a different spot, I wouldn't object."

"Tactful."

"Thank you."

Luke got a beer and leaned against the kitchen table, admiring Charlotte's profile as she scrolled down a web page. Charlotte was a historian, from a well-to-do D.C. family, who'd made her own quirky paths through life, often defying her parents' expectations. Marrying Luke, for instance. Luke had been raised by roaming, working-class parents, mostly out West. Before joining the seminary, he'd been a paramedic and EMT for several years, while cultivating all sorts of odd interests, from rock climbing to sketching to wok cooking. They were opposites in many ways but temperamentally similar. Charlotte possessed a gentle inwardness that had always appealed to him. Although she played the role of pastor's wife to a T, she harbored her own peculiar spiritual ideas, drawing from sources as diverse as Greek mythology, Buddhism and Rastafarianism. She abhorred the phrase *new age*, although some in the congregation regarded her, disapprovingly, as a closet new-ager.

Most days Charlotte worked at home alone, though she dressed as if she were in an office full of coworkers, not just her and Sneakers. Tonight she wore crisp tan capris and a short-sleeved white blouse, her ash blond hair up in a claw clasp.

"We were going to have that conversation," Luke reminded her.

"Past tense?"

"Not necessarily."

Charlotte glanced at him and smiled, parenthetical grooves appearing on each side of her mouth. Then she looked back at the screen.

Luke edged a little closer to see what she was doing.

"The only negative I find on Nick Champlain is that he developed a condo project nine or ten years ago with a man who'd been convicted of cocaine possession. And later this man was charged with fraud and extortion."

"Nice combination."

"Yes." Charlotte clicked to a different page. "Otherwise, he seems to have done all the right things. Makes a point of giving to charities."

"Including the Tidewater FOP, I understand."

"Yes, and paramedics. He's a former city councilman in a small town in Pennsylvania . . . Has a grown daughter. He married Susan Wilkins four years ago, it looks like. Right after divorcing his second wife. She's thirty-six now. Looks like—let's see, twenty, twenty-one-year age difference." *An older man.* "How's your arm, by the way?"

"Getting better. Beer helps."

She turned and smiled at him.

"I'm getting used to you in a sling, actually. It kind of suits you."

"Thanks," Luke said. "Although that feels like a left-handed compliment if I've ever heard one."

"Ha-ha."

"Sorry."

"So, how worried is she?"

"On a scale of one to ten?"

"If we must."

"Eleven."

"And it's not possible she's embellishing a little—because she feels ignored and wants someone to take greater interest in her?"

"I wondered that at first," Luke said. "But, no, I don't think so. I think the fear's real. Although I, also, think she may have left out part of the story."

"Which part?"

"The main part. The part about what she's really afraid of."

Charlotte gave him an appraising look, with her intelligent pale blue eyes. "You know that there are some people you can't help, right?" she said, repeating something he'd told her.

Luke sighed but smiled. They'd been through this before. Charlotte knew he struggled sometimes with the disengaged attitudes of many churchgoers.

Sneakers sat up and began to scratch his side. He walked lazily around the chair and nudged Luke's leg. Sneakers was a rescue dog whom Charlotte had brought home from the Humane Society; he tended to become restless when he was excluded too long from conversations.

"What is it?" Luke said. "Didn't we already do our male bonding?" They had, in fact—very thoroughly.

"You want to know what I think?" Charlotte said. "I think he's bucking to lead the pet blessing service."

"Pastor Sneakers."

"Yes."

"I guess we'd better go out and discuss it, then. You ready?" Luke opened the front door and Sneakers galloped out across the lawn. It was drizzling, but that didn't bother Sneakers, who ran willy-nilly alongside the marshlands, stopping to water the grass and to raise his nose several times at the seafood smells drifting across the harbor.

Luke walked to the edge of the bluff, recalling the haunted look on Susan Champlain's face. He gazed down at the Bay, and heard the loud but distant sounds of summer people dining by the water, feeling the cold truth of what Charlotte had said to him . . . *Some people you can't help* . . . It was a strange evening, and he looked back in the direction of their cottage, thinking for a second he'd seen something wild running through the marsh grasses . . . Just the wind . . . Luke took a deep breath of the wet air and began to walk back.

"She has a website, you know," Charlotte said, as he came in. Sneakers was at his water bowl already, lapping with abandon.

Charlotte got up to give him a look while she went into the kitchen to pour a glass of white wine. It was a modest website, self-constructed from a template. Luke remembered, as he clicked through it, that he had visited here once before, early in summer, the first time Susan had mentioned she was a photographer. Three samples of her art were posted now, each showing what seemed to be a reflection—or a photo-shopped image—on a human eyeball. The first, *Light of Awareness*, was of an elderly Asian-looking couple seated on an iron scroll bench in an overgrown tropical garden at night. The second, *Child's Eye*, was the only color picture—bright balloons, candles, and presents from a child's birthday party in a woman's black-and-white eye. The third, *Trapped*, was of a seagull in flight, its wings extended upward, sunlight fringing the edges. Not trapped at all. Several lines of wavy script appeared to be superimposed on the bottom right corner of the image.

"I sort of know what you're thinking," Charlotte said, coming in with her wine and leaning against the doorway. Hovering.

"What am I thinking?"

"As soon as you saw the photo on her camera, you felt you'd become involved."

"Kind of, yeah."

Luke stood, relinquishing the chair.

"Have you thought about mentioning something to your friend Hunter?"

"Well, that's an idea," he said, as if he hadn't been thinking it.

Charlotte gave Luke a scolding glance as she sat back in front of the computer. Amy Hunter was the state police's chief homicide detective for Tidewater County. Young, independent, energetic, attractive. Charlotte had a small jealous bone, which grew more prominent whenever the topic of Amy Hunter came up. Suggesting he talk with her meant that she considered what Susan Champlain had told him to be serious business.

"Maybe I'll go see her in the morning," he said.

"Good." She turned off her computer and let the room darken. "Are we ready?"

They took their drinks and settled on Adirondack chairs under the deck awning, to watch what there was of the sunset, their evening ritual. It had been an unusual summer on the Bay, with lots of weekend storms and uncharacteristic cool fronts—although as Manfred Knosum, the church's pastor emeritus, had told Luke when he first arrived, "Every summer's unusual in Tidewater County."

Their home was an old cedar-shingled captain's cottage, owned by the church, small but charming, with a lovely view of the Chesapeake Bay from the back deck. The Bay was the country's largest estuary, where salt water met fresh, and this time of year the air off the water was often so salty it felt like sea breeze.

"To gratitude. And falling," Charlotte said, tipping his beer bottle with her wineglass. Gratitude was going to be the theme of Luke's sermon this week, an appropriate topic for the end of July, with the cash registers all ringing, the crops headed for harvest. But he'd decided to amend it to talk about falling, too, after his own mishap.

"Will you still be in your sling on Sunday?"

"I'm thinking not. I may retire it before our dinner with your parents tomorrow, in fact."

"It'd be a nice prop."

Luke said nothing. He watched the fog moving across the wetlands.

"You're still thinking about Susan Champlain, aren't you?"

Luke saw her blue eyes watching in the dark.

"I am, too," she said and gave him a smile that struck him as slightly sad. "How about if we talk about our future tomorrow?"

"Yes," Luke said. "Good idea."

NINETY-ONE MILES AWAY, on a jag of land near Delaware Bay, Walter Kepler sat at a corner table in a little restaurant called Kirby's Fish House waiting for Nicholas Champlain.

Three hours earlier, Champlain had called him on a throwaway phone and said, "I'm picking the Phillies tonight."

"So I'll go with the Braves," Kepler replied.

In truth, Kepler didn't follow baseball and never had. But

Champlain was talking in code. If he'd said he was choosing the Braves, they wouldn't be meeting.

He watched as Champlain took long strides through the light rain, not bothering with an umbrella. Nick Champlain was a large, sturdy man with a boyish smile and a thick head of dark hair going gray on the sides. He'd been a fullback in high school and might have played college ball if he hadn't quit to run his family's business. Kepler, who had the build of a smaller athlete, a wrestler or middleweight boxer, had learned all he could about Champlain since their previous meeting.

Kepler stood to greet him as Champlain was led to the table. Then, while the two men settled and began to peruse the menu, Kepler fought a familiar apprehension: having to negotiate his way through the carnival of mirrors again in order to make this deal work. Having to trust people like Nick Champlain.

Kepler glanced out at the rain. He thought of his father, walking hell-bent down marble corridors past the "dispensable galleries" to the masterpieces; and he thought about the "miracle," how it would be construed and covered by the news media in another week—things he couldn't share with Nick Champlain.

He waited until they had ordered their entrées—speckled trout for both, a late-summer specialty at Kirby's—and then he said, "So your message indicates we have a deal."

Champlain showed his assent with a flat smile.

"Both?"

"Both have authorized it."

"Good."

They talked around it for a while, making conversation. Champlain bringing up Anthony Patello, the man who, indirectly at least, had brought them together. Everyone in the region had read about Patello, a seventy-seven-year-old retired mechanic, who was living quietly in a modest suburb of Philadelphia, trying to blend in, spend his last years on his own terms. But eleven months ago, FBI agents had raided Patello's home on a concocted search warrant. The media had been all over it, dredging up Patello's purported organized crime ties, and his thirty-year-old felony conviction.

The raid was part of a larger strategy—and that had been reported, too, bottom front page of the Philly *Inquirer*: The FBI and the Philadelphia state prosecutor believed that the raid might lift the cover on a twenty-five-year-old crime—the Isabella Stewart Gardner Museum heist of 1990, considered the largest property crime in American history. A haul the papers liked to say was "worth" $500 million. Although, as Kepler knew, stolen art at that level was nearly worthless. There was no street value for stolen art.

The feds still didn't want to concede that the raid had been a mistake. They'd based the warrant on a statement given by a onetime Philadelphia capo, John Luigi, who had once run his family's New England operation. Luigi gave the FBI details about Patello that turned out to be true—what they'd find if they were to raid his son Dante's pool hall in South Philadelphia, for instance. So the feds also believed the rest of what he told them, which *wasn't* true—that Anthony Patello and his son not only knew about the stolen Gardner art, but that one or both of them could tell investigators where it was.

Luigi had made a mess of his own life by then and was dying of bladder cancer. But he hadn't lost his vindictive sense of humor.

The feds didn't seem to recognize how unlikely it was that Anthony Patello, who never set foot in an art museum, would be hoarding stolen paintings in his suburban Philadelphia home.

It was apparent now that Luigi had simply been looking out for his own interests. But what the feds hadn't figured out—and Kepler had—was that he'd also been shielding his nephew, Vincent Rosa, who really *did* have knowledge of the stolen art.

Kepler had hired Nick Champlain as his bridge to Rosa. Champlain had done business with Rosa and his brother Frank on half a dozen projects in the Philly area. And Champlain was a reliable and reputable developer who flew under the feds' radar, making him a perfect intermediary. The only concern Kepler had with Champlain was women; the man had a little issue with women.

"So let me tell you what we need to do," Kepler said at last, as they dug in to their blueberry cobblers. "And let me give you the time frame."

Chapter Four

*W*eird morning, Amy Hunter thought, watching heavy fog
float through the pine woods outside the Public Safety
Complex.

Hunter's first thought that morning had been to text her partner, Ben Shipman. Suggest they meet up for breakfast at McDon-
ald's to talk about Marlena Eden, a twelve-year-old cold case
from the next county: a thirty-six-year-old mother of two found
hanging by an electrical cord from an oak tree in the woods by
Pike Creek. It was a case with a good suspect but still no good
evidence. Hunter had been wanting to turn up the heat on it for
several weeks, wanting to figure something out before the end of
the year, although she hadn't yet said that to anyone.

It'd been a long time since she and Ship had talked about Marlena Eden. Too long. And then, lying in bed, watching the boat
masts outside her marina apartment, the idea of calling Ben Shipman dissolved. She remembered: Ship was gone. There were still
times when Hunter reached for her phone to call him, to get his
advice or to bounce an idea off him, even though he'd been dead
more than a year. Ben Shipman had lost his life helping to solve

the most notorious murder case in Tidewater history, involving a man named August Trumble. The Psalmist. A man now serving multiple life sentences at Allenwood Penitentiary for murder and racketeering.

Ship's funeral had drawn hundreds of cops and service people from all over the region, who'd formed a mile-long procession of official vehicles on the two-lane roads to Tidewater Cemetery. It had been an apt tribute to a good man. But his death, and nearly everything else about the case, troubled her. None of it had ended in Hunter's comfort zone. Or her frame of reference. There were still times when she heard the bizarre timbre of Trumble's voice in her head, like some sinister music from earlier times.

Hunter never forgot the faces of homicide victims, but the perpetrators didn't usually stay with her like that. Most were variations of the same person, anyway; not monsters, as the media liked to make them, but self-absorbed misfits who'd traded their lives for a few dumb—and usually cowardly—choices, which had also ruined the lives of others.

Hunter headed the Maryland State Police Homicide Unit for Tidewater County. She was thirty-one years old, although most people thought she was younger. Some in Tidewater's tradition-rich old guard had problems that an outsider—who also happened to be young and female—had been put in charge of Homicide. But she didn't particularly care and that was one of Hunter's secret weapons. She was paid a salary by the Maryland State Police, but liked to think that she really worked for the victims of the crimes that she investigated. It was a way of keeping her priorities straight, and steering herself around local politics. So far, it hadn't gotten her into too much trouble.

She was still thinking about Marlena Eden on Wednesday morning when Pastor Luke Bowers called. Always a pleasant surprise.

"I wonder," he said, "if we could meet for a couple minutes today? Whenever you're free."

"Okay," she said. "How about now?"

It'd been several weeks since she'd talked with Luke Bowers and something about his voice gave her a lift. Hunter liked the way he had of seeing things from several perspectives at once—close up and from a distance—an instinct she was trying to hone, and she liked his irreverence. Bowers had a cop's curiosity, she'd always thought, but without the jaded skin that many in law enforcement grew. And there was something else—an unusual capacity to listen, to make other people feel comfortable by taking interest in what they were saying. Hunter had been planning for a while to ask for Luke's input on Marlena Eden. She hadn't expected for him to seek *her* out.

She closed the file on her screen a few minutes later and walked down the long corridor to meet him in the lobby of the Public Safety Complex. The PSC, opened two years ago, consolidated municipal, county, and state police departments; fire companies; EMS; and district and circuit courts.

"Hey, what happened?" Hunter folded her left arm into an air sling.

"Nothing serious," Luke said. "I was cleaning the gutter on the roof drain and slipped. Well, one leg of the ladder went into a sinkhole, I toppled over."

"Oww."

"It's okay. It only hurts when I breathe."

She smiled and got him a visitor's badge and they walked back to Homicide. Luke was tall and thin, with slightly unruly dark-and-light blond hair, ten years older than she was.

Gerry Tanner looked up from his desk in the next office as they came in—Ben Shipman's old office. Tanner was the newest member of the state police homicide unit and one of three investigators based in Tidewater County. The other was Sonny Fischer. Tanner had transferred to Maryland from New Mexico two months ago, and was still trying to fit in. He was an old-school cop who believed in collecting information through face-to-face interviews; Fischer was the opposite, a skilled assimilator of electronic data who didn't especially care for people.

As soon as Luke sat, Tanner was standing in the doorway, asking Hunter if he could borrow a highlighter.

"Highlighter?"

"If you have one."

Tanner took the opportunity to introduce himself, energetically shaking Luke's hand. Some locals considered Tanner's eager manner a little strange, an impression accentuated no doubt by his appearance—long, lanky, dour-faced. But there was a hard-edged intelligence under the surface, which was what Hunter liked about him.

She waited a moment after he left, seeming to have forgotten all about the highlighter, then she got up to close the door.

"Highlighter," Hunter said to Luke.

They shared a quick smile. Then Luke drew a deep breath and sighed.

"We have a woman at church," he began. "Her name is Susan Champlain."

"Okay."

"You know her?"

"I know who she is."

"She came to see me yesterday afternoon. Seemed scared to death about something. She said that her husband had threatened her, but no one would believe her if she told them. She asked me not to go to the police, so I'm not reporting her here, I'm just talking. Seeking a professional opinion."

"Okay."

The story he relayed to her was one that Amy Hunter had heard before: young woman, older man; control, repression; two people who probably shouldn't have married, constantly making adjustments. In a selfish way, hearing it made Hunter glad that she wasn't in a relationship herself at the moment.

Then Luke got to the part about Nick Champlain threatening to make his wife disappear. And Hunter had a bad feeling. This was a story she'd heard before, too, one that didn't end well.

"And the argument was over a photo?"

"Well, I'm sure there was more to it. But that's what she said."

"It would be interesting to see the photo."

"Yes. I did, actually," Luke said. "She showed it to me."

"Oh." Hunter frowned. "So she still has it."

"Yeah. That's what worries me."

Luke described the photo she had showed him—the faded elegance of an empty room, two men talking.

"Did she say who these men were?"

"Her husband's clients evidently. She didn't particularly want to talk about it beyond that."

"Except she made a point of bringing it to your attention."

"Yeah. I know."

Hunter leaned back and let her eyes drift, out at the woods. "I worked on a case several years ago," she said, "in rural Pennsylvania. Roxie Hadley. The man said almost exactly the same thing—told his wife that he could make her disappear, and no one would ever find her body."

"And—?"

"He made good on it. No one ever did. They finally convicted him without a body. But it wasn't easy."

Luke's face tightened, watching.

"I'm thinking I'd like to talk with her," Hunter said. "Maybe we can figure a way to do it so it doesn't seem like an actual meeting."

"Okay."

"Maybe she comes in to talk with you about volunteering, and I stop by."

"That might work." Luke's blue eyes brightened. "This afternoon? Tomorrow?"

"Whatever you want," Hunter said. "I'm pretty open right now." She thought of Marlena Eden again, hanging from an oak tree in the woods. "Just let me know."

"I will. I'll try to reach her this morning."

"Good."

"Maybe it's just a phase they're going through," Luke added, as he stood, sounding pastor-ish all of a sudden. Hunter didn't believe it, nor did he. He wouldn't be here if he did.

"One other thing she mentioned: She says her husband maybe has some connection with the sheriff here and the state's attorney. I don't know if he knew them before or just became friendly since coming down."

"Okay." Hunter felt her neck bristle. Sheriff Clay Calvert had worked against her throughout the Psalmist case, and held a nasty grudge because she'd gotten most of the credit for solving it. Calvert was a fourth-generation Tidewater Countian who stubbornly refused to take Hunter seriously.

"Anyway, let me know," she said, willing herself not to think about the sheriff. "I'll do some checking in the meantime."

Luke smiled. It was a warm, selfless smile. If Hunter had to wake up to someone, that would be a nice face to see in the morning. Although Winston, her longhaired tuxedo cat, wasn't so bad, either.

"What's your sermon going to be Sunday?" she asked as they stood in the lobby.

"Falling." He held up his sling.

"Of course."

Chapter Five

Luke drove the scenic route back, over the snaking creeks and tributaries of the south county, the rising sun shimmering through the loblolly pines. Even in this most picturesque corner of Tidewater, the human signs of summer were on full display beside the road. Luke stopped on the oyster-shell lane at Crawford's Neck, where nine empty Bud Light cans had been dropped in a sequence. He kept a litterbag in the back of his car and got out to pick them up.

About a half mile farther on, near Man Ray Point, he spotted what looked like a woman's one-piece bathing suit. Over the next mile, various items appeared—an athletic sock, an old pillow, more beer cans, a single deck shoe in the center of the road, jockey shorts, pieces of a Styrofoam cooler, a green rubber glove. When he stopped at the flashing light intersection by Bayfront Drive, he caught a faint whiff of throw-up in the breeze.

Ah, summer.

Summer brought strangers to Tidewater County and sometimes strange crimes. This year, someone had supposedly been peering through apartment windows in the middle of the night, although for some reason nothing had been reported yet in the local media. The problem with a small town is that it's a small town, Luke sometimes thought—similar to other small towns in the obvious ways, but at the same time thoroughly unique in ways that only a native could fully appreciate.

He turned left, onto a long gravel drive that dead-ended at the old cedar-shingle church where Luke had served as head pastor for the past six years. It was going to be a busy day, with an afternoon meeting of the Outreach Committee and a lengthy phone call with Mrs. Crowley, the church's major donor. And then in the evening, Luke and Charlotte were scheduled to have dinner with Charlotte's parents, always an interesting challenge.

He keyed in Susan Champlain's number as he sat in the parking lot, gazing out at the Bay, the runabouts and sailboats and, farther out, the freighter ships headed from Baltimore to the Atlantic Ocean. Seeing Hunter had given him a charge, reminding Luke a little of his own more idealistic inclinations before he'd gone into the seminary.

He wanted to ask Susan if she would come in at the end of the day, to talk with him about volunteering. But there was no answer, just an automated male voice, so Luke left a message.

"J. MICHAEL BUNTING called," Aggie announced as he came in. "And Mrs. Crowley. And a Dr. Edward Fengler."

"*Dr.* Fengler?" Luke said. "No, I don't think he's a doctor."

Aggie looked defensively at her notes. "That's what he said. Dr. Fengler."

Eddie Fengler was a boat captain who for some reason wanted Luke to publicly endorse his eco-tour back-bay charters.

"Is everything all right?" Aggie said, suddenly looking ill herself.

"Yes, sorry, fine," Luke said. He summoned a smile. "I think Sneakers is going to apply to be head pastor for the pet blessing service."

"Is he qualified?" she deadpanned.

"Probably as much as I am. If not more so."

Aggie nodded. Often she ignored, or missed, his attempts at humor. But occasionally she went with him. She was being playful today, he suspected, because she still didn't know why Susan Champlain had come in the day before and was hoping he'd tell her all about it.

Luke went in his office and closed the door three-quarters of the way. He'd prepared a statement about the church's policy on pet worship, which he now polished and e-mailed over to J. Michael Bunting at the *Tidewater Times*. Then he returned the call from Mrs. Crowley, who spoke for close to an hour, often without pause. She had a harsh, emphatic voice, which reminded some, including Luke, of Donald Trump.

At noon, Luke was beginning to edit through his sermon on Gratitude and Falling when Aggie knocked twice and poked her head around the door.

"Surprise," she said. She had a crab-cake sandwich she'd picked up for him at the Old Shore Inn, along with sides of Shore Slaw and curly fries in Styrofoam containers.

"You didn't need to do that," Luke protested.

"Oh, no, no trouble," she said. "I was there, anyway. My treat. I can tell it's a very busy day for you."

"Yes."

She hurried out to get him a bottled water from the refrigerator in the lunch room. Sometimes, Aggie did things like this out of a genuine kindness. This time, he knew, it had something to do with the three-quarter closed door. But he was gracious, and didn't mention that the Old Shore was where they were going for dinner that night with Charlotte's parents.

"Oh, I saw Susan Champlain, by the way," she said, as she returned. "Over at the inn. I was going to say hello, but she seemed deep in conversation with someone and didn't notice me. Let me get you some extra napkins."

When she came in again, and set out his napkins, Luke said, "Who was it, I wonder?"

"Pardon?"

"The person she was talking with, I mean."

"*Oh.* You mean Susan Champlain? I don't know. A gentleman I'd never seen before. A nicely-dressed man, with elegant shoulders. One of the guests, probably. They were in the club room there." She stepped away. Luke felt his curiosity outwrestling his resolve.

"Anything else?"

"No, thanks," Luke said.

Gratitude and Falling, he told himself, gazing back at his sermon notebook.

THE AIR WAS breezy on the bluff at Widow's Point that night, tossing the pine branches against the oily, dimming sky. Sixty feet below, two dozen gulls had gathered by the edge of the water, although much of the sand wharf had been covered by incoming tide.

By the time the 120-pound object thudded on the beach—several minutes past eight—the birds were gone, flapping frantically to the north and to the west. Belasco was in flight, as well, walking through shadows down the sheltered access road, feeling a brief, unexpected giddiness. Killing was mostly a process now, a learned skill, which Belasco sometimes traced to childhood, to brothers and friends who'd thought it was funny to shoot at stray dogs with a .22 rifle and to douse the tails of cats with gasoline and light them on fire. Belasco regretted all that at times, because of the costs that came due later. But there was something different about tonight; tonight was lovely. The eastern sky was darkly majestic, bruised shades of backlit charcoal. It reminded Belasco of a painting, a seascape. But then, these days, what didn't?

Chapter Six

Besides splitting Maryland geographically, the Chesapeake Bay also serves as something of a social and imaginative divider. The Eastern Shore is the more casual side, with old wood-frame houses, crab shacks and fish fries, cattail marshes, oyster-shell roads and a thriving seafood industry. The Western Shore, where Charlotte's parents kept their sailboat, has a more cosmopolitan energy, with yacht clubs, boat harbors, townhouse developments and boutique shops.

Tidewater County's Old Shore Inn was something of an anomaly, its Victorian-style elegance suggesting the early 1900s. It was by far the priciest hotel in Tidewater and the only one that asked men to wear jackets to dinner.

As they walked over the narrow polished floorboards to the dining room, Luke peered in the club room—all leather and old brass—and he imagined the chair where Susan Champlain had been sitting earlier in the day, talking with a "gentleman" Aggie had never seen before. Obviously, Aggie had come here looking for her, Luke decided.

"What are you doing, exactly?" Charlotte asked, sidling up

against him, and holding Luke's good arm. He'd decided not to wear his sling tonight, mostly because of the comments it would elicit from Charlotte's father. Charlotte looked fetching but casual in a beige dress and jacket.

"Me? Nothing."

She steered him toward the dining room, where Lowell and Judy Carrington—Charlotte's parents—were at a window table, early as always, her father leaning way back and waving them over. Lowell Carrington was a tall, urbane-looking man, his white hair fashionably disheveled. Luke could see from the way his chair was turned that he'd been watching the pleasure boats come in; Judy, small and hunched over, frowned at her menu as if it were written in Mandarin. Charlotte's parents lived in an old-moneyed suburb of D.C. Once or twice each summer, they sailed across the Bay to Tidewater County and docked near the Old Shore Inn, so they could visit with their daughter and a couple of old friends who kept second or third homes here. Lowell Carrington had once been an economics professor at Georgetown and had served as a White House advisor during the Bush 41 administration. He was long retired now although he "dabbled" in real estate, as he put it, buying and selling luxury properties in the Bahamas, where the Carringtons owned a winter home.

These dinners followed a pattern—the four of them greeted one another with exchanges of "Great to see you!" and "You look wonderful!" then sat and began the process of evaluating the specials and new entrées—taking turns picking an entrée for discussion, something someone would say "sounds good"; in each case, Charlotte's mother would then say "Where's that?" and her father would invariably find something wrong with it.

Midway through the standard entrées discussion, Luke weighed in: "I wonder what rosemary-infused cannellini beans are like."

"Where's that?" Judy said.

"The rockfish." Luke pointed to it on her menu. "It says it comes with rosemary-infused cannellini beans."

"Maybe they'll let you switch it out for french fries," Charlotte said. "Ketchup-infused."

Lowell Carrington gave her a mock scowl over the top of his menu, probably not realizing that Charlotte was serious. Luke decided he'd stick with cannellini beans.

They were well into their entrées—the butter-poached lobster for Judy, filet mignon and lobster tail for Lowell, lump crab cakes for Charlotte and the rockfish for Luke—when Lowell Carrington said, "So, Luke, have you ever thought about going on television?"

"Television? No. Not seriously."

"Because I met a fellow the other week, he's done this successfully in other markets. You broadcast your Sunday service—live or delayed—and begin to build an entirely new audience. From what he says, you can get in some markets now for just a few thousand dollars."

"Interesting."

"Then at the end of the broadcast, you sell your CDs or DVDs and direct people to your website—that's where you recoup the upfront. And, of course, at the same time, you'd be spreading your message to a larger audience. It's a business model that's worked in a number of markets."

Luke nodded, forking a cannellini bean.

"I'll give you this fellow's name, if you'd like to talk to him."

"Appreciate it," Luke said. "Although, I don't know the congregation is quite ready to go in that direction."

"Well. You won't know until you ask." He smiled, his hard hazel eyes giving Luke a pointed look.

"Yes. We *have* asked, actually. Over the winter. The congregation was asked whether or not they wanted to broadcast the Sunday service online. It was more than three-to-one against. The feeling was, it might discourage people from coming to church."

Lowell frowned, as if Luke had just made a serious math error.

"Because from what this fellow says, it's just the opposite."

He went back to his food and an awkward silence replaced the camaraderie. Luke heard distant sirens, then saw red and blue emergency lights whirling along the coast; no one else seemed to notice.

"So are they going to keep the church where it is, or move to a new building?" Judy asked Charlotte.

"Still up in the air," Luke said. "Eventually, we're going to need a larger building. I don't think we're quite there yet."

"It's funny, we were looking at it today," Lowell said, "and from certain angles it's even more run-down than I thought. Judy was saying it looks like something from an old horror movie." A flush rose up Judy Carrington's neck. "But with a little work, you could make her a pretty elegant old building. You know, it's all cyclical, that kind of thing. First they say you're old and worn out; before long, they're calling you a classic. Kind of like us, right, Jude?"

Judy Carrington, although caught by surprise, smiled and glanced at Luke.

"Will you two be getting away at all, once the season is over?" she asked.

"Probably, yes," Charlotte said. "Although we haven't decided where yet."

Charlotte's mother took a long sip of her vodka and tonic.

"Us three," Luke said.

"Yes. Technically, we're a family of three," Charlotte said.

Lowell hissed good-naturedly.

Something was going on, Luke saw—more police lights speeding toward the coast road.

"A dog is fine, but it's never the same as family," Lowell said, "your own flesh and blood."

"He *is* flesh and blood, though," Charlotte said.

"And fur," Luke added.

"Yes. And fur."

Charlotte's father surprised them both by laughing. He could be a good sport when he wanted to be. Charlotte gave him her sweet sideways smile in reply, and Lowell patted her hand. It was a rare tender moment.

Over dessert, Lowell turned to Luke: "You know, Lucas, I've mentioned this before, but if you ever get tired of what you're doing, consider coming down to the Bahamas. I could set you up in real estate down there, luxury properties, you could pull down some very nice commissions."

Luke gave him an arch look. "Get tired of what I'm doing?"

"No, I don't mean your work, of course. I mean—the *circum-stances*. Living here."

"Ah." The salary, in other words. Luke was content, though, to be a servant, as he thought of it, earning a servant's wage. But he knew better than to argue the point with Lowell Carrington.

"The crowds here in summer," Judy said, her nose crinkling as if she'd caught a bad smell. "The traffic."

"Summer people," Charlotte said. "They bring strange things."

"It's true," Luke said.

"Case in point." Lowell set down his drink, stretching his chin forward. "I drove our rental car down to check on the boat before coming here and saw a lovely sight on the way back—not more than a half mile from where we're sitting now. I was crossing one of those creeks back there with the little bridges? And this fellow was out in his boat—fishing, I assume—and as I drove over the bridge the man stands up and begins to urinate off the side. I tooted my horn at him and the fellow just waved. Kept urinating."

"Oh, my," said Judy.

"Yes, a very lovely sight."

"And, of course, that would never happen in the Bahamas," Charlotte said.

"Well, it might. But let's not compare this to the Bahamas."

"Do you know who lives down there?" Judy said, to Luke. "One of our neighbors?"

"No. Who?"

Charlotte said, "Anna Nicole Smith *used* to live there, I know."

"Sean Connery," Lowell said.

"Really," Luke said.

"Really. Good man." He signaled for another drink. "But no, I'm just throwing the idea out, something to think about. Come down and have a look, if you'd like. You're always welcome."

"We will," Luke said.

"Think about it, that is," Charlotte added.

"Yes."

"I just wish we didn't have to go back on Saturday," Judy said, turning to Luke. "We so wanted to see your service."

"Anytime. We'd love to have you," Luke said cheerfully. But, in fact, missing the Sunday service was as much a part of the Carringtons' visits to Tidewater County as was dinner here at the Old Shore Inn.

As they walked out into the parking lot, Luke saw more police lights down the coast. He clicked on his phone and checked messages. Nothing from Susan or Hunter. Nothing from anyone.

"Can't beat that breeze, can you?" Lowell Carrington said.

Luke just nodded and they breathed it together. He had a point.

SNEAKERS WENT INTO the usual gyrations as they came in the cottage, getting down on his side in the foyer, wiggling and thumping.

"He's getting better at that," Charlotte said.

"Yes, he must've been practicing."

Luke let him out the front door and they both jogged toward the bluff, Sneakers stopping periodically to sniff and to water the lawn. Coming back, Luke felt weighed down again by the previous night's thoughts, recalling the pitch of concern in Susan Champlain's voice, the haunted look in her eyes. The house was dark when he came in, except for the stove surface light in the kitchen. Sneakers was lapping energetically at his water; Charlotte's classical music played very faintly from her office.

"Char?" he said. Where was she?

Luke checked the living room. He walked down the hallway to the bedroom, letting his eyes adjust, his heart tightening a little.

"Pastor?" a voice called. Luke stopped. "Is that you?"

"Yes." He smiled. The voice sounded very much like Charlotte's. "Who is it?"

"It's me. Dr. Nicely."

"Oh, yes. I thought I recognized you." It was Luke's sex therapist, who made house calls. He sat on the edge of the bed and undid his shoes. "I'm actually rather glad you're here," he said.

"Yes. I am, too," said Dr. Nicely.

Luke's cell began to ring as soon as he got his shoes off, making the sound of an old rotary phone.

Charlotte reached for it on the nightstand. "Hmm," she said, glancing at the readout while she handed it to him.

Amy Hunter.

"Interesting timing," she said.

"Yes."

"Maybe she's watching through a telescope."

Luke glanced out at the Bay. "Not likely."

"I guess not."

"Hi, Amy," he said.

Hunter exhaled, rather than say hello. Not a good sign.

"Bad news," she said.

Luke made eye contact in the dark with Charlotte.

"What is it?"

"Susan Champlain," she said. "They just found her on the beach. She's dead."

Chapter Seven

Hunter got the call at 8:51. It was Gerry Tanner, who often monitored police radio traffic through the night, although there was, on average, less than one homicide a year in Tidewater County. "There's a ten–seventy-nine at Widow's Point," he said. "I'm heading over."

"What is it?"

"Woman in the surf. A couple walking their dog found her. Looks like she might have fallen from the bluff."

The code 10–79, Hunter knew, was "notify coroner." The fact that Homicide hadn't been called directly probably meant that the first responders thought the woman's death was accidental. But with a fall, it was often hard to tell. Three possibilities: fell, jumped, pushed.

"See you there," she said.

It wasn't until she'd parked along the access road, where cop cars had lined up with their light bars flashing, and was walking out onto the hard sand that Hunter realized who it was.

The beach had already been secured with police barricades

and crime tape—two layers, one to isolate the death scene, the other to keep away spectators; a dozen or so had gathered by then behind the police tape.

The dead woman's fall had left her in a contorted position, her head jammed sideways into the sand, her torso jutting at 45 degrees, rump in the air, her left arm trapped beneath her.

"The girl's name is Suzanne Champagne," sheriff's deputy Barry Stilfork told Hunter, as she stood looking on. "Summer resident. Too much to drink, apparently."

Hunter felt a rush of disbelief. She'd assumed for some reason that it was a teenager, a summer guest who'd been partying too hard with friends.

"You know her?"

She shook her head and moved to the police sawhorses, for a better look at the body and to get away from Stilfork, who gave her the creeps. In fact, she'd been thinking about Susan Champlain much of the afternoon, processing what Luke had told her and expecting him to call. She'd run DMV and data searches on both Champlains. She'd also driven by the house they were renting, about a mile and a half down the coast road.

The investigating officer on the scene was Captain John Dunn of the state police, a burly man in his mid-forties with pocked skin and small, jaded-looking eyes. He was always friendly with Hunter in a distant sort of way. Five people had been allowed past the single entry to the death scene, she saw; the others were the coroner, two evidence techs and a police artist. The artist was doing a triangulation sketch.

Dunn shrugged when Hunter finally caught his eye. "Go on," he said, nodding her in. There was an official protocol in

Tidewater County, and there was also a working protocol. State police did the photos and the initial investigation, but the sheriff and municipal police liked to be involved. Hunter expected the usual jurisdictional conflicts.

She nodded thanks and stepped closer, keeping a respectful distance from the state tech who was taking pictures. She crouched in the sand and studied Susan Champlain, who was barefoot, dressed in white cotton shorts and a matching blouse. Despite the body's contorted position, she wore a disturbingly innocent expression—eyes open, mouth closed; the ashen face of a child, it seemed, something that had fallen from the sky. Rigor hadn't set in yet. Hunter looked closely at the hands: one broken fingernail, something under several of the other nails.

Dunn lowered his voice conspiratorially as Hunter walked back over: "Coroner said ninety-six point five degrees."

"So, the last hour or so."

"Mmm."

She looked up at the bluff, where Susan had fallen, or been pushed over, fifty or sixty feet up. The uneven edge of the land was backlit with police floodlights, creating an eerie wedge against the pine trees and the night sky. Hunter gazed at the shadows down the beach, where a state police tech was halfheartedly combing the sand with a metal detector.

"What are the markers?" Hunter indicated the yellow vinyl evidence markers that had been placed on the beach.

"Sandal," Dunn said, pointing to Number 1. "Some footprints that've probably been there awhile," pointing to Numbers 2 through 8. "The others are debris that she may have caught on the way down."

"Just one sandal?"

"So far."

"How'd you ID her?"

"Driver's license, credit card in her shorts. Along with a house key."

"Purse, or phone?"

"Not down here. They're processing up above."

Hunter thanked him and moved away.

Every unattended death should be handled as a homicide until it is determined that no crime has occurred. That was basic law enforcement procedure, and also common sense. But Hunter could tell that the coroner and some of the police investigators had already made an assumption about this one.

She saw Gerry Tanner's long, stubborn face as she came around the tape, his eyes fastening on hers.

"Sight her family won't want to see," he said.

"No," Hunter said, "they won't."

"Anything?"

"Not yet. I doubt if we'll know much tonight. Any idea where the husband is?"

"They're with him now, apparently. He'd been out of town since yesterday. Just returned."

That could be an interesting detail, Hunter thought, noticing that the sheriff, Clay Calvert, was moving their way, with his halting shuffle, upset no doubt that Hunter had been allowed so close.

"Strong smell of alcohol on her person," Calvert said in his throaty voice, stopping on the other side of Tanner, making sure that Hunter heard. Physically, they could've passed for a vaudeville duo, the sheriff thick and squat, Tanner tall and lean. "I've been saying for months we ought to have railings up there. God forbid, but it takes something like this." He turned his head and spat in the sand for emphasis. "Don't know that you people need to be here," he added, squinting at Hunter.

Hunter said nothing. This was SOP for the sheriff: decide what happened, then look for evidence to support it. Hunter slipped off into the shadows, putting some distance between her and the police and emergency responders.

The air felt warmer in the damp sand along the cliff side, shielded from the wind. It had been just before high tide, probably, when Susan had fallen. The tide was going out now and there were several feet of beach that hadn't been visible then.

Walking south, she spotted a few things in the sand, but nothing of consequence: small odd-shaped pieces of driftwood, a circle of metal that seemed to be the rusted top of a crushed soda can, a smooth-edged piece of glass. Then the nearly full moon caught an angled coin as the surf receded, a quarter, faceup. And a few yards beyond it, she saw another glitter in the sand, just past where the tech had been walking his metal detector. Hunter reached down and pinched it between her fingers. A long cable chain from a necklace emerged out of the wet sand, what appeared to be a broken eighteen-inch gold chain.

Hunter looked up again at the bluff, figuring the trajectory of Susan's fall. *Three possibilities.*

She walked back to tell John Dunn, and to have another look at Susan Champlain's neck. Dunn sent a tech with her to photograph and mark what she'd found. Number 13 was the quarter. The necklace, Number 14.

"Has anyone gotten pictures of the crowd?" Hunter asked the tech as they returned. He was a young, pale-skinned man.

"I don't think so. Why?"

Hunter shrugged. "Sometimes a perpetrator returns to the scene to watch."

He stopped, his brow furrowing as if her suggestion were absurd, then grudgingly took several quick crowd shots. There were twenty or twenty-five people gathered now, staring silently at Susan Champlain. It was a sight that struck Hunter as more grotesque in its way than the contortion of her body.

"I'm going to have a look up top," Hunter said to the tech.

"What?"

She drove back around, up the dark shoulder-less road to the bluff, parking her Camry behind a line of four police cars, two marked, on the dead end of the road.

A rusty chain blocked the entrance to Widow's Point with the warning "No Trespassing." It was a law that was almost never enforced. Hunter had seen city officials picnicking here.

She walked a thin, well-trod dirt path through the weeds to the open wedge of the overlook, which was lit up with flood-lights. Two state police techs were processing the scene. A diesel engine ground away behind them, powering the lights; the air smelled like an old bus depot.

Investigator Frances Neal came out to see her in an officious, slightly territorial manner. Neal was a large, slow-moving woman who didn't abide by the invisible hierarchies of Tidewater's old guard. Hunter liked that about her. She and the other tech had been taking shoe-print impressions by the edge.

"Any sign of a cell phone or purse?" Hunter asked. "There's nothing below."

"Nope."

She showed her what they had found: a plastic bottle in an evidence bag. "Something sweet. Wine, probably."

"The other sandal?"

"Not here."

"Anything else?"

"Nope." She could see from the twist in Frances Neal's face, though, that something about the scene wasn't sitting right with her.

Hunter looked out at the Bay. It was a dramatic view: the moon a column of light, glimmering on the water; traffic moving silently back and forth over the twin arcs of the Bay Bridge. She tried to picture what had happened: Susan, sitting on the rock by the edge, or leaning over to set up a photo, had somehow tripped or lost her balance, and fallen over. There was nothing she could see, though, that she'd have tripped over.

"Hers?" she said, nodding at the bicycle leaning on a pine tree, taped off behind a police barricade.

Neal turned and nodded. "Be my guest. We haven't processed it yet." Hunter walked over to look. It was a rental bike from Tidewater Cycles, she saw, a clunky old single-speed 24-incher. There was a basket hanging crookedly from the handlebars and a pouch below the seat. Hunter ducked under the tape. She lifted the pouch flap carefully with the edge of her finger, saw a paperback book inside. She looked out to the point, where the police techs were bent over, talking, neither paying attention to her.

The diesel engine droned. The book, she saw, was a biography of photographer Diane Arbus. Hunter flipped through it, and found something—a receipt, being used maybe as a place marker. She leaned down and looked closer: it was a sales receipt from a health food store in town called Cool Beans, date-stamped that morning at 8:17. Susan Champlain's breakfast: Egg biscuit and orange juice. On the back, someone had scribbled in swirling penmanship what looked like *Kairos48*.

Hunter closed the book and the pouch. She walked over to tell Frances Neal.

"We haven't processed it yet," she told Hunter, an unexpected note of irritability in her voice.

Hunter thanked her and walked along the edge. She looked down at the emergency responders and spectators on the beach. Finally, police were setting up a partition to block the view of Susan Champlain's crumpled body.

Susan had bicycled here from her rented house before sunset. The book maybe meant that she had come to read, that it was still daylight when she'd parked her bike. Or not. Maybe the book had just been there, from an earlier bike ride.

Returning to her car, Hunter recalled the only time she had spoken to Susan Champlain, if it could be called that: They'd crossed paths in a hot parking lot by the raw bar outside Kent's on a weekday afternoon. Susan Champlain had said "Hi" with a surprising familiarity, as if Hunter were a friend. Maybe she'd mistaken her for someone else. Hunter had then realized that she was with someone, a younger man with dark, floppy hair, walking just behind. But when they reached the sidewalk, they veered off in different directions, exchanging a glance, but not saying goodbye, and she wasn't sure.

Pulling away from Widow's Point, Hunter called Henry Moore, who was the commander of the State Police Homicide Unit, and Hunter's boss. "Who's handling notification?" she asked.

"Dunn's people. They're on it."

"They've found him?"

"Evidently." Moore sighed. He was an Eastern Shore native with a lot of old-fashioned wisdom about law enforcement; but he gave Hunter slack, knowing she worked best without much supervision. "What do you think?"

She told him, relaying the gist of what Pastor Luke had said to her that morning about Susan Champlain and then her own observations from the scene. State police troopers trained in death notification had already handled that end of it, she knew; Hunter would have liked to see his reaction.

Three possibilities. The fact that Nick Champlain had threatened his wife days before ratcheted up the odds that this was a homicide. But there was one aspect of her death that made Hunter think it *wasn't* the husband. Nick Champlain's alleged threat had been "I could make you disappear and no one would ever find you." But what had happened was different. What'd happened was very public: the opposite, in a way.

Hunter drove down to the wide-porched house the Champlains were renting, a mile and a half farther along the coast road at Cooper's Point. It was a large Victorian-style place with gabled windows and gingerbread latticework. A front light had been left on but there were no lights inside. Hunter parked and walked a loop around the property, through the night shadows of a big oak in back.

She took the rural route to the PSC, figuring what might've happened. Tidewater was a resort town this time of year, but there were still a lot of large, dark spaces—farm fields and marsh-lands and back bays. The image of Susan Champlain's crumpled body was stuck in her head now; it would never go away for good, she knew.

She was almost back when Moore called again. "The husband's on his way over to give a statement," he said. "Voluntary. They caught up to him having dinner at Kent's. Just got back into town around nine, supposedly. If you want to walk upstairs, you can see him."

TWO HOURS AFTER the incident, Belasco still heard the police sirens, racing with false urgency through the night. Belasco had watched the official activity from a distance for a while, and then returned home, confident that tonight's event would become nothing more than it seemed: an unfortunate accident.

It was a warm, breezy evening, with a trace of fog coming in over the water. Belasco was driving into town, still feeling a spike of adrenaline, and the lingering thrill. Killing, done right, could be an art form, an activity that aroused the higher emo-tions. Belasco had nearly forgotten that. Tonight's work, which had been carried out quickly, with purpose and precision, but also with passion, had been a reminder. Kepler would appreciate that. There had been a sense of inevitability to it, as well: Susan Champlain's recklessness had become a threat to everything they had planned. Belasco had confirmed that tonight in going through her cell phone.

Normally, Belasco was better at killing men than women; but tonight's incident had unfolded with a surprising ease, as if guided by some divine force. There had been just one small mistake, a hitch that Belasco should have anticipated; but it wasn't likely that local law enforcement would pick up on it. Belasco wasn't going to mention it to Kepler when they spoke in the morning. What would be the point? There were far more important, and practical, things to discuss. And anyway, Belasco had a knack for making mistakes disappear. This one was already beginning to seem insignificant, an undetectable flaw in the finished work.

Chapter Eight

Susan Champlain's husband, Nicholas, was upstairs in the interview room at the Public Safety Complex, wearing a royal blue golf shirt, his eyes lowered, his right hand over his left on the tabletop. John Dunn and Kyle Samuels, the sheriff's investigator, were with him.

"Two questions?" Hunter said to state police troop commander Gary Martin. They were standing in the adjoining room. Martin was a blond, round-faced man with a rosy complexion.

His eyes turned to Champlain through the one-way glass. Champlain was gesturing now, looking surprisingly put together.

Okay, he nodded. "He'll probably enjoy the change of scenery, anyway."

Hunter decided to let that one go. *Pick your battles*, her father used to tell her.

She took a seat and waited, watching through the glass as Nick Champlain fielded questions. It didn't take long to see that, for whatever reasons, investigators weren't pushing him as hard as they should be. Part of it was the fact that he had an alibi. But some of it was his manner: Champlain was cool and sort of interesting to watch. Hunter was reminded that he'd been a politician, a one-term city councilman in a small town in central Pennsylvania, not far from where she had been raised. Maybe the donations he'd made to the local FOP had something to do with it.

"You're up," Martin said seemingly arbitrarily, coming in and gripping one of her shoulders.

Hunter walked in and John Dunn came out. She took a seat at the table beside Kyle Samuels, the sheriff's detective, and nodded hello.

"Mr. Champlain, Amy Hunter, Maryland State Police. I'd just like to ask a couple of follow-ups."

His face softened with cordiality even as his eyes gave her a quick once-over. It was warm in the room. Hunter caught a trace of expensive cologne. She glanced at her notes.

"Sir, I just want to clarify, we need to ask these questions: You said it didn't surprise you that your wife had gone to the bluff at Widow's Point to watch the sunset this evening. She went there frequently, you said?"

"Sporadically."

"Sporadically. And she would take pictures of sunset there?"

"Sometimes. Sometimes the Bay. Or the trees. That's correct."

"Okay. And you're aware there's no evidence of a camera or a cell phone at the scene."

"No, they just asked me that," he said, his eyes turning, with a flicker of annoyance, to the other detective. "I'm guessing it fell in the Bay."

"In fact, your wife didn't normally use a camera, did she? She used her cell phone as a camera, isn't that right?"

"That's correct."

"And as I understand it, a lot of her artwork came from photos she'd taken on her phone, isn't that right?" His eyes gave her another quick up and down. Hunter cleared her throat and checked to make sure her shirt was buttoned properly. "And sometimes, she'd take pictures of people when they didn't know it."

There was a tiny delay in his response. "Sometimes."

"Was that ever a source of friction between you?" Hunter asked.

"Was that—?" Crinkles formed around Champlain's eyes and then he smiled; for an instant she saw something he didn't want her to see. "I don't understand the question."

"Didn't you argue earlier this week about a particular photo she'd taken on her cell phone?"

The other detective squared up his papers perpendicular to the table.

"Say that again," Champlain said.

Hunter felt her heart accelerate. She said it again.

"No."

"Hadn't you and your wife been arguing in recent days, sir? And hadn't one of those arguments been about a photo on her cell phone?" Champlain watched her evenly. He said nothing. "And during one of those arguments, hadn't you said that if you wanted to, you could make her disappear and no one would ever find her?"

He looked at the other detective, who was making a subtle sound in his throat. "No," he said.

Hunter was about to ask him about the necklace when Martin came into the room, waving a folder as if something had just come up. He handed it to Kyle Samuels and touched Hunter's shoulder. Meaning she was relieved.

She looked back before closing the door. Champlain gave her a shrewd, wide-eyed look. It could've meant anything.

" 'Two questions'?" Martin said. He looked like a dad about to upbraid his teen daughter. "Can you put that in writing, about the photo?"

"Of course."

Gerry Tanner came into the room a few minutes later and sat down. The three of them watched the interview in silence for a while, jotting notes.

"If he's not guilty, he's a good actor," Tanner said, to Hunter.

"Even if he *is* guilty," she said. In fact, the whole thing resembled a performance, Hunter was thinking. When Champlain let his guard down, his wife's death seemed an inconvenience more than anything else—than a tragedy or a personal loss.

"He's cooperating," Tanner said, after Martin left the room, "but he wouldn't turn over his phone. Did you hear that?"

"Why?"

"Claims confidential business transactions. He gave Dunn his business manager's name."

"What is it?"

Hunter wrote it down and filed a mental note to ask Dunn about this. She stayed for the remainder of the interview and then, after Tanner left, she stayed while state police investigators recorded interviews with Joseph Sanders, Elena Rodgers, and Sally Markos, all of whom had worked for Champlain.

Sanders, Champlain's driver and "assistant," was a large, gruff-speaking man with a beat-up-looking face who seemed to struggle with some of his sentences. He had been out fishing alone in his runabout that afternoon, he said, then stopped at a bar called the Harbor Loon, at about 7 P.M., to have "a couple" beers. He was "off duty" today, he said three or four times.

Elena Rodgers, a personal assistant to Champlain, was an athletic-looking woman in her late thirties, wearing a dark windbreaker and a slightly sullen expression. She had been in her room at the Old Shore Inn all afternoon reading, then joined her boss in the private dining room at Kent's Crab House several minutes past nine. It was a "business meeting slash dinner," she said. Rodgers was terse and businesslike and several times flashed a look of impatience—an upside-down smile—as if disgusted that the detectives had found it necessary to interview her.

Sally Markos, Champlain's house cleaner, was a dark, waifish-looking woman with frizzy shoulder-length hair. She couldn't get through more than a few words without crying, a response that became almost theatrical at times, Hunter thought. She'd been home with her husband, she said, watching television tonight. She named the shows: *Wheel of Fortune*, followed by *Jeopardy* and back-to-back episodes of *Forensic Files*.

None of the interviews was very useful, although something about Sanders's story felt off. The detectives picked up on that, Hunter noticed. Some of it may've been that he was drinking and had to sober up to talk with them. But there was a discrepancy in his recollection of times—when he'd arrived at the bar, when he'd left—that sounded as if he was spontaneously trying to invent an alibi. And when this discrepancy was pointed out, his face colored and he said, "I can't remember exactly."

It was past midnight when Amy Hunter swiped her badge into

Homicide. Inside was a reception desk and four small offices—one for Tanner, one for Fischer, one for her; the fourth was open, used as a conference room and sometimes by their supervisor, Henry Moore. She was surprised to see that Tanner and Fischer were both still here. Tanner's door stood wide open, Fischer's about two inches. It was only a couple of minutes before Tanner was in her office.

"The alibi seems to check," he said, resting a hip on a corner of Hunter's worktable and opening his worn-out leather notebook. "We're pulling highway surveillance."

"Alibis are sometimes overrated, though."

"Yeah." Tanner studied her. "Why, what are you thinking?" Hunter shrugged. "You think the husband did this."

"I think it's possible he was involved. Whether he was here or not."

Tanner waited for more, staring with his long wooden face. He had a spiel he gave about how cheap opinions were. *My daddy used to say you ought to have a license before they allow you to carry an opinion.* It was ironic considering how much he liked to hear other people's opinions.

"Sanders's story had problems."

"I know," she said.

"You think he was involved?"

Hunter shrugged. "What do *you* think?"

"Maybe Champlain *arranged* it?" he said. "Made sure he was out of town when it happened?"

"Why, though?" she said.

"The usual, I guess. Maybe he saw the writing on the wall. D-I-V-O-R-C-E?" He spoke each of the letters, like in the song.

Tanner's voice had a wide, expressive range, but his face never changed. The effect could be slightly comical. "Save him a ton of money if she had an accident before that happened."

"Maybe," Hunter said. "Except I don't know that they were at that stage in their marriage. I don't think they were."

"Speculation."

"I know. It's too early for that. We'll know more when we hear from the M.E. There was a broken nail," she added. "Something under her other nails, might be skin cells."

"Lump on the back of her head, too, right?"

"Yes. Although she may have just hit her head on the way down."

"That's what the sheriff's saying," Tanner said. "Of course, maybe it *was* an accident."

"Maybe." Hunter gave him a cursory smile. "But I don't think so." Tanner stared, expecting her to say more. But Hunter wasn't ready to do that yet.

Several minutes after Tanner left for the night, giving her his "Hasta la Vista," Fischer emerged. He filled his coffee cup with cooler water and then leaned against Hunter's doorway.

"How's Geronimo?" he asked. Gerry Tanner's real name was, in fact, Geronimo, although no one called him that. Hunter shrugged, knowing better than to get between them. Fischer was a fitness and organic food nut, half Cuban, half African-American. He was one of the most meticulous and focused investigators Hunter had known. But, unlike Tanner, he wasn't a people person. He was great at sorting through information, finding a story in piles of data.

"What can I do?" he said.

Hunter had been waiting for him to ask; she was as pleased to give Fischer an assignment as he was to receive it. Fischer readied his pen to write on his steno pad.

"I'd like to know more about Champlain's whole setup here."

" 'kay."

"Who he's with and why. Backgrounds on everybody. Sanders is his bodyguard, supposedly, Elena Rodgers his personal assistant. There's a part-time housekeeper named Sally Markos. Where are they from? Can we run checks on all of them?"

" 'course." Fischer was writing.

"I'd like to pull security tapes, too, anything we can find for the past week."

"M'kay." Where Tanner would've asked "Why? What're you thinking?" Fischer just listened and jotted notes.

Hunter told him then about the necklace she'd discovered on the beach. "It's possible she was fighting with someone and, in the process, the perp ripped off her necklace. There seemed to be scrapes on Susan's neck and upper right arm. I didn't have a chance to ask her husband about the necklace, but I will. In the meantime, let's see if it turns up in any surveillance pictures."

"M'kay."

Afterward, Hunter sat at her desk, trying for some time to fit the details of Susan Champlain's death into some kind of pattern that made sense. She couldn't. She printed out a photo of Susan, the only one she'd found online: taken four years ago, at a fundraiser, with her new husband, "Philadelphia developer Nicholas Champlain." Hunter cut Nick Champlain from the picture and tacked the image to her corkboard. She printed a second one to take home. Something maybe to replace the one in her head—

Susan Champlain's body contorted on the beach, in front of a gallery of onlookers, before the partition went up.

She was driving out of the parking lot at last when Henry Moore's number came up on her phone.

"Wow," she said. "Surprised you're calling so late."

"I wouldn't be, except I just saw you leave the building."

"Oh. You're still there?"

"Getting ready to leave." *That* was odd.

"Why so late?"

Moore sounded tired. He was a brusque man with a soft center, who often skipped over the niceties. "I was talking with Dunn. I'm told we're not getting directly involved in this one. They're going to push that it was an accident."

Hunter felt her heart begin to beat faster. "Not surprising, I guess."

"Not surprising." She suspected Moore had talked, too, with State's Attorney Wendell Stamps; Stamps was the silent arbiter in Tidewater County, where too many competing agencies worked the same turf. "Except," he said, "I think we probably should be involved."

"I do too," Hunter said. *Good.* She listened to him breathing. There was a saying she'd heard years ago: homicide investigation is God's work. It came back to her at times like this. "Why, what are you hearing?"

"Nothing specific. I think there's another shoe that's going to drop."

"Literally," she said.

"What?"

"I mean, there's literally another shoe," Hunter said. "They only found one of Susan Champlain's sandals."

"Oh. Yeah." Hank Moore chuckled. "I was thinking figuratively."

"I know."

"It's late. Let's talk in the morning."

"All right."

LOOKING UP FROM his laptop, Luke followed the thin white line of surf that traced the shoreline down to Widow's Point, where it suddenly vanished into darkness. The early-morning air was cool and unsettlingly quiet, the moon veiled by drifting clouds. Unable to sleep, Luke had come out onto the back deck to sip a glass of bourbon and to ponder his Sunday sermon. Falling was no longer a feasible topic.

Yesterday, Susan Champlain had come to him asking for help. Luke had advised her to rely on faith, to surrender her fears and troubles to God. *Ask and he will reveal himself to you.* He'd prayed with her, and for her, and quoted lines from Psalm 37, the psalm of patience. The next evening, Susan Champlain was dead.

Luke knew he wasn't supposed to explain that. Tragedies happened every day for no evident reason, the result of cruel or random violence, indiscriminate disease, other people's carelessness. "Why does God let them happen?" was for many people the defining question, the simplest and most persuasive argument against the existence of God. There were good answers in Scripture, but not the sorts of answers people wanted to hear. The good answers required patience, and the long, slow learning of a new language, a language of faith. There were better *questions*, too. Better than, "Why does God let them happen?" But that was a question that never went away; and on nights like this, when the tragedy felt personal, Luke even found himself, against his better judgment, trying to answer it.

He surfed through the local news again, seeing that there was a short item now on the Channel 14 website: "Tidewater PD Investigates Fatal Fall."

An unidentified woman died tonight in an apparent accidental fall from the bluff at Widow's Point in Tidewater County. The woman was discovered on the beach by a couple walking their dog at around 8:30. Details are pending.

The bulletin was followed already by a couple of anonymous posters: "RIP." And: "Sad story. Supoosely the lady'd been drinking?" Which drew another reply: "SUPOOSELY? *WHOSE* been drinking?"

Luke glanced again at the darkness where Susan had fallen, thinking about the famous passage from James 4:14, comparing life to "a vapor that appears for a little while and then vanishes." Maybe *that* would be his sermon.

Realizing he hadn't checked e-mails for several hours, Luke called up his AOL account. Perhaps Susan Champlain had responded during the day, he thought. But she hadn't.

He logged on to his church account, checked e-mails and spam, for something else to do.

And there it was, in spam: an e-mail from SWilkins79. Sent to him at 2:47 P.M. that afternoon.

Wilkins was Susan Champlain's maiden name.

Luke's heart began to race. He clicked open the e-mail, and read the brief message she had sent him: *Pastor Bowers, I'll call this aft. Thanx for listening. These are the pix. Please keep in STRICT confidence until we can talk. SC.*

There were three photo attachments with the e-mail, which was probably why it had been kicked into spam.

Luke clicked on the first: side view of a large, paint-chipped Victorian house. The second was a mangy field of weeds; in the distance a chain-link fence and a basketball hoop, beyond it some buildings.

The third he recognized right away: it was the image she'd shown him from her phone. The empty wooden room, two men talking, a mirror, a slant of sunlight.

Moments later, the screen door squeaked, startling him. Sneakers's toenails clicked enthusiastically onto the porch. Just behind him was Charlotte in her silk bathrobe and flip-flops. She hadn't turned on any lights.

"What are you doing?" she whispered. Her nose twitched and she made a face, detecting the bourbon. "Come to bed."

"Can't sleep."

Charlotte leaned down so her face was touching his. Her skin felt warm and smooth.

"That's the photo," she said.

"Yeah. She sent it to me at church this afternoon. I just now found it."

"How about that." She straightened up, breathing in the air. Luke looked down at the line of surf again, to the darkness at Widow's Point. "You better send it to Hunter," she said.

"Yeah, I know."

He looked at the clock on the bottom of the screen. "Probably too late to call her now."

But, of course, it wasn't.

Chapter Nine

Amy Hunter looked more disheveled than usual Thursday morning, wearing a wrinkled blue men's shirt, tails out, faded jeans, work boots, her dark medium-length hair sticking up in back. A can of Diet Coke was on her desk, two empties in the recycle can.

It was seven and a half hours since Luke had discovered Susan's images in his church e-mail account, and he was now looking at them blown up on the three monitors in Hunter's office at the PSC. The FBI had them, too, she said; she expected she might hear something back later in the day.

Luke hadn't come in to talk about the pictures, though. He'd come in to tell her what he hadn't said yesterday. And to hear what *she* thought might have happened to Susan Champlain.

Before he'd ever met Amy Hunter, Luke had heard this about her: that she could look at a crime scene and tell what was there, what wasn't and what should've been there. She'd proven that several times over in the Psalmist case. But there was another thing about Hunter, something that was harder to figure—an intuitive intelligence about people's darker motives, a surprising quality at odds with her wholesome, youthful appearance. Hunter picked up frequencies that most people couldn't access. She was also the most single-minded person he'd ever known, for better and for worse.

"Two things," she said, nudging him.

"Right." Hunter flipped through her steno pad full of scribbled pages, looking for a page with space enough to write. Notes were jotted every which way, on each page—sideways, diagonally, even upside down.

"A couple hours before the e-mail was sent," Luke began, clearing his throat, "our office manager, Aggie—Agnes Collins—" Hunter's brow crinkled involuntarily; Aggie and Hunter didn't much like each other. "—saw Susan Champlain at the Old Shore Inn. This would have been about 11:45. Talking, very intently, she said, with someone. A man."

"Any idea who?"

"No. She said she'd never seen him before. Which is sort of odd, since Aggie tends to know everyone. She described him as well-dressed. With elegant shoulders."

A single line creased Hunter's smooth brow. "What are elegant shoulders?"

"No idea. Her phrase."

Hunter wrote something down, and underlined it. She reached for the Diet Coke, her large light brown eyes never leaving his as she drank.

"The other thing that's been sort of bothering me is the odd word choice she used. She told me she was afraid some*one* was going to get hurt. Not that *she* was going to get hurt. Some*one*." Hunter set down her soda. "It just struck me as odd."

"What do you think she meant?"

"At the time, I guess I thought she was talking about herself. But I've begun to think maybe she was talking about something else."

"Something to do with the photo."

"Maybe."

Luke could almost see the ideas networking inside Hunter's head.

"You think this was a homicide?" he said.

"Probably."

"The husband?"

"I think he was involved." Her eyes turned to the window. "I don't know how yet." She looked back to him. "Did you ask her, by the way, if she had mentioned the photo to anyone else?"

"Indirectly."

She raised her eyebrows, meaning, "And—?"

"She said no, she hadn't. It's funny, though. For some reason, I got the feeling that she wasn't telling the truth about that."

Hunter nodded, as if she'd been thinking it, too, although he didn't see how that would have been possible.

"This puts us in a small club, I guess, doesn't it?" Luke said. "With just three members."

"Oh, with your wife, you mean, yeah." Hunter wasn't quite tracking with him. She scribbled a word on a corner of her note page and underlined it.

"Three that we know about, anyway," she said.

STATE'S ATTORNEY WENDELL Stamps called a Police Commission meeting for four o'clock to discuss Susan Champlain's death.

The PC was made up of the state's attorney and representatives from the sheriff's office, state police, and municipal police. The purpose of this meeting, Hunter knew, was to agree on a story to tell before the real one was known. That gave Hunter several hours to conduct follow-up interviews. A copy of the preliminary autopsy report had been promised Homicide by 2 P.M.

She walked down the hall first to talk with Frances Neal, the state investigator in charge of gathering evidence at the bluff. Neal looked tired this morning, more tired than Hunter felt.

"You were right about the book," she said, giving Hunter an accusatory look from behind her metal desk. "Kairos forty-eight."

"What does it mean?"

"A password?" She had a photocopy of the receipt right in front of her. "The way the forty-eight is flush against the *s*?" She pointed with her middle finger, her nails all bitten to a nub. "Don't know what forty-eight means. *Kairos* is an ancient Greek word. Meaning 'opportune moment.'"

Hunter nodded; she'd already looked it up.

Susan Champlain's other sandal hadn't turned up and there was still no sign of a phone or a purse, Neal told her.

"Footprints?"

"Three separate imprints on the bluff trail besides Champlain's. It also looked as if someone may have tried to smooth over the dirt on the bluff itself. But that's a guess."

"What size impressions?"

"I got a ten and a half Reebok," Neal said. "The others aren't clear, one larger, one smaller."

They'd also taken tire impressions from the edge of the road, and footprint impressions down below, near where Susan's body had been found—which, judging from the length of the stride and the size of the foot, were probably a woman's.

"What time's your meeting?" Neal asked.

"Four o'clock."

"I'll call you before then if we have anything else."

Hunter drove to the Old Shore Inn and talked with the manager and the lobby bartender, both of whom were cautiously helpful, telling her that Susan Champlain came in several times a week, always by herself, to read and drink iced tea; neither remembered seeing her on Wednesday, though. The manager told her that Sonny Fischer from Homicide had already contacted him about surveillance video and that they'd turned over what they had.

Elena Rodgers, Champlain's "personal assistant," who'd been renting a room at the Inn for the summer, was out. Hunter left her card at the desk with a brief note asking her to call.

She walked beneath the fluttering awnings of Main Street to talk with Carly Talbot, a poised, chalk-skinned woman who managed Cool Beans, the health-food store where Susan had bought breakfast the day before. Talbot had been described by the bartender at the Old Shore as a "friend" of Susan Champlain, who'd met her for tea a couple of times at the Inn. But Talbot smiled dismissively at the characterization.

"Not really friends." Her eyes fixed on Hunter's for a long moment. "I talked with her after church a few times, and she came in here occasionally. Never stayed, always picked up something to go. We met once to chat. I liked her. We kept making plans to do things, and then Susan would always back out. It got to be kind of weird, actually. I hate to say."

"Why was that, do you think?"

"I don't know, she was just very private. And, I thought, scared about something."

"Did she ever give any indication what it might be?"

"Not really. I almost got the impression that—she acted like someone was following her. But I don't know. Her husband's so-called bodyguard, maybe? That's a total guess. Probably not fair." She exhaled dramatically, looking at the street. "I don't know, just the idea of someone having a 'bodyguard' gives me the willies. You know? I can't imagine that kind of lifestyle."

"Did she ever talk with you about her husband?"

"Never."

"Did you see her at all this week?"

"Sunday. That was it."

"Not yesterday?"

"No."

"Supposedly Susan came in here for breakfast yesterday."

"I wouldn't know, I wasn't working." She exhaled again, as if she was very tired all of a sudden. "I thought she was a sweet person, with a lot of style. But hard to know."

"What *did* she talk about with you?"

"Oh, just—Not a lot, really. Her family. The weather. Growing up in Iowa. Her artwork. She did tell me that one of her photographs had gone on display for a couple of days at the Empress Gallery in town, and then was taken down. Which struck me as kind of weird."

Hunter thought so, too. Considering what she'd heard about Nick Champlain monitoring her activities.

"Taken down why?"

"I have no idea. She wouldn't talk about it. That's how she was.

"Oh, and she talked about animals," she added. "She'd always had cats and dogs growing up, she told me, and I think she really wanted to have a pet here in Tidewater. But her husband was allergic, she said. That's about all she ever told me about her husband."

Hunter thanked her and walked to the Empress Gallery at the other end of Main Street. But the gallery didn't open until noon. She cupped her hands and looked through the glass. It was mostly Eastern Shore art, paintings and wood carvings, along with abstract glass sculptures.

Her interview with Agnes Collins at the church went about as expected. Collins was prickly, hesitant to answer questions the way Hunter phrased them. Amy tried to be patient, and finally came away with a better description of the man with "elegant shoulders." But not much else.

She left a voice mail with Susan Champlain's parents in Iowa, with condolences, saying she'd like to ask them a few questions if they felt up to it. She introduced herself as a Maryland State Police officer, not mentioning Homicide, and gave them her direct number.

Joseph Sanders, the bodyguard, she found in the shade beside the house the Champlains were renting. He was shirtless, doing something under the hood of a Ford pickup.

"I really have nothing to say," he told her, as soon as she'd identified herself, wiping his hands on a rag. His bald head glistened with a thin layer of sweat.

Sanders repeated what he'd told state police the night before at the PSC, how he'd gone out fishing alone and then stopped at the Harbor Loon bar. He smiled impatiently at one point, showing several misshapen teeth.

"I really have nothing to add beyond what I said last night."

"What do you think happened to Susan?"

"No idea." He frowned, continuing to wipe his hands. "What I heard was she fell. I don't know any different."

"What was the nature of your relationship with her?"

"Ma'am?"

Hunter asked again.

"There was no relationship, ma'am," he said, giving her a steady look under hooded eyes. "I work for her husband. I explained all that last night. Otherwise, I have nothing to say."

He was standing facing her, arms at his sides now. Hunter watched his belly go up and down as he breathed.

"Do you know any reason anyone might have wanted to hurt her?"

"Hurt her? No, ma'am."

It went on like that for a couple of minutes. Hunter left with the idea that she'd come back to him once she had something more specific to ask.

The Champlains' housekeeper, Sally Markos, was a petite, pretty woman with olive skin who wouldn't look Hunter in the eye. She'd met the Champlains at the beginning of summer, she said, and worked for them only once a week.

"It's just awful," she said repeatedly, sitting on a narrow bed in her cottage looking out toward the cove, her eyes misting over; she seemed more composed, though, than she had the night before. The air was dusty, a warm breeze puffing out the sheer curtains.

"Do you know anyone who may have wanted to hurt her?" Hunter asked.

"Mrs. Champlain? Oh, God *no*, I can't imagine. No. It's just awful. They were good people. I just hope nothing happens to Mr. Champlain."

Hunter cleared her throat, trying not to seem surprised. "To Mr. Champlain? Why do you say that?"

Her eyes were downcast. "Because he's my *employer*."

"No, I mean: why do you think something might happen to him?"

"I didn't say that. I said I hope it doesn't."

"But what makes you think it *might*? That something might happen."

"I didn't say that. I said I hope it *doesn't* happen."

"Okay."

Hunter glanced at her notes. She'd be back to her, too.

She picked up an oyster sandwich from Kent's Crab House on her way back to the PSC. The place was bustling with sunburned tourists, cracking crabs and drinking beer in the sun on the decks, oblivious to what had happened the night before at Widow's Point.

The preliminary autopsy report was back by the time Hunter returned. Fischer had placed it on her desk in a sealed envelope.

She skimmed through the findings as she ate her sandwich: Susan Champlain appeared to have a contusion at the back of her head, and a slight swelling of the brain. BAC level was .09, just above the legal .08. Her injuries were "consistent with a fall," the summary claimed, with "multiple traumatic injuries" including a broken left arm. Hunter flipped through the death photos again, the disturbing way she'd ended up crumpled on the beach. Pending toxicology and final autopsy, the ME was calling her cause of death "inconclusive."

The State Police had also sent over a report, requested by the state's attorney, Wendell Stamps, for those attending the Police Commission meeting. It was exactly what she'd expected: wordy generalities with a strong bias bolstering the state's theory that Susan's death was accidental.

She finished her sandwich, crumpled the wrapper and tossed it in the trash bin. A minute later, Gerry Tanner was sitting on a corner of her worktable, his leather notebook opened on his left knee, several printouts in his right hand.

"Well, the husband's left the building," he said. "Just confirmed."

It took Hunter a moment. "As in Elvis has left the building?"

"Yep." Tanner's long expressionless face reminded her of a mask. "His business manager just called me back. The man's on the road, back to Philly. His assistant's alone in the house."

"Elena Rodgers?"

"No, I meant Joey Sands. Joseph Sanders. That's what they call him, Joey Sands." Tanner glanced at his notes. "He did say that Champlain will fully cooperate and answer any questions we have."

"Didn't Dunn ask him to stay put?"

"He should have. His business manager said he cleared it with the sheriff and the state's attorney."

Hunter felt a prickle of anger. The state's attorney was making a point, as he sometimes did.

"What's a business manager, exactly?"

"That's what he calls him. John McCoy is his name."

Hunter nodded, instructing herself to stay cool. "Anything else?"

"The man's grieving, he said. Champlain. He, uh, asked if I had any reason to think it *wasn't* an accident." He looked at his notebook—lines of minute, carefully printed writing. "*Evidence*, rather. To think it wasn't an accident. Not reason." His dark eyes lingered on hers.

"Anything more on the alibi?" she asked.

"Yeah, video confirmation. Champlain was on the road last night when she was killed. Didn't return until after nine."

He leaned across the desk and laid out three printouts. This was what he'd really come in to show her. She felt him breathing on her arms. "That looks like him," he said: Nick Champlain driving his dark Mercedes sedan through a toll plaza on Delaware Route 1, and then at a four-way intersection entering Tidewater County from the north, at a few minutes before nine.

"So, time frame," Tanner said, flipping another page. Hunter leaned back in her chair. "The victim rides her bicycle over to Widow's Point, we think, about seven P.M., give or take a half hour. No one sees her. Joe Sanders—Joey Sands—is supposedly drinking beer at the Harbor Loon, from about seven oh five to nine thirty. The husband returns to town around nine, drives straight to Kent's Crab House for dinner, where he meets Elena Rodgers, his assistant. Mr. Kent, the owner, joins them. And, I'm told, the sheriff may have been there, as well."

Hunter scribbled a note about the sheriff on her desk calendar. "And police weren't able to reach him right away," she said. "What was the delay about?"

"No one had his cell phone number. But I've confirmed he was there—he came in the restaurant at nine fourteen. They first left a message with his office, then they tried the landline in the house he was renting. No one had his cell." He glanced at his notebook again. "So. And then he comes in for the interview, voluntarily, at eleven oh seven."

"After being notified by who? Dunn?"

"Dunn, that's right. Found him at Kent's, they rode together to the M.E.'s office, where she'd just come in. So that added to the delay."

"Oh." Hunter should've asked about this before. "So he'd seen her when I talked to him last night."

"Yes. He'd just ID'd her."

Hunter thought about that. "What was his demeanor when he was notified? Any idea?"

"Cool," Tanner said. "He's a cool customer."

"Yes, I know," Hunter said. "Who did the transfer, then?"

"Byers Funeral Home. Police rented a hearse, took her to Baltimore."

Tanner stared at Hunter, his wide mouth shut tight. "People are saying it was a fall."

"I know," she said. "It wasn't."

"Okay." His eyes glanced at Fischer in his office, working with earbuds in. To his credit, Tanner never said anything negative about Fischer. "When's your meeting?"

"Four o'clock," Hunter said. "If you get anything else, let me know."

"Ten–four."

It always freaked her out a little when Gerry Tanner said "Ten–four." Those had always been Ben Shipman's parting words. Had someone told him that, or was it just coincidence?

Tanner didn't leave immediately, though. He turned a couple of pages in his notebook, as if they were in a reading room at the library.

He glanced up finally when her cell phone rang.

Area code 202. It was the FBI.

"I'll need to take this," Hunter said.

"Okay. Hasta la vista." Tanner stood and marched out.

"Hunter," she answered.

"Well, you've done it again."

It wasn't the call Hunter had expected, from John Marcino, her contact at the FBI. It was Dave Crowe, an FBI special agent and Hunter's onetime mentor. Crowe had reappeared in her life during the Psalmist case.

She took a breath. "Well, hel*lo*," she said, forcing a greeting.

"How are you?" he said. "What's the deal with this photo?"

"I didn't know there was a deal."

"Techs here are taking unusual interest."

"Why?"

"I thought you were going to tell *me*."

"No," Hunter said. She got up and closed the door. Tanner was in his office with his head tilted back, trying to listen. "I can't," she told Crowe, calling up on her computer the images Susan Champlain had sent Luke. "Why are they taking interest?"

"It's complicated," he said. Crowe often did this with her, talking with a slightly heightened sense of drama. Eight years earlier, they'd gone out on a date together, followed by a couple of near-dates. Hunter wasn't as good in personal relationships as she was in her work.

She studied Susan Champlain's three images, which she'd forwarded to the FBI that morning, as they talked. *Why would the Bureau have any interest in these cell-phone pictures?*

"Between us?" Crowe said. "You'll probably be hearing from a guy named Scott Randall in another day or two. Okay? He's been asking about you."

"Has he? Why?"

"And frankly? You may regret it if you become involved with this guy. Okay? Just a friendly warning," he said, only stoking her interest further. "Call me once you've heard from him, if you want to talk about it."

It was Crowe who hung up first, skipping the goodbyes.

Eleven minutes until the Police Commission meeting.

Hunter called up an FBI directory. Scott Randall, she discovered, was the new director of the FBI's Stolen Art Division based out of D.C.

Now things were getting really weird.

Chapter Ten

When she arrived at Conference Room B, Hunter found a sheet of computer paper taped to the door: *Police Com. mtg moved to State Aty's Office. 4 P.M.* The peculiar left-slanted felt-penmanship she recognized as the work of Connie Elgar, the state's attorney's executive assistant.

"Scheduling conflict," Wendell Stamps explained as Hunter took a seat in front of his immaculate glass-covered desk. The others crossed legs and shuffled papers, giving the impression that the meeting was already under way, although Hunter was in fact a minute early.

"I thought it might be more useful if we just went ahead with the four of us."

"That's fine," Hunter said. At this point, she didn't have anything, anyway; she wasn't ready to talk about the photos.

Stamps was a big, shrewd man with thin blond hair and a wide, impassive face. He was dressed, as always, in pinstripes. In many ways, Stamps ran the justice system in Tidewater County; it wasn't uncommon for people from one or more agencies to gather unofficially in his office to chart out some slightly clandestine course of action.

The other two in the room this afternoon were the sheriff's public information officer, Kirsten Sparks, and Stamps's investigator, Clinton Fogg, who was doodling arrows onto a yellow legal pad.

"I understand from Gary Martin that you have information the husband may have made a verbal threat of some kind in the days preceding the incident?"

"It came up in an interview," Hunter said. "I wrote a report and submitted it this morning."

"We've got it." It was on top of his small, neat stack of papers. "Are you going anywhere with it?"

"Not at this point, no."

"Champlain has an airtight alibi, supposedly," Stamps said. "Right?"

"That's what we're hearing," she said. "Although time of death is not an exact science, sir. As you know."

"No, it isn't."

Stamps showed his perfect poker face. Fogg continued to doodle, turning an arrow into a triangle.

"The preliminary autopsy," Sparks said, "I'm told, is leaning toward accidental?"

"Yes," the state's attorney said. Sparks sat forward, making it clear that she was asking him this, not Hunter. Then sat back again, watching Hunter with a small smile, emboldened slightly by the state's attorney's affirmative answer. Sparks was blond and attractive, with a hard outer shell and lots of insecurities. She became defensive whenever Hunter spoke to her forcefully, compensating at other times by either ignoring her or looking at Hunter with a silent, slightly superior expression, as she was doing now.

"Well, no," Hunter said. "Inconclusive or undetermined."

The state's attorney half shrugged, meaning *same difference*. "Inconclusive" meant they could sell it as accidental if they wanted. They were really here just to see if she had anything they didn't.

"But you have no reason to think this was homicide?" Stamps said. "That's the issue."

"No, sir, not at this time."

He slanted his eyes very slightly as if he didn't understand. "But—you have something you're looking at?"

"Not at this time, sir," she lied.

"Understood. But at a later time?"

"No, sir. Not that I'm aware of."

Fogg kept his head down, as if not listening, doodling arrows again. Hunter knew he was hearing every word. The S.A.'s office didn't want to pursue this; but they also didn't want to be caught flat-footed.

Wendell Stamps tried again. When he couldn't get Hunter to say anything, he closed the meeting, and the other two left the room. Hunter stood too, but didn't leave.

"Why do I get the feeling you're holding something back?" Stamps asked.

"I'm not, sir. My only issue, if you want to call it that, is I'm concerned that Nicholas Champlain was allowed to leave town when there were still questions to be answered."

"Questions."

Hunter cleared her throat, realizing she shouldn't have used that word. "Yes. Questions of timing," she said. "Even if he's not involved, he could help clarify time frames. Help us determine whether or not this was an accident."

He looked at her with a trace of frown or, maybe, smile. It was hard to tell. He glanced at the antique German wall clock. Hunter was thinking about the photos on Susan's phone, about the necklace in the sand, about what Dave Crowe had just said about the case being "complicated." But she wasn't ready to share any of that. She had a strong feeling about Susan's death, but no good explanation yet.

"I did speak with his business manager thirty-five minutes ago," Stamps said. "Who told me that Mr. Champlain wants to cooperate fully."

"I've left a message with him."

"He'll talk with you I'm sure, whenever you want. Just give him a day or two. He's dealing with the funeral arrangements right now. I also spoke with Hank Moore, this morning."

Hunter's supervisor. Making it clear he'd covered all the bases. Hunter watched him.

"But nothing else I need know about?" Stamps tried again. Hunter shook her head, deciding to act dumb. With Stamps, he assumed it anyway. In fact, Hunter wanted to keep her own investigation separate until she had a clearer idea what had really happened to Susan Champlain.

"No," she said, showing a smile. "Nothing at this point."

"Are you recommending we hold off saying anything on this preliminary, then?" Stamps, to his credit, was a diplomat, if a self-serving one.

"No, sir. Although, if you're asking me, I'd say it might be smart to wait a couple of days. And maybe have a moratorium on saying it was an accident. But that's only a suggestion."

"You know I can't control what people are *say*ing."

If only that were true. Hunter decided to leave it there. He knew what she meant.

The FBI's number had come up again on her phone during the Police Commission meeting. Crowe. She tried him as she walked down the corridor to her office but had to leave a message.

Tanner had placed a note on her desk: *Out doing interviews.*

Hunter also had an e-mail from attorney John McCoy. Nick Champlain's "business manager."

Mr. Champlain is currently making arrangements for his wife's funeral. He will be able to meet with you on Monday at 1 P.M. at his office in Philadelphia. If this is acceptable, please confirm.

It was an odd, impersonal way to tell her, but Hunter wrote back, accepting.

Minutes later, Sonny Fischer came out. He leaned in her doorway, to give her an update on what he'd found. For some reason, he didn't like sitting in other people's offices.

"Not a lot yet. Problem with two: Markos and Rodgers," he said, speaking in his quirky verbal shorthand.

"What's the problem?"

"Basically, don't exist."

"Okay," Hunter said. That could be a problem. "Meaning—?"

"No DMV, birth, property records. I can dip into tax reports if we need to."

"How about the necklace?"

"Not yet. Security tapes to go through."

"Maybe work on that a little first?"

He nodded. Fischer was good, thorough to a fault sometimes. Hunter didn't want him data-mining into places that could potentially be legally challenged. Not yet, anyway.

She worked in her office until several minutes past six, when she realized she needed to feed Winston, her eccentric tuxedo cat. Winston let Hunter know immediately—with his sashaying walk and bizarre howling—that she was half an hour late.

She fixed a frozen enchilada dinner for herself and poured a tall glass of red wine. Then she settled in to review what she had, starting with the notes Fischer had prepared. One detail led to another and she lost the thread of time on several occasions, pausing only to commune with Winston and, once, to listen to a song by the Pogues through earbuds, dancing in her living room to let off steam. Winston sat on the sofa arm, watching as she did, a perplexed and not very happy expression on his face.

It was a misty night and the wind made a loud sound through the trees that resembled human breathing. Hunter fell asleep with her windows and deck doors open. She'd made a list of three things to follow up on in the morning: ask Luke about Kairos; ask Champlain's business manager about the necklace; determine who Joey Sanders was and what sort of relationship he might've had with Susan Champlain.

But by morning, the list wouldn't matter.

Chapter Eleven

The death of developer Nicholas Champlain's wife was news, much as Walter Kepler had feared. But it was passing news, a regional wire service short with the shelf life of a single news cycle. The words "apparently accidental" helped; they'd head off potential innuendo, as would Nick Champlain's aversion to publicity. But what really concerned him now was what *Champlain* thought, and whether or not it would affect their plan.

Nick was staying at one of Kepler's condos on the Delaware coast tonight, letting his business manager handle inquiries and condolences. Kepler was eleven miles to the north in a larger apartment, although Champlain didn't know that.

"Nick, I'm sorry," he said, conjuring a sympathetic tone. "I wanted to give you a chance to get your bearings. Just know I'll do whatever I can."

"I'm letting my business manager handle it with the media," Champlain said, talking on one of the disposable phones Kepler had given him. "We've issued a statement."

"I saw."

"That should take care of it." He added, "This doesn't affect our arrangement?"

"No. Should it?"

"No. That's why I'm asking."

There it was, then: *He* was asking the question. Everything was fine. Kepler breathed more easily, turning to look at the Atlantic Ocean. Nick Champlain had probably loved his wife very much on the day they were married, four years ago, he imagined—but not on the night she died. By then, Susan Champlain had become a liability to him. That's why she was down in Maryland for the summer—to keep her out of the way. Although, according to Belasco, who had been Kepler's eyes in Tidewater, that hadn't worked out so well.

"You understand, I wasn't there," Champlain said. "It was an accident. That's what the police are saying."

"I hear it," Kepler said. "And I appreciate you telling me. I really do."

Kepler looked at the fast-moving night clouds over the water. Thinking: They were in the storm now, weren't they? He felt the change in the air, the miracle only a week away now. "You're going to the funeral?"

"I'm paying for it," Champlain said. "They don't want me there. The sister doesn't."

"We'd like you to *tell* people you're going," Kepler said. "It would work into our new time frame."

Champlain was silent.

"Okay?"

"Okay," he said. Then: "What's the new time frame?"

"My client would like to move the whole thing up by three days. Is that possible?"

"Three days," he repeated.

"You said they just needed twenty-four-hour notice."

"That's right."

"Good." In fact, from what Kepler knew of the Rosa family—who controlled the painting and were now selling it to him through Nick Champlain—he suspected they didn't *want* a lot of notice. They wanted this deal to go quickly, to collect their $5 million and move on. "So can we just pick up where we were, then? We'll meet Tuesday. I'll have the rest of what you need then."

"All right."

"Take care of yourself, Nick. Again, I'm sorry."

Kepler only hoped that Belasco hadn't waited too long.

Chapter Twelve

That was the night that Luke and Charlotte finally had the talk about their future—the real topic of which was whether or not to enlarge the Bowers family from three to four. It didn't come off quite as Luke had imagined. First, he prepared dinner—roasted salmon with slivered almonds, prepared in butter and lemon juice—while Charlotte made the salad, chopping tomatoes and onions she'd picked from their garden.

As the fillets were simmering, they slipped into the bedroom and made love, which had become a fairly regular Thursday night activity at the Bowerses' domicile. In bed afterward, savoring the cross breezes, Luke had spontaneously brought it up. Not as the question he'd been formulating in his thoughts for several days. But as a statement that came to him in a flash of inspiration: "I think we ought to have a child."

Charlotte leaned on her elbow, looking at him with the tiniest of smiles. "Okay," she said.

"Okay?"

"Yes."

"Really?" Luke said.

"Really."

"Okay. That was easier than I expected," he said, wondering if the death of Susan Champlain had nudged them a little.

The decision was one thing, of course, the details another. Those would be a much longer discussion, he knew, which they began to have that night over dinner, and a couple glasses of white wine. It involved deciding where to live (not enough room in the parish house), how long they would stay in Tidewater (Methodist ministers averaged only four to six years at one location) and also how long Luke wanted to remain a pastor.

They sat on the deck afterward, talking about it over another glass of wine. But eventually their thoughts drifted to more private places and more mundane concerns.

"I'm going to check something online," Charlotte said vaguely a few minutes past nine. Luke gravitated to his own space in the sitting room, glad to work on his sermon for a while—reading several times through the passage in James about the brevity of life.

Charlotte came in with Sneakers and a glass of wine later to check on him, and to say that she was going to review her notes for a few minutes. Charlotte was writing about Delmarva-region Indian treaties from the 1600s and 1700s—including the famous treaty of 1722, which professed to be binding until "world's end."

He could hear her later talking to herself, which she sometimes did, as if alone in the house with Sneakers, her voice occasionally rising on a phrase or a word. "Now, *that's* interesting," he heard her say at one point and he wondered if she might be on the phone. Charlotte had a phone voice that was slightly different from the tone she used with him; she tended to gesture with her arms while talking on the phone, too, as if the person on the other end could see her.

Then she went quiet. Luke looked at the clock when he heard her again: 9:47. "Are you *kidding*?"

"No way," she said, at 10:19.

Feeling left out, Luke decided to see what was up.

"Everything under control in here? You two behaving?"

Charlotte turned, surprised. Sneakers, too, raised his head and looked up. She was deep into something, he could see; she'd tacked all kinds of printouts to her bulletin board.

"Sorry," he said, "I just wanted to make sure you weren't indulging a secret porn habit."

What Luke saw on her computer was only slightly less surprising, though. Blown up on the screen was one of the images Susan had sent him the day before. Was *this* what she'd been working on so diligently for the past hour or so, while Luke assumed she was researching Indian treaties?

"You're looking at Susan Champlain's pictures."

"Yes."

"Why?"

She sighed and clicked a new image onto the screen. "See this?"

"Okay."

"And this." She pointed to a printout on the bulletin board, what looked like a dark abstract painting, or maybe a drapery pattern.

"Looks like an out-of-focus early Rothko."

"No," Charlotte said. She collapsed the image on her screen, to show most of the room again, from Susan Champlain's photo.

"Now this is the reflection of the next room," she said, closing in on just the mirror. "See this? What looks like a giant piece of wood here, leaning on the wall?"

"Okay."

"Now, this is a stretch, admittedly," she said, "because it's so blurry, but this image"—she enlarged the screen image further—"looks quite a bit like this one," indicating the abstract printout. Charlotte pointed to similarities in the color and paint patterns with the assurance of a forensics expert in a murder trial. "Doesn't it?"

"They *are* similar blurs."

"Yes, more than similar, actually. They're matching blurs."

"Matching blurs."

"Yes."

"Sounds like a rock band."

"Ha-ha."

"You're saying that piece of wood leaning on the wall in the mirror might be a *paint*ing?"

"Might be." She called up a different, sharper image that he vaguely recognized—a dark oil painting of a ship tilted in rough seas. "The color's off a bit, but the shapes are almost an exact match. See?" She brought in a close-up of the painting, and compared it with another printout, detail from Susan's cell-phone photo. Despite the distortion, there were clearly similarities in the patterns and colors.

"Why does that painting look so familiar?"

"It's an early Rembrandt," Charlotte said. "Called *Storm on the Sea of Galilee*."

"Oh."

"It's one of the most famous stolen paintings in the world. Missing now for some twenty-five years."

"And how did you manage to figure *this* out?"

Charlotte shrugged. "A couple of glasses of wine helped. Sneakers gave me moral support, of course." Luke frowned at her, but admiringly. "Actually, I've written about this painting," she said. "We've talked about it. Several times."

"The Gardner Museum."

"Yes."

"Sorry, I'm a little slow tonight."

In fact, they'd visited the Gardner in Boston twice together; he'd looked at the empty frame where Rembrandt's masterpiece had lived for decades.

"Of course, even if that's what this is, it could be a reproduction," he said.

"Could be." But Luke wasn't thinking that. He was thinking of Susan Champlain, the urgency and evasiveness in her eyes as she'd told him her story.

He pulled up a chair and listened as Charlotte recounted what had happened at the Isabella Stewart Gardner Museum in Boston on St. Patrick's Day night 1990, a tale he'd heard many times over the years, although he'd forgotten some of the details: how two men dressed as Boston police officers had been allowed in the museum that night on the pretense that they were responding to a reported disturbance. How they'd tied up the night guards with duct tape in the basement, disabled security cameras and spent eighty-one minutes in the galleries, removing thirteen works of art worth an estimated $500 million, including a Vermeer, three Rembrandts, and a Manet.

Two men police believed played a role in the theft were murdered shortly afterward and countless leads in the case had fizzled over the years. One investigator said there seemed to be a "curse" surrounding the Gardner art.

As Charlotte talked, Luke continued to think of Susan Champlain, seated in his office wearing a white sleeveless blouse, her hands gesturing anxiously, her voice momentarily thickening at one point. He wondered if she'd had any idea what she'd photographed. If she suspected what her husband had meant when he'd said "people could get killed waving this thing around." Or if she had died without knowing any of that.

Sensing that he was no longer paying attention to her, Charlotte stopped talking. They just looked at each other for a while, and then at the matching blurs. By that point, Luke could tell they were thinking the same thing: this may have been the reason that Susan Champlain was killed.

"The question is," he said, "what are we going to do about it?"

Chapter Thirteen

Hunter's cell phone woke her several minutes before sunrise on Friday. It was Scott Randall, from the FBI's Stolen Art Division in Washington.

"Are you able to meet this morning?"

"I am," she said, blinking herself awake. "Where are you?"

"Headed your way," he said. His voice had the pitch of a female and Hunter wondered at first if "Scott" might be a woman. "Could you meet me in front of the Captain's Table at nine thirty?"

She gazed at the boats in the marina, just turning visible again, a slight breeze moving in the trees. She'd been up much of the night running Internet searches, ever since Luke had called and e-mailed over the Rembrandt image. Hunter had forwarded it on to John Marcino, of the Criminal Investigations Division, her longtime contact at the FBI. By the time she'd fallen asleep ninety minutes earlier, Hunter had become an expert on the Isabella Stewart Gardner heist. "I'll see you there," she said.

The Captain's Table was a breakfast/lunch diner in a strip of

storefronts along the highway, known for creative breakfast selections such as oyster omelets and blue crab muffins. At 9:30,
Hunter was standing out front.

A Honda Civic pulled to the curb a few minutes later. The passenger window slid down.

"Hunter?" Randall leaned across the seat, showed his ID, and
reached to shake her hand. "Hop in."

He was a tall, rangy man with a good-natured face and receding hairline, his eyes hidden behind aviator sunglasses.

"Sorry to do it this way," he said. "I'm not a fan of offices."

"No, me neither."

"Thanks for sending over the photo." He smiled as he pulled
onto the highway, and Hunter noticed that his middle front teeth
protruded, one longer than the other, giving him the affable
smile of an overgrown high-school kid. He was wearing a black
golf shirt and light-colored sports slacks and loafers, an inch of
white flesh showing above his beige ankle socks.

"I hope you understand we need to keep this whole thing contained," he said.

"Sure," Hunter said. "Which whole thing, exactly?"

"The photo."

"Okay," she said. "Which would make me think that this
painting is the real deal."

"Well." He made a throat-clearing sound. "Maybe. Hard to tell
from the cell photo, obviously."

He turned off Highway 50 onto a two-lane state road and
pushed down on the accelerator, heading toward rural Delaware.
"Who else knows about it?" he asked her.

"The painting? Or the photo?"

"Both."

Randall's nose wrinkled as soon as she mentioned Dave Crowe. Not a lot of people liked Crowe, even though he was a skilled investigator.

"And, of course, Nick Champlain, too," she added.

Randall briefly let his foot off the gas. "How do you mean?"

"I mentioned the photo to him. Two nights ago. The night his wife died. During police interviews. Of course, I hadn't seen the images yet at the time. I didn't know about the painting at that point."

Hunter told him the rest of it, about Susan Champlain's conversation with Pastor Luke and about Nick Champlain's cool denial. Randall listened, leaning back, both hands flexing on the wheel, Hunter noticing his long clean fingernails. Several times he started to reach for something in his left shirt pocket, although there was nothing there to reach for; and no pocket, for that matter. He also lowered and raised the window twice. Hunter suspected he'd recently quit smoking.

"And no one else?"

"No one else."

The painting, though, was different. A smaller club. Only Hunter, Charlotte, and Luke knew about it. And John Marcino, at the FBI.

"And my cat," Hunter added. "He knows the whole deal."

Scott Randall either didn't find her comment humorous, or didn't understand what she was saying. Sometimes Hunter suffered timing issues when she tried to be funny. Randall drove on through the tall cornfields, passing an old barn and a roadside produce stand.

"You're going to explain what this is all about, I presume," she said.

"What I can, yeah."

"Because, I ought to point out, my concern is the death of Susan Champlain," Hunter said, "not the whereabouts of a stolen painting. Not even one that's worth a hundred million dollars."

This, surprisingly, got a rise from him. He grinned over at her, a little maniacally, it seemed. "Who told you it was worth a hundred million dollars?"

"No one. I saw it online," Hunter said. "The whole theft, supposedly, is worth five hundred million."

"Yeah, right," he said. "That's an estimated auction price. If it ever went to auction. But stolen art doesn't go to auction. So saying it's 'worth' something is nonsensical."

"Okay."

"The media invents these numbers. Sometimes assisted by so-called art experts, sometimes not," he said. "Matter of fact, there was a famous theft at the Kunsthal Museum in Rotterdam in 2012. The media reports all said the art was, quote, worth five hundred million. The number was repeated over and over like it was the Holy Grail. Indisputable. But then later they had to adjust it down to fifteen million. They'd talked to the wrong 'experts.'" He smiled at her again, in his element now, Hunter could tell. Randall had all sorts of facts and figures about stolen art at his disposal, she sensed. His voice had taken on a new assuredness, and speeded up; he had a way of crowding his words, dropping syllables—*matter of fact* sounded like *ma'fak*. *Holy Grail* was *Ho'grell*. Once he got going, he reminded her a little of Chris Matthews on *Hardball*.

"They want to find someone who'll say it's worth some big, astronomical number, right, because that's what sells, makes for a good story. But does it help the cause? No. It doesn't. I'm sort of an amateur collector myself. It amuses me, but it angers me a little at the same time."

The road turned into the sun through the cornfields and Hunter pushed down the passenger visor to block it. "You know what that Rembrandt's been worth for these past twenty-five years? *Storm on the Sea of Galilee*?"

"No," she said. "What?"

"Nothing," he said. "Zilch."

"Because it couldn't be sold, you mean."

"That's right, because it couldn't be sold. High-end stolen art is priceless—which from the standpoint of a thief means the same thing as worthless. The idea that stolen masterpieces are worth anything is a myth. They aren't. You can't take a masterpiece from a museum wall and sell it. It can't be done."

"But you're saying this case is different."

He gave her a cagey sideways look, thrown off momentarily; Hunter caught a glimpse of his eyes for the first time. "I'm asking," she said.

"Well, yes, in a way," he said. "In a way." But rather than explain, Scott Randall dropped back into silence.

"WHICH MAKES ME wonder," Hunter said, a minute or so later. "I was told yesterday that the FBI had an interest in the photos I sent over—but this was *before* we figured out they might have anything to do with this famous Rembrandt."

"That's right." He took his foot off the gas again.

"And I was told you'd be contacting me in the next day or so," Hunter said.

"Right."

"But then I sent over the image last night and you called me right away, before the sun was up, even," she said. "So something must've changed."

His face colored. "Did I wake you?"

"No, that's all right. My point is, you were interested in the photo be*fore* you knew about the painting."

"That's correct, yes." Randall slowed. They were coming to a rural four-way stop, with a convenience store and gas pumps. Randall braked and then pulled over in front of the store, the only vehicle there. "You mind?"

"No," she said. "I don't mind."

Hunter got out and stretched her legs, walking to the edge of the road while Randall went in. A slow breeze rustled the cornstalks, stirring the tassels.

Randall came out looking around for a moment as if he'd lost his car. There was a picnic table around the side, between a Dumpster and the cornfields. He pointed his coffee at it. His right hand went to the invisible shirt pocket.

"This okay?" he asked.

"Sure."

His leg made a wide arc over the bench as he sat. The coffee seemed to energize Scott Randall a little. He told her some more about the business of stolen art, his eyes seeming fixed on a spot down the road, although it was hard to tell with the sunglasses. He might've been talking with anyone, Hunter thought, expounding on the business of art theft, how stolen paintings on the black market sell for only 5 to 10 percent of what they'd draw at auction; how the Bureau calls stolen art a $6 billion- to $8 billion-a-year business. "But those numbers aren't based on actual transactions," he said, "they're based on 'market value,' so who knows? It's very misleading.

"At the highest level? It's a business that has its own rules. Which it sometimes makes up as it goes along." He backhanded the air as if flicking away a fly. "But back to your question? Yeah, you're right, we *were* interested in that picture before we knew about the painting."

"Why?"

"Because of one of the men in the picture. Okay? We think we know who one of the men is." He turned his aviator lenses to her. "And that's strictly on the q.t." He lifted his coffee cup and looked at the cornfield. "What's that stand for, anyway—'on the q.t.'? I've always wondered."

"I think it's just a slang for quiet," Hunter said. "The first and last letters."

"Is that right?" He took a long drink of coffee. "So, anyhow, yeah. There's reason to think one of the men in the picture has a connection to this painting. What you sent over last night seems to confirm it."

"And this is someone with ties to the Philadelphia mob?"

He grinned. "You saw that online, too?" He backhanded the air again. "We didn't necessarily want all that out there, but, yeah, okay. Of course, organized crime is a different animal now than it used to be. In Philly, we're not even talking about the families anymore, we're talking Nigerian stolen-car gangs—they steal luxury vehicles, load them onto big-box freighters, ship them across the Atlantic to sell in West Africa." *Ship them across the Atlantic* came out as *Shipacroslanick*.

"Okay," Hunter said, "but getting back to the painting. You think Nick Champlain has some connection with these people. And with the stolen painting."

"It's possible. Champlain is not the man we're interested in, though, okay? But what we think—what we hope—is that he may *lead* us to that man."

"Who is—?"

He smiled again, the easy, big kid's smile, and made her wait.

"The man's name is Walter Kepler," he finally said. "He's basically just a high-end art fence, although full of grand ideas about himself. He's a narcissist, a real piece of work." Randall's tone stiffened as he said this. She saw the crow's-feet form beside his eye as he turned his head toward the road. "Stolen masterpieces are essentially worthless. It's a myth that there's any market for them."

"You said that."

"But there's one exception. And that's what we're dealing with. *Who* we're dealing with."

"Kepler."

"Mmm-hmm." He finished his coffee, tilting his head way back. "His business isn't stolen art, he likes to say, it's stolen masterpieces. That's *his* characterization, now, not ours."

"The difference being—?"

"Numbers." His hand reached for the phantom cigarettes. "There are four hundred thousand stolen works of art out there, okay? Stolen masterpieces? Less than three dozen. Some would say less than two dozen, maybe closer to ten or twelve works that actually still exist. Depends on how you define *masterpiece*. So—a much more specialized market. Kepler's the only one who's ever been able to work that market in any kind of sustained way. And we haven't been able to catch him, to make a case that sticks. For that, I give him credit. I don't give him credit for how he goes about it."

"And you have information that Walter Kepler is in the process now of obtaining *this* particular masterpiece. That's what your case is about?"

"No, I didn't say that," he said, an irritability leaking into his voice. His feelings about Walter Kepler were personal, Hunter could tell, probably more than they should be. "And understand, Kepler's almost never the buyer. He's the buyer's agent, a broker basically. He's the dealmaker. People come to him, wanting to acquire a painting. Kepler puts the deal together."

"Okay."

"Typically, there is a seller and a buyer, and each is represented by an agent who does the negotiations directly. Typically, buyer and seller never meet."

"So you think Nick Champlain may be the seller's agent in this case? The connection to the stolen painting?"

"Well, I didn't say that, either. But, yeah, it's a reasonable assumption. That's been one of the missing pieces. I'm grateful that you brought this to our attention."

He nodded to her and smiled momentarily. Hunter still hadn't seen his eyes. "Ready?" He stood. He stuffed his coffee cup through the hatch of the trash can and pulled out his keys.

"So why are you interested in me?" Hunter asked as they headed south again through the cornfields, a rural route into

Maryland. "I mean, I hope you don't think of me as a path to finding this stolen art."

"No, not at all." He breathed out deliberately. "But, think of it this way. What if our cases are intimately entwined, okay? In other words, what if solving one case solves the other?"

"Okay," she said, feeling skeptical all of a sudden. "And you're going to explain that. You're going to tell me about this man Walter Kepler."

"Of course," he said. "That's why we're here. That's why I called you."

Chapter Fourteen

Luke was thinking about the vapor, from James 4:14, and the similar, earlier passages from the Psalms about the brevity of life, his topic now for Sunday's sermon. The discussion with Charlotte the night before—the decision to start a family—had filled him with new energies and optimism, and he'd sat down this morning with the idea of writing Sunday's sermon in a single sitting. But his thoughts kept straying from the sermon to the unknown details of their future—they would need a larger house, surely, but how long would they stay in Tidewater? Would they take up in a new part of the world, as they'd occasionally discussed? And what would Sneakers think?

He looked out the window, surprised to see J. Michael Bunting's Jeep parked in the church lot beside his car.

Almost simultaneously, Aggie appeared in the doorway.

"Do you want me to tell him you're in a meeting?" she asked in her breathy voice.

"No, that's all right," Luke said. It would be sort of a tough sell with no other cars in the lot.

By then, Luke had all but forgotten about the pet blessing

proposal. The plan to give dog and cat owners the opportunity to bring their pets to church two or three times during the off-season was in line with what other churches were doing around the country. A quick online search would've confirmed that. But J. Michael, as he liked to be called, was still trying to make it seem like a local controversy. Luke had declined to be interviewed by him, instead preparing a statement, which he'd run by the staff parish committee for their approval (after making their usual three or four word changes). He had sent the statement over to Bunting the day before.

That should have been the end of it.

But here he was, sitting in Luke's office, opening a badly wrinkled copy of what he'd e-mailed to him. "So you got our statement, I see?" Luke said.

"I did. Thank you."

He rattled it in the air for a moment and then tucked it back under his notebook. "But I just wanted to clarify a few things."

"Okay." Luke watched him cautiously and laced his fingers on the desk. J. Michael was a short, wiry man with curly hair, who wore thick-lensed, black-frame glasses. "Although as I said to you before, I don't want to make any public comment," he said. "The statement will have to stand on its own. That's the position of the church, and it's now been approved by staff parish."

Bunting stared at him, his brows frowning, as if Luke had said something inappropriate.

"Off the record, though," he said. "I wonder if I could just get your response to a comment I've been told."

"It would have to be off the record."

"I've been told that your wife has been lobbying for this. That the idea may have in fact come from her? And that's caused some people to suggest there may be a conflict of interest."

Luke cleared his throat. This was a new one. J. Michael kept looking, his expression far too serious for the discussion at hand. Luke was fairly certain that he'd made this up, an excuse to get him on the defensive.

"I'm just repeating what I've heard," Bunting said.

"Well, the answer is no," Luke said. "Not true." He was tempted to say something like "Why don't you ask her?" but he knew that J. Michael would use it as a reason to drive over to their house and bother Charlotte.

"So, you're denying that there's any conflict, then," he said, his pen now poised.

"I don't think there's anything to deny, really," Luke said, trying to smile. "But since we're off the record, I'll tell you, Charlotte—my wife—had nothing to do with suggesting this, that's correct."

"Even though she does work at the Humane Society."

"She volunteers there, yes. Once or twice a week. But this was suggested by two other women, who are members of the congregation. And, as I said before, there really hasn't been any opposition to it that I've heard."

"Other than Mrs. Elliott."

"Well, but she isn't a member of the congregation. And in her letter to the editor, she was just posing the question about whether pets should be allowed in church. It's actually a growing national trend, as I told you the first time."

He nodded, scribbling a jagged line on his pad and then several parallel lines over it; not real notes.

"But you do understand the opposition."

"Actually, no," Luke said. "What I understand is that there isn't much. Or any. As the statement says, these blessings will be held separate from the regular church services, just once a month. And, obviously, only for those who choose to attend."

"Okay." J. Michael was giving him his too-serious look again. "And, I mean—and this may sound kind of naive, but people are asking it—the pets wouldn't actually be expected to *worship*, obviously, would they? Or how would it work?"

Luke coughed once and shifted in his chair, trying not to laugh. It usually didn't take long for J. Michael to ask a thoroughly inane question, mostly because he hadn't bothered to research the issue or think it through.

Luke decided to try a different tack. "Do you have a dog? A cat?"

"Not at the moment."

"But you have had?"

"You mean—in my *lifetime*?"

"Yes." *When else?* Luke wondered.

"Okay."

"Good. Then I'm sure you can understand how people become very attached to their pets. How they become like family members. How they share their lives with them."

"Mmm-hmm."

"And so this would just be a way of showing gratitude for this blessing that our pets have been to our lives." J. Michael raked his pen slowly over the pad. He seemed to be stifling a yawn. "Maybe if you waited to see the first service yourself, see what it's about. Because I don't think there's any issue here. I mean, other than that one letter to the editor—"

"Well, *five* letters to the editor, actually. That we've published." His mouth flattened.

"Yes, but only one was critical of the idea," Luke said. "And she obviously misunderstood the concept, thinking that, as you just suggested, the pets would be expected to pray."

J. Michael stared blankly back at Luke. There would be no resolution to this today, Luke saw.

Walking to the door, J. Michael capped his pen and slipped it into his pants pocket. "Anything more on Susan Champlain?" he asked as they stood on the gravel out front.

"Not that I've heard, no."

He looked at Luke intently, as if he were a police investigator. "There's some talk now that it might not have been an accident?"

Luke sighed. There was a scent of cut grass and gasoline in the breeze. The sound of motorboats carried up the bluff. "People say all sorts of things, don't they?"

His brow clenched. "Supposedly she left behind a note? Had you heard that?"

"Nope. Nothing like that," Luke said. "Where'd you hear it?"

He shrugged. Sometimes, J. Michael made up details in order to get people to talk to him. It was more a nervous trait than anything malicious. "Anyway, Hunter hasn't been a lot of help," he added.

Luke smiled to himself at this. Amy Hunter categorically

avoided the media, referring all inquiries to the public information officer. That was smart of her. *He* should hire a PIO, just to deal with J. Michael Bunting.

"Well, thanks for stopping by," he said. "I hope you're able to attend the pet blessing and see for yourself what it's about."

J. Michael opened his mouth and showed his tongue like he was about to be sick. Then he smiled and reached to shake Luke's hand.

"Poor man," Aggie said, holding down a Venetian blind slat with her finger as the Jeep started up. "Supposedly he's having problems at home. And their youngest son is ill. Although I probably shouldn't be saying anything."

"No."

"You know what he said about the note?" Luke's eyes went to the window; he saw the air on the screen. Aggie must've heard their whole parking lot conversation. "Sorry," she said. "I wasn't trying to eavesdrop. But I've heard the same thing."

"Which—?"

"That she left behind a note of some kind, I mean."

"Saying what, I wonder?"

"Oh, I don't know. I just heard there might've been a note."

"Hmm." Luke grimaced and went back to his office and the Sunday sermon. It was something else he had to share with Hunter.

Chapter Fifteen

There are bad men and there are bad men," Scott Randall said, driving slowly past corn and soybean fields back to Tidewater.

"Okay," Hunter said. "And so which would he be? Kepler?"

"Bad," he said. "Very bad."

Hunter nodded, trying to grasp the distinction.

"Kepler was a legitimate art dealer at one time," Randall went on. "Which is how he got into this: he inherited his father's business in New York. His father studied art in Israel, wrote about art, wanted to be an artist himself. But—this is the way Kepler described it—he loved great art too much to produce merely good art himself. He opened a modest art gallery in New York many years ago, and did okay. Kepler ramped it up after he died. I actually *knew* Kepler briefly, years ago. So I know a little about him personally. And he *was* good at what he did. The man had an ability to make people believe a painting was worth far more than it really was. You have to understand, that's what the art world is, in a lot of ways—a high-level game of illusion. And he became a very accomplished BS'r, the kind of person who takes on the color of his surroundings." He glanced over at Hunter, to see if she was with him. "And, so, what happened was, he eventually stumbled into a deal that set him up for life. Mostly, it was dumb luck. But I give him a lot of credit for being able to pull it off."

"What was it?"

"He'd brokered the sale of a small private collection, which included two Picasso paintings from the nineteen fifties. Befriended the buyer, who had no immediate family, and became the man's friend, as well as his dealer. When the man died several years later, Kepler somehow wound up in possession of one of the Picassos. It was challenged by the deceased's estranged granddaughter—who was as unsavory, but not as sophisticated, as he was. They tried to claim he'd forged the man's signature on his will, etcetera, etcetera, it went on for a while. But the courts ruled ultimately in Kepler's favor. He sold the painting a year after the dust cleared, for sixteen point five million. You can look it up. A couple of years after that, he flipped a lesser Picasso to a well-known casino owner and picked up another seven or eight mill. That sort of thing happens in the art world. But for a very small number of people. Do you know the most ever paid for a painting?"

"I don't know," Hunter said. "Two hundred million?"

"Two hundred *fifty*." Both hands kneaded the steering wheel. He was disappointed, she could tell, that her guess was so close, although it wasn't a guess. "Cézanne's *The Card Players*. One of five, actually. It sold in twenty twelve to the royal family of Qatar for two fifty."

"That's hard to imagine, anyone paying that much for a painting."

"Yeah, well, that's the point, isn't it?" he said. "It was $100 million more than anyone had ever paid for a painting before. Is *The Card Players* really worth two hundred fifty million? No, of course not. But that's the nature of the business. It's worth what people are willing to pay.

"I think those deals gave Kepler an inflated sense of himself," he went on. "After that, he changed his M.O. and became a dealer in *stolen* art. Or *lost* art, as he called it, as if that gave some legitimacy to what he was doing. He began to style himself for a while—still does, probably—as this great *retriever* of stolen masterpieces."

"Rather than as just a dealer or broker."

"Right, that's how it evolved. He's made the claim that he can find and purchase any stolen masterpiece still in existence," Randall said, and Hunter heard an echo of bitterness in his voice once again. "Some years ago, he supposedly handed out business cards with just his name and the initials RSM. That's the story, anyway."

Hunter thought about it for a moment. "As in 'retriever of stolen masterpieces'?"

"That's right. He likes to think he's serving some higher calling, I guess, saving these art treasures, finding them a home where they'll be properly cared for. Sometimes in museums, sometimes not. If the museums had cared for them properly in the first place, they never would have been stolen, that's the idea he wants to project. To me? He's a high-level fence, who's just been lucky so far. End of paragraph, end of story."

Hunter noticed his lashes fluttering behind the sunglasses.

"But he *has* retrieved stolen art?" Hunter said.

"He has. Yes. Three or four times that we know of."

"What were they?"

"The paintings?" He seemed to become more tentative all of a sudden. "There were a couple of well-known cases. One in Zurich, where in 2008 a Degas, a Cézanne, van Gogh, and Monet were all taken off the walls of a small museum. No security. They were recovered four years later in Serbia. Kepler and his attorney played a role in negotiating their return, by setting up a dummy buyer.

"And also one of *The Scream* thefts in Oslo. The more recent one. He was involved in the recovery. But understand, he was very well paid, in both cases.

"I'll tell you what I *do* respect about Kepler," he added. "The problem with stolen art at this level is getting the thieves together with the potential buyers. That's always been the issue. We're talking two completely different social classes, two kinds of people. Neither of whom trusts or understands the other. There's a huge gulf there. That's why people who've dealt in stolen masterpieces have nearly always failed miserably. If I give Kepler any credit, it's that he's been able to bridge those two worlds."

"So Kepler has nothing to do with the thefts themselves."

"Oh, no," Randall said. "Most—all—thefts of masterpieces are carried out by people who don't know their little toe from their elbow. They don't respect the art, they only respect what it's supposedly 'worth,' and mistakenly think they can get some of that. We're talking low-level organized crime, in many cases. This one, for instance—the Rembrandt—the thieves cut the canvas out and left the frame on the floor of the Gardner. The painting was damaged goods before it even left the museum.

"Some very famous paintings—by Picasso, by Caravaggio, many others—have been destroyed because the thieves couldn't find a buyer. A few years ago, some men in Rotterdam stole seven works—Gauguin, Monet, Matisse, among them. They tried to sell them a couple times, couldn't get any serious offers and one of the thieves' mothers ended up burning them in her kitchen, to protect her son from prosecution. You can look it up."

"Yes, I have," Hunter said. "So Kepler wants to save these masterpieces before the same thing happens."

"Well. That's what he says."

"And so if a Cézanne could be sold privately for two hundred and fifty million dollars, presumably other paintings could also be sold privately for a sizable amount?"

"Yes, in theory." He smiled, turning to give her an enigmatic, possibly admiring look. "Of course, the art does carry a certain stigma, being stolen. The Cézanne wasn't stolen. But I think he may be able to use that in a perverse way to add to their value."

"So who's the buyer in this case, if it isn't him?"

When he didn't respond, Hunter said, "Do you have any idea?"

"Do I have any idea? Of course. There are a handful of people who operate at that level, a few predictable players: there is a collector in Dubai we know about who would like to own it. There is the Qatar royal family, as I mentioned. There's a Corsican dealer. There's someone now doing this very quietly in Silicon Valley.

"But what concerns us, you see, is that this buyer *isn't* one of the usual suspects. We have good intelligence that there may even be terrorist money in this deal. *That's* what concerns us." His voice rose with a new, more urgent inflection as he said this.

"Why would terrorists have any interest in a Rembrandt painting?"

"Well. That's the part I can't get into," he said. "But in general terms? The information we have is that he's working this deal for a Middle Eastern businessman who collects art. He, also, happens to be a supplier of arms to Sunni rebels in Iraq and to terrorist interests throughout the region. That's why this concerns us more than any other deal."

He went silent again. Hunter flashed on Dave Crowe's warning: *You may regret it if you become involved with this guy.* She watched his long fingers, tightening and loosening on the wheel again as if doing hand exercises.

"And there's one other problem, which goes even beyond that," Randall said. "Many of the deals Kepler's been involved in? Have been dirty, in a different way. The man has a problem, and his wealth and success have only exacerbated it: He doesn't care about human life. He always values the art over people. People's lives aren't going to last; these masterpieces will. That's one of his sayings." Randall's voice had a bitter edge again. "In each deal that we know about, there has been some collateral, human damage. 'Collateral' is his term."

"As in people who've been killed," she said, sensing that this was what the conversation had been turning toward.

"At least four," he said. "Although there's some disagreement over this within the Bureau. But—we know of three cases, unsolved, that have his fingerprints: one missing person, two homicides. And another accidental death that I'd put in the same category. That's four. This Susan Champlain may be number five." There was a sudden catch in his voice. "As I say, he's a man without a moral compass."

"Hmm." *Had* he said this? Hunter wondered.

"We've tried twice before to make cases against the man. Put good time and manpower into it. But we couldn't bring charges. And right now, some in the Bureau are a little reluctant to go up against him a third time, even though we're building a case."

Hunter waited, then realized he wasn't going to say any more. "So he hasn't been charged with anything, you're saying, not even in relation to stolen art?"

"Not yet. Right now, Kepler has a perfectly legal presence in the world. He pays his taxes, owns property, keeps a primary residence near Dover, Delaware, and owns some beach property. Although he's not there right now. Whenever Kepler's working a deal, he goes mobile, he rents rooms in various places, for himself and the people working for him. When Kepler's not home, it usually means something's happening."

"So something's happening now, you're saying," Hunter said.

"That's what we think. But we're limited in what we can do. It's a little bit of Catch-22: we don't have the resources to go after him properly because we haven't been able to make the case; and we can't make the case without the resources. You say the words 'stolen art' and some people in the Bureau roll their eyes; it's not a high priority, never has been. Stolen art is the Bureau's orphan child. And that situation's only made him bolder. This deal, in particular, worries me."

"Why?"

"Because of the terrorist connection, first. And because of the

painting itself. Walter Kepler loves this painting, he's made re-
marks about it over the years. He told one of our people last year
this is not only the greatest stolen work of art in the world, it's
also the greatest *painting* in the world."

Randall went silent, then. They were coming back to the
highway.

"And so you want me involved why? Because I can talk with
Nicholas Champlain?" she said.

"In part," he said. "You're in an unusual position. You have a
legitimate pretense to approach him and ask questions."

"Homicide isn't a pretense, though."

"No. Sorry, you have a *reason* to approach him. And he's not
going to think that you have any interest in the larger case."

"I don't know that I do."

"Or knowledge of it, let's say."

This confirmed what Randall was up to, anyway: he was recruiting her. Hunter needed to know more about him, even if it
meant getting in touch with Dave Crowe again. "So? What do
you have in mind?" Hunter said.

Scott Randall told her his idea, then, his real reason for contacting her. He wanted Hunter to meet with Nicholas Champlain—
which she already planned to do on Monday afternoon—and to
talk with him while wearing an electronic transmitter. He wanted
them to discuss the death of his wife, Susan Champlain—which
she planned to do anyway—and, also, to ask him about the stolen
painting and about Walter Kepler.

Hunter watched the scenery. She wondered how much there
was here that he wasn't saying. She'd worked with the FBI
several times before and found that mistrust and misdirection

were institutional. The feds had a little attitude toward state and local cops; their investigations tended to become unnecessarily convoluted and bureaucratic, she'd found. Still, Hunter had learned from them, and her instinct was to say yes, even though this Randall worried her a little. She couldn't quite figure him out.

"I've already talked with Henry Moore," he added, as if hearing her doubts. "He's on board with me."

"Is he?" Hunter was surprised. "When did you talk with him?"

"Right before I came to see you."

Oh. He shifted, then, to a more companionable tone: "It's a wonder they've got you out here in the bean fields of Tidewater County, anyway," he said.

"Is it?" Hunter said, a little defensively. "Homicides happen everywhere, though," she said. "It doesn't matter a lot where you are, does it?"

"Well, you proved that last year," he said, alluding to the Psalmist case. "I'd've thought you could've written your own ticket after that."

"If you mean more high-profile cases, that's not why I do this," Hunter said, fighting down a bubble of anger. "Homicide is homicide. People are people. The borders of the county are just an invisible fence around people."

Hunter genuinely believed this, although it wasn't an idea that always translated well to conversation. Also, it seemed beside the point. She was lucky to have a supervisor—Henry Moore—who let her do what she wanted, within reason. Hunter had her own ways of running an investigation and a freedom she'd never have at the FBI.

"All right," he said, sounding mildly amused. "Point taken. I just happen to think you'd make good Bureau material."

Hunter sighed. There were ways to flatter her; this wasn't one of them.

"What do you say? Will you do it?"

"I think so," Hunter said. Not right away, but she said it. They rode back in silence, through the marshlands of northern Tidewater County, past old farmhouses, grassy fields, horses, bedsheets flapping on clotheslines, Hunter's thoughts chewing up the scenery.

"I'll try to call you on Monday," Randall said. "I'll be down in Virginia visiting my mother for a couple of days. In the meantime, just keep all this between us."

They shook hands back at the shopping center, cordial like friends.

On her way to the PSC, Hunter stopped at Kent's Crab House to pick up a carry-out sandwich. The air smelled of fries and steamed crabs, sun-scorched dock boards. Large blues were going for $45 a dozen today, according to the chalk board. The summer waitress's face was blistered from an afternoon in the sun.

Travis Kent, the owner, came over to greet Hunter, draping his arm across her shoulders as she stood in the shade by the carry-out window.

"So how *you* been? Can I get you some iced tea, a soda, birch beer?"

"No thanks. I'm just here for carryout."

"Keeping everybody in line?" He winked. Kent was a good-hearted soul who knew how to make most people feel welcome. Hunter bantered with him for a few minutes, as she always did.

Then she noticed that Sheriff Clay Calvert was across the deck, watching her, having lunch with two of his fishing cronies. For a tense few moments, it was like two nervous dogs eyeing each other.

Finally, the sheriff got up and walked over with his limping gait, pretending to be on his way to the men's room.

"Hey! How's your *investigation*?" he said with false bravado. He never wore his uniform except for official events, so Hunter had no idea if he was working or not. It was clear he'd been drinking.

"I feel bad for him," the sheriff said, coming closer, staring her down accusingly. "The man's lost his wife, now he's got Homicide on his ass acting like he was *responsible*. Jesus Christ!" He spit over the rail into the water to emphasize the point.

Hunter edged away from him. "Just doing my job," she said.

"Your *job*?" The sheriff crowded her against the carry-out window, smelling of beer and Old Bay seasoning. "Leave the man alone. For Christ's sake."

Fortunately, a server came out with her sandwich before things got any worse.

Calvert gave her his usual parting line as he walked away, "Tuck in your shirt!" grinning as if it had all been a joke. Once he'd pushed on into the men's room, Hunter felt her shirt just to make sure it *was* all tucked in. The first time he'd said this to her, a couple of years ago, it hadn't been. She still hadn't figured the perfect comeback, mostly because it wasn't a priority. Someday, she would.

FIVE DAYS TO go, and Walter Kepler was grocery shopping at Food Lion, stocking his condo for the weekend: cheeses, wine, bread, salad stuff, the makings for white clam linguine and tomato-broth shellfish stew. All was good, except for the news that Belasco had just delivered by phone: the predator appeared to be recruiting someone new, a female homicide investigator this time. He'd just met with her, they'd gone for a drive. It was Belasco's problem, of course, to watch her and determine if she was a threat. Kepler trusted Belasco. But it gave him pause, just the idea that Randall would be introducing a new complication so late in the game.

Kepler opened the door of a frozen food case and reached in for a loaf of bread. The cold vapor rose to his face and he suddenly had a very strange sensation, the air like fog, transporting him to another place, two years earlier: *Oslo*. Kepler and Belasco, on vacation, hands and ears numb as they hurried through the run-down Toyen district to the Munch Museum. Standing in the dusty gallery air, observing *Madonna* and *The Scream*, two paintings that had been easily stolen from the walls in 2004 and remained missing for two years. He was reminded of the 1994 theft of another version of *The Scream* from the National Museum across town, the thieves leaving behind a note reading, "Thanks for the poor security." It was Kepler who had secretly negotiated the recovery of the Munch Museum paintings in 2006, on condition that museum security be improved so that their theft could never happen again. A condition that had been met. The paintings were today as secure as the *Mona Lisa*. But did Scott Randall even know about that? Did he know the good that Kepler had done?

He closed the door, shutting the memory. But he carried a lingering unease as he pushed his cart down the aisle—that Randall still thought he could stop him; not that he could, but just that he *thought* he could.

By the time Kepler cleared the store checkout, the feeling had passed. Walking to his car, carrying three sacks of groceries, Kepler recalled one of his favorite sayings: *A wise man gets more use from his enemies than a fool from his friends*. Five days to go.

Chapter Sixteen

I guess there's no news?" Luke said, reaching Charlotte.

"About—?"

"Our daughter? Sneakers's little sister?"

"Funny," she said.

"Sorry."

"You're the one who always preaches patience."

"I know."

"But I did speak with my doctor. I'll tell you all about it."

"Good. I'm leaving in fifteen minutes."

"We'll be waiting."

Luke left the church at 1:15 for what he told Aggie would be "a late lunch with Charlotte," which was in fact an excuse to work on their "project," as they were calling efforts to enlarge the Bowers family. He wondered how long it would be before Aggie figured out what was going on.

"I'm home!" he called coming in, reminding himself of Ward Cleaver or Howard Cunningham. *Was he already beginning to play the role of father?* Sneakers came trotting down the hallway, as usual, his toenails clicking on the hardwood floor. But his head hung in a peculiar way, as if he disapproved of what Luke and Charlotte were about to do and yet didn't want to make a fuss over it.

"What's the matter, boy?" He sat for his usual neck rub, his ears pulled back, although there was a halfhearted quality to this, too. He wouldn't look at Luke.

"Char?"

Sneakers stood up and led him into the kitchen, where Luke saw the real issue: there was a strange man seated at the kitchen table with Charlotte, tall, balding, with a long, narrow face, sunglasses on top of his head.

"Oh," Luke said. "Hello."

"This is—" Charlotte began.

"Scott Randall," he said, standing and giving Luke a meaty handshake. "Special agent with the Federal Bureau of Investigation."

"Oh, okay. Hi."

Luke squinted out the window. *Where had he parked?*

"You're Luke Bowers."

"So I'm told."

Randall sat back at the kitchen table, and Luke joined him. Charlotte had set three bowls. They were all going to have soup, it looked like.

"I called the church and the woman said you'd left for home some time earlier."

The woman, Charlotte mouthed, giving Luke a sly glance.

"Yes," he said. "That's true. Where did you park?"

"I took a cab, actually."

"Ah."

"Hungry?" Charlotte said. She was up getting the lunch.

"A little."

She brought them bowls of wild rice soup, along with buttered raisin toast.

"I think I picked up a nail in my tire," Randall explained. "They're fixing it in town. I thought, I have some time, I'll come out and visit you for a few minutes."

"Where'd you take it?"

"The car? I think it's called Lenny's?"

"Lonny's," Luke said. "Yes, he'll take care of you."

He exchanged a smile with Charlotte. Sneakers got up, turned in a circle readying to lie down. But then he seemed to lose interest and scratched his side instead. He looked at Randall, then, as if waiting to be noticed, and finally walked out of the room.

"So, how can I help?"

"I just wanted to ask you about the photo Susan Champlain e-mailed you. Get your impressions." He paused to taste the soup. "I can't go into a lot of specifics but the photo does seem to dovetail with an active case we're working on. I was just talking with your wife about it—"

His eyes turned to Charlotte's. Sneakers, in the next room now, whimpered.

"Go ahead and eat," Charlotte said.

"I understand the photo was sent to you on Wednesday afternoon," he said, to Luke, who noticed that he was slightly cross-eyed.

"Sent to me, that's right. I didn't discover it, though, until late that night. After she'd died."

"Can you give me the time frame on all that?"

"Sure." Luke went through it all, as they ate their soups and toast. Randall's eyes kept turning to Charlotte; he was a little charmed by her, Luke could see, as people sometimes were, but a little bit more than seemed appropriate.

"So you must have reason to think it's the real thing?" Luke said. "The Rembrandt, I mean."

"Oh, I have no idea," he said, and smiled disingenuously. "As I told your wife, it's an ongoing investigation. And I'm going to ask that anything we've discussed today remain in confidence."

"Sure." Luke spooned the last of his soup. "So you talked with Amy Hunter, I gather?"

"Just finished, yeah. Sharp kid."

Charlotte's eyes lifted and locked with Luke's briefly; she silently mouthed the words *sharp kid.*

"Yes, she's very good. Very bright."

"Kind of a firecracker."

"That, too," Luke said.

Randall was stingy in telling Luke what *he* knew, though. There was a subtle aggressiveness about him that was unsettling, as he tried to get Luke to tell him more about Susan Champlain.

After finishing lunch, Randall crumpled his mostly shredded paper napkin into a ball and set it on his plate. Luke offered to drive him back into town.

"Thanks. Appreciate it," he said. "Could I use your facilities?"

"Of course," Charlotte said. "It's just down the hall there."

Luke sighed as Randall disappeared in the facilities. "I guess that constituted today's lunch date," he said.

"Not quite what I expected, either. Nor did Sneakers."

"Sneakers actually seemed to have a little attitude," Luke said.

"I noticed. He's not used to being ignored."

"Anyway: we'll make up for it."

She leaned across the table and kissed him.

Randall came out looking recharged, smelling of hand soap.

"Ready," he said, rubbing his hands.

AFTER LETTING HIM off, Luke drove back to Widow's Point. He parked in the shade on the access road and walked out onto the beach below the bluff, to the spot where Susan Champlain had died. It was low tide again. There were no signs anymore of what had happened here. Susan's phone had never been found; her second sandal hadn't washed ashore. Luke spent a half hour walking the beach, barefoot, searching the sand and looking out at the sails on the glittering Bay. Then he closed his eyes for a few minutes and felt the sun warm his face, the tide coming in around his ankles, his feet sinking into the sand. He expressed gratitude for all that he had and then drove back to work, feeling uneasy and a little guilty.

Chapter Seventeen

Hunter fought the urge to call Dave Crowe for much of the day. She ran data searches on Walter Kepler instead and did a background check on Scott Randall. Kepler was an enigmatic character who'd grown up in New York City and seemed to have moved among residences in Delaware, New Jersey, New York, Pennsylvania, France, and Switzerland over the past twenty-five years. He still owned at least two properties in Delaware, one a house in the country with an assessed value of $895,000, the other a beach condo worth about half that. There were several records of lucrative art deals, including the $16.3 million sale in 1995 of a Picasso painting called *Femme et de Fleurs* and a 2001 sale of a late Picasso for $7.1 million. In 2012, the *New York Times* ran a story about the return of six Impressionist paintings stolen in Zurich four years earlier. The article quoted sources claiming that "Walter Kepler, an elusive figure in the world of high-end art, reportedly helped negotiate the return of the paintings . . . Kepler is reputed to have recovered—and traded in—high-end art (including, by some accounts, stolen art) for more than fifteen years. He declined, through a spokesman, to be interviewed."

Early in the afternoon, Hunter paid a visit to the Empress Gallery on Main Street, where Susan Champlain had supposedly displayed her photographic art for several days earlier in the summer.

A trim man with floppy black hair and arresting blue eyes emerged from a cubicle space. "Good afternoon," he said, bouncing out to greet her. "Welcome to the Empress Gallery. Can I help you find anything—Eastern Shore landscapes? Photography?" he said, guessing at her taste.

"I'm on business, actually." Hunter showed her badge. "I understand this gallery represented Susan Champlain?"

One side of his mouth made a funny downward wiggle, as if a worm were inside his lips. "Susan Wilkins," he said, correcting her. "She wasn't represented here, no. Although I believe she may have had one piece for sale." His blue eyes had an attentive, otherworldly quality that reminded her of a husky dog's. "May I ask where you heard that she was represented here?" he said.

"You may," Hunter said. "But, unfortunately, I'm not able to answer."

This caused him to smile, in a quick, passive-aggressive way. "It was just up for a few days, as I recall," he said, his tone turning more businesslike. "We routinely rotate the selections."

"Did it sell?"

"I couldn't give out that sort of information."

"Okay." She snuck a glance at his shoulders; not bad, but she wouldn't call them elegant. "Did you know her?"

"Did I know—?"

"Susan Champlain. Wilkins."

"I believe I *met* Miss Champlain, yes. But, no, I didn't know her. May I ask what this is regarding?"

"Just part of a routine investigation."

He gave Hunter a curt smile and she suddenly recognized something—this was the man she'd seen walking behind Susan Champlain that hot afternoon several weeks ago, in the parking lot outside Kent's, her sandals making a clip-clop sound, oil stains glowing in the sun. The only time Susan Champlain had spoken to her.

"How did it happen that her work was on sale here?"

"I couldn't comment on that. You'd have to talk with the owner. Excuse me," he said. He pivoted and walked back to his cubicle. Hunter waited, glancing around the gallery. He came out again with two business cards, one in each hand. One for the owner, Darian Empress; the other, him: Marc Devlin, manager, Empress Gallery.

"Let me know if there's anything else I can help you with," he said, meaning the art.

Hunter gave him *her* card, which he looked at as if it were filled with a paragraph of text. "Would you have Ms. Empress call me?" she said.

"I will leave Mrs. Empress a message, certainly."

"Thank you."

Hunter browsed for a couple minutes before leaving. She could see quickly that Susan Champlain's art wouldn't have fit here. The paintings on the walls were mostly oils of Eastern Shore landscapes and sailing scenes. There were also waterfowl carvings and small colored-glass sculptures.

Devlin gave her space, pretending to be checking a wall text across the room, but keeping an eye on her. Hunter noted the prices, which were mostly in the $2,000 to $6,000 range. She saw one for $24,000, and stepped back to study it more carefully. She didn't get it. Was it really worth $21,000 more than the landscape next to it?

Hunter enjoyed going through the Philadelphia Museum of Art, seeing the Impressionists, some of the Hudson River School paintings; she liked the ancient Greek and Roman art at the Penn Museum. Things that lasted: she was a sucker for that. But the world of art galleries was a mystery to her.

She turned to say goodbye to Marc Devlin, who immediately raised his right hand.

Hunter stood under the awning on the sidewalk and was surprised when the door creaked open behind her. Devlin stepped out, squinting at the light.

"Your ID said Homicide," he said, in a quieter voice.

"That's right."

He glanced both ways up and down Main Street. "I thought Miss Champlain's death was an accident."

There was a note of compassion in his question that made Hunter suddenly like him.

"It may have been. We don't know yet."

Her card was still in his hand, and he pretended to read it again.

"Could I call you later?" he said.

"Sure, if you'd like."

"Good. I will." Devlin looked at her with those blue eyes, then made a pivot and went back inside.

FISCHER AND TANNER were in their offices at the PSC, heads down. But Tanner's eyes lifted subtly as Hunter walked into her office.

He gave her a minute to settle before coming in. Hunter knew she'd eventually have to tell them about the photo, and the Rembrandt painting, but for now she was going to honor Scott Randall's request not to talk about it with anyone, other than Henry Moore, her boss, and Pastor Luke. At least until Moore told her different.

"Anything?"

"Not a lot. You?"

"Possible witness."

"Oh?" Hunter nodded him in. "To Susan's fall?"

"I wish. No. But someone saw a pickup driving away from the bluff road Wednesday night. Where it forks off onto, I guess, Route 11?"

"12."

"12. The woman came forward after the fact, talked to one of Dunn's investigators. She got a partial on the license plate. The interesting thing is, it matches three of the numbers on Joey Sands's truck."

"Joe Sanders."

"Right. The lifeguard—I mean, the bodyguard."

"Right."

"And where is *he*?"

"Sanders? I'm still following up. He may have left town already."

He studied her with his dark, liquid eyes.

"Nothing more on the footprints, either? Cell phone, computer, sandal?"

"None of it, no."

"Strange."

"Yeah, I know."

Joey Sanders was becoming more interesting to this case, Hunter thought. She made a mental note to ask Randall about him.

"Let me get this," she said, as her phone began to ring again.

But there was no one there. So she thought. Then she realized that someone was breathing on the other end.

"Amy *Huuun*-ter?"

"Yes? Hello?"

A deep, splintery breathing sound, in and out, in and out. Then nothing. The caller had hung up.

Hunter sighed. She closed the door and called Dave Crowe, at the FBI building in Washington. 4:02. It was almost two days now since Susan Champlain's body had been found on the beach at Widow's Point. There was too much still that she didn't know about what had happened; and too much she wasn't supposed to talk about. If Susan had been killed because of a stolen painting, then it probably wasn't Hunter's business to solve the case. But she kept thinking back to what Randall had said: *what if solving one case solves the other?*

"How was your meeting?" Crowe asked, in a tone suggesting he already knew.

"Have you talked with him?"

"Randall? Just briefly, yeah. He asked me a few questions about you."

"Great. What did he want to know?"

"I, eh, need to be careful. Talking on this phone."

Hunter sighed. "Let's meet, then."

IT WAS EASY by then for Belasco to get close to Joey Sanders. He was an open book with some people, closed up with others. But there was a lot about him that was predictable. He was like Belasco's brothers. There was a cocksure steadiness in the way that Sanders looked at you, chin up, an entitled quality to his smile. He was a man who counted on things going his way; and if they didn't, no biggie. He didn't wrestle a lot with angst. He worked hard, he played by the rules (those he had to). He liked to drink at night, beer and vodka. He was seducible, but thought he was doing the seducing. A lot of people were raised that way; it was an attitude that they never really shed, not completely.

But he was also smart, in a deceptive way, and that worried Belasco. That's why they were doing this, before Belasco left for good at the beginning of the week. They were headed now to pick up Belasco's car; but taking a circuitous drive first, down through the protected marshlands. Sanders had something he wanted Belasco to see.

Sanders was driving, only too pleased to help, windows lowered a third, cool air streaming from the vents. It was a hot afternoon, the outdoors making their clothes stick. Sanders's face eager like that of a much younger man; like he was pretty sure something was going to happen. That was the game, the anticipation: shared desire. Just let it sit there, and simmer a little in the summer heat.

Sanders turned onto a rural route, which would take them to Virginia eventually if they kept going. He picked up speed again, laying rubber at one point, but doing it responsibly, like a forty-something-year-old man. The marshlands were sparkling in the distance all around. There was a motel ten or maybe fifteen miles up ahead.

"A beer'd sure taste good," Sanders said.

"Okay."

"Want one?"

"I could have one."

Sanders slowed. He eased off onto the shoulder of the road in the shade, by a narrow creek. He had a cooler of Budweiser in the truck bed. Belasco opened the passenger door. The air was still under the leaves, buzzing with insects. A small plane flew toward the beaches, towing a banner.

As Sanders let down the tailgate, Belasco stuck the needle in his neck. Sanders had no time to do anything but look surprised. Then he tried to swat at it for a moment like a mosquito had bit him. Belasco always enjoyed seeing that transformation, that instant when someone you know turns out to be someone you don't know.

Eventually Sanders's eyes and his arms stopped moving. He was fully paralyzed as Belasco heaved him up into the bed of the truck. Sanders should have known better than to let things get personal. In that instant before the tarp went over his face, Joey Sanders's open eyes reflected the blue sky, and it reminded Belasco of Kepler's eyes the first time they'd met, at the museum in Philadelphia: It had been like peering into a magnificent house full of elegant furnishings where nobody actually lived. That's how it had seemed. Now Belasco knew better. It *was* a vast house with many rooms still unknown. But it wasn't uninhabited. It was now the place where Belasco lived.

Chapter Eighteen

Hunter fed Winston and began the drive west, across the narrow creeks and farm fields toward the Chesapeake Bay Bridge. Dave Crowe had agreed to meet with her at Fred's Crab House on the water in Anne Arundel County. Not "halfway" to D.C. as he called it, but close enough.

Crowe was a different man after a few drinks in the evening than he was sober behind his desk downtown during the day. Night and day, literally and figuratively. Hunter had benefited from this transformation in the past, when he'd told her more than he should have about the FBI's investigation into what became known as the Psalmist case, for instance. But she also worried about him drinking and driving, and vowed she would end this at a reasonable hour.

She'd just started up the eastern ramp to the Bay Bridge when her cell phone rang. Marc Devlin's name came up. Hunter raised her windows, so she could hear.

"Miss Hunter? I just wanted to apologize."

"For?"

She thought for a moment that Devlin had been the heavy breather; that he was calling to say he was sorry.

"I couldn't talk openly in the gallery earlier," he said. "The place is wired, for audio and video. Everything that happens there, she sees it. Mrs. Empress." A truck whooshed by, and Hunter missed a few words of what he said next. "I wonder if I could meet with you, just for a couple minutes. I have a few things . . . Are you busy tonight?"

"Actually, I'm on my way over the Bay Bridge right now on business. What's it about?"

"I just wanted to say—that I sort of *did* know Susie Champlain. I told you I didn't know her. Well, I sort of did."

"Okay."

"I mean, not *intimately* or anything. But—I'm the one who put her art up in the gallery, to be honest with you," he said. "And Mrs. Empress took it down. I wasn't authorized to do that. She made that very clear."

"When was this?"

"Beginning of July."

"Why'd she take it down?"

"It wasn't a good match with our clientele, she said. She was afraid it might scare people off. If it's not duck decoys or sailboat pictures, they tend to become very uncomfortable."

Devlin sounded much more natural than he'd seemed in person. Hunter liked the slow cadence of his voice, which had some sideways Southern inflections.

"So how'd you come to know Susan?" she said, gazing at the brightening lights of the Western Shore past the bridge.

"Oh, I didn't *know* her. But I ran into her a couple of times, and we got to talking. I mean—a total of maybe four or five times, at most. Just chitchat, mostly, you know."

"When was the last?"

"The last? Oh—the last time? Was . . . Tuesday morning, I guess, outside the library."

The same day she had talked with Pastor Bowers.

"And what time was this?"

"Well, the gallery opened at noon and I open the gallery. So, it must've been eleven thirty. Eleven thirty-ish."

"So, the day before she died."

"Right."

"What did you talk about? What was her state of mind?"

"Actually, we didn't. She was kind of jammed up that day, like she *couldn't* talk."

"Jammed up."

"Well, yeah, stressed out. She kind of gave me the cold shoulder, if you want to be honest. I was kind of like—ohhhhhh-kay."

"Any idea what caused it?"

"Caused it? No. Not a clue. I'd never have taken her for doing that kind of artwork," he added incongruously. "I think she must've had a *very* abstract mind. She was a mystery girl, really, that's what I thought. You know that Roy Orbison song?"

"Mmm-mmm," Hunter said. She knew *Pretty Woman*.

"The other thing is, if you're interested, I could probably tell you a few things about Mrs. Empress."

"Oh? What sorts of things?"

"Fraudulent appraisals? Faked provenances? I mean, if you ever wanted to look into it. I'm probably not going to stay there beyond the summer, anyway."

"Okay. Thanks," Hunter said, "but I do homicides, I don't investigate art fraud. I'll be in touch about Susan, though. Can I call on you for follow-up?"

"Oh. Of course. By all means."

He sounded quite happy about the prospect.

"I'M A LITTLE worried about Amy Hunter, if you want to know the truth," Charlotte Bowers said.

"Really?"

Luke turned from the stove, where he was sautéing scallops. Charlotte was sitting at the table, drinking wine, keeping him company. Luke had stopped at Kent's on his way home and was preparing his seared scallops with mango salsa, one of Charlotte's favorites, to celebrate their decision to introduce a new Bowers into the world.

"I just worry that she's too independent and it's going to catch up with her before long."

"Well," Luke said. "I think Hunter's pretty good at handling herself, actually."

"Oh, I know you do," she said, giving him a saucy look.

Luke turned back to his scallops. "So," he said. "Is that one of the things?"

"Things?"

"You said you had two things to tell me tonight."

"Oh. No." Charlotte laughed. "It's just that I wonder about this Scott Randall and what his intentions are. I had a funny vibe about him."

"We all did, didn't we?"

Perhaps coincidentally, Sneakers raised his head then and looked up at Charlotte. Then he returned his chin to the floor.

"I wonder what Amy Hunter thinks about him."

"I guess we both do," Luke said, stirring the scallops.

"So how about we invite her to dinner? She's never even been to the house. At least as far as I know."

"Really?"

Charlotte eyed him mischievously. "To which part?"

"Inviting her."

"Yes. Really. That was one of the things."

"Okay. Good." He liked that Charlotte was suggesting this.

"Let's see if she's free over the weekend."

"I'll ask her," he said. "Good idea."

Charlotte smiled at him, ambiguously. They ate Luke's dinner on the back deck, drinking wine, talking about the future. The sun deepened to a warm orange-copper shade that seemed to settle into the wetlands before dimming into darkness. *A year from now, we might be living somewhere else, raising a child*: it was an exciting feeling.

"You said two things," Luke reminded her.

"Oh, yeah," Charlotte said. "The second was just that I thought we could work on our project later. After dinner."

Luke smiled, looking at the long, brightening stretch of the Bay Bridge. "Another good idea," he said.

DAVE CROWE WAS seated on the large screened porch by the docks. Behind him a cabin cruiser was coming in, blasting a familiar country music song. The restaurant was something of a cliché, with a captain's wheel, dark wood tables covered with butcher paper, fishnets hanging from the ceilings, lots of neon beer signs behind the bar. It wasn't the place Hunter would've picked for a quiet conversation.

"Why doesn't it surprise me that you've gotten yourself involved in this?" Crowe said, giving her his self-assured smile as she sat.

"A question only you can answer, I suspect," Hunter said.

Crowe watched her unfazed. He was a small, good-looking man, with nice hair, nice bone structure, dark eyes. He was also married, although, like a number of cops and Bureau agents Hunter had known, he seemed comfortable blurring the lines between what was allowed and what wasn't.

"I received a letter from our old pal, by the way," he told her, once they'd ordered drinks. "About a week ago."

"Who's our old pal?"

"August Trumble."

"Oh." Hunter went cold. This was the way Crowe did things, his dark eyes nailing her across the table, his cheeks creasing as he smiled. Trumble was the serial killer Hunter had helped put away for life, a man the media had christened the "Psalmist." It should have been a sore subject between them because Crowe had waged a tug of war with Hunter throughout the case. But he was reinventing the past as he talked, which was one of his specialties.

"He asked how I was. And he asked how *you* were. Fortunately, we don't have to deal with him anymore."

"Tell me about Scott Randall," Hunter said.

His eyes did a dance for a moment. "You first. Tell me *your* impression."

"My impression is that he cares very much about making a case against Walter Kepler. Too much, maybe."

Crowe was smiling. "There you go. That's it, in a nutshell."

"Why?"

"Because he can," Crowe said, touching his drink glass with his fingertips. "Randall's headstrong, and he's finally carved out his own little domain, chief dog of the Stolen Art Division. But keep in mind, this is his third case involving Walter Kepler. Did he tell you that?"

"He did."

"And Kepler won the other two. My impression? I think this is Randall's last big shot. And he knows it. And frankly? I think he's worried that Kepler's the better chess player. I think the boy's running scared."

Drink often added a tone of condescension to Crowe's speech, so that he used terms like "the boy" and "the kid," words he'd never use when sober. It also made him sloppy with his metaphors. Clearly this wasn't his first drink of the day.

"I know a little about that," Crowe added, "because I worked the last case. Down in Florida. Randall and Selwyn actually were talking about starting a task force to go after Kepler at the time."

"David Selwyn was the head of art crimes before Randall."

"That's right. Then Selwyn got kicked upstairs, mostly because there wasn't room for the both of them. Selwyn got to the point that he didn't want to look at Randall's face anymore, that's what he told me." His cheeks creased as he grinned.

"Randall made Kepler out as a bad guy," Hunter said. "He told me he thinks he has ties to terrorism. True?"

Crowe tilted his drink glass. He seemed briefly fascinated with how the light changed in the whiskey. "It's a big point of contention within the Bureau," he said. "I don't think so. I think Kepler is smart. Randall thinks he's just bad. Bad draws more resources. He wants to Escobar-size the man to gin up interest. Did he try to recruit you?"

Hunter shrug-nodded.

"The reason I warned you yesterday," Crowe said, "is because someone else did what you're doing and it didn't end up so well. You ought to know that."

"What am I doing?" Hunter said. "I'm investigating a homicide in Tidewater County."

"No. I mean, someone else got involved with Randall, on a deal having to do with Kepler. Up in Philadelphia last year. Someone Randall thought could get him things he couldn't get on his own."

"Okay. Tell me about that."

"I wish I could." Crowe's hands circled his drink glass. He gave her a flinty look. "Actually I'm going to put you in touch with a woman who'll tell you all about it, all right? Ex-Bureau. She lives out on the Shore, so you won't have to go far. It'd be worth your while. I just need to clear it with her first."

This, too, was typical Crowe, drawing out the drama.

"Why is Randall so fixated on Kepler?" she said. "I don't get that."

"Obsession." Crowe shrugged, gripping his drink. "He's got it in his head that the man's a killer. And I'm sure it pisses him off that Kepler sees himself as some kind of Robin Hood of the art world."

"*Is* he a killer?"

"No." His eyes took in the deck, then returned to her. "*I* don't think he is. But . . . There *is* another theory. Which Randall, I'm sure, didn't mention to you." Hunter nodded. "It's the theory that Kepler has a partner. And it's the partner who does the dirty work. That's the real point of contention. Helen Bradbury, this woman I'm going to put you in touch with, tried to push that agenda. I did, too, insomuch as I could. But Randall fought her every step of the way. Every *step*.

"Now, I'm not saying Kepler *isn't* a bad guy," he went on. "But he's also a smart guy, like I say. I'd be more concerned about the smart than the bad. He's a very hard man to pin down, you'll find." Crowe took a long drink of his bourbon. "Let me ask you slomething," he said. "You know how many objects were stolen in that Gardner deal?"

"Thirteen? I think." Did he just say *slomething*?

"That's right." He smiled up at her for an instant. "The works were split up. The Vermeer went overseas, it was sold off in the South of France, we think, in the late nineties. Two of the others were sold to a Corsican group. And one of those two, the Manet, was down in the Miami area for a while. Kepler tried to broker its sale there last year." This was the sort of information Crowe wasn't supposed to talk about and never would have if he hadn't been drinking. "That's the deal I was involved in."

"So this isn't Randall's first connection with Gardner art."

"No, second. Kepler was the broker. He represented a buyer who was willing to pay two or three million for the Manet, if Kepler could locate it. The day Kepler's seller was supposed to show the work, he disappeared. It ended right there. I think Kepler saw red flags, took the money and ran."

"Who was the buyer?"

"Supposedly some sultan type in Dubai." He gave her a quick, sly smile. "That was the cover story, anyway. The real buyer was Uncle Sam—although you didn't hear that from me. *That* was the real problem. It was supposed to be run as a sting. But Randall got overconfident, and sloppy. He thought he could get the painting and Kepler in one swoop. They got nothing, and Kepler walked away with some of the government's money—an upfront broker's fee, basically. We don't know for sure that Kepler really even had the painting; my guess is that he didn't. That's when Selwyn parachuted out, right after that; he thought Randall was too much of a loose cannon. Randall blamed others, of course, as he always does. And he was promoted, as a result."

"So you're saying the buyer was a straw man the FBI created?" This seemed a little incredible to Hunter.

"Did I say that?" He grinned into his drink and then downed what was left.

"And so what about *this* deal? The terrorist interests he talked about: Is *that* real?"

"Well," he said, "that's another point of contention. After what happened before, we thought he was ginning this one up, too. But he's got a CIA liaison involved now, supposedly, so I don't know. Did he mention that?"

Hunter shook her head.

"Might be real, might not be. Either way, I think Kepler *does* have a bead on the painting this time. That's what I hear."

"The Rembrandt."

"Yeah. But that's all just between us."

"Who *is* Scott Randall?" Hunter said. "Do you know him?"

"Not well, no." He shook his drink glass, tinkling ice. "Career Bureau type, been involved with stolen art for a lot of years. He's one of these obsessive guys you don't *want* to know too well. Or maybe you do—but it turns out there isn't a lot there to know. You follow? He doesn't have many friends, if any. Long-suffering wife, not much of a marriage. Second marriage. He takes care of his mother in Virginia, who has advanced Alzheimer's."

He signaled new drinks for both of them. Hunter was still working on her wine and tried to wave off her order but was too late.

"He's an obsessive mama's boy, is what I think," Crowe added. "Probably gay."

Soon Dave Crowe was trying to shift the conversation to her, but Hunter didn't let it go there. So he talked instead about himself, about his daughter, about his wife wanting to get back to work. Things weren't so good at home for him lately, he said; but then he always told her that.

The air had grown misty over the water and it was much cooler by the time they left. They stood for several minutes in the parking lot looking at the moored sailboats. "You want me to drive you?" she asked.

"What?"

"You want me to drive you home?"

"Of course not," he said. "What are you talking about?"

Hunter drove herself home slowly, her windshield wipers clicking on the slow cycle in the mist, which was thick over the Chesapeake. She felt better traveling through the dark spaces of Tidewater County, seeing stray lights from farmhouse windows and the wavy reflections of the moonlight and open sky on the water. There were two slogans the tourism bureau pushed about Tidewater—"a land unto itself" and "a land apart." Pretty trite; but this evening they felt appropriate. There were quieter rhythms to life here, different from anywhere Hunter had lived, and she was growing comfortable with them, even if she didn't particularly fit in the community.

She lay awake in bed for a while that night, communing with Winston, her cat, listening to the breezes rattling the sailboats, the creaking of the docks, going over her conversation with Dave Crowe. There were still a lot of questions to answer; but Hunter didn't know how far Henry Moore, her boss, would want to take this. The more complicated it became, the more the state's attorney would push the idea that Susan's death was accidental, she knew. Tidy solutions were a tradition in Tidewater County. Hunter decided she'd get Pastor Luke's input in the morning.

She was sound asleep that night when her landline woke her. The effect was like an explosion and Hunter instinctively reached for her state police-issued Glock .22 in the drawer of the nightstand before realizing what it was. It rang once more and she picked up, expecting Crowe. It was 1:12 in the morning.

"Hello?"

"*Huuuun*-ter."

She listened to the breathing on the other end, the same as before. Her heart suddenly felt as if it had doubled in size.

"Hello," she said, sitting up. "Who is this?"

"You're lucky," the caller said. "You still have a chance to step away. You *understand* me? *Huuuun*-ter?"

He was trying to make his voice gravelly and menacing but

there was a slurred, high inflection that sounded familiar—the way he said "still" and the last syllable of "away."

"Who is this? What do you want?" she said, trying to draw him out.

"You know who I am."

Yes, Hunter thought. *I do.* But he hung up before she had a chance to say anything else.

This time, Hunter called the state police barracks officer and asked him to run a trace on the call. Then Hunter put in her ear plugs and went back to sleep. She slept soundly for another six hours, before Winston woke her up by walking back and forth over her face, ready for his morning tuna ration. "Thanks a *lot*," she said, finally tossing back the covers. Winston jumped down and ran into the hallway, squawking as if the building were on fire.

She went on a hard run along the marina road to Waterman's Bluff, feeling good, the Beatles blasting on her iPod, then came home, opened a Diet Coke and checked through her e-mails. Fischer had prepared a file of new material on Joseph Sanders, which Hunter skimmed at the kitchen table. As she was doing so, Henry Moore e-mailed her to say that he wanted to meet as soon as she could come into the office. Saturday wasn't going to be a day off.

She called Pastor Luke after showering, wanting to share with him some of what Crowe had told her, and to feel the anchor of his thoughts. He sounded unusually upbeat this morning. "I just wanted to run a few things by you," she said. "Maybe later today? Or tomorrow after your service? Whatever works for you."

"How about if we make it tomorrow evening," Luke said. "We'd like to invite you to dinner."

"Oh," she said. "You don't have to do that."

"No, we'd like to. Nothing fancy. Just crab cakes and a salad. Say, six o'clock?"

Hunter looked at her posture in the kitchen window and didn't like what she saw. She sat up straighter. For some reason, the invitation made Hunter uncomfortable. She'd never really talked with Charlotte, who occasionally seemed to have a little attitude toward her. Maybe this would be a chance to get to know her better. Still, she kind of regretted that she had to wait another day to get Luke's input.

"Sure," she said. "That'll be nice."

"Great," Luke said.

Hunter printed out the file on Joseph Sanders and read it as she drove in to work, holding the sheets of paper up on the steering wheel. Dave Crowe called her cell as she pulled into the parking lot.

"Interesting conversation last night."

"It was," she said, glad that he was all right. "Thanks for talking with me."

"Have you said anything to Randall?"

"I haven't talked with him."

"Don't," Crowe said. "Well, it's Saturday, he's probably with his mother, anyway. She has advanced-stage Alzheimer's."

"Yes, I know."

His voice sounded normal, maybe a little thicker than usual. Crowe never seemed to suffer hangovers in the traditional sense. "Anyway," he said, "reason I'm calling: I just talked with this woman. She's got someone visiting for the weekend, but she'll see you first thing Monday, okay? Her name's Helen Bradbury. She's no longer with the Bureau, but she knows a lot and stays connected. She's full of piss and vinegar. She can tell you more than I can."

"About Kepler and Randall."

"Yeah, all that," he said vaguely, and then he gave her Helen Bradbury's address. "She'll see you at eight thirty Monday. I've already set it up with her."

"Does she have a phone number?"

"She doesn't give it out. Just show up, she's expecting you."

Chapter Nineteen

Henry Moore was in the little conference room in Homicide working, papers spread out across the table, his transistor radio playing easy listening music as Hunter came in. Until she'd met Moore, Hunter hadn't realized that transistor radios still existed.

"Morning," she said. Moore waited before acknowledging her. He was a ruddy, outdoorsy-looking man, with squinty eyes and a sly, lopsided smile. Hunter liked him a lot, although he could be a taskmaster. She wondered if he was going to scold her now for talking with Crowe.

"Hunter," he said, his usual greeting. He turned off the radio, pushed the papers aside and pointed at the chair across from him. "How are you?"

"Fine."

He breathed in heavily. "I thought you should know," he said. "Joseph Sanders has been reported as a missing person."

"Really."

"Supposed to be home last night, didn't show up. His wife reported him this morning. He left here yesterday afternoon, evidently, hasn't been heard from since. Police say his truck was spotted on surveillance camera about twenty miles north of the Virginia line. Which doesn't fit with any route he would have taken."

"Wrong direction."

"That's right, wrong direction." Moore leaned forward, shifting his weight to his left side, tapping his left hand over the table as he often did, as if the transistor radio was still playing. This wasn't what she'd thought he wanted to talk about.

"Was he alone?"

"Don't know. The picture doesn't show much." He pulled out a printout and pushed it toward her. "Maybe we'll get something better. It's still early." He took another deep breath, his favorite punctuation. "Thoughts?"

"Well. It may complicate things," she said.

"Yep. May." Moore started to smile, his eyes receding.

"Fisher's been running data," she said. "I just got some new information from him this morning. Sanders worked for Nick Champlain off and on for the past year or year and a half. He also worked construction in Pennsylvania."

"Is it possible this was something he might've done *for* Champlain?"

Hunter frowned. Tanner had suggested the same thing. "Killed Susan while Champlain was out of town, you mean?" she said. "I guess it's possible."

"But you don't think so?"

"No."

"Why?"

"I don't see motive. I don't know why Champlain would want

her killed. It doesn't seem consistent with what we know." She added, "Of course, there's still a lot we don't know."

"I understand Sanders may've had a gambling problem? Spent some time in the casinos up in Atlantic City?"

"In the past."

"Problems come back. Maybe he needed the money?"

"Maybe. But I don't think so," she said. "Nick Champlain is a careful man. It doesn't make sense that he would have paid someone like Sanders, who supposedly has a drinking problem, to do that."

"But he paid him to be his bodyguard."

"That's different."

"So, what *do* you think?"

Hunter shrugged. "I think it's something we don't know yet," she said. "Give us some more time. I'll have a better answer in another day or two."

He nodded, straightening his papers.

"What does the state's attorney think?" Hunter asked.

"About Sanders? He's not concerned. He's going to consider her death an accident until someone tells him otherwise."

"And he's still unaware of Susan's photo, I take it."

"Yep. We'll just keep it that way for the time being." He showed his sly smile, just the right side of his mouth. Moore was an adept navigator through the politics of local law enforcement. He was acting as if the photos were unrelated to Susan's death, even if he didn't believe it. Moore liked to keep information in a tight circle for as long as possible, which was why he wasn't quite ready to bring Fischer and Tanner in, she suspected.

"Oh, and I talked with Scott Randall yesterday," he added, almost an afterthought. "He stopped in to see me."

This was what Hunter had been expecting.

"Yes. And?"

He made a face and rolled his eyes. "He tried to push an agenda on me and I told him we couldn't really help him. Although I don't have any problem with you talking with him."

"He said you were on board with what he wanted to do."

His nose scrunched. "I'm not on board with him at all. I said I didn't *mind* if he listened in on your conversation with Champlain. If *you* didn't mind. He left the electronic device, if we want to do it. But that's up to you.

"Our case and his case are two separate things," he added. "I told him that. I made that clear."

"Good."

"Just use your own best judgment."

"I will."

"And you want my honest assessment? The guy's kind of a bozo. Something about the man just rubbed me the wrong way."

Hunter nodded. Further warning about Scott Randall.

She told him then about the two threatening phone calls she'd received. Moore breathed heavily, showing mild interest.

"Any idea who it might be?"

"Not really." For some reason, she was thinking about Barry Stilfork, the deputy sheriff who patrolled overnight. But she also mentioned Marc Devlin.

"You know what I think?" he said, giving her his inscrutable, squint-eyed stare. "You're interviewing Champlain in Philly on Monday, right?"

"One o'clock," Hunter said.

"I think it might do you good to get out of town for a day or two. Doesn't your mom live up there?"

Hunter just looked at him. She often couldn't tell what he was thinking until he told her.

"Stay a couple days if you want," he said. "It wouldn't hurt you to get away from here. Recharge the batteries a little. We'll carry the slack."

The conference room phone buzzed before Hunter could respond. Moore answered it. He said, "Yep." Then again, twice: "Yep. Yep." He hung up. "Anyway, you got two visitors up front," he said, and winked.

NANCY WILKINS ADAMS looked like a stockier, more subdued version of her dead sister, Susan Champlain, with the same rounded cheekbones and lively blue eyes. Susan's brother Brian had even more of her in his face—the nicely shaped nose, the compelling downward smile—although he, too, was heavier than she'd been.

"We just had a drive around the town. Nice place," he said, sounding like a tourist, shifting his weight from one leg to the other.

"Yes, it's very charming," Nancy added, not so upbeat.

"It is." Hunter welcomed them into her office. They'd been to Baltimore first to see their sister's body, then to the Champlains' home in Philadelphia to collect some of her possessions. They came back through Tidewater to get the rest of her personal effects from the rental house at Cooper's Point. But Hunter sensed that they were also here because they wanted to see where she had lived out her final days, and where she had died.

Nancy said, "Nicholas has already left, we hear."

"He wasn't at the house in Philadelphia?"

"No." Nancy Adams had a slightly startled expression, which it took Hunter a minute to recognize was built into her eyes, as if life itself caused it.

"But he did talk with you—?"

"With me," Brian said, raising his hand. "We had a decent talk."

"I won't speak with the man." Nancy turned her head to the side, gripping the chair arms.

Brian exhaled, puffing out his cheeks, slumped in the other guest chair. "We disagree on this a little," he said. "For whatever reason, I always got on with him. Not that we had a lot in common."

"Football," Nancy said.

"Well, that's right, although we disagreed a little there, too," he said, trying to keep things light. "I'm a Chicago Bears fan. He's Eagles. Of course, we don't actually have a home team in Iowa. We have some folks who are diehard Packers fans. What's the home team here? I was trying to figure that out—Ravens or Redskins?"

"Either one," Hunter said. "Although I'm partial to the Eagles."

"He offered to pay for the funeral," Nancy said, crossing her legs, uncomfortable with the football talk.

"He can pay half," Brian said.

"We were pleased to learn that you're investigating this," Nancy said.

Hunter shrugged. "It's a routine investigation at this point."

"But you're Homicide." Nancy glanced at the door as if for some kind of confirmation.

"Yes. Do you think it was homicide?"

"I'm sure it was," Nancy said.

Brian's nose twitched. Hunter had already looked them up. Brian was the middle child, Nancy the oldest.

"When was the last time you talked with your sister?" Hunter asked.

"It was intermittent," Brian said.

"*Really* talked with her?" Nancy said, her voice rising to a dominant level. "Was about two weeks ago. She was quite upset. She didn't let on what was happening, but I could kind of read between the lines." Her eyes moistened, went somewhere else. "She told me about this thing that she was afraid of that was going to happen. That's what she called it. This *thing*."

"She didn't say anything about it to me," Brian said factually.

"What do you think it was?" Hunter asked.

"I don't know, I wish I did. She wouldn't—Susie just always had this—it was like a heightened awareness, really, almost a sixth sense, from when she was a little girl. I'm not saying it was supernatural or para*normal* or anything, but it was a gift. Even when she was little." Hunter glanced at Brian, who was pulling lint from his shirt. "She just had this, I don't know, sensitivity, this greater *aware*ness than most people have."

"But you don't know what specifically it was that was bothering her?"

"No. I don't."

"Susie was always kind of a dreamer," Brian said, picking it up.

"From when we were kids. She was the youngest and I guess she just felt she needed to be a little different. To stand out, maybe."

"Our parents are devastated, naturally," Nancy said, as if he hadn't spoken. "They were sort of waiting for her to make her mark. We all were. Which she would have done. They didn't expect she'd want to be an artist, of course, but they always supported her. Although they were never real comfortable with Susan marrying *him*."

"She was actually quite shy," Brian said. "But she had this great imagination. And she really wanted to be an artist. She had that idea all her life. Be an artist and live in New York City, Greenwich Village. She romanticized it in her mind."

"Bright lights, big city," Nancy said.

"To the point that, when she finally got there, I think it was kind of a letdown."

"She had some troubles there," Nancy said. "She went broke. My father wired her money once and it seemed to disappear in a few days. She did fall in love, though." Nancy's eyes became teary and she glanced toward the Bay. "I was sure she was going to marry him."

"John," Brian said.

"Yes, John Linden. But then Nicholas came along. And I guess she was more drawn to the *allure*. Not that I have any right to stand in judgment of anyone, least of all my sister."

Brian said, "I think she saw Nick as someone who was very worldly and maybe could fix her problems."

"She believed that life was supposed to be that perfect summer," Nancy said.

"How'd they meet?" Hunter asked Brian.

"She just answered an ad, and went to work," Nancy said. "That was the kind of deal he was running: He hired secretaries. Probably still does. He had a business on the Jersey Shore and ran ads for secretaries. I think it was a racket."

Brian's face contorted as she said this. Every time she became emotional, he looked as if he was suffering mild chest pains.

"Will you tell us honestly what you have?" Nancy narrowed her eyes at Hunter. "As far as an investigation goes? Is there anything implicating him? Any evidence yet?"

"I can't say," Hunter said. "It's an active investigation. Although I can tell you, Nicholas Champlain has an alibi. He was out of town when it happened."

"Well, I don't believe it," Nancy said, crossing her arms.

Brian sighed.

"I'd like to hear more about this boyfriend. John Linden," Hunter said.

"John? He lives in Delaware now," Nancy said. "I just received an e-mail from him, actually."

"So you've stayed in touch."

"Oh, no, not at all," she said.

Brian said, "I think he just heard Susan had passed and sent condolences."

"Had *he* stayed in touch with Susan, do you know?"

"I think he may have," he said.

"Do you know how I might reach him?"

"John Linden?" Nancy said. "Why would you want to do that?"

She looked at her brother, who nodded. "Go ahead."

"He's an attorney in Delaware now," she said. "Near New Castle. I'm sure he's listed."

"Is he married, too?"

Brian coughed and looked at his sister.

"I understand he did finally marry, yes," Nancy said. "My feeling is that Susie probably regretted it in a way that she didn't stay with him."

"So did *she* break things off?"

"Well—"

"She was always a little vague about that," Brian said. "They both said it was 'mutual.'"

"Which is another way of saying they don't want to talk about it."

"I think maybe she wore him down a bit," Brian said, smiling privately. "She did that."

"Maybe," Nancy said, disagreeing.

"Are you staying in town overnight?" Hunter asked.

"We are," Brian said. "We're at the Old Shore Inn. We're going to church in the morning and then we're driving back."

"Well, I'll probably see you in church, then. I hope you say hello to Pastor Bowers. I know he thought very highly of your sister."

Hunter found John Linden's listing a few minutes after saying goodbye to Susan's siblings and left him a voice-mail message. She surfed for Linden online. He was a tax attorney who collected antique clocks and owned a house in the suburbs appraised at $324,000. She found just one image of him, taken at an American Cancer Society fund-raising dinner in New Castle. He was a wide-cheeked man, well-dressed, posing with his arm around his smiling blond wife. Hunter looked at it for a while and felt pretty sure about one thing: John Linden was the man with the elegant shoulders.

LUKE'S FAVORITE MUSIC was silence. Often his best thoughts came late at night when he should have been sleeping. He'd open his eyes in the dark sometimes and think up an entire sermon while Charlotte and Sneakers slept soundly beside him— although he was lucky if he remembered half of it in the morning. Some of those sermons were inspired by his parents, who had expected big things from Luke and seemed quietly disappointed at times that he hadn't achieved them by the time cancer began to eat away at his father. Luke still abided by some of the simple wisdom his father had given him as a boy, his rules for better- ment: *whenever you think you've finished with something*, he'd say, *look at it one more time and ask, how can I make this even better? How can I give it more meaning?*

Luke practiced today's sermon in his head as he lay in bed waiting for daylight. But his thoughts kept drifting to Susan Champlain—the look of expectation in her eyes seemed as vivid in his mind as it had in his office five days earlier. Luke couldn't get back to sleep. When dawn broke over the marsh- lands, he was outside trotting slowly with Sneakers along the bluff, the sky turning silver-blue above the farm fields. It was a gorgeous day, reminding him of the mornings when he first felt called to the ministry, walking along the beach in North- ern California. He thought of the prayer of St. Francis, with its peculiar inverse logic—in dying we are born; by giving we receive; comfort rather than be comforted; love rather than be loved. Luke had always been interested in things he couldn't see, from when he was a boy, gazing up at the dark infinities from his backyard. It was his job now to talk about them, to try to explain them in ways that encouraged and inspired people. The death of Susan reminded him of the enormity of that task, of making Biblical ideas live beyond the twenty minutes of his Sunday sermon. How do you make them resonate through the week?

Chapter Twenty

It's not often that we don't have enough parking spaces," Luke told the congregation, which was full to the rafters that morning. "I'm reminded of the old story about the man who was late for an important meeting and couldn't find a parking place. He kept going around and around the block but nothing opened up. Finally he said, 'God, if only you'll let me find a space, I promise I'll attend church every Sunday and read the Bible every night.' Miraculously, it seemed, a parking space opened up right in front of him. So the man told God, 'Never mind, I just found one.'"

The congregation chuckled, although there was a somber undercurrent in the room this morning, which seemed to expand when the chuckling stopped. Everyone knew that a member of the congregation was missing.

"When I think of the events of the past week," Luke said, beginning his sermon, "I'm reminded of something the apostle James said. He was talking to a group of businessmen who were making plans, as all of us do. And James said, 'Now listen, you who say, today or tomorrow, we will go to this or that city, spend a year there. Why, you do not even know what will happen tomorrow. What is your life? You are a vapor that appears for a little while and vanishes.'

"It's a theme that recurs throughout the Bible, Old Testament and New. First Chronicles tells us that our time on Earth is like a shadow. Job says, 'My life is a breath.' In Psalm 102, we're told our days 'vanish like smoke.' Psalm 103 says, 'Our days on Earth are like grass, the wind passes through it and it is gone.'"

Luke glanced up and noticed the sheriff was seated alone in the third row, making faces. Was he trying to suppress a sneeze?

"I'm also reminded of what David said, in First Samuel 20: 'There is but a step between me and death.'" He paused, glancing to the other side of the room, seeing Charlotte and feeling a tender emotion flow through him, thinking about their project. "There is only one step separating each of us from death. One step.

"Most of us here this morning have had to deal with the loss of someone close in our lives, whether a parent, a brother or sister, a neighbor, a best friend. Many of us have known someone who died suddenly and we've recognized—painfully—the truth of David's words.

"This week, we unexpectedly lost a friend and congregation member, Susan Champlain. And we were again reminded how close each of us is—just one step—from death. A week ago, Susan sat here with us in our sanctuary, as she did every Sunday. And three days later, she went to be with the Lord.

"Susan liked to sit on the right side, close to the front, often in the fourth row," Luke said, pointing toward the pew where she sat. "We welcome her brother and sister this morning, Nancy and Brian, who are visiting from Iowa, and we share their enormous loss."

An explosion erupted in the sanctuary, a single guttural sound like the roar of a lion. Luke blinked several times. It was the sheriff, finally sneezing. "Je-sus! 'Scuse me!" he said.

Luke waited a moment for heads to swivel back. "One step," he continued, pleased that much of the congregation chose to ignore the sheriff. "Susan visited with me this past Tuesday. We talked a little about faith, a little bit about her life, a little about her art. As many of you know, Susan was a talented photographer, and she had many plans for her future. As all of us do.

"If we knew how close that one step was, would we live our lives any differently? Would we look at our limited time here through a different lens? Would we place a higher value on the presence of God in our lives? On our interactions with one another?

"What is value?" Luke asked the congregation. "The pearl merchant asks that in Matthew. Often what Scripture says about value and what our society values are two very different things. And too often our society gives value to the wrong things.

"If I asked you today to rank the most valuable things in your life, how would you respond? Most of you would say your family. Your health. Your home. Financial security. Your freedom, perhaps. Then what? Some of you might mention some prized possession or other, a vintage car, mementos.

"But where would you put your relationship with God? Why wouldn't you put that first?"

He looked out and saw the sheriff shifting uncomfortably in the pew, his face lowered and contorted like he was about to sneeze again.

"We've all heard the saying 'a rising tide lifts all boats.' God's like that, too. When we put God first, it lifts the value of everything else in our life. It gives us a greater appreciation for all of the other things that we value. We need to remember that, in good times and in difficult times. And in times of tragedy."

He talked some more about value and then closed the sermon with a prayer for Susan Champlain, drawing from Psalm 139 and its parting message of darkness becoming light. Afterward, Charlotte helped him greet the congregants as they filed out. There were many people there he hadn't seen in weeks, or months, among them Jackson Pynne, the swaggering businessman whose new restaurant/bar, Jackson's, was having problems with the liquor license board again; Tim and Marty Sparrow, a retired couple whose surname had always struck him as a perfect fit; gift shop owner Roberta Tilghman, with her clangy bracelets and theatrical gestures, telling him how her parakeet Andy was "so looking forward" to the pet blessings; Anne Renault, a true-crime journalist, who tried to interest Luke in helping her tell "the real story" about Susan Champlain, as Luke pretended not to notice the enormous stain on her blouse; Talmadge Lantern, a gaunt, white-haired scarecrow of a man who'd once played drums with Bob Dylan; Donald Rumsfeld, the former secretary of defense, visiting with his wife Joyce; Gab Bunting, the wavy-haired publisher of the *Tidewater Times*, who still wanted Luke to go goose hunting with him sometime; Gabe Knoll, a retired astronomy professor and former atheist who now believed that science and religion were simpatico; and the pastor emeritus Manfred Knosum and his wife, Mabel, who lived in Florida but returned to Tidewater in summer to visit with their seventeen grandchildren.

After all of that, and saying goodbye to Charlotte, Luke noticed Sheriff Clay Calvert ambling toward him, coming down
the corridor from the restrooms. He'd been lingering, evidently,
wanting to be the last to leave.

"Well, that was sure a nice sermon, Pastor," the sheriff said,
gripping his hand a little harder than necessary and then not letting go. "But I gotta tell you, call it my prejudice, but I don't
know as I like what I'm seeing so much out there anymore."

"What is it you're seeing?" Luke said, trying to stay upbeat.

"A fear. Is what I call it," he said.

"A fear?"

"A fear. Yes, sir."

Luke held his smile as long as he could. There were several
theories about the sheriff—that he was becoming prematurely
senile, that he was drinking too much, that he was having financial or marriage troubles (all of these Luke had heard from
Aggie). Luke didn't think it was senility, but there was definitely
something different about the sheriff lately.

"We've had it before, don't misunderstand," he said, finally
letting go of Luke's hand, "but not in a while. And not like this.
And the thing is, it preys on itself. *Preys* on itself," he said, liking
the sound of that phrase. "There's a fear now that accidents
happen and people start to talking like they're not really *accidents*. And it *preys* on itself."

"Well," Luke said. "That's interesting. I'm glad you could
come today."

Calvert grimaced, and turned to the parking lot. "What you
and I need is to go out fishing one of these weekends," he said.

"We should do that sometime, yes."

He clapped Luke hard on the back and walked away to his car.

Luke helped the custodians to clean up and close the church. He didn't realize until he was in the parking lot that Susan's brother and sister had been waiting at their car for him to come out. Nancy Adams gave him a long hug and Brian Wilkins shook his hand slowly but firmly. It was touching to see how grateful they were. They talked for several minutes, Nancy becoming emotional again. He invited them to visit with him in his office but Brian Wilkins said they needed to get on the road.

"It's almost like she knew this was coming," Nancy told Luke. "She had an acute awareness that other people never had. I hate to think this, but she almost *knew* ahead of time what was going to happen."

She gave Luke another hug before leaving. Brian was already in their rental car by then. Nancy had begun to mythologize her sister a little, Luke sensed. That was okay. It was one of the ways people dealt with death.

"Have a safe drive," Luke told her.

HUNTER WENT ON a long run after church, around the commercial harbor and up along the bluffs, Radiohead in her earbuds, ending it with a wind sprint along the flat marina road. It was a hot, cloudless day and it felt good to work up an honest sweat.

She called out Winston's name as she came in—"Hey Winnie! Ready for a lunchtime snack?"—but heard nothing in reply. Normally, Winston squawked immediately, either proud of whatever hiding place he'd found or just wanting to announce his presence. She walked through all of the rooms of her apartment, sweat sliding down her face and neck, trying his name in different voices.

She got down on hands and knees and peered under the bed. She looked in the closets, the washer and dryer, behind the sofa and in the bathtub. She searched each room carefully, first the places he favored and then everywhere else, beginning to worry that something had happened; that somehow Winston had gotten loose. Had she left the door open while she was lacing up her running shoes? Or when she was using the bathroom? It didn't seem possible. Hunter spent another fifteen minutes searching the apartment, retracing her steps and trying not to panic, her priorities suddenly falling away; she wanted nothing more in her life now than to find Winston. She began to imagine him outside, darting across the marina road, his mind in chaos mode; or cowering in the bushes near the seafood restaurant, too scared to do anything. She imagined finding him on the side of the road, after he'd been hit by a driver who didn't bother to stop or maybe didn't even notice. Hunter went outside, anxiously pacing the parking lot, shouting his name, walking onto the docks, her eyes combing the lawns and the boats. "Winnie! *Win*nie!" Probably sounding a little foolish. She went back inside and searched again, all the places she'd already looked and then places she hadn't, where he couldn't be; although with Winston, it was hard to tell. She opened the refrigerator. She felt along the upper shelf of the study closet and the kitchen counters, even though they were taller than she was. She lifted the toilet cover. At one point, she opened the middle drawer of her bedroom dresser, looked down and there he was—lying on a white T-shirt, curled up like a black half-moon, asleep. It took a moment for it to register: had she really closed the drawer before her run and not noticed that Winston was inside?

She lifted Winston from the drawer and hugged him, cooing as if he were a human baby. Finally, he squawked disapprovingly. She set him down and he trotted away to his water dish, tail straight up in the air. Hunter followed him to the kitchen, feeling enormous waves of gratitude. Not only for Winston, but for everything else. She thought of Luke's story—about the parking space. About how tempting it was *not* to be grateful.

Hunter took a ten-minute shower, and then returned to normal life. She checked her messages: John Linden had finally called back, while she was outside frantically searching for Winston. She got a Diet Coke from the kitchen, and went to the back porch with her phone and notebook.

"You called me," Linden said, in a guarded tone. "How can I help you?"

Hunter explained that she was investigating Susan Champlain's death.

"And how'd you get my name?"

"It came up in the course of interviews," she said. "Could I come out and talk with you?"

He let some silence pass. "How did my name come up in the course of interviews, if you don't mind me asking?"

"Does it matter?"

"I'm curious. You're investigating her death?"

"That's right." She scribbled *Doesn't want to meet* in her notebook. Then decided to push it into another gear. "The reason I'd like to talk with you is that I understand you were with Susan here in Tidewater County on Wednesday, the day she died. In fact, as far as I've been able to tell, you were the last known person to see her alive."

Another silence followed. But this was a different kind of silence. The long, endless kind. "Hello?" Hunter said.

JOHN LINDEN SEEMED to be dressed for prep school: blue oxford shirt, pressed khaki slacks, natty burgundy loafers with tassels. His clothes were unwrinkled, despite the seventy-mile drive from Delaware; Hunter wondered if he'd stopped nearby to change. His cheeks looked even fuller than in the picture and he had less hair, but what struck her most was how short he was. Probably an inch or two shorter than Susan Champlain. Hunter hadn't picked up on that from the photo, where he was standing beside his even shorter wife. Fooled by the elegant shoulders, evidently.

"So. Am I in trouble?" Linden asked, seated on the other side of Hunter's desk. Linden's dark eyes had a steady, attentive quality but the smile spoiled it a little, giving his face a crooked, indecisive look.

"I don't know," she said. "Is there any reason you should be?"

"No, of course not. Who told you I was here on Wednesday?"

"Someone who saw you with her," Hunter said. "I understand you used to date Susan?"

A flush rose up his cheeks. "You've talked to the family, then."

"Her brother and sister, yes."

Linden shifted in the chair.

Tanner walked by, hesitating as if he was going to ask Hunter something.

"Hello," he said, nodding to Linden.

Linden just looked blankly back at him.

"So: You used to date her?" Hunter asked.

His eyes assented. "Years ago, yeah."

"How many?"

"Six. Five or six."

"But you stayed in touch."

"Occasionally. Not a lot."

"So how did you happen to be with her here in Tidewater on the day she died?"

"How did I happen to be with her," he said, echoing her tone. He leaned back and cleared his throat again. "Okay: Susan e-mailed me the day before. Said she wanted to talk, could I meet with her? I drove down in the morning, Wednesday morning, we met, and I left here at about one thirty that afternoon. I was back in my office before the end of the day. You can check."

"I will," Hunter said. "Why did she want to meet with you then?"

"Why? She just wanted to talk. She said she was worried about something, and needed to talk."

"Was that something she'd do—ask to meet with you when she wanted to talk?"

"Almost never."

"So what was different on Wednesday?" she said. "What was she worried about?"

"When she contacted me, you mean? Or—? She didn't go into specifics. Just—that she wanted to talk and—We were going to have lunch, but she was real nervous when I got here so we talked at the Inn for—I mean, just a few minutes, walked out to the water, and I left. That was it."

John Linden cleared his throat again, unnecessarily.

"That's a long way to drive just to talk for few minutes."

"It is."

"And so what was she worried about?"

"Oh, well, I don't know. I mean—her husband, mostly. There were tensions in her marriage, as you probably heard."

"Over—?"

"Over—" He had to think about that. A thin film of sweat had formed above his chin. It was as if he'd over-rehearsed and suddenly become tongue-tied. Finally, he said, "I mean—this is kind of getting into a personal area, asking about our conversations."

"Not anymore," Hunter said. "The details are part of a police investigation now. You were seen here with her the day she died. There's going to be video footage of you talking with her. It's part of our investigation now."

Suddenly the blood seemed to leave his face and his eyes flashed a look of panic. Moments later, John Linden leapt to his feet and gasped several times. He flapped a hand up and down in front of his face and dropped back into the seat as if he was about to faint. Was he having a panic attack?

"Are you okay? Can I get you water?"

Hunter rushed out to the watercooler. Tanner waved from his office as she walked by, but she kept going. When she returned, he was better, standing again and shaking out his right leg as if the problem had just been his foot going to sleep.

"Are you all right?"

"Sorry," he said. He took a couple more deep breaths and they both sat. "I just sort of got dizzy there for a second. Dehydrated, probably."

"Take your time." Hunter let him drink the water. He gulped down three-quarters of it and set the cup on her desk. "Start from the beginning," she said. "What did you talk about with Susan Champlain? Why did she call you?"

"All right," he said. He sat forward and exhaled audibly. "She wanted to talk because—she was worried, like I say, about her husband. And I guess it had to do with—she had learned something that she wasn't supposed to know, about her husband's business."

"Go on."

"And she was afraid it might have something to do with organized crime—or that's what she said, anyway." He gave her a tentative smile. "She was afraid he was being used and that he was going to get hurt. She was actually more concerned about her *hus*band's welfare, I think, than her own."

"Okay. Go on. What kind of business are we talking about?"

"I couldn't tell you that."

"You could," Hunter said and he looked up at her for a moment like a scolded child. "You're saying she didn't share *any* of the details?"

"No, I mean—not many of them."

"Okay. Tell me the ones she did share."

He sighed, reached for the rest of the water, and drank it, setting the cup back on her desk.

"She believed—this is what she told me—that she thought it maybe involved stolen art," he said. "And, possibly, that this deal had something to do with organized crime, like I say."

"Her husband's business."

"Yes." He drew in his lips and sat back.

"Okay. And why did she think that?"

He lifted his palms to show he didn't know. "I have no idea. I mean, that's what she said. That's what she *thought*. She did kind of overhear things. She was smarter than people give her credit for. A very astute observer."

"She could read signs, I understand."

"What?"

"Did she ever tell you that?"

"No."

Hunter nodded and waved away the subject. "So she told you she'd overheard him talking about this deal?"

"On the phone, yeah, two or three times, making comments, talking—*cryptically*, sometimes, I think was how she put it. Like I say, she picked up pieces here and there—"

"Had they been arguing about it at all, Susan and her husband?"

"Arguing?" He reached for the cup again, saw that it was empty and left it on her desk. "I mean— She didn't get into that part with me, really. She could be very guarded about certain things. And probably a little paranoid, because of the organized crime thing." Hunter waited. "She was afraid they were 'shadowing' her husband. That's a word she used."

"Why would someone be shadowing her husband? Who did she think it was?"

"Oh, I don't know."

Hunter nodded. She could sort of understand why Susan Wilkins and John Linden hadn't stayed together. They were two nervous people who probably made each other a little crazy.

"It seems strange to me that you chose to meet in such a public place, at the Old Shore Inn," she said. "Had you met there before?"

"No. I mean, it wouldn't have been *my* choice. Of course, her husband was away at the time. So—"

"And I don't understand why you didn't come forward and say something after she died."

"You mean to the police?"

"Yes."

"I don't know. I mean—" He sighed. Sweat glistened on his forehead and his chin. "In retrospect? I probably should have. Obviously, I'm devastated by what happened, as her family is. But. I guess I just didn't want to get in the way. And I didn't think it would help, anyway."

"How would you have gotten in the way?"

"I just didn't want to confuse things."

"Confuse things—meaning because you're married and she's married?" Hunter said.

"Well." He cleared his throat and shifted in the chair, his face turning scarlet. "That probably entered into it," he said. "But, I mean—if I thought I could have shed any light on what happened? I'd have been there in a heartbeat."

"What do you *think* happened?"

"Oh, I don't know," he said. "No idea."

"Then why are you so sure that nothing you said would've helped?"

"What?"

"Why are you so sure nothing you said would have helped?"

He began to fidget with a cuff button on his shirt. Hunter had seen all kinds of affairs and knew what they did to people, including some that weren't technically affairs; those, at times, were worse than the real thing. "I mean, I just didn't think it would have mattered," he said, as if this explained it. "Also, I didn't come forward because I don't think she would have wanted me to."

"Were you having an affair with her?"

"No. Absolutely not," he said, sounding too adamant. "But that's what I mean. That's what people would have thought. It would have just confused things. Who told you, anyway?"

"A guest who saw you talking with her. They said you appeared to be in a very intense conversation."

"No."

"How would you characterize it?"

"Friendly. Just a conversation. I think I was always kind of a sounding board for Susan, in a way. But it was perfectly innocent. Half the time she wanted advice about her husband."

"But what was it, specifically, on that day, that made her want to meet with you?" Hunter said, circling back to the key question.

"I guess—I mean, I think she just thought that something had changed."

"With her husband?"

"With her husband, yeah." Hunter nodded for him to go on. "He'd been acting, I don't know, a little erratically, he was angry at her, and I think that just worried her. But, I mean, she couldn't really pinpoint *what* it was."

"And you never thought that you ought to tell the police about that?"

He shook his head, almost imperceptibly.

"No?" Hunter said.

"No."

"Because you thought it would confuse things."

"That's right, yeah," he said. "And also—I mean—"

"Yes?"

"And also I was—I guess I was kind of advised against it."

His face went pale for a moment, then slowly reddened. He cleared his throat.

"By?"

"By the FBI."

Oh. "You're saying you did go to the FBI about this?"

"No." He shifted again in the chair, showing a nervous smile. "I guess I wasn't supposed to say that. No, I didn't *go* to them, I just made a call. After the fact. I made a phone call."

"After which fact?" Hunter asked.

"After Susan died. I'd offered to do it beforehand, but she didn't want me to. That's what we were arguing about, okay? I called Thursday, the day after she died. Maybe I shouldn't have. I just felt like I had to do something, okay? I didn't think there'd be a local investigation."

"Why the FBI?"

"That was actually her idea. We'd talked about it a couple of times. She knew they had a Stolen Art Division. She thought this might have something to do with stolen art. She thought maybe we could do it anonymously. Although when I did call, they actually discouraged the whole idea."

"Who did?"

"The fellow I talked with."

Hunter studied his face, still flushed and oily now with sweat. "Was this fellow's name Scott Randall, by any chance?"

"No," he said.

"The fellow you talked with?"

He frowned past her out at the woods as if trying to think harder. "His name . . . yeah, *Scott Randall*. Was that it? I think so."

Jeez-us, Hunter thought. She felt a twinge of anger. Why didn't *he* tell her this?

"Why—do you know him?"

"Not really." Hunter forced a smile. "How'd that go, by the way? What'd you tell Randall?"

"Basically, nothing. I mean—I told him what I knew, which wasn't much."

"Tell *me* what you know," Hunter said. She sure could've used a bad cop/good cop partner about now. "Tell me what you told him."

"Okay." John Linden sat forward and summoned a new, more authoritative tone: "I did tell him this: Before things changed, early in the summer, I guess it was, Susan's husband evidently said something to her that he probably shouldn't have—that he didn't mean to."

"Go ahead."

"He said something, in passing, about a famous stolen painting. He said that he knew someone, or had heard of someone, who knew where it was and was going to help recover it. It was just one conversation that lasted about a minute and a half, she said. After that, Susan and her husband never discussed it again. It never came up. But she never forgot it."

"What did she think it was? This famous painting?"

"She thought it might be the art stolen from the Gardner Museum, in Boston. Which, of course, would make it a big deal."

"Why would she have thought that?"

"I don't know, I guess because he said something about it

being a big take or a big heist or something. And that was one of the biggest. I think she Googled 'art thefts' and that one comes up pretty quick."

"Did she tell you anything about a photo she'd taken? Something her husband had found on her phone?"

Linden's face remained expressionless. "No."

"Sure?"

"Sure."

Hunter had a different idea, then. "You know what the reward is for those paintings, I'm sure, don't you?"

"The reward? No." Linden made a faint choking sound. "I mean, yeah—I saw *something* about that, I think, yeah." Hunter wondered if Linden might be interested in the FBI's standing $5 million reward for information leading to the return of the stolen Gardner art. "I mean, are you saying *that* could somehow pertain to her *death*?" he asked.

"I don't know," Hunter said. "What do *you* think?"

"I have no idea. I'm asking you."

"And I'm asking you."

"Okay," he said.

Hunter waited.

"What else?" she said finally. "What else did she tell you?"

"That's it," he said. "That's all."

He smiled uncertainly.

"And is there anything else you'd like to tell me?"

"About?"

"Anything."

Linden made a face.

"No?" she said.

"No."

"Okay." Hunter kept her eyes on his. "I'll be back in touch with you, then."

She stood.

"You will?"

This seemed to bother him as much as anything.

"Or you with me," she said. "Whichever comes first."

Chapter Twenty-one

Hunter went home to spend some quality time with Winston before visiting Luke and Charlotte Bowers for dinner. Winston didn't know it (or perhaps he did), but she was going to be away overnight on Monday and he would be tended to by Grace Pappas, a crotchety older neighbor whose voice scared Winston something awful. The quality time was more for her than for Winston, of course, although he didn't mind. They communed on the back porch, watching the marina activity, Hunter stroking the sides of his face and beneath his chin.

Then she showered again and got dressed. *Nothing fancy, just crab cakes,* he'd said. Still, she'd ironed a dress shirt and pulled out her gray slacks. Somehow, she'd forgotten that the slacks fit funny, a little too tight at the waist and sort of bunchy around her thighs. But her usual selection of well-worn jeans didn't seem appropriate tonight. She had never been to the Bowerses' house, which was more of a cottage, a "parish house," he called it, whatever that meant.

As soon as Luke opened the door that evening, the Bowerses' dog Sneakers was all over her. Hunter went with it, getting down on one knee as he rolled onto his back and turned to jelly, his tail thumping wildly on the hardwood floor.

"Looks like we've got some competition," Charlotte said to Luke as she came in, holding a glass of wine.

"That's actually quite unusual," Luke said. "He doesn't often act that way."

"Tell her what happened when the FBI man came by."

"Well, it wasn't pretty," Luke said. "Sneakers isn't used to being ignored."

Hunter straightened up.

"FBI man?" She felt a shiver race through her. "Was Scott Randall here?"

"Yes. I probably should have told you that."

"He ignored Sneakers," Charlotte said. "Can I show you the house?"

"Sure," she said. Then added, "Yes."

There wasn't a lot to show. The house was small and neat, with antique wooden furniture, nautical knickknacks, little embroidered pillows, photos. Hunter's place was neat, too, but she didn't go in for knickknacks. Sneakers followed, sniffing at her ill-fitting pants each time they stopped. It was starting to make her self-conscious.

Back in the living room, she sat across the sofa from Luke. A baseball game was on television, the sound off. Charlotte came out, leaning in the doorway. Hunter told them about John Linden and some of what Randall had shared with her about Walter Kepler. Both Bowerses listened with great interest, not moving, as if any undue motion would interrupt her story.

"I guess it goes without saying, this is all just between us," she said in conclusion.

"Yes."

Luke said, "Charlotte was saying before you came over that we're kind of a secret society now."

"Yes."

"We might even need to come up with a secret handshake," Charlotte suggested.

"We'd probably have to include Sneakers in that," Luke said.

"Of course," Hunter replied. *And Winston*, she thought, but didn't say.

"He *has* learned to shake," Luke explained.

"I'm not surprised." Hunter smiled. She hadn't really expected this degree of banter, which seemed to be the natural way they communicated.

"So you're going to see Nick Champlain tomorrow?" Luke asked, once Charlotte had brought out the salads and Luke had said grace. "Will you press him about the photo?"

"I think so. It's one of my topics, yes."

"Is Randall feeding you any questions?" he asked.

"No. He gave me a few suggestions." Hunter took a drink of wine. "I keep having to remind myself why I'm doing this."

"Which is?" Luke said.

"Susan Champlain. Not stolen art."

"Right."

"But you're going to ask about the Gardner art?" Charlotte said.

"I think so, yes." Hunter picked up a cherry tomato and popped it in her mouth. "Although it's a sensitive area, obviously," she said. "I mean, if it has something to do with what happened, then, it's part of the . . . Oh, my God! . . . Whoops!"

Hunter stared in horror at the table. She'd bitten on the cherry tomato and squirted juice all the way across the table and onto Charlotte's salad plate. For a moment, there was silence, all of them staring at the line of tomato juice and seeds.

"No worries," Luke said, bounding up. "We do that all the time, Charlotte in particular."

She punched him in the arm as he passed by.

"Luke taught me," she said. "He used to be quite good at it."

Hunter did the usual "Let me help" and "I'm so sorry" as Luke sponged away the juice, impressed how deftly they were able to leapfrog her faux pas.

"No harm," Charlotte said, in a tone that was reassuring but also seemed to be asking her to cool it with apologies. These Bowerses are full of surprises, Hunter thought.

Charlotte commandeered the conversation as Luke prepped the crab cakes. Telling her about something called the Coriolis Force, which she said caused the saltier water in the Chesapeake Bay to move toward the Eastern Shore rather than the Western Shore, particularly in late summer. "That's why the breeze this time of year feels like sea air," she said.

"I didn't realize that."

"No, most people don't."

"Coriolis was a French engineer," Luke added, bringing in the dinners on expensive-looking china plates. "He's one of the seventy-two names inscribed on the Eiffel Tower. Scientists, engineers, mathematicians."

"Really," Hunter said. "This is becoming quite an education."

"Aren't you going to tell her the names of the other seventy-one?" Charlotte asked.

"I was saving it. Maybe during dessert?"

They ate in silence for a while, Hunter careful not to make any mistakes. The crab cakes were delicious, crisply cooked with lump fin crabmeat and no detectable filling. Hunter praised them to Luke, who smiled quickly and shifted the subject back to Susan Champlain. "You know, I've sort of been rethinking a few things that Susan told me," he said. "I'm not sure I believe the circumstances under which she took those pictures, for instance."

"Oh?"

"Having had some time to reflect."

"Which circumstances?" Hunter asked.

"The story about stopping off at that house on the way to the airport, where the painting was. I'm not sure I quite believe that."

"Why?"

"Because the way she told it was funny." He glanced at Charlotte, then back at Hunter. "I realize, from an investigative standpoint, that may not be the soundest reason—"

"Although it surprised me a little, too," Hunter said, "that he'd take her so close to the painting. To something that valuable."

"Or that such a great painting would just be sitting out there in the open like that," he said.

"Well, it was in a side room," Charlotte said. "And anyway, people who deal with stolen art are notorious for not exactly caring for it the way a museum would."

Hunter nodded. "Stolen masterpieces have been recovered in storage sheds and behind Dumpsters."

"That's right."

"One other thing I heard," Luke said, "is that Susan may have left a note behind. That's not true, is it?"

Hunter frowned. "Where'd you hear that?" she asked, suspecting Aggie, the receptionist.

"J. Michael Bunting."

"The newspaper guy?" Even better. They shared a quick smile around the table. "No," Hunter said, "no note yet. Although she did have a book in the pouch on her bicycle and there was a receipt inside that she'd scribbled on."

Hunter saw something change in Luke's face as she told them what Susan had written. *Kairos48.* "Does that mean anything?"

"Well, yes, maybe," he said.

"Kairos and Chronos," Charlotte said.

"I gave a sermon on Kairos and Chronos early in the summer," Luke explained. "Chronos is man's time, Kairos is God's time."

"Well, that's interesting."

"Yes."

"I wonder how much Susan actually knew," Charlotte said. "Do you think she knew what was in that photo—that she may have inadvertently taken a picture of the stolen Rembrandt?"

"From what John Linden said, no," Hunter said.

"I'd vote no, also," Luke added. "I think she would have said something if she did."

"It's interesting what John Linden said, though," Hunter said. "He made it sound like she was afraid *for* her husband rather than *of* him."

"Yes, I picked up on that, too," Luke said.

"So maybe she *was* starting to figure it out."

"Whatever *it* is," Luke said.

"Yes."

They all smiled at that. By the time Charlotte brought in dessert, they'd finished up with secret society business. Hunter was feeling good after a couple of glasses of wine; the tomato incident was ancient history.

"How'd you get into this, anyway?" she said, slicing a fork through her apple pie. "I don't know that I've ever asked you." With Luke, it seemed, any question was fair game.

"I want to hear, too," Charlotte said, pretending to be a little girl.

Luke smiled. "Not much of a story."

"You were working as a paramedic, right?" Charlotte prompted.

"Yes, out West, some years ago. Taking a couple of graduate courses. It's rewarding work, paramedics, but with a high attrition rate. We were the first responders to emergencies. Let's you see how fragile life is."

"How we're all one step from death," Charlotte said.

"Well, yes."

"To be honest, I related more to the story you told about the parking space," Hunter said. "That's me, at times."

"It's most of us at times," Charlotte said.

"It was me before I was called to do this," Luke said.

"A long distance call if ever there was one," Charlotte said.

"Ha-ha."

"What did your parents raise you to be?" Hunter asked.

"Independent."

"Did you have brothers and sisters?"

Luke shook his head. "Still don't."

"I liked Susan Champlain's family," Charlotte said, to Hunter. "Her brother and sister."

"Me, too."

"I think Susan saw herself as having a calling, and a gift," Luke said, "and she really wanted to make the most of that."

"Her art."

"Yes. I think so."

"We all have our own unique gift," Charlotte said, "and we need to find what it is."

"Yes. Paul says that," Luke said.

"Paul—?"

"St. Paul. The apostle."

"Oh." Hunter was thinking for some reason of Paul McCartney.

"In Romans and again in First Corinthians."

"Does he say just one gift?" Hunter asked.

"One above others," Luke said. "And I think, with that, we have two obligations: to find what it is. And then, more important: figure out how best to use it."

Hunter was gazing at the darkened Bay, thinking about Susan Champlain's final hours, feeling extremely comfortable now. Pleased that neither of them had asked much about *her* past and confident that neither of them would.

"Anyone ready for more wine?" Charlotte asked.

BELASCO WATCHED AMY Hunter's window from a bench in the shadows on the Bay end of the marina. Her bedroom lights went out at 11:45. Came on again at 11:52. Then went out at 12:01, for good. *Amy Hunter.* Belasco had identified her now as a potential obstacle. She had spent her Sunday evening with the pastor and the pastor's wife. Susan Champlain had gone to the pastor, too, on Tuesday afternoon; the day she should have had her fall. Then on Friday morning, Hunter had met with Scott Randall. They'd taken a drive. All of those were reasons for concern.

Belasco waited in the dark, feeling invisible, enjoying the breeze over the water, thinking about what would happen in a few days: Kepler's "miracle." Not wanting to be here. Wanting to be back in Philadelphia.

This was Belasco's self-appointed role, however: to watch, to make sure that nothing threatened what Walter Kepler planned to do. In Belasco's world, obstacles were to be avoided; threats to be eliminated. All of a sudden, Amy Hunter was becoming an obstacle. Not yet a threat. But that could change fast.

PART 2

A Good Bad Man

I am now as a tramp who has the Sun all to himself.
  —Isabella Stewart Gardner, 1898, to art dealer Bernard Berenson,
 after purchasing Rembrandt's painting *The Storm on the Sea of Galilee*

Where you come from is gone, where you thought you were
going to never was there and where you are is no good unless
you can get away from it.

—Flannery O'Connor, *Wise Blood*

Chapter Twenty-two

The notion of getting away for a couple of days gave Amy Hunter an anxious pause, which was enhanced by the fact that it was Monday, the beginning of the work week for everyone else. Her plan was to meet Helen Bradbury at 8:30 at Bradbury's home near Easton, and then drive up to Philadelphia to interview Nicholas Champlain at 1 P.M. After that, she was going to visit with her mother overnight in the Philly suburbs and attempt to relax for a few hours: have dinner with her mom, maybe walk the hiking trail near her childhood home, drink a little wine, watch a true crime show on television. It was Henry Moore's idea that she do this, take a day or two off after interviewing Champlain to "recharge the batteries," although taking time "off" had never been one of Hunter's strong suits. Especially not in the early stages of an investigation.

Helen Bradbury lived in an old, two-story clapboard colonial, isolated on a large creek-front property, with a decrepit, falling-down barn out back. The exterior paint of the house was peeling and the gutters drooped from years of neglect. But there were stunning views of water and wetlands in all directions.

Four dogs of various sizes rushed in a tangle down the driveway to greet her. They were followed by Bradbury, a large woman who wore a long green muumuu-style dress and rubber flip-flops.

"Come on in," she said, stopping halfway down, waving her up the drive.

The house looked and smelled like a historic site inside, with creaky wood plank floors, cracked ceiling beams, dusty heat registers. The rooms were cluttered and musty; 1960s jazz played in her study, which was lined with ceiling-to-floor bookshelves.

"We'll just go in here," she said, leading Hunter to the kitchen, where a teakettle was steaming on a white porcelain gas stove. A warm stewy smell filled the room. "So," she said, motioning for her to sit, "did Dave Crowe send you to me?"

"Kind of."

She grinned broadly, revealing gums, as she poured tea into delicate old china cups. Bradbury was a round-faced woman with a silvery bowl haircut and large, watchful brown eyes. "Always looking for new ways to cover his ass, isn't he? And so," she said, sitting, her knees spread out, "what's your particular interest?"

"I'm investigating an unattended death in Tidewater County," Hunter said. She sipped the tea, which was hot, strong, and slightly disagreeable in taste. "A woman named Susan Champlain."

"That's not what I asked you, honey," she said. "What's your interest in the Stolen Art Division? And in me?"

"Well. I believe that Susan Champlain's death may have had something to do with stolen art," Hunter said. "A stolen painting." In fact, Hunter was hoping that Helen Bradbury could help fill in some of the blanks in the story Dave Crowe had told her Friday, two blanks in particular: Who was the man who "got involved" with Randall last year, in a deal that "didn't end up so well"? and who was Kepler's so-called partner?

"You think her husband's doing some work for Walter Kepler, in other words?" Helen Bradbury said, peering over the top of her teacup. She was sharp, Hunter could tell, and not one to suffer fools.

"Yes."

"And you've talked with Scott Randall."

"I have."

"Bootsie!" She clapped her hands twice, startling Hunter. Bootsie, a black mixed Scottie, who'd been tentatively sniffing Hunter's shoe, scooted out of the room.

"Well, you got one side of the story, then, didn't you?" she said. "I just caution you, be careful. He can be a very duplicitous man."

"Kepler, you mean."

She tossed back her head and let out a quick, bawdy laugh. "No," she said. "Randall. Well, both of them, if you want to get technical. There's a big divide in the Bureau over Walter Kepler right now, as you may know. Randall's put himself in the middle of it. Crowe probably told you that."

"A little. What's the divide about, exactly?"

"In plain English?" Hunter nodded. "Scott Randall wants to bring down Kepler, any way he can. And he's in a position now to do it, being in charge of the division. My side—the other side of the argument—thinks he's too willing to cut corners, and maybe hurt a few people along the way, to get that done. We think he's puffed up this current case against Kepler to make sure that he gets the funding. Stolen Art Division, as you may have heard, is the redheaded stepchild of the FBI."

"Yes," Hunter said. "Randall said something like that."

"So . . . Let's cut to the chase, then," she said. "My view—and it's shared by others—is that if we're going to put our resources into pursuing someone, we'd better make damn sure we're pursuing the right man. And for the right reasons."

"And you don't think Kepler is the right man?"

"I'm not convinced of it. I certainly don't think he's responsible for the things that Randall *says* he's responsible for, no. That's where we finally parted ways, the Bureau and me. And that's why I'm talking to you."

"Okay."

"I think it's clear, if you take an honest look at the evidence, that there's nothing tying Walter Kepler directly to any killings. That's all been puffed up. So has this story that he's dealing now with terrorists or terrorist financiers. The man's a high-end art trader, that's all. I think he may have dealt *occasionally* in stolen art, but he's not what Randall says he is. And so you have to wonder why Randall's doing what he's doing."

Bootsie was back in the room, lying on the floor in the doorway, his eyes gazing up at Hunter's. When she smiled, his tail flicked once. Hunter tried the tea again, and then set her cup on the kitchen table.

"I was told Kepler has a partner," Hunter said. "Could the partner be responsible for these things? The killings?"

"He does have a partner, yes," she said, eyeing Hunter soberly. "Randall didn't tell you that, did he?"

"No."

"Crowe."

Hunter shrugged. "Was the divide over this partner?"

"No," Helen Bradbury said, "the divide is over Kepler. But, in part, yes, it involves his partner. The Bureau could have gone after the partner, and probably could have made a strong case against him. But there were strategic differences. Randall didn't want to do that. Categorically. Randall thought that if we went after the partner—or anyone else at a lower level—we'd lose the big prize. Making Kepler the bull's-eye—linking him to murder and, now, terrorism—made the case simpler and stronger. And easier to sell to Randall's higher-ups. It, also, became part of his own ascendency within the Bureau."

"Do you know who this partner is?"

"I do." Her big eyes watched Hunter as she sipped her tea; momentarily, they seemed to twinkle.

"You know the partner's name? His back story?" Hunter asked. "I mean, if we're cutting to the chase."

"His name is Belasco," she said. "I can't tell you a lot about him. We're not even sure about his first name: Edward or Edwin. The name came up last summer. There's a file on him, which Randall did all he could to suppress. We think Belasco may have some loose connections with an organized crime family in Philadelphia. The Patellos." She sipped again and set her cup down. "To be candid? I think it's quite possible Belasco was the person who killed your Susan Champlain."

Hunter felt a chill race through her. "Why do you think that?"

"Because I do."

"Killed her for what reason?"

"To help Walter Kepler. Because they're 'partners,' as you say. And also, possibly, from what little we know about Belasco, I think that he probably also enjoys killing, and finds it easy to do.

That's what we're told. He may be someone who has gotten away with it for years and just assumes he'll never be caught. You'd be surprised how many of those there are out there."

Not really, Hunter thought. "But what specifically makes you think Belasco might have killed Susan Champlain?"

"Nothing specifically. It's a hunch," Bradbury said. "There's some evidence he's done it before, to protect Walter Kepler. It's all in the file. It was. You ought to get ahold of his file."

"Any suggestions how I'd do that?"

"Well, no, honey, that's the problem: Randall's running the show now, and he's not interested in going after Belasco. He questions whether he even exists. Which I think is a big mistake."

Hunter glanced out at the morning sun dazzling the wetlands. "He did it to *protect* Kepler? Why?"

"Well—you have to delve deeper into the nature of the partnership, I guess, don't you? We never had the support within the Bureau to pursue that question adequately; Randall always tried to keep the focus on Kepler. Understand, Kepler *is* dirty in some ways," she went on, echoing what Crowe had told her Friday night. "But he's not the bad guy Scott Randall says he is. The question you have to ask is: is he a good bad guy or a bad bad guy?"

"I didn't know the Bureau divided them that way," Hunter said, still marveling a little at the turns this woman's mind was taking. Hunter decided she liked Helen Bradbury.

"No, honey, *I* divide them that way. What I'm saying is—" She stopped to drink her tea. "He *has* dealt with terrorists, but only in the process of recovering stolen art. And only once that I know of. He helped negotiate the return of a Degas and a Cézanne in 2012 that were in the possession of Serbian terrorists. He and his attorney, a man named Jacob Weber, set up a straw buyer, we think, who contacted the art thieves and then trapped them. I'm told he was remunerated quite well by the insurance companies for what he did.

"To me, it's really a moral question that's dividing the Bureau," Bradbury continued. "Because morally, I think Kepler's closer to being on the side of right than Randall is. Which can be a big problem when Randall's heading the division. It's complicated. But I can simplify it for you. I can boil it down to one man—a man named Eddie Charles."

"Okay," she said.

"Eddie Charles was tangentially involved in Kepler's last deal. The one that fell apart."

"The Manet."

"Yes. That's right." This, Hunter realized, must be the man Crowe had been referring to when he'd warned her about Randall; the man who "got involved" last year. Bradbury smiled at how much Crowe had shared; it was a feeble smile, showing small gray teeth and pink gums. "Eddie Charles was an innocent man who happened to have done business with someone the Bureau was watching. No more than that. He came to Scott Randall's attention last year, and Randall went out and tried to recruit him, to be an informant, to help make Randall's case against Kepler. This man didn't want to do that, which stuck in Randall's craw."

"This was the government sting?"

"Yes." She grinned. "And then, after the deal broke down, after the Bureau showed its cards and Kepler backed away, Scott

Randall blamed this guy. He thought this guy had given him up. And a couple weeks later, Eddie Charles turns up dead on a Philadelphia street corner, with crack cocaine in his pockets."

"What happened?"

"That's the moral tale," she said. "It's something that Randall caused but he will never have to pay for." She drank the last of her tea and set the cup down. "Sometimes," she said, "you can do things that are legal but not moral. Randall understands that. There's a man in Pennsylvania, in a little town called Scattersville. He can tell you Eddie's story. You need to set up an appointment to see him. Mention me if you want.

"He's a sentimental cop," she added, showing her gums, "but he has a deep-rooted sense of right and wrong. You'll like him."

Hunter took down the name: Calvin Walters. Chief of Detectives.

Hunter wondered what Henry Moore would think about her driving out to Scattersville to pursue a "moral tale" on her day "off."

"Just be careful."

"I've been told that several times now," Hunter said, smiling, thinking she might elicit a smile in return from Bradbury; but the former FBI agent looked at her stone-faced.

"The trouble is, once Randall has you in his orbit, it's not so easy to get out."

"Well. I don't think I'm in his orbit," Hunter said, feeling suddenly defensive, remembering how he'd drawn her into this: *What if solving one case solves the other?*

"No. I didn't say you were."

"Sorry," Hunter said.

"But just keep in mind," Bradbury told her, walking with some effort back toward Hunter's car, the four dogs in tow. "There's always a tiny possibility that Randall's right."

"Okay," Hunter said. "What do you mean? Right about what?"

"About Belasco."

She stopped walking and looked at Hunter.

"I'm not following. What do you mean?"

"Randall claims that Belasco doesn't really exist. That's why Randall says he doesn't want to pursue a case against him. He thinks that Kepler's made him up, as a diversion. Belasco *is* his partner, yes. But he's not real. He's simply the darker side of Walter Kepler's personality, his alter ego, which Kepler would prefer to keep hidden."

Hunter squinted at her in the glare of the morning light. "That's kind of creepy," she said.

"Yeah, I know. It is, isn't it?" Bradbury smiled.

SHE CALLED SONNY Fischer on his private line as she drove Route 301 north to Philadelphia. "I need to find everything you can get me about someone named Belasco."

"Spelling?" She heard him writing it down. Hunter loved this about Fischer. "First name?"

"Not sure, Edward or Edwin. And I also need to know everything about a man named Walter Kepler. He's a high-end art dealer. And, in particular, any connection there may be between the two. Belasco and Kepler."

"Walter Kepler."

Hunter spelled it. "And, I'd like to see any security images we can get of Nick Champlain, Sally Markos, Joey Sanders, or Elena Rodgers. At Kent's or at the Old Shore Inn."

"Going through them now."

"Okay, good." Hunter realized that she probably sounded wound up. Probably she *should* take some time off. But not now. "Sorry," she said. "Whatever you can get to. Belasco and Kepler first."

"No problem. I'm on it."

Twenty minutes later, a mile into Delaware, Hunter called the number Helen Bradbury had given her, in the little town of Scattersville, Pennsylvania.

"Calvin Walters," a friendly voice answered.

Hunter explained who she was, mentioning Susan Champlain and telling him that Helen Bradbury had recommended she call. "I'd like to talk with you about Eddie Charles, if you can spare a few minutes."

He seemed unsurprised. "Well, okay," he told her. "I can't guarantee I can tell you a lot. But, sure, I'll talk with you."

"Are you free tomorrow?"

He chortled. "Well, I ex*pect* to be free. What time you-all want to stop by?"

"Ten? Eleven?"

"Eleven o'clock tomorrow morning," he said, stretching out the syllables as he wrote it down.

"I'll see you at eleven, then."

"Don't know that I can tell you a lot," he said again, "but I'm glad to meet with you."

WALTER KEPLER WAS floating in the Atlantic Ocean on a clear plastic mattress, doing the numbers again in his head, his taut body undulating pleasantly with the pulse of the water, the sun warming his skin. He savored the freedom he had to just float for a couple of hours, disconnected from everyone. Much of Kepler's work involved thinking—and he especially liked doing so on the ocean, where he couldn't be interrupted.

"The cost of a miracle," he said aloud, enjoying the sound, and the irony, of those words, the way his voice folded into the rise and fall of the waves.

He cast his eyes back to shore. Kepler's attorney, Jacob Weber, would be coming to visit tomorrow, with news from his trip north. If Weber brought good news, as he fully expected, then Kepler was going to push the schedule so that all three phases took place in a single twenty-four-hour period. Wednesday. Which had been his intention all along, although he had kept that detail to himself.

There were reasons all around why this new time frame would be acceptable. The sale would make Vincent Rosa five million dollars wealthier and free him of an albatross. Champlain, too, was restless, wanting to take his profit in cash and return to Philadelphia, to his shopping center deals and his girlfriends, with the promise of an even bigger transaction down the road. Kepler was the only one who'd be losing anything financially. But making money wasn't the point this time; the point was creating a "miracle." Kepler had long ago set up accounts to comfortably finance the rest of his life. This time, money wasn't an issue.

Champlain would recite the authentication details to Kepler

again when they met tomorrow: five identifying characteristics (a pinprick hole in the upper right corner being the most recent), proof that this painting they were buying was the real thing.

Once Rosa had led Champlain to the work, and he had authenticated it, Champlain would call Kepler. The rest of the payment would then be transferred to Rosa's account through a holding company in Bermuda. Afterward, the painting would belong to Champlain.

The second phase would be on Kepler's terms. Champlain would sell him the painting and walk away with three million dollars of Kepler's money.

The third part would be up to Jacob Weber. It would cost Kepler nothing.

LUKE WATCHED CHARLOTTE as she rose from their bed to get a bottled water from the kitchen, feeling a long moment of gratitude as he listened to her footsteps in the hallway. He was home for lunch to work on their "project," which was going to be a regular activity for a while; or so he hoped.

"I was at the shelter this morning and talked with Claire," she said, coming back, along with a tired-looking Sneakers, who'd been napping in her study. "She told me she knows the whole story about Susan Champlain."

"Well, there's a teaser for you," Luke said.

"Yes, I know."

Charlotte sat on the bed, leaning against the headboard. She handed Luke the water.

Sneakers hopped up and settled against Luke's leg.

"Do you believe her?"

"No. But you know Claire."

"Sort of," Luke said. "If you insist."

Luke took a drink and handed the bottle to Charlotte. Claire French was an eccentric Tidewater native in her late sixties, a tall, sinewy woman who dressed in jeans and tank tops and wore her long gray hair in twin braids, like Willie Nelson. Charlotte knew her only because they both volunteered at the Humane Society. Claire, who lived several miles inland on a small farm with a menagerie of animals, was probably one of the most knowledgeable residents of Tidewater. But she was also a strident atheist who occasionally took preemptive strikes against Luke, pointing out the contradictions of Christianity as if these were topics Luke had never considered before.

Luke maintained what he considered a healthy skepticism toward atheism, particularly with people like Claire, whose certainties approached fanaticism. Most atheists Luke had known experienced profoundly religious moments on occasion, he had found; they just chose to define them as something else.

"I didn't think she even knew Susan," Luke said.

"I didn't either. She said Susan had worked at the shelter one afternoon and they'd gotten to talking. Which was news to me. Her name wasn't on the volunteer sheet."

"Did you ask her what the 'whole story' was?"

"I tried," Charlotte said. "But Claire's always in a rush to be somewhere, so she couldn't tell me. I called her back before you came over and, naturally, she completely downplayed what she'd said earlier. By tomorrow, she will deny she even said it."

"Such is the life of an eternal nonconformist," Luke said. "Why do you think she said it?"

"Conversation. Some people like to invent stories that make their lives momentarily more exciting."

"Yes. I know."

Charlotte set the water on the bed stand. She snuggled against Luke and held him, pushing Sneakers away, laying her head on his chest. They stayed like that for a long time, listening to the silence, the occasional squeak of the weather vane on the back deck.

Luke went for a drive after Charlotte woke him, feeling grateful for the family he had and the one that he might have in the future. He drove along the coast road, stopping for a minute at the Gray Inlet overlook, then heading south past the oyster reefs and the seafood processing plant, and turning inland, passing Landrum's Boatyard and the mini-market and the storage bays where Luke had rented a small locker years earlier and then had all but forgotten about what he'd left there—his papers, books, notebooks, family letters, photos and keepsakes; his life before Charlotte, in effect.

He wound up at Widow's Point again, where he parked on the access road and walked out onto the beach. It was just past low tide. Luke took off his shoes and walked along the edge of the water, thinking maybe he'd find something this time: the other sandal, perhaps, or Susan's cell phone. He stopped in the shade below the bluff and gazed out at the Bay, which glittered brilliantly in the afternoon light. There was no one on the beach in either direction; and no visible reminders of what had happened last Wednesday. Luke closed his eyes and thought of Susan Champlain. It was his third visit here alone. He left finding nothing, with the same empty feeling he'd carried away the other two times.

Chapter Twenty-three

Nicholas Champlain's spacious eleventh-floor office overlooked the Benjamin Franklin Parkway with a view of the Rodin Museum, the Barnes Foundation building and the Philadelphia Museum of Art at the other end. In the old days, "wearing a wire" meant having an electronic microphone attached by adhesive to one's body. Now voice recordings could be transmitted digitally from a pin-sized device and streamed to a remote computer. Hunter carried the transmitter on her shirt pocket. Scott Randall, presumably, was at the other end, and would be listening in and recording their conversation.

Champlain's receptionist, a fetching but very serious young woman with full red lips and lots of black hair, ushered her into Champlain's office, a large paneled room, with dark, expensive-looking furniture.

"Mr. Champlain," Hunter said.

Champlain stood, nattily dressed today in a navy business suit. His expressive, good-natured face seemed pleased to see her, although his manner was more hurried than before.

"I'm sorry I've been difficult to reach," he said, gripping her hand. Hunter sat. "I've been making arrangements for this funeral. I'm going out there this afternoon."

"Oh." This surprised Hunter, considering how Susan's sister felt about him; she wondered if he was making it up.

"I must confess, I was surprised to hear from you. I thought we'd covered everything the other night."

"Most," she said. "There are a few things we didn't get to."

"Okay." His eyes gave her a once-over. An eight-by-ten smiling headshot of Susan stood on the cabinet behind his desk, along with several smaller pictures that she assumed were his daughter. "I understand you're Homicide."

"Yes."

"So . . . are you saying you think my wife's death may've been a homicide?"

"No, I'm just investigating the circumstances."

"I assume you've checked my whereabouts. You're satisfied I couldn't have had anything to do with it?"

"Yes, sir. We understand you were here on Tuesday in a business meeting and returned to Tidewater County on Wednesday, just after nine in the evening."

"That's correct. More like nine fifteen, I'd say. I'm sure they have video that'll confirm the time."

"You went back and forth a lot, I understand," Hunter said.

"Pardon me?"

"Between Tidewater and here."

"Correct." He summoned a pleasant smile, surprisingly detached, Hunter thought, from the topic of his wife's death, although part of it was just the easy way his face worked. "Tidewater was a nice getaway. That's what we thought, Sue and I. Good place, good people. But, naturally, I couldn't put my business on hold entirely."

"No."

"This shopping center, they're bringing site plans for a zoning review next month. My wife, though, she likes to get off by herself sometimes. And, of course, she has a little history down there on the Shore. So it was more for her than anything else."

"History?" Hunter asked. She hadn't heard this before.

"I'm not even sure what it is exactly," he said, waving the subject away. "She vacationed there with her family, I think. My business manager found the house, figured it'd be a good place for her to relax. He's from that area. Lovely region. Although I wish now I'd never seen the place.

"I might just mention, too, Amy," he said. He scooted forward and spoke in a more hushed tone: "That because of Sue's love of the region and the tragedy that occurred, I'm thinking about funding an arts center down there in her name. Not a museum, but like a photography center. Where people could display their photographs. That kind of thing."

"I see."

Hunter suspected he'd already talked with J. Michael Bunting at the newspaper about this.

"But anyway," he said, leaning back again, "I know you have to do your job. And I don't want to impede that in any way. So I'm here for you, Amy, anything you need to know."

"Okay, I appreciate that."

"But—have you had lunch, Amy?"

"I did, actually."

He was trying to flirt with her, she suddenly realized, which felt kind of icky considering the circumstances.

"I do have a few questions I need to get to," Hunter said, paging through her notebook.

Champlain nodded, once.

"Your wife gave indications in the days before she died that she was concerned about a business deal you were involved in."

"Did she?"

"That's what I'm told, yes. True?"

"What—you mean, the *shopping center*?"

"No. Something else," she said, still flipping through her notes. "Something she said you two had argued about. Something you became angry about after you saw a picture on her cell phone."

His expression stiffened. "You already asked me that once," he said. "What, is this something the pastor told you?"

"No. Why would you say that?"

"Process of elimination." He swiveled in his chair to look out the window. "I know she was talking to him. It wouldn't surprise me."

"Wasn't that an issue between you, though? A photo she'd taken."

"No. Look, as I told you the other night, Amy. And, I mean, come on—even if it was, we're talking ancient history. And the issue wouldn't have been about taking *pic*tures. It would've been about respecting people's privacy."

"It *was* something that came up in recent days, then."

"No, not at all." He said it too quickly and seemed to be reassessing her a little bit, put off by how serious she was, how un-charmable she must've seemed. "I mean, the *subject* may've come up."

"Of the picture."

"No," he said, "there *wasn't* any picture. As I said before."

HUNTER OPENED THE file folder she had brought and pulled out copies of the images from Susan Champlain's cell phone. She set them one at a time in front of Nick Champlain, whose face tilted one way and then another. It told her something about him: that he was guilty of something, although she wasn't sure, yet, what it was.

"Okay," he said, displaying his smile. "I give up—what are you showing me here?"

"These are pictures your wife took. Which had evidently become an issue between you."

"These?" He made a dumb face, looking at them while shaking his head dismissively. "I have no idea what this is. Why are you showing me this?"

"Do you remember where these were taken? Whose house it is?"

"No idea. I have no idea what you're showing me here, Amy."

"It's Sergeant Hunter."

"Oh, okay." He smiled faintly.

"You don't recognize this?"

"Not a clue, no."

Hunter left the images sitting in front of him as she flicked through her notes. He seemed nervous now, moving the paperweight on his desk, to one place and then, moments later, to another.

Hunter pulled out the last image from her folder, showing the gold necklace she'd found in the sand at Widow's Point.

"How about this? Does this necklace look familiar? Was this your wife's?"

His eyes stared at it strangely.

"No," he said. "Why?"

"This doesn't look familiar?"

"No. My wife, frankly, didn't wear a lot of necklaces. To be honest."

Hunter nodded, leaving the pictures in front of him.

"How long had Joseph Sanders worked for you?" she asked.

"Joey?" His voice went up an octave; it seemed to surprise him more than it did her. "Not long. Why?"

"How long is not long?"

"Off and on, a couple of years. He wasn't planning to stay on after mid-August anyway." His lips aligned and smiled. "The man makes more money in construction than I was ever able to pay him."

"In this area?"

"Pittsburgh."

"He was your bodyguard?"

"No, he was my driver. My assistant."

"Was there ever an issue, sir, between Joe Sanders and your wife?"

His face contorted, an exaggerated show of confusion. "Who said there was?"

"I'm asking you."

"No," he said.

"Sure?"

"Of course I'm sure. Joey was always respectful. I had no problems with Joey Sanders. Ever."

"Aren't you also working with a man named Walter Kepler?"

His eyes narrowed. He seemed unable to speak for a moment.

"Sir?" Hunter said.

"I'm not sure I understand what you're asking me here."

"Walter Kepler," Hunter said. "Do you know who he is?"

"I don't know."

"You don't know *him*? Or you don't know?"

"No. I don't. Know him." His face looked very naked right then. Hunter let the lie sit there.

"Belasco?"

"What?"

"Does that name mean anything?"

"Nothing."

"Did you ever have a discussion about stolen art that your wife may have overheard? Possibly involving works stolen from the Isabella Stewart Gardner Museum in Boston, in nineteen ninety?"

"Now you've lost me."

But Hunter could almost feel the blood pulsing in his neck, the anger roiling below the surface. She bought some more time by paging through her notes.

"You say you're planning to attend Susan's funeral in Iowa. Do you know that the sister thinks you had something to do with Susan's death?"

He grinned broadly and swiveled to face her directly. "Is that what Nan told you? I guess that shouldn't surprise me."

"Why do you say that?"

"Some people have a harder time accepting reality than

others," he said. His smile was still doing a slow fade. "Nan's one of them. Good little farm girl, married a good little farm boy. I'll leave it at that."

Hunter continued to watch him, feeling the invisible presence of Champlain's anger crowding the room. He was upset about Nancy Adams's accusation; but more so, she thought, he was upset that Hunter had brought up Kepler's name. She glanced at his sparse desktop, wondering if Kepler might be listening in, too.

"Did you have anything to do with your wife's death, sir?"

"Come on." Hunter waited. "Of course not. Of course I didn't."

"Do you think there was foul play involved?"

"Unfortunately, no. Well, not unfortunately. *No.* I mean, no, I don't."

"All right." Hunter closed her notebook and they stared at each other. "Well, if you think of anything else, sir, feel free to call. As I say, I'm just doing a routine follow-up."

Champlain walked with her to the elevator, the quiet clinging to them. He pushed the down button twice as they waited. Hunter felt that she probably shouldn't have said so much. He'd told her more in his evasions and silences than in his words—and now she needed to sort through it. She looked across the parkway to the "Rocky steps" at the Philadelphia Museum of Art. She'd rattled him a little bit, and wasn't sure how she felt about that.

WALTER KEPLER LISTENED to the conversation on his computer, surprised by the aggressiveness of this homicide cop and the fact that she'd brought up *his* name. So Belasco was right about her. Kepler saw where this was likely headed: The predator, Scott

Randall, had recruited this woman, not to make Kepler nervous, but to make *Champlain* nervous. It was a clever ploy, in that sense; Kepler was sure that Randall would try to use her again, playing on Champlain's weaknesses. They'd whittle away at him until he felt so vulnerable that he would agree to negotiate with the FBI. Then Randall would offer Champlain a deal, trading immunity for giving up Kepler. That was surely his strategy.

Unfortunately for Scott Randall, it would never reach that point. There simply wasn't enough time. The miracle was less than three days away now.

Chapter Twenty-four

Either Scott Randall was upset and trying not to show it or else he was acting, trying to make it *look* like he was upset. Hunter suspected it was mostly the latter.

She met him on the eighth floor of the William J. Green Center in Center City, Philadelphia, where he walked her to a small conference room, buttoned down in dark suit pants, a blue dress shirt and loosened tie. Randall had worn sunglasses throughout their meeting on the Shore. This was the first time she'd seen his eyes, which were unusual, a dark olive color, and slightly off-kilter, the left eye leaning to one side, the eyelid drooping slightly. His physique was surprising, too. He was a tall, thin-framed man, but the shirt he wore today fit a little too snugly, accentuating a pronounced gut that she hadn't even noticed the first time.

"I left several messages for you," Hunter said. "I thought we were going to touch base again before I talked with Nick Champlain."

"I got the messages." He closed a folder, what he'd been working on before she arrived. "Didn't I did tell you I'd be out of touch for a couple days? I was down in Virginia visiting with my mother."

Hunter nodded, although this sounded like an excuse more appropriate for the 1990s before cell phones.

Randall smiled. "You scare me a little sometimes, Hunter, you know that?"

"Why's that?" Randall scared *her* a little, the fact that he was acting now as if she worked for him. She'd have to nudge him away from that.

"Because you're good. You did a nice job. Thank you," he said, rushing his words, sounding more patronizing than gracious. "I like that you pushed him a little on Sanders."

"Is that why you recruited me?" His eyebrows rose and his lashes fluttered rapidly. "When you said we could help each other, was that the point? You sent me in there to carry a message to him?"

"Message," he echoed, pretending not to understand. She could see him consciously changing his expression from confusion to amusement, wanting to smooth her feathers. "For what purpose?"

"I don't know, to worry him a little? So he'd be more apt to make a deal?"

"No." He seemed to be considering what she'd said, though. "I mean, if it ever came to that? Sure, of course we'd like to make a deal. But no, we don't have any grand plan. Although, as I told you the first time, I do believe that solving one case will solve the other. I feel that even more strongly now."

"Well, you need to tell me the rest of what's going on, then," Hunter said. Randall waited. "John Linden, for instance."

"Okay." His eyes began to blink.

"Linden was friends with Susan Champlain. He's her former boyfriend. On the day she died, last Wednesday, they met in Tidewater County. The next day, Linden called you." Randall nodded, his eyes continuing to blink. "Didn't John Linden make an inquiry about the Gardner reward?"

She was guessing, but Randall's face reddened slightly. There was a $5 million reward for the return of all thirteen stolen works in good condition. It would never happen, considering that some of the art had almost certainly been damaged, but Linden probably didn't know that.

"I *talked* with him, yes. Frankly, you're right, he probably *was* fishing around about the reward money." He sighed, lowering his eyes for a moment. "All right, Hunter. Here's what it is, here's what I *can* tell you: Do you know what Walter Kepler looks like?"

"I've seen his picture."

"Let me show you some photos of him, then. I've got some images here for you." He opened his folder again: inside, under some official-looking memos, were printout images of Walter Kepler. The first two she had already seen. He was a midsized, nice-looking man with silvery hair who wore a faraway look in three of the photos. It was the fourth one that Randall wanted her to see.

"We've got *our* candid camera shot, too," he said, handing it to her.

It was a blurred picture of two men walking on a narrow street, shoulders turned toward each other.

"This was in Amsterdam six months ago. You don't recognize the man he's talking to, do you?"

"No."

"Ayman Al-Bulawi is his name. He's a terrorist agent, based in Jordan. He represents one of the largest private funders of Middle East terrorism, a man named Garrett Massoud. He's negotiating the purchase of the painting for Massoud, okay? Al-Bulawi had been under surveillance for several months. Not by us, initially, by another intelligence service."

Hunter absorbed that for a moment. "For what purpose? Why would a terrorist financier want this painting?"

"Well, he's a collector. And this painting's a prize, the crème de la crème of missing art." He frowned at the image of the two men. "There is, also, some intelligence indicating that Massoud would like to use this acquisition for political purposes."

"How would he do that?"

He displayed his adolescent's smile. "Without going into details: obviously, it would have a certain symbolic value if he could show the world that this masterpiece—which was stolen from the walls of an American art museum twenty-five years ago—is now in his hands and that we won't be able to touch it ever again. Kind of like kidnapping a high-profile Western target.

"And, frankly," Randall added, "we're not sure that their goal isn't then ultimately to desecrate and destroy this masterpiece in view of an international audience."

Hunter felt dizzy for a moment, recalling Crowe's warning about getting involved with Randall. "Kepler wouldn't allow that to happen," she said.

Randall tilted his head. "Kepler may not know about it. That's the problem. We don't think he does."

"And where are you getting this information?" she said.

"I told you, we're working with national intelligence on this." Implying the CIA, as Crowe had said. Or was this an invention, like the earlier straw man scenario in the Miami deal? He took the image back and closed the folder. "But that's the part I can't get into," he told her. "I shouldn't be telling you *any* of this, really. But there it is."

Hunter breathed in and out deliberately. She sensed that he was still recruiting her, but in a different way, for another round with Champlain.

"Where's the painting right now?" she asked. "When do you think this is going to happen?"

Randall shrugged. "Honestly? I suspect it's within a hundred and fifty miles of where we're sitting right now. That's what we're being told. I think it's going to happen in two to three weeks. Probably it's going to be flown out of a private airfield to the Middle East. Maybe Jordan. And within a few weeks of the sale, there's going to be some sort of international incident. Obviously, we'd like to prevent that from happening."

They sat in the quiet dusty sunlight for a while, Randall's strange eyes staying with her.

"Let me change the subject for a minute," Hunter finally said.

Randall nodded.

"Tell me what you know about Walter Kepler's partner," she said.

"When do you sleep, exactly?"

He laughed, wanting Hunter to laugh, too. But she didn't.

"Okay," he said, "yes, there have been reports for years that Kepler has a partner. But, truthfully? We have no proof that the partner exists. I don't think he does. I think it's more likely he has a bodyguard, or someone who handles security. I don't, frankly, think there *is* a partner."

"His partner's name, I'm told, is Belasco," Hunter said. Randall suddenly began to blink again. "You know that name."

"Heard it." Clearly, this subject made him uncomfortable. She wondered why. "Where is all this coming from, anyway, Dave Crowe? No wait—don't tell me. Okay, I can imagine where it's coming from."

"Where?"

Randall shook his head. He wasn't going to say Helen Bradbury's name. Hunter looked down at the city—working women and men in business attire. She thought about Susan Champlain's fall, the way her body had landed, below the bluff, and reminded herself whom she was working for.

"Anyway." Randall made a pretense of straightening the papers in his folder. "You want to go down and grab a hot dog?"

"No."

"Or a cheesesteak? When in Philly . . ."

Hunter shook her head. There was a whooshing sound of the air-conditioning coming on. Sunlight slanted across the room. She felt the indoors closing around her a little. Hunter *was* out of her element, but she needed to find out who it was she was really pursuing. And she needed to stay on good terms with Randall, even if *he* was the bad guy.

"How about if we touch base again tomorrow, then, see how things shake out," he said.

"All right."

"Just see how Champlain is once he's had a chance to digest everything. Were you planning on calling him again?"

"I'm sure we'll talk."

"Good. Good idea."

His hand went to her back twice as they walked to the elevator. The second time, she stopped and turned to look and he quickly pulled it away.

"I'll be here in the city a couple of days," Randall said. "If you want, we can meet in one of our satellite offices. Where's your mother? You said you were staying with your mother?"

She told him reluctantly, although it wouldn't have been difficult for him to find her.

"Look, in a way I did recruit you, okay," he said, a note of contrition in his voice as they rode down to the lobby. "But our cases *are* tied together, as I said before. I told you that from the beginning."

This time, Hunter let silence change the subject.

Chapter Twenty-five

She almost didn't recognize her mother's face in the late afternoon light, as Joan Hunter looked out the kitchen window at the woods behind their old house. There was a leathery quality to her skin and a new fullness to her cheeks. It was as if someone had taken her mother's place while Amy was away, living down in Tidewater County.

She had prepared breaded fish sticks, the traditional dinner whenever Hunter returned home. It had been Amy's favorite when she was in grade school, although it didn't do much for her now.

Joan Hunter offered her green tea, but Amy poured herself a tall glass of red wine instead. Hunter's mother, although a teetotaler, always kept wine and a twelve pack of discount beer in the hall closet.

"What sort of business brings you all the way up here, anyway?" she asked, once they'd moved to the living room for their traditional predinner chat. "A case, you said?"

"Yes. I wish I could talk about it."

"Oh, no, I wouldn't expect you to. It's just as well that you don't."

Hunter's mother always tiptoed around the subject of her work, knowing that Amy's job was bound by confidentiality. She was proud of her independent nature to a point, but didn't really approve of her work, which Hunter understood: she dealt with unseemly people and motivations, and there was also an inherent danger in what she did.

Amy still thought of this as her father's house; there were times when they would glance at each other and it seemed both were waiting for Joseph Hunter to return home. There'd been the usual bittersweet feeling of nostalgia driving into the old neighborhood, past the familiar brick houses with chain-link fences that never changed and the shopping center that did, past the high school where she'd run track for three years, and where she'd also been assaulted on the athletic field in the spring of her junior year.

Amy's mother worked as an administrator for the county school system. As the backyard darkened, they caught up on the latest school issues: bus safety, french fries on the lunch menu, Wi-Fi in the classroom and various other topics, many of which hadn't existed when Amy was in school. "Otherwise, nothing to report," Joan Hunter said, and she smiled contentedly at her daughter. It was what Hunter's father always said—*nothing to report*—and it still carried a reassuring ring.

Hunter gazed out at the backyard trees as if it were twenty years ago, as if she could go outside and pick up right where she'd left off. Her mother liked to sit in the living room and watch the night come in, keeping the lights off until it was fully dark outside. Hunter couldn't remember if it had something to do with saving energy or if she just liked the sensation of darkness seeping in; she kind of liked it, too, the enclosing feeling.

"I guess I didn't even realize you drank," Joan said, as Amy poured a second glass of red wine.

"Not a lot." She stopped pouring, though. The first drink was fine; the second usually drew a comment. In truth, Hunter could have used a shot of bourbon and Coke right about then. There'd been a bottle of Jim Beam in the closet on one of her visits and it was gone now. Hunter suspected her mother had dumped it. "I just like a glass of wine sometimes at the end of the day, a way to relax."

"My sister was that way, too," Joan Hunter said as Amy returned to the living-room sofa. "I don't know that she always handled it so well."

"Hmm."

Hunter sipped more slowly, thinking about her cat Winston, who seemed to enjoy her better when she drank.

"Will you see Glenn while you're here?" she asked, meaning Hunter's brother and his family, who lived near Pittsburgh.

"No, I don't have time this visit. We'll do it another time. How *is* his family?"

"Oh, they're well. Although the children are so grown up all of a sudden. I feel I've missed so much of it, living here." Hunter's brother had two children and ran a thriving software business. Only when she was with her mother did Amy compare her life with his and come out feeling on the short end.

"Dad would've been calling the team right about now, wouldn't he?" Amy said, looking at the tributaries of the oak branches, as familiar as these rooms and this furniture. "The seniors."

"Oh, I know." Her father always called the seniors in early August to see what kind of summer they'd had and what sort of shape they were in, then to invite them to his one-day football camp in mid-August. "You know I'm going to a baseball game on Saturday," her mother said. "Did I tell you? A friend has asked me. A gentleman."

"Good."

"Does it surprise you?"

It didn't, really. Joan Hunter was still sort of feeling her way through life. She met people online now. This man she'd met on Christian Mingle, she said, which she belonged to because she considered it "safe," even though she was only nominally a Christian herself.

"What does he do?"

"Oh, he's retired now. He worked for years for the postal service. In a management position. A very nice-sounding man."

"Meaning you haven't *met* him yet?"

"No, well, we talk on the phone. It's an afternoon game, anyway," her mom added, as if this made it more legitimate.

Hunter took a baby sip, thinking about a third glass of wine. Most of the trees out back had blended into the darkness.

"Well, I guess we ought to have our supper now."

Amy's mother got up and turned on the kitchen light. She served up the breaded fish sticks with broiled potatoes and asparagus. They drank ice water with the meal, poured from a glass pitcher that sat on a porcelain potholder on the table, condensation sliding down its sides, just like when she was a girl.

They chatted some more about Joan's job and Hunter's life in Tidewater County, and then her mother asked the inevitable question, her eyes zeroing in on her daughter's. "Have you met anyone new there?"

"No one new, no," she said, forking a potato. "It's just been very busy."

"Mmm." Joan gave her a worried smile. Being here always reminded Hunter of things she didn't want to be reminded of, like the wide gulf that had existed between her parents during her high school years. Hunter had been close to her father; she'd enjoyed letting him rev her up with his pep talks and inspirational sayings. She'd carried a quiet confidence in those days, keeping to herself, doing well in school and in sports; her mother had struck her as a bit weird and still did, interested in the strangest minutiae, managing to spend hours every day cleaning the house. The pauses in their conversation now felt like a musical combo missing the main instrument.

"Remember when you and Glenn used to catch fireflies out there?" her mother said, nodding past the window.

"Yeah, I do. Although Glenn did all the catching. I'd usually just watch."

"Well, they're still there," she said, meaning the fireflies. "Although Glenn was telling me that he read somewhere there aren't as many now as there used to be."

"Really? There aren't as *many*? I wonder why that would be."

"Oh, I can't remember, something to do with the climate

change? Global warming, I think. Although, I guess that's pretty much been discredited now, hasn't it?"

"Global warming? No, Mom."

"I thought it had."

Hunter's phone rang; her mother's head jerked up as if a firecracker had gone off under the table. "Oh, my goodness, what is that?"

"Sorry," Hunter said. "My phone."

"*Goodness*, that startled me," she said.

Henry Moore's number. "I better take this," she said, pushing from the table. "Thanks, Mom, the dinner was fantastic."

Her mother's smile was quick. *Fantastic* was a word Amy had stopped using around 2000, although it reentered her vocabulary whenever she came home and got to talking with her mom.

She opened the screen door and walked into the side yard. The air was still warm. Through the woods she saw the kitchen light of a neighbor's house.

"Just checking in, how did it go?" Moore asked.

Hunter gave him a summary of her meetings with Helen Bradbury, Nicholas Champlain and Scott Randall. She could tell from the beats of his silence that Moore was really calling to give *her* news.

"I wasn't going to bother you but I thought you'd want to know. Two things," he said. "I've had a closer look at the prelim and talked with the M.E.'s office. The injuries to Susan Champlain's arm are from an altercation, and there *are* skin cells under her nails. We'll see how that turns out."

"Okay."

"Second." There was a greater-than-usual gravitas to his

intake of breath. "Joseph Sanders was discovered this morning in a rural wooded area about fifteen miles from the Virginia line. Local PD's treating it as suicide."

Hunter felt her heart speed up. She had anticipated the possibility that Sanders was dead; but not like this.

"What happened?"

"They found him in his truck, parked there in the woods. The ignition switched on, a hose attached to the exhaust pipe and in through the front window. The truck had run out of gas."

"How long ago?"

"Couple of days, probably."

Hunter was stunned. She took a deep breath, surprised to see the air twinkling with fireflies; if anything, there were more of them than ever. "What does the state's attorney think?"

"Wendell Stamps is still not concerned. Different jurisdiction. Of course, if this is what you think it is, if it has anything to do with organized crime, that'll kick it into a whole different level. Federal investigation."

"Okay. And what do you think?" Hunter said, feeling the case sliding away from her.

"That may be true, but it doesn't change what happened here last Wednesday," he said. "Susan Champlain was killed in Tidewater, it's a Tidewater case."

"Good," Hunter said. She'd misunderstood.

"I spoke to the state's attorney about an hour ago. He asked me where you were, by the way. Said he heard you'd interviewed Nick Champlain this afternoon in Philly."

"Oh." He let Hunter absorb that for a moment. *Where would he have heard it?* Champlain? Champlain's business manager?

"Don't worry about it," Moore said. "I just wanted you to know. Fischer's just sent you the report on Sanders. No rush on anything. How about we meet first thing Wednesday?"

"All right." So much for taking off a day or two.

"I want to bring Fisch and Tanner in after you come back," he said. "I want us all in the game."

"Good," Hunter said. Meaning Susan's death would become a homicide investigation. "Will do. Thanks."

Hunter tucked away her phone and walked into the woods, feeling better about the case. A breeze moved slowly, high in the trees, and then a cooler air trickled down through the leaves reminding her of currents in river water. She imagined a possible scenario: Sanders had been harassing Susan Champlain, making advances on her while her husband was away; her death had been a crime of passion; afterward, Sanders had felt remorse, or felt that Nick Champlain was going to come after him, so he'd taken his own life.

Hunter didn't quite believe that. But she didn't have a better story yet. She thought about her minimalist conversation with Joey Sanders on Thursday: Sanders standing shirtless beside his truck, the hood propped up, parked by the house where Susan Champlain had spent her summer. Not wanting to talk with Hunter, his eyes squinting into the distance, his thoughts already somewhere down the road.

She turned to the house and saw her mother for a moment, in the rectangle of kitchen light. The song "Silhouettes" began playing in her head as she walked back across the lawn. Where did that come from? Hunter needed to return to Tidewater County, she knew. She probably shouldn't have come here at all.

The air-conditioning felt good as she slid the glass door closed to the living room, the artificial kitchen light startling her eyes.

"Sorry, Mom. Work."

"Everything all right?"

"Fine." She smiled. Her mother had already set out dessert, ice cream and wafer cookies, the ice cream beginning to melt. Cherry vanilla, scooped from a quart carton, another tradition. They ate mostly in silence, Hunter's thoughts far away until she realized the silence had become awkward for her mother. Afterward, she helped clear the table and excused herself. She wanted to check the report on Sanders's death.

Amy's bedroom had been preserved more or less as she'd left it fourteen years earlier—unlike her brother's, which had been emptied out and redesigned as a den and guest room. Hunter's track trophies were still on the chest of drawers, the brainteaser books her dad had bought her still lined up on the shelf with old math and geography schoolbooks. Some magic Wi-Fi was at work, too, she sometimes thought, able to pick up 1999 every time Hunter visited. She only had to be there a few minutes and "Livin' La Vida Loca" or "Genie in a Bottle" would begin playing in her head. Or she'd have some vivid recollection from *Friends* that she hadn't thought of in years.

She logged on to her laptop and quickly found the file that Sonny Fischer had sent. Not much yet. Routine unattended death report. Hunter ran some searches on Sanders, feeling sort of silly working at this old desk where she'd done her seventh-grade geometry homework. At one point, she heard a creaking of floorboards and froze. A shadow moved under the door. She heard a tapping: her mother knocking on the door.

"Are you okay, dear?"

"Fine. Just doing some work, Mom."

Hunter stayed up until after one o'clock sifting through data about Sanders and the Champlains. Then she lay in bed sorting the case in her head until she finally fell asleep. It was eerie, the sounds this old house made; all kinds of thoughts lived in these walls. Later, Hunter dreamed she was walking in a long, creaking hallway that curved through darkness like a funhouse maze, past miniature rooms lit by slants of moonlight. And then somehow she was seated in the rear of a small boat in rough seas, watching as a tall man in a black raincoat tried to steady Susan Champlain; but Hunter could see what was really happening—that the man was actually positioning her so he could push her off into the waves: when he turned to glance at Hunter, she saw who it was—Randall. Hunter woke in darkness and heard crickets chirping in the yard.

She woke again much later, smelling bacon through the air vents. There was light now in the oak branches. Her mother had her breakfast going, the *Today* show on television. Matt, Al and Savannah.

"Morning," Hunter said, coming in the kitchen in her sweats.

"How'd you sleep?"

"So-so." She got herself a Diet Coke and sat at the table. "I forgot how hard that little bed is," she said, trying to sound lighthearted.

"Oh, really?" Her mother, dressed for work in a nice cream-colored pants suit, frowned at her. "Well, it never bothered you when you were growing up."

"I guess I had nothing to compare it with, then." Hunter smiled.

Her mother cracked eggs for her, another custom. "So what are your plans? Can you stay with us one more night?"

"Actually, no, I can't. I have business in town this morning and then I need to get back." Her mother stood stock-still, looking at Hunter over her shoulder. "I'm sorry, Mom. This was probably ill-advised timing on my part. My fault. But I'll come visit for a week when we finish all this."

"Well. Okay," she said, sounding more disapproving than disappointed. She brought Amy a plate of scrambled eggs and buttered wheat toast.

Hunter popped open her soda.

"I wish you wouldn't drink that for breakfast," Joan Hunter said. "I'd like to see you start drinking coffee in the mornings."

"Okay," Hunter said.

"I think you're old enough now."

"Yes, I probably am."

Her mother gave her a kiss on the cheek before setting off.

"Just be careful," she said.

"I will."

Amy watched her mother pull out of the driveway, her old Camry disappearing around the corner. As she ate her eggs, she was struck by their role reversal—Amy seeing her mother off to work like her mother had seen her off in school days.

WALTER KEPLER WAS in the study of his beachfront condo reviewing travel itineraries when his attorney called from the parking garage to say that he had arrived. "Come on up," Kepler said. "I'm in the Italian Room." It was one of Kepler's small jokes. The Baroque painting in his little study was by Bernardo Strozzi, among his favorite artists, and so he called the room his Italian Room. Next door in the bedroom were small paintings by Joachim Patinir and Pieter Aertsen; he called that his Flemish Room.

"Come in." Kepler nodded hello and ushered the smaller man in. They sat at the round mahogany table, Jacob Weber dressed in his attorney suit, smelling faintly of menthol shaving cream and breath mint. Kepler knew him well enough to know that the news was good, even though he appeared grim.

"Well," Weber told him, opening his binder. "We've reached terms."

"Good," Kepler said. "All through the one man."

"That's right."

"And is he on board with the wording?"

"All of it. Yes."

"Very good."

Like a miracle. Anonymously. Kepler's words, from the script.

"And you trust him."

"Yes, of course. He seems to want this as much as you do."

"I'm sure." *Of course, he does.* They were in the game of suppressing emotions now, all around; emotions were a distraction at this stage, at best a waste of time. Kepler understood what his attorney must be feeling, though: Weber had been negotiating terms for three months now, walking a tightrope, and he was about to reach the other side. "It's in everyone's best interest to move quickly, then," Kepler said, and Weber agreed. *Everyone, of course, except for Scott Randall.* The predator would be caught by surprise, as they had intended. Randall was still convinced the painting was being readied for a passage to the Middle East.

Kepler smiled inwardly at that, while gazing somberly toward the Atlantic Ocean. It was easy to plant a story, although there was an art to planting one well. Kepler had worked up a new one, to keep himself busy and to keep Randall busy, too, in these final days. At Harlan Antiques in Dover, Delaware, which the FBI had been watching for several weeks now, he had arranged the delivery from London of a painting on Thursday afternoon measuring 50 inches by 63 inches—which happened to be the exact size of the Rembrandt. Kepler had then placed an anonymous tip to the FBI's Stolen Art Division informing them that a stolen work, "possibly a famous painting," was en route to the antiques store.

But the primary decoy was the story the CIA was banking on, which Kepler had helped set up one afternoon in Amsterdam: Ayman Al-Bulawi, the terrorist middleman, representing the infamous financier and art collector Garrett Massoud.

"The question he wants to know now, obviously, is when," Jacob Weber said. "We're saying tentatively on Friday."

"They can do it with twenty-four-hour notice, though."

"That's the understanding, yes."

"Okay," Kepler said. "Let's give them that, then."

Jacob Weber frowned.

"Meaning overnight Wednesday," Kepler said, to clarify.

Weber said nothing. Kepler watched his precise dark eyes taking this in. He'd anticipated that Kepler would change up the schedule, but probably not so dramatically. Kepler needed to shift hard now, in order to make this happen.

"Will that be a problem?"

"It's sooner than expected," Weber said.

Kepler grimaced. "That's how it has to be, I'm afraid," he said. "It's the only way we can make this work."

"All right," Jacob Weber said. "We'll do it, then. We'll make it work."

"Good. I know you will."

All three phases in a day; the truncated schedule lessened the possibility of sabotage; it also gave them the advantage of surprise. Kepler's risk was that he could lose $5 million, if things fell apart in the first phase. But that was *his* gamble.

"I'm meeting with Nick in a couple of hours. We'd like to commit to that."

"All right," Weber said. "Are you comfortable with everything else?"

Kepler knew that he meant Belasco. Weber didn't approve of Belasco, even though they were, in essence, all partners—all in it together. But Belasco made Weber uneasy. "Yes," he said.

"It'll be in the news Thursday, then."

"Yes."

Two days from now, everyone would be talking about the miracle.

"How about if we go over the details once more," Weber said. "With your new time frame."

ON THE WAY to her meeting with Calvin Walters in the town of Scattersville, Pennsylvania, Hunter took a call from Dave Crowe.

"How did it go with Bradbury?" he asked.

"Interesting."

"She's a trip, isn't she?"

"I guess," Hunter said. He sounded out of breath.

"She's gay, you know. I forgot to tell you that. Not that it matters."

"No, it doesn't."

The suburban traffic was heavy and moving faster than she had imagined. She switched lanes abruptly, almost rear-ending a Mercedes, which had braked suddenly. She glanced at her rear-view mirror, understanding why handheld cell phone use while driving had been banned in Maryland and many other states.

"It's interesting, though," she said, "from what she told me, there's some question about whether or not Belasco—the so-called partner—really exists."

"He exists. The Bureau doesn't know much about him because we haven't had the resources to really pursue him. But he definitely exists."

A car jerked in front of her and Hunter slammed on her brakes again, dropping the phone. "Dammit!"

The phone was on the floor now, sliding toward the accelerator. She could hear Crowe's voice talking to her but couldn't reach it.

"Dammit," she said, trying to move it with her right foot, afraid it was stuck behind the accelerator pedal.

She slowed and undid her seat belt, reaching to the floor, feeling for the phone. Finally she managed to lift it between two fingers. The car behind her whipped into the left lane as she straightened up, its driver holding down on his horn. Hunter glanced over as he passed: a bald, red-faced man. Hunter read his lips: "Learn how to drive!!!" it looked like.

"What's going on?" Crowe said, back in her ear. "Are you all right?"

"I'm all right," Hunter said. "Traffic. Let me call you later."

She got another call several minutes later, this one from her mother, but decided against taking it. She was pulling into the small town of Scattersville by then, and wanted to make sure she didn't miss her turns.

She drove past the small brick police station and made a U-turn, pulling into a Wells Fargo lot. She parked there and listened to the message her mother had left for her: "Honey," Joan Hunter said gravely. "I had a call for you, dear, here at work. It was very strange. A very strange man. He wouldn't give his name, but he said you were expecting him to call. He said, and this is a direct quote, I wrote it down: 'Tell Amy Hunter she still has a day to extricate herself.' Do you know what that means? He wouldn't let me say anything or ask anything. So, I can only imagine." She sighed dramatically. "Anyway, it was good to see you again. Call and tell me everything's all right. Okay? I love you."

Hunter set her phone on the seat, willing herself not to think about it until she had finished her meeting with Calvin Walters.

Chapter Twenty-six

Scattersville was an old suburban community about seventy miles from Philadelphia. It reminded Hunter of her own home town: fifties and sixties houses with small yards, sidewalks and telephone poles, mature oaks and elms, the downtown built around a four-block Main Street.

Calvin Walters had worked for the city of Philadelphia for thirty-six years before seeking a quieter life out here, battling a quieter type of crime. He was a lanky, bony man, with small patches of white hair on his head. He favored one hip as he walked, but there was a steadiness in his dark, bloodshot eyes, and something gentle and immediately likable about him.

"Nice town," Hunter said, as she sat in the creaky wooden guest chair in his windowless office.

"It'll do," he said. "It's the place where old police detectives go to pasture." He showed her a playful smile. "So how can I help you?"

"Eddie Charles," Hunter said. "I understand you knew him?"

He acknowledged it with a sideways tilt of the head.

"He died last September," Hunter said. "His death was thought to be drug related."

"Thought to be. That's what they tell me."

"You don't believe it."

"I don't." He rotated his swivel chair and reached over the desk for a clipping on the bulletin board. The board was layered haphazardly with notes, photos and faded newspaper clips.

What he handed her was a photocopy of an *Inquirer* story. SOUTH PHILLY DEATH MAY HAVE CRIME TIES was the headline.

There was a photo showing a wide-faced African-American man wearing a loosened tie, beaming at the picture taker. Hunter had read about the case before coming here. Eddie Charles's body had been found dumped in a small parking lot near Fifth Street and Jackson in the city last September 27. Hunter knew the neighborhood, long considered a "drug corner," before the spread of cell phones.

The Philly police maintained a website that anyone could access with grainy videos of shoot-outs, abductions, and other unsolved crimes, caught on cameras mounted around the city. Many of them were years old. Hunter had already watched and rewatched the website video of two men leaving Eddie Charles in the lot and driving away.

Detective Walters let the unedited footage run now on his computer. He'd had it queued up to go before she'd come in. They both watched: a car stopping, two men pulling from the trunk an object wrapped in a sheet. Dropping it in the lot and jogging back to the car. It was filmed from behind, almost a block away, much of the incident obscured by a store awning. The make of the car was impossible to determine.

"There was a baggie with crack residue in his pants pockets, but no drugs in his system," Walters said. "They knew what they were doing. Knew where the cameras were."

"So it was a setup."

"That's right."

He rocked back in his swivel chair, hands gripping the arms, studying Hunter. "I don't see a lot of similarity between what happened with Eddie and what you're investigating," he said. She knew he'd probably spent a little time looking up Susan Champlain.

"Except both deaths seem to be something they aren't," Hunter said.

He tilted his head to one side thoughtfully and showed a slow crescent of smile.

"The thing about that neighborhood," he said, "was that it came to represent something to Eddie. That was a place Eddie'd climbed out of. He'd gone on. Started his own business, raised a family. We used to talk about it. In his mind, that was a place that didn't exist anymore. That's how he'd come to think about it. You can't choose where you're born, but you can choose where you live your life. He did."

"So he was dumped there to make a point."

"That's right."

Someone had put Eddie Charles back in the neighborhood he'd escaped from, the place he'd risen above. Nullifying the rest of his life, in a sense.

"Who would want to make that point?" Hunter asked.

He showed her his right palm. "That's the question, isn't it?"

"I'd like to help answer it."

The crescent smile emerged and quickly faded. "If it was easy to do, we'd've done it months ago, believe me. It was meant that way, not to be figured out. It was meant to send a message. To make a point."

He reached up to tack the clipping back onto his bulletin board and sat down again.

"You knew Eddie Charles a long time, I understand."

"Twenty-five years." The chair creaked when he rocked back. "His story was nothing unusual when I met him. Same story you hear a million times on the streets. Raised by a single mother, picked on growing up. Bumped into drugs for the first time when he was thirteen or fourteen. For a while, drugs gave him what he didn't have. An *in*ternal life," he said, with a strange, drawn-out emphasis.

"It's a cliché," Walters went on. "But being a cliché doesn't stop it from happening. You try to warn these kids, tell them exactly what's going to happen to them and they all think, Nope, not me. And two years later, they've become the cliché."

He sighed and leaned forward.

"Eddie had four or five arrests before he was eighteen. He made several attempts to straighten himself out and get clean in his twenties. Of course, that doesn't often take."

"But it did with Eddie."

"No, ma'am. Not for a while. Not until he got older and recognized how much of his life he'd lost, how many doors'd closed that were never going to open again. You get older, people stop giving you chances, stop looking at you in ways you want them to look at you. Eddie went past that point and his choices narrowed down to two: he could die, he could live."

"And he decided to live."

"Well, no," he said. "I don't think I'd use the word decided. He got scared into it finally; and when he did, he turned his life around. But what *was* different about Eddie was that once he crossed that bridge, he never went back. Never. How did he do it? He got involved with better people, joined the church. And then he met a young lady, Maureen, who saved his life. Gave him a family. Helped him start his business."

"So this isn't something he would have ever gone back to."

"No, ma'am, that's what I'm telling you."

"What happened, then?"

He rubbed a hand down his narrow face, feeling the contours of his bones. "What happened was, Eddie walked into a hole. He stepped into something he couldn't get out of. Drugs was one hole, but there's other kinds of holes you can step into."

"What happened, exactly?" Hunter asked. "What was the hole, in this case?"

He winced and seemed to close up a little, leaning to one side. "The exact details of what happened with Eddie, I couldn't tell you. And I'm not going to speculate. All's I can say is that he must've met up with the wrong people. Or the wrong *person*."

Hunter asked, "Did what happen to him involve organized crime?"

He flicked out his left hand dismissively. "I couldn't tell you that. Although——" He paused and went on. "Eddie was an electrician. A very good one. He had a lot of clients. One of them was a fellow named Dante Patello. You may've heard about him. Or his father, Anthony. And also a fellow named John Luigi. So I guess you could say that put him on the fringes of it. But, no, I don't think those people were the ones who betrayed Eddie."

"*Someone* betrayed him."

"Yes, that's right, someone betrayed him."

"Who do you *think* it was?"

"My business isn't to think," he said, smiling at her. "It's to solve cases or shut up. In this instance, I'll take the second option."

"Did it have anything to do with stolen art, what happened to Eddie?"

"May have." The look on his face became more nuanced. "Are you asking me that or do you know that?"

"I'm asking."

"Then my answer is, I don't know, I couldn't tell you. I've *heard* that. But I can't tell you if it's true or not."

For the first time, he sounded disingenuous.

"When did you last hear from Eddie?"

"Three days," he said. His eyes turned back to the bulletin board; Hunter looked at the crooked clipping: Eddie's face beaming. "Three days before they found him," he said. "My feeling is . . . someone got the wrong idea about Eddie, and they planted a story about him that wasn't true. Not the Patello family, though, someone else. But that's all speculation on my part. I'm not going to talk about something I don't really know."

"Do you know anyone else who might talk about it?"

"I'd have to think about that."

He was pulling back from her, Hunter sensed. She opened her folder, then, and laid out Susan Champlain's cell phone pictures, side by side on his desk.

Calvin Walters leaned forward. He looked closely at the images, lifting them up one at a time.

"Could that be him?" Hunter asked, standing beside him.

Walters didn't answer right away. He picked up one of the three again and held it inches from his eyes. Then he set it down, and pointed a yellowed fingernail at something. It was the photo Susan had taken from beside the house. "You see that? That tower there?"

"Okay."

"That's Revel," he said.

Hunter moved in and looked closer. She didn't know what he was saying. "What's Revel?"

"Casino hotel. That's where the NFL player knocked his wife unconscious in the elevator."

"Oh." She looked again. "You're saying this is Atlantic City?"

"That's right. Revel was the tallest building in A.C. Still is, I guess. Although it shut down a couple of years after they opened. Which tells you something about Atlantic City."

He turned the picture over, looking for some kind of ID. So the house *wasn't* in the Philadelphia suburbs, as Susan had said; it was on the New Jersey coast. Luke was right about that. The Rembrandt, then, had been in Atlantic City.

Walters slid his chair to the side and hit some computer keys, as if he were alone in the office. A minute later, a photo came on the screen.

It was Eddie Charles, wearing what appeared to be the same jacket as the man in Susan Champlain's photo, an aqua Member's Only, which looked a size or two small.

"That's him," he said. "Eddie did business down there. Him and his wife. Mo. Rented an apartment there. Not in A.C., but in Margate. Although I couldn't tell you whose house this is."

"Do you know who the other man is?"

"Nope."

He leaned back and was watching her again, she realized.

"Tell me about your case," he said.

Seated again, Hunter told him who Susan Champlain was, and how she had died. She told him how she'd been led to Helen Bradbury while pursuing leads about Susan's death and then what Bradbury had told her about Eddie Charles. Calvin Walters listened intently, his right ear cocked as if it helped him to hear better. She didn't say anything about Kepler or Belasco. Or the Rembrandt painting.

"I'm told there was a moral issue involved in what happened to Eddie," Hunter said. "A moral story."

"Yeah, that's right," he said, showing his smile. He'd had this discussion before. "And that was the funny part about how Eddie ended up, and the part I still don't understand: his daughter says he saw the whole thing coming before it happened. Saw it as clearly as a train coming his way on a cloudless afternoon. It was that certain, to the point where there was nothing anyone could do to stop it. Eddie told her exactly what was going to happen. And a week later, it'd happened. He was dead."

He pushed the images together and gave them back to Hunter.

"But, the thing of it is," he said, "Eddie didn't do anything wrong. All he did was he fell into a hole. And it wasn't a hole he dug. And therein lies your moral issue."

"I'd like to talk with her," Hunter said. "The daughter."

He nodded. "Who else've you talked with about Eddie?"

"No one yet, other than Helen Bradbury."

"She's something, isn't she?"

"I was going to talk with the son," Hunter said. "I have an address for him in the city."

"Cyril? Cyril won't talk to you. The daughter probably won't, either. But she might. Thelma knows the whole story. More of it than I do. But the thing of it is, even if she were to tell you anything, what good do you think it would do now? It's not going to do Eddie any good."

"Except it might clear things up for his family. It might clear his reputation," Hunter said.

"It might."

He rocked back and forth very slightly, considering that. "I did a little background check on you, by the way," he said.

"And—?"

He shrugged and slapped his hands on the arms of the chair. "Do you have a card for me?" he said. Not in a dismissive way; in a way that meant he wanted a number, to call her back. Hunter pulled a business card from her pocket and handed it to him.

He got up, then, rubbing his hands on his hips, and began to walk her down the narrow hallway to the front door of the storefront police station.

"And if you do talk to Cyril," he said, "don't mention that you talked with me. If you don't mind."

"No. I won't."

"All right. Just be careful," he said, shaking her hand. There it was again. Outside, he looked up and down the street as if someone might be watching them. Hunter walked back to her car.

Chapter Twenty-seven

Kepler arrived early, choosing a table in the shade on the back deck at Cap'N Vic's Grille. The place smelled of fried onions and river water, the ceiling fans spinning warm air, the sun making dozens of bright creases on the water.

He watched a young couple industriously eating a late breakfast across the deck, not speaking, heads down, each staring at a separate section of *The Philadelphia Inquirer*. *Married a while*. In two days, they'd be reading about the miracle. Kepler could feel a shift, the faint rumble of what was coming.

Being a deal maker has a shelf life, and for Kepler, this would be it. He'd structured the Rembrandt deal more carefully than his others, and with extra precautions. When it was over, Kepler would retire into the life he'd been shaping in his imagination for years—a life of traveling, visiting great museums, reading good books, living with his passions.

Still, there was some unfamiliar apprehension this time, the feeling that all of his precautions carried their own vulnerabilities. Part of that was Belasco, he realized.

He looked up, surprised to see that a waitress was standing

beside the table. A little blond with big teeth, her skin flaking from sunburn.

"Bring us a pitcher of ice water, please," Kepler said. Her eyes quickly went to the empty place across from where he was sitting. "And a bowl of chips with crab dip."

She smiled at him and walked away without saying anything. Occasionally, Kepler enjoyed places like this, far from the poseurs of the art world. He enjoyed sitting at a bar and striking up a conversation, inventing his identity as he went. It was easy to convince a stranger you were someone else; he'd been doing it all his life. It was a form of recreation to him, unchaining his own burdensome past, and giving in to the lure of the ordinary. He craved the big deals, but when he was in them he sometimes craved ordinary life just as much.

Officially, Nick Champlain was in Iowa now. The funeral was today. Weber had arranged for a man to carry his ticket and his passport, to check in to a hotel in Cedar Rapids under his name. Vaguely a look-alike, if anyone was watching.

Unofficially, Champlain was here. Kepler gave him directions from the freeway when he called: "You see Exit 12? . . . Not yet? You keep going, you take exit 12 . . . Turn right off the ramp, okay, then get in your right-hand lane . . . until the light . . . no, that's Glenbrook . . . You see Glenbrook? . . . Okay, and turn right toward the water. Last lot . . . Good . . . now, park . . . no, I'm looking at you . . . Come across the street and join me on the deck for a drink of water."

He lifted his hand slightly to wave. Champlain wore a ball cap, loose jeans, a T-shirt, two days' growth of beard. A disguise, in effect, although he still walked and grinned like a cocky Philadelphia businessman. This was their penultimate meeting, Kepler expected, although Champlain didn't know that; he probably didn't even know what that meant.

Kepler poured water for both of them as Champlain sat at the table.

"You look like you're ready for a Phillies game," Kepler said.

Champlain displayed his winning smile. "I am. I just wish they were playing better."

"We're ready, though?"

"Sure." His expression sobered quickly.

"You told me these people are set to go," Kepler asked, after the niceties. "Anytime?"

"That's right."

"My client says he needs to move it up another couple days. He wants to go tomorrow. Can we make that happen?"

Champlain breathed out through his nostrils.

"He'd like to do the whole deal in a day," Kepler said, speaking more softly now. "Rosa sells it to you in the morning, you sell it to me in the afternoon."

Champlain continued to breathe through his nose.

"Yes? No?"

"Yes."

"All right. Let's talk about the numbers, then. One more time."

Champlain nodded.

"I deposit another five hundred into Rosa's account overnight," Kepler said. "That means he's sitting on a rock."

"Right." A million dollars down.

"Which will set the first phase in motion in the morning."

"Right."

"Then you pick it up from there."

The first part of the plan was between Champlain and Vincent Rosa. Kepler's only role would be to wire the remaining payment, four million dollars, to Rosa's Bermuda account, and cover the rest of Champlain's fees, $500,000. The second part of the plan would transfer the painting from Champlain to Kepler, at a cost of two million dollars, plus the million already paid.

The third part, the miracle, he didn't mention.

"We do this right, we both go home tomorrow and enjoy the rest of our lives," Kepler said. "And then, you're still interested, we can talk, in another four or five weeks, about the other deal."

"Of course I'll be interested."

"Good."

Catnip. Kepler had dangled this from the start—the idea of a second, larger deal. The other prize from the Gardner theft had been Vermeer's *The Concert*, one of only thirty-four Vermeer paintings in existence. The Vermeer exchange would be more complicated; but it had also passed through the Rosa family before finding a temporary home with a collector in the South of France. The collector died in 2006, and the painting had again come under the control of the Rosas. Kepler had told Champlain he had a buyer willing to pay $25 million for it. Which meant Champlain could probably more than double what he was making this time as an intermediary to the Rosas. That's what Kepler told him.

When he finished talking about the deal, Kepler began to talk about art, the natural drift of his thinking process. He'd been to Amsterdam in the spring, he said, and told Nick what it had felt like to stand again in front of Rembrandt's magnificent *Night*

Watch, which took up most of an entire wall at the Rijksmuseum. "It's his most famous painting, you know, but it's misnamed, because it's actually set in the daytime. Not Rembrandt's title, obviously."

Champlain subtly adjusted his facial expression several times to indicate his interest. Kepler liked that.

"Rembrandt always had a soft spot for the criminal class, did you know that? For people like the Rosas and Luigi."

"Van Gogh called him a magician, I read," Champlain stated.

"Well, yes, that's right." Kepler smiled, pleasantly surprised by this. Nicholas had prepared this time; he'd spent a few minutes reading a Wikipedia entry, probably, about Rembrandt van Rijn. Brownie points. "You know, there's a painting called *Self Portrait as Zeuxis Laughing*," Kepler told him. "It's in Cologne. You have to see it someday. A very heroic painting, from the last years of his life. The laugh—it's quite stunning, words can't describe it. It's the most remarkable laugh you'll ever see in a painting."

"I'll put that on my bucket list," Champlain said, holding his smile. He was a brutish man, Kepler saw again, although there was something—an amused cruelty—about his manner that appealed to him.

"The life of a painting like that," Kepler said, "if cared for, it's indefinite. Whereas the life of one of us, a human being, it's what, seventy-five years? If we're lucky?"

"If we're lucky."

Kepler set his elbows on the table then and leaned forward. "There are two other things I need to mention, Nick. First: the photos this homicide cop showed you."

Champlain shrugged with exaggerated emphasis, as if he didn't know what Kepler was talking about.

"You don't have copies."

"No."

"But they came from your wife's camera." Champlain's eyes suddenly appeared nervous, which was the response Kepler had wanted. "Tell me about them."

"There's nothing to tell. That was the first I heard of them."

Kepler nodded, figuring: Hunter had copies, the police had copies. How far would this go? "We're just concerned that this woman, the homicide detective, may be talking with the FBI. Or vice versa, they may be talking to her."

Champlain's expression never changed. "Why would that be?" he asked. "Why would they think I have anything to do with it?"

"Well, they don't. It's no cause for concern." Kepler smiled, reassuring him. "They think you're in Iowa for the funeral, right?"

"But how do they know *anything*?"

"Because they're tracking someone connected with your friend, Vincent Rosa, I imagine," Kepler said pointedly. "They don't know anything about *you*. Or me. And we want to keep it that way. I'm just saying, if she should try to reach you again, I trust you'll refer all inquiries to your business manager."

"Already doing it," he said.

"Good. Good." Kepler felt satisfied. "Then we'll do our business tomorrow and we'll all go home happy."

Chapter Twenty-eight

Hunter headed back toward the city, taking the Schuylkill Expressway over the river. Driving past Fairmount Park, then through a series of turns into a sketchy neighborhood of row houses where Cyril Charles lived. Eddie Charles's son would be a long shot, she knew, but she decided she'd make this one last stop before returning to Tidewater. She was off track, clearly, taking a detour on the chance that Eddie Charles's children might be able to tell her something about Belasco. Or Kepler. Something that might tie back to the killing of Susan Champlain.

Fischer had sent her updates, she saw as she drove. The state police computer forensics lab had gone into the computer of Sally Markos, the Champlains' summer housekeeper, and found e-mails and phone numbers belonging to Joseph Sanders and Elena Rodgers. *Still processing all*, Fisch wrote.

Hunter parked on the street below the row house listed in property records as belonging to Cyril Charles, behind a new-looking maroon Lexus.

She rang the doorbell three times before Cyril answered. He was a rail-thin man with a lean face and stubbly whiskers, wearing shiny warm-ups that were several inches too long.

Hunter introduced herself and showed her badge. She told him she wanted to talk with him about his father. Cyril looked at her, keeping his left hand on the door.

"You don't want to be here," he finally said, which was more or less how Hunter felt by then. "Okay?"

"Why not?"

"Because we don't talk with no po-lice," he said. "Okay? You understand what I'm saying?"

"Not really," Hunter said.

"What do you want to ask me?"

"I'm just doing some follow-up on another case," she said. "Your father's name came up. I'd like to help find out what happened to him."

"Oh, no, you don't. You don't want to do that," he said. Hunter smelled alcohol on his breath now. "Okay? We have nothing to tell you about that." The door opened wider. Hunter was surprised to see a heavyset, pouty-looking woman leaning against him, her arms crossed. "Because we already said more than we need to say, you understand what I'm saying? There's been enough trouble over all that, we've put all that behind us now."

"What sort of trouble?"

"Trouble you don't want to know about. Okay?"

Hunter's phone began to vibrate in her pants pocket. She ignored it.

"Also, I'd like to share some information with *you*," Hunter said, trying a new tack, but Cyril was no longer looking at her. The woman was speaking tersely to him, saying, "Just close the door!"

"We're not interested in talking to no po-lice," Cyril said again. "Okay, you understand what I'm saying? Thank you."

He closed the door.

Hunter walked down the steps to her car. Three children—two boys and a girl—who'd been kicking a soccer ball froze in position down the street, staring at her. Hunter waved. She turned back to the row house and saw Cyril Charles and his wife looking out the window at her.

Driving away, she slid down the windows and pulled out her phone. At the end of the street, she stopped, hearing it again: the breathing sound, high in the trees, wind inhaling and exhaling through the leaves, sweeping subtly back and forth.

It was Calvin Walters who'd called while she was standing on the stoop with Cyril Charles. She called him back as she drove toward the river.

"Hey you," he said, "you still in town?"

"I'm just leaving."

"Think you could scoot over to the art museum?"

"Which art museum?"

"The big one. If you can be there at four, she'll meet with you. Eddie's daughter. She can talk for ten minutes in the Cafeteria. It's on the ground floor."

"Okay."

The Philadelphia Museum of Art.

"Keep it to ten minutes, all right? Her name's Thelma. Be gentle."

Hunter punched in the Philadelphia Museum of Art on her GPS, and let it guide her back into the city.

SHE PICKED OUT Thelma quickly. Conservatively dressed, a professional woman in a dark suit that fit a little snugly. Mid-thirties, probably, with long, thin hair over her shoulders and strong, symmetrical features. She was seated at a table against the wall, looking slightly self-conscious as she spread butter on a bagel.

Hunter bought a bottled water and sat diagonally across from her. She spoke her name as a question. Thelma acknowledged her by lifting her eyes.

Speaking softly and conversationally, Hunter told Thelma who she was. "I'm interested in what happened to your father," she said.

Thelma finished buttering her bagel. She took a small bite and kept it in her hand.

"I'm investigating a case that I think may be connected to what happened to your father. I'd like to know about him. I'd like to help establish a more truthful explanation for what happened."

She looked at Hunter with eyes that were startlingly direct but vulnerable. Hunter felt that she was treading a line, not wanting to push too hard or promise anything; but wanting to help. Thelma had agreed to meet, after all, so she must have something to say. *Let it come naturally.*

"My father," she said, "was a good man. The police never tried to catch the people who killed him. They made up their minds what happened and never considered it might be anything else."

"The police treated your father's death as drug related."

"Yes."

"I'd like to hear what really happened," Hunter said. Thelma kept her eyes down, both hands holding the bagel. "I was told he saw it coming?"

Without looking at her, she said, barely audibly, "Yeah. He knew."

"Okay."

She took another small bite and pushed the plate to the side, no longer interested in eating. "He knew a week before it happened," she said, looking up again. "He sat me down and he told me what all was going on. He said he was in a jam that he probably couldn't get out of. He wanted me to know that."

Hunter nodded for her to continue. Thelma glanced around the cafeteria first. "I don't know that I'm really comfortable telling it like this. I'm only doing this because of Mr. Walters."

"I understand. Any way you want to do it," Hunter said.

"If I tell you, do you guarantee you're not going to get me in trouble?"

"I'll do everything I can . . . If you want to do this later, in a different location—"

"No." She lowered her eyes and began: "A week before my father died, he told me that he was afraid he was going to be killed. He said it could happen anytime. A week, a few days. It could happen the next day."

Hunter nodded. "Okay."

"He told me he'd learned some stuff and was afraid it was going to get him killed. Which put him in a tough position, because once you learn something you can't just unlearn it. You know what I mean?"

"Okay. What was it he had learned?"

Thelma glanced at her watch. Hunter saw the second hand sweep around.

Six minutes twenty seconds.

"This can't come back to me in any way."

"No." Her eyes held Hunter's—deep almond ovals, a secret world opening up to her momentarily.

"My father, he was an electrician," she said. "It was a one-man business. He worked for some important people, in the city and on the Shore. People like Mr. John Luigi and Mr. Dante Patello and Mr. Frank Rosa. Those men were very generous to my father over the years and he always respected their privacy.

"But the thing that happened was because of that, because of his association with those men. It wasn't anything he did. It was more like guilt by association. And maybe my father made a mistake along the way. But it wasn't something that he should have lost his life over." Her eyes had moistened.

"What was the mistake?" Hunter asked.

"My father had one conversation where he might've said something he shouldn't have. And after that, this other man came along and hired him. A man he didn't know."

"To do what?"

"Well. To wire an apartment. That's what he said. But the man was acting funny right from the beginning, asking him questions about the Patello family, and my father began to think he might be a cop or something. He tried to cut it off."

"And—? What happened?"

"That's when this other man started to play rough with my father."

"How so?"

"He tried to force him to talk about the Patellos—or, the word my father used, *coerce*. He'd have a conversation with my father and then, later, my father found out that he had recorded the whole thing. And then he tried to use the tape to threaten him."

"Threaten your father."

"Yes."

"How so?" She was going fast now, leaving things out. "How was he going to use the tape to threaten your father? What did they talk about on the tape?"

"There was nothing in*crim*inating. But they were—my father said if it was taken out of context, it might *sound* incriminating; it might sound like he was saying something he really wasn't. And this man just began to threaten him with it. Said he could make that conversation available to Mr. Dante Patello if he didn't cooperate. He made my father feel like he was in a trap that he couldn't get out of."

"What exactly was this man asking your father to do?"

"Find out some things about the Patellos."

"Why? Who *are* the Patellos, exactly?"

"They have several businesses in the city and Dante has some apartment buildings on the Jersey Shore. My father'd done work for them for years. Anthony Patello, Dante's father, lent my father some money at one time, that helped him get started in his business. So my father wanted no part of this. He was planning to go to Mr. Patello and come clean about it, tell him what was going on. But I don't think he ever had a chance to do that."

Her eyes were glistening with emotion. She was nervously twisting a corner of the napkin.

"But he never did what this man asked him to do."

"No."

"Did he say who this man was? Did he give you a name?" Her thoughts seemed to lose focus then, her eyes staring at a spot on the table. "Thelma? Did he give you a name? Did your father say who this man was, who he worked for?"

"He said he worked for the government."

"The government."

"Yeah."

Thelma glanced at her quickly.

"This was the government putting pressure on him, you're saying?"

"That's what he told me. That's why he didn't think he could ever just walk away from it."

"What government? State? Federal?"

"Federal government. FBI."

Hunter felt her heart ratchet into a higher gear. "Okay," she said, concentrating on keeping her voice even. "This man was with the FBI."

"Yes. My brother's warned me not to talk with anyone. I'm only here because Mr. Walters called me."

"I know that."

"I've got four children at home. I can't afford to get involved in any kind of trouble, you understand?"

"I understand," Hunter said. "You won't. Believe me, this is strictly between us. But it's important that you tell me all you can about what happened." Hunter glanced across the room. An older woman seated alone averted her eyes. "Why did your father think the government was interested in Mr. Patello and his family?"

She breathed more heavily but didn't answer.

"Did this have to do with stolen art?"

Thelma raised and lowered her chin, their eyes connecting for a long moment. "Yeah, that's what it was. This man wanted my father to find out about stolen art. He wanted to pay him, thousands of dollars, he said, if he'd just ask three or four questions. That's how he put it."

"But your father wouldn't do it?"

"Never. Not for a second. They wanted him to go in and be a snitch, and my father would never do that. Never. My father was an honorable man."

"So he said no."

"He said no. But that only made this man come on stronger. I don't think he knew what kind of person my father was. And then, of course, the government raided Mr. Patello's house and it was in all the papers, and I guess maybe my father got tied in with that."

Hunter sighed, understanding now. "Was this all just one man? Or was there more than one?"

"One man."

"Okay. Thelma, can you tell me who this man was," Hunter said. "Did he give you a name?"

She kept her eyes down now. Hunter took a breath, knowing she had to be careful or Thelma might close up.

"Was his name Scott Randall?"

She lifted out her chin affirmatively. It wasn't a direct answer, but close.

"Was it Scott Randall?" she asked again, and this time she nodded and looked at her, her eyes glistening, letting Hunter all the way in for a moment.

"Did your father tell you anything about this deal specifically? With the stolen art?"

"No," she said. "Other than what this FBI man said to him."

"Which was what?"

"He told me someone was going to make a deal for a stolen painting that was worth several million dollars. That's all he knew."

This must have been the earlier deal that fell apart, Hunter figured. The Manet. The FBI sting that Kepler had walked away from, taking some of the government's money. Maybe in the end, Randall blamed Eddie Charles for sabotaging it.

"And so, what happened?"

"Just like I say. He didn't want any part of it. But he was scared because this man wouldn't let go. Told him he was replaceable, all kinds of shit," she said, her voice suddenly angry and trembling. "And he said, if my father, or any of his family members, even think about going to the police, they'd regret it."

"That's why you haven't talked with anyone other than Mr. Walters?"

"Yeah. I mean—I didn't exactly think they'd believe me, either. But also." She hesitated, and went on: "Also, someone paid my brother some money after my father got killed. An attorney contacted him, said it was from a fund my father had set up. But I think it may've just been payment to keep him quiet."

"How much was this?"

"I don't know. He gave me five thousand. Said that was my half of it. I don't necessarily believe what Cyril tells me."

Hunter glanced at her watch, seeing the ten minutes were up.

"When your father talked with you, what did he say about this man? This Scott Randall?"

"He said he was corrupt. He said all kinds of things, tell you the truth," she said, showing a quick smile for the first time. "But my father was very afraid of what he was going to do. My father was an honest man. Anyone will tell you."

"I know," Hunter said. "I know that."

"There was a lot of loyalty in my father. Maybe Mr. Patello, the son, thought my father had betrayed him with the FBI, I don't know. I hope not. But it was wrong, that the story got out there."

"I know it was."

Thelma glanced at her watch. "Anyway," she said. "I need to go."

Hunter understood some of what she was feeling, the sense of injustice and powerlessness. *You can do things that are legal but not moral,* Bradbury had told her. Was there any direct connection between what had happened to Eddie Charles and what had happened to Susan Champlain? Hunter didn't know yet. But Eddie had been in the photo that Susan had taken, in the same frame with the stolen Rembrandt. Maybe he'd just been there as an electrician, to wire an old house. Maybe the fact that she'd taken the photo had just been a coincidence.

"Did he ever mention a man named Belasco?" Hunter asked. "Or Walter Kepler?"

"Kepler," she said.

"Yes. Do you know that name?"

"Uh-uh."

Something had changed. Thelma's eyes had glazed over and all of a sudden she wouldn't look at Hunter. For a few moments she wasn't there.

"Thelma? What is it? What did he tell you about Kepler?"

She exhaled and finally looked at her. "That's who this is about, isn't it? Kepler?"

"How do you know that?"

"My father mentioned the name. He wouldn't talk about him. That was one thing he wouldn't talk about."

"But he mentioned the name."

"Yes. Once. The FBI man asked about him, too."

"Okay." Hunter thought of Randall's snaggle-toothed smile, his dark, asymmetrical eyes. Had Randall put out the word that Eddie Charles was an FBI informant as a way of exacting revenge?

Thelma was looking at Hunter squarely again, ready to leave. "I don't really know why I'm talking with you," she said. "I don't expect the real story about my father will ever come out."

"What would that story be?" Hunter asked. "How would you like it to come out?"

"I'd just like to hear someone say the truth. That it was the murder of an honorable man. That it wasn't some drug deal. Those articles in the paper, that's the way they left it."

"I know," Hunter said. "I'll do everything I can to get the real story out, Thelma," she added, but her promise sounded hollow.

They walked together to the west entrance lobby, stopping by the information desk. Hunter asked a final question: "When you said your father knew he was going to be killed, what exactly did he think was going to happen? Who did he think was going to kill him? Someone connected with Mr. Patello's business?"

"No."

"The FBI man."

"Yes. That's what he said. The FBI was going to do it. Maybe not directly. But he said it didn't matter. The FBI man was setting him up, putting him in that trap, and there was no way he could get out of it unless he did exactly what the man asked him to do. By then, it was too late."

She looked at Hunter and she saw the raw hurt in her eyes, her cheeks reflecting the afternoon light through the tall museum windows.

"Okay," Hunter said. She reached out and gripped the backs of her hands. "If you want to talk again, you know how to reach me."

"Yes. Mr. Walters."

"Yes." Thelma lowered her head. She walked outside, onto Anne d'Harnoncourt Drive, and quickly disappeared.

BELASCO FINALLY TURNED away from the Dali painting in Gallery 169. *Self-Construction with Boiled Beans (Premonition of Civil War)*, a grotesquely fascinating portrait of a dismembered creature in the throes of doing battle with itself. There was a terrifyingly morbid fascination to the scene, set against a lovely Catalonian sky and a barren countryside. The beans an offering to the gods. A painting depicting the Spanish Civil War, supposedly, although it had become a much more universal symbol over time. The little professor wandering the landscape had always reminded Belasco of Walter Kepler, barely noticed and barely noticing, as he went about his business.

Belasco was killing time today. A lovely phrase. Tomorrow, it would be time again for killing, in the more literal sense. Belasco walked out through the main entrance, to the so-called Rocky steps, having no idea that Amy Hunter, the homicide investigator from Maryland, was one floor below, on the ground level, about to exit through the west entrance.

The real art of killing, of course, was to make it seem like something else; an accident, a suicide, death from natural causes, a random killing. As long as you could do that, you kept moving; you were free to act again. As soon as it was seen for what it was, everything changed; the investigators identified a pattern and it was a matter of time before the perpetrator self-destructed, becoming like Dali's self-mutilation. *A matter of time*. Another lovely phrase.

Belasco had spoken briefly to Kepler before coming here. The transactions would happen tomorrow. Belasco would drive a white van to the Pennsylvania countryside in order to participate. On Thursday, they would both be back here, at the museum, this time together.

It was a delicious late afternoon in Philadelphia. On the walk back to the hotel, Belasco saw a man seated on a bench reading the newspaper. Funny: Belasco already knew what would be on the front page of that newspaper Friday morning. Almost alone among the 1.5 million people in Philadelphia, Belasco knew. With that knowledge came feelings of both power and impotence; feelings that canceled each other out, becoming something more like humility. It was Kepler's story that would be told. Walter was the storyteller. He understood the potential of image and story as well as anyone. Belasco's role was to be in service of that story; it was a mostly selfless role and a necessary one.

Tomorrow one more person would have to die. Possibly two. Belasco didn't know yet. But it was starting to look like two.

Chapter Twenty-nine

Walking along Benjamin Franklin Parkway to her car, Hunter felt a potent adrenaline cocktail working on her nervous system. She'd thought that this detour—the meetings with Calvin Walters, and now with Eddie Charles's daughter—might get her closer to Belasco; that they might provide new clues to Susan Champlain's killing. But they hadn't done that at all. They'd circled her right back to Scott Randall and his obsession with Walter Kepler—back to her instinct that something about Randall was seriously not right.

Driving back to the freeway, Hunter called Fischer, wondering where he was on the backgrounds of Kepler and Belasco. She asked him to add Randall to the priority list. Fischer, as usual, sounded pleased to receive a new assignment.

"Also," she told him, "I'd like to know what sort of relationship there was—or is—between Walter Kepler and Scott Randall. Anything connecting them. And anything connecting either one with Belasco."

"I'm not finding a lot on Belasco, unfortunately," he said.

"Whatever you can do."

She listened to the scratch of his pen on paper. "When do you want it?" he said.

"Tonight? Tomorrow morning? Whenever you can get to it."

"M'kay."

Twenty-some miles down the freeway, Hunter felt hungry, and remembered she hadn't eaten since breakfast. She stopped at a turnpike restaurant, where she ate a turkey burger with fries and a large Diet Coke. She watched the highway, feeling anxious to get back to her team—Moore, Tanner, and Fischer. For a while she sensed that she was being watched: a booth of four smooth-skinned young girls across the room. They went quiet as soon as she looked. One of the girls' smiles reminded Hunter of her mother when she was young. She glanced over at them as she ate, imagining how each of their faces would change as they aged, how their cheeks would loosen and lines would etch into their skin. She only stopped doing it when her phone buzzed. This time it was her boss, Hank Moore.

"We got a trace back from one of your crank calls, Hunter," he said. "From Friday night?"

"All right."

"We've ID'd the phone. A woman named Leslie Kue. She works here, in Records."

"It wasn't her, though."

"No. How do you know?"

"I'm guessing."

"No, she lost her phone that night. It turned up Saturday morning. The thing is, she knows where she lost it. She was out at Kent's Crab House after midnight. There's security tape. We should have an ID in the morning."

"Okay." Hunter looked out: a semi-trailer truck pulling in. "I'll be back tonight."

"Let's meet at nine thirty in the a.m. I want Fischer and Tanner in now."

"Okay." *Good*, Hunter thought. This meant that Moore was going to bring the full resources of the homicide unit into play.

Hunter let her mind drift as she drove south. She was in central Delaware when her phone rang again; she was pleased to see Fischer's name on the readout.

"Got a few things."

"That was quick."

"This a good time?"

"Perfect."

Fischer was in his element, data-mining, although sometimes he went places he shouldn't. Hunter heard an energy in his voice that she liked.

"Okay, Kepler and Scott Randall. Just preliminarily. Found a couple things . . . Evidently they may have met in their twenties. At college."

"Really."

"Both went to Columbia. Took same art class. This was thirty-two years ago," he said in his verbal shorthand. "Early Modernism . . . which means, pre–nineteen twenty. Picasso. Matisse."

"Not Rembrandt."

"Rembrandt was earlier. Sixteen oh one to sixteen sixty-nine."

"Okay."

"Randall's first wife, maiden name Catherine Collins, was also in the class. Art history teacher now, Cornell. She worked for

Kepler, too, at one time, and may have dated him. Remarried twelve years ago."

"Good."

"I did find more on Kepler's background, too."

"Go ahead."

Papers rustled. "Okay. Kepler. Grew up, Brooklyn, New York. Only child. His father was an art writer. Opened a small art gallery. When Kepler was twenty-two, his father died of heart disease, and he inherited the gallery."

Ten years later, he went on, Kepler sold his interest in the gallery and became a private art dealer. He became rich when he sold an inherited Picasso for $16.3 million. Kepler then married a painter he had once championed; it broke up after two years. Bitter divorce.

"And nothing on Belasco?" Hunter asked.

She heard him turning a page. "Not yet. Just getting started. I find one hundred eight Belascos in the United States. Stephen Belasco, in Philadelphia, who may be an art dealer. There's a Darren Belasco, who's done time for burglary, including stolen art. I'm still running it down."

"No connection with Kepler, though, or with Randall?"

"Not yet."

"What kind of name is it?" she asked, mostly because she was curious, and because she suspected he'd checked on this.

"Spanish. Basque origins."

"'Kay."

Hunter tracked with the shades of the night sky, letting the details Fischer had recited assemble themselves in her thoughts. "And how about the images?" She had asked for security-camera tape of Nick Champlain, Sally Markos, Joey Sanders, and Elena Rodgers.

"Still coming in. I just left a first round on your desk. And we're getting another batch of phone records and e-mails, too. New source. I'll have more in the morning."

"What do you mean, new source?"

"Joe Sanders's wife. Widow. Provided e-mail and phone accounts voluntarily. We're going through them. I'm working from home."

"Terrific. Great. Great work."

"M'kay," he said, cutting her off.

The countryside had turned foggy by the time Hunter rolled back into Tidewater County. Tompkin Creek wound like a smoky serpent through the marshes and farm fields, crossed by three separate bridges along Route 12.

Hunter was formulating a new idea about the case now. It was probably wrong, but it might explain the part that most troubled her. She kept thinking about the image from her dream the night before: Susan Champlain on the front of the boat, about to be washed overboard; Scott Randall pretending to steady her but actually preparing to push her over. Why *had* she gone to Pastor Luke? And why had she told him what she did?

Some*one*'s going to get hurt.

Chapter Thirty

Hunter followed the sound of Winston's deep-toned "meow" to the linen closet, where he'd managed to jump from the hamper onto the third shelf, and was stretched out on a pile of clean sheets, very proud of himself. It was another first for Winston.

"Well, that looks mighty comfortable," she said, rubbing under his chin. Winston squawked, pretending to be mad. But she continued to rub and he purred, forgetting himself for a few blissful moments. "I envy you a little, Winnie, you know that. If I could just perch in a linen closet all day, life would be so much easier. But someone has to go out and solve homicides."

This drew another, disapproving, squawk.

Winston stayed in the closet as Hunter went to her computer and checked messages, but he continued to make noises, no doubt hoping to lure her back, while making it clear that he wasn't going to simply forget that she had left him alone with Grace Pappas.

When she did try to rub him again, Winston let out a high-pitched warning, which sounded like the single note of a seagull. "Okay, now quit that," she said.

But she knew what he wanted: a healthy dollop of Fancy Feast

Tuna Florentine, in a Delicate Sauce, even though he'd already had dinner.

So she gave him a generous serving, setting his plate right there in the linen closet, and headed out the door. "Sorry, Winston," she said. "I need to get back to work for a while."

He was eating intently, and paid her no attention.

It was 9:41 when Hunter walked into the PSC, anxious to see what Fischer had left on her desk. She was surprised to see the lights on back in Homicide.

Tanner was in his office, his door wide open, hunched over his notebook.

They exchanged "Hey"s as Hunter came through the reception area. Fisher's envelope was on her desk, as promised. Sealed.

"Welcome back," Tanner said, coming in with his notebook. "Surprised to hear about Sanders."

"I know."

"Suicide?"

"That's what local PD says."

Tanner watched her, his dark eyes glinting with interest. "You've already connected some of the dots, haven't you?"

"Some," Hunter said. "I could use some help getting the rest of them."

"What do you want me to do?"

"I'd like to know more about how Sanders spent his time here," she said. "Who he talked with. And also more about Sally Markos and Elena Rodgers. I'd like to have a better idea of what their life was like here in Tidewater County. I'd like us to trace their movements as closely as possible on Tuesday and Wednesday."

He was writing in his notebook, still standing, each assignment on a separate line, in small, neat print.

"And someone else: Marc Devlin. He's the manager of the Empress Gallery in town. Can you find out where he was at the time Susan was killed?"

"Sure."

"And finally: I wonder if there's any record of Scott Randall being in town around the time of her death."

His pen hand stilled. "Who's Scott Randall?"

"The FBI man who contacted me last Friday. He's head of the art crimes unit."

"Oh." He added it on a new line.

"That can go to the bottom of the list," Hunter said.

"It is."

"Whatever you can find, we're meeting in the morning."

"I know, I heard." He flipped back several pages. Hunter knew he'd already gotten started while she was away, getting a leg up on Fischer, probably.

"I found a little background on Sally Markos already. The housekeeper," he said. "Want to hear?"

"Please."

Hunter nodded for him to sit and he did, folding into one of the guest chairs. She leaned back and waited as he found it in his notebook. "Okay, Sally Markos: married, lives here year-round, rents an apartment with her husband at Piper Inlet. No children. She was hired by Nick Champlain at the beginning of summer. Cleans the house once a week. She also cleans apartments and does general maintenance at Oyster Cove. Worked at Oyster Cove for about six years. People like her. Good personality. Plays the lottery. Picks up odd cleaning jobs where she can. She's thirty-seven. From Baltimore originally."

"Who's her husband?"

"Rob Markos. Oysterman. He's a native of the Shore, grew up near Cambridge." Hunter kept glancing at the sealed envelope Fischer had left for her. "Apparently, he's gone out flounder fishing in the Bay with Joey Sanders a couple of times."

"So they knew each other."

"Not well. Sanders liked to drink and fish, I was told. A lot of people knew him down at the docks. Markos likes to drink, too."

"Did this Rob Markos know Susan Champlain?"

"I don't think so. He knew who she was. Fisch sent you those photos, right?"

She tapped the envelope once.

"How about Elena Rodgers?" Hunter asked. "Anything on her?"

His eyes lowered. He flipped back a couple pages. "Not much, no. Came here from Philly in mid-June to work for Champlain. Worked as kind of a personal assistant for him."

"So that would have been after *he* came down?"

"A week or two after, that's right." Hunter studied his long, unrevealing face. "And, as of yesterday, Champlain's business manager tells me, she doesn't work for him anymore."

"Really. Do we know why?"

"Nope. Wouldn't comment."

"There are rumors Champlain and Elena Rodgers were having an affair, right?" Hunter said.

"It's possible," Tanner said. "Except people say she wasn't the usual type Nick Champlain hired."

"What's the 'usual' type?"

He frowned at his notebook. "He tended to hire certain physical types: thin, young, lots of hair." Tanner kept his eyes down, uncomfortable saying this. "Elena was a little older. There was something maybe a little tough about her manner. Not her appearance, but her manner. Like you didn't mess with her."

"Where is she now?"

"Gone. Champlain's attorney says she moved back to Philly Friday morning. But, so far, I'm not finding anything on her there. There's no address, no DMV record, no social, no employment records. Fischer may be checking on tax records."

"Maybe Elena Rodgers isn't her real name."

"Maybe."

That was interesting. Hunter glanced out at the night fog moving through the pinewoods. "I guess no one checked her room at the Old Shore Inn?"

"I was there this afternoon. It's been rented out twice since she left. People knew her, but not well. She was always polite. Made a nice enough impression. I still have a couple of folks to talk with."

"Okay, good."

He was looking at her intently, waiting for Hunter to bring him in.

"You're acting like Sanders is a homicide," he finally said.

"Yeah," Hunter said. "I think it is."

"Who? Why?"

"I don't know yet." Hunter knew that he had his own ideas about the case and he'd been waiting for her to see if they meshed with hers. "What do *you* think?"

"What do I think? I think maybe Susan Champlain was a crime of passion."

"Perpetrated by—?"

"Joey Sands."

"Okay," Hunter said. "Why?"

His eyelids lowered a fraction. "I'm told he had a hair-trigger temper. And I found there was an assault charge against him in Pennsylvania in two thousand four. Involving a woman he'd allegedly been harassing. Also, his story didn't hold together very well when he was interviewed."

"Okay."

"And the ID on the pickup."

All of that made sense.

"But why a crime of passion with Susan Champlain?"

"Maybe he'd made an advance on her?"

"Maybe."

"Or. Maybe she'd just looked at him wrong, and it got him upset. The husband was out of town at the time, Sanders had been drinking."

"Although no one ever saw anything between them before, right?" Hunter said. "In fact, he was very careful around her, wasn't he? Champlain was his livelihood."

A slight tilt of his head conceded the point. "I'm just saying, I think he was capable of it," Tanner said.

"And so, what—? Then he felt remorse and took his own life?"

Tanner shrugged. "Or maybe the husband came after him."

Hunter nodded, although she didn't believe it.

"I did talk with someone who'd seen her out there at Widow's Point before. Jason Glasser, who works for the county parks. He says he saw her there twice. She'd ride her bicycle and sit on the rock behind the growth of bushes on the ledge. I went out and had a look. It's a very dangerous spot."

"I know," Hunter said.

But he could see that she wasn't buying it. "You think it was premeditated," Tanner said.

"I don't know, I'm leaning that way. A crime of passion, but a different kind of passion." He lifted his head alertly, waiting for more. "Of course, these are often difficult cases to prove," Hunter added, "as you know. Anyway, we'll pick it up in the morning. Thanks for all your great work."

"Okay."

His eyes lingered a moment after he stood. Then he nodded at the envelope. A trace of smile lifted the corners of his mouth.

"Got that sealed tight, I see."

"Yep."

He moved toward the door. "I'm not sure Fisch has quite warmed to me yet."

"Acquired taste, probably." Hunter smiled up at him.

"Probably."

She hadn't indicated *which* was the acquired taste. Both, really. Tanner lowered his voice. "I hope that's all it is," he said.

"Why, what else would it be?" Hunter asked.

"I don't know. I'd hate to think racism has anything to do with it."

Oh. His long face was like a mask again. Hunter had no idea what he meant, or if he was putting her on. But she was tired and didn't want to know. She wanted to see what was in the envelope.

She was glad when Tanner finally said, "Hasta la vista," and she heard his footsteps echoing down the hallway.

Hunter opened the envelope. She skimmed through the report the techs had prepared, the phone messages and e-mails from the ISP. Sally Markos, the housecleaner, and Joseph Sanders's widow Beth, had both voluntarily let investigators access their cell phones; they'd found numbers and e-mail addresses for Joey Sanders, Elena Rodgers, and Nick Champlain. Tomorrow, she hoped, Moore would file warrants to access *their* phone and e-mail accounts.

She stayed another hour in the office, until she could barely remain awake. Walking to her car, Hunter stopped and listened to the night air. There it was again: that restless back-and-forth sound high in the trees that she didn't quite remember from any other summer. She heard it later, too, waking in the middle of the night in her bed, with Winston snoring softly beside her head, the boat ties creaking on the docks and a soft cry of the rusty hinge on the old Texaco sign at the harbor: the wind back and forth in the trees like human breathing, the night inhaling and exhaling, as if someone else were there with her.

Chapter Thirty-one

Luke dressed quietly in the space they called the sitting room, careful not to wake Charlotte, who liked to sleep in until 8 or 8:30 and then stay in bed for another half hour or so reading.

But when Luke and Sneakers came in from their walk to the bluff, he was surprised to smell coffee and hear a rousing crescendo of violins.

Charlotte was at the kitchen table in her white silk bathrobe, listening to her classical music and gazing at the front page of the *Tidewater Times*. Sneakers trotted to his bowl and began to lap loudly.

"Did you see this?" she said, tapping the front page. "Iran wants to negotiate now?"

"I heard," Luke said. "Which, to me, is nearly as surprising as you being up at seven fifteen in the morning."

"Well, I must've caught what you had overnight."

"Which is?"

"I don't know. Restless brain syndrome?"

"Oh, that."

She nodded out the kitchen window at the marshlands. "Beautiful morning, isn't it? I thought we might take a drive down to Widow's Point after breakfast and have a look. The three of us."

"Widow's Point?"

"Mmm-hmm. Isn't that where you're heading? Or will you wait until later. Two oh three, perhaps?"

Sneakers lifted his head and looked at Luke, as if following the conversation.

"How'd you know?"

"I called the church yesterday afternoon," she said. "I was told you'd just gone out for an hour."

"Why do you say two oh three?"

"Low tide?"

"I see." Not much got by Charlotte. "You haven't been spying on me, I hope?"

"No. But Aggie knew, somehow. She said she'd seen you there."

Luke snorted and smiled to himself. He shouldn't have been surprised that Aggie would know, but he was.

Fifty minutes later, he parked along the access road and the three of them walked in silence out across the isolated beach where Susan Champlain's life had ended. The air was cool and salty, smelling of wet sand. There was a couple way down by the south point, walking the other way; otherwise, the beach was empty. Luke had that same unsettled feeling as he'd had before, a sense that some unfinished business had been left here. The beach was wide, slick with receding waters; seagulls screeched, diving through the shadows, the morning sunlight giving the cliff fringe a fiery yellow glow.

"How many times have you come here?" Charlotte asked as they walked through the shade.

"Three?"

"Not including this one."

"No."

"So, four."

"Okay."

"What are we looking for? The phone?"

"Not really." Luke stopped and turned to the water, the light causing his eyes to squint. "At first, I guess I was."

"Something more intangible, then, now."

"Probably."

"Okay."

Charlotte reached for his hand. She swung it slightly as they walked down the beach out of the shade. It'd been a while since they'd done this and it felt good.

"You wanted to come here alone," she said. "I'm sorry."

"No, I'm glad we're doing this," Luke said. Adding, after several steps, "I'm disappointed in a way that more people haven't come here. It feels like Susan's life has receded too quickly. As often happens."

She tightened her hand on his. Sneakers charged ahead chasing seagulls, acting as if he might actually catch one.

"Should we try throwing him a stick?" Charlotte suggested. "I don't know that we've ever tried that."

"You know what they say about old dogs."

"Old?"

"Middle-aged."

Charlotte managed to find a stick, a branch that must've fallen from the cliffside. She pulled her hand over it, pruning the leaves, and then shook it enticingly in front of Sneakers's eyes. "Want this?" she asked. She shook it a few more times, and then feigned a throw. But Sneakers just sat, pulled back his ears, and made a sound like he was hungry.

"Want the stick?" Charlotte said. "Want the *stick*?!" She wound back and hurled it, a pretty good throw, Luke thought. "Go on, Sneak! Go! Go get it! Retrieve!"

The excited tenor of her voice caused Sneakers to run several steps, but they were in the wrong direction. He stopped, looked down the beach, then turned around and trotted to Luke.

"He's not a stick dog," Luke said, crouching as his ears pulled back.

Charlotte looked momentarily stricken.

"I think the fad of chasing sticks may be passé now, anyway," Luke said. "Like Frisbees and bandannas."

"You think?"

"It's an idea, anyway. Chasing sticks always struck me as kind of dumb to begin with."

"Well, yes," Charlotte said. "But you could say that about most human activities."

"True."

Luke gave Sneakers what he really wanted—a vigorous neck and chin rub—and Sneakers soon got on his side, turning it into a full belly rub. Charlotte began to walk away by herself up the beach, into the breeze. Luke sat in the sand and watched her for a while, a little spellbound by her shadow and silhouette against the blue sparkles of the Bay.

Sneakers broke away from him and galloped off in Charlotte's direction. Seagulls, again. Charlotte turned to him, walking backwards. She made an exaggerated shrug, turning her palms up. Luke smiled and stood. He looked up at the bluff, the fan of sunlight reminding him of the police floodlights last Wednesday night, the crowd gathered to look. Would it ever be possible to come to Widow's Point and not think about Susan Champlain, about how her life had ended?

Luke began walking, scanning the surf for a while, rubbing his feet in the sand. The dead don't come back; but the objects they've left behind don't just disappear, either. Susan hadn't come here wearing one sandal. And it wasn't likely she'd come without her cell phone. Something had happened to them.

They searched the beach separately for close to twenty minutes, Sneakers staying mostly with Charlotte, although at one point he sprinted back to Luke like a greyhound racer.

"What is it, Sneak?"

Sneakers made a small circle in the sand and then just sat down and stared at him, breathing wildly. He trotted back, at a more reasonable pace, to Charlotte.

A few minutes later, Luke noticed Charlotte moving her arms overhead in semaphore-like motions, her voice lost in the blue expanse between them. Luke began to jog to her.

Sneakers was half circling a spot in the sand when he got there, as if *he'd* discovered something. "What is it?" he said. "A giant meat bone?"

"No." Charlotte showed him what she had found with her toes in the sand by the surf. She held it out and dropped it in his hand: a pendant, heart-shaped, covered with diamonds. Probably worth hundreds of dollars.

Luke had an idea what it might be before she said anything. They both stared at it in the folds of his hand.

"Maybe it goes with the necklace?"

"I was going to say that."

"Which would mean she fought with someone," Charlotte said.

"Yes."

"Who tore off the necklace in the process. The clasp was broken, wasn't it?"

"I think so," Luke said.

He felt a sudden, inexplicable affection for Charlotte. As they began to walk back, he stopped and gave her a hug, feeling the breeze lifting her hair. And then he kissed her, and she made the kiss go on for a while.

"I'm glad we did this," he said. "Thank you."

"Me, too."

They walked to the car holding hands, thinking about what she'd found, and then drove home along the coast road without talking. At one point, Charlotte reached over and wrapped her right hand around his left. He didn't realize at first that she was trying to open it, to have another look at the pendant.

"I guess I ought to take this over to Hunter," he said.

Charlotte smiled.

THE PENDANT FELT to Luke like a puzzle piece. And the idea of a puzzle seemed like a suitable container for Sunday's sermon: the puzzle of how to best live our day-to-day lives; the puzzle of faith, of God's "secret wisdom," from First Corinthians; the puzzle of desire: wanting to fill the church each week with people who cared deeply, who took the message of the sermon home with them.

Sermon ideas came in flashes like that; sometimes they panned out, often they didn't. He was mulling over the puzzle idea as he walked into the Public Safety Complex.

Hunter was in the lobby, waiting for him. "Morning," she said, bounding up from a chair. "Sorry, I can't ask you back."

"No, that's—"

"We're meeting in a few minutes. It's a busy morning," she said, setting her hands on her hips. "I really enjoyed dinner the other night."

"We did, too. No, that's fine," Luke said. "I just wanted to show you something. It won't take more than a minute."

Hunter seemed a little frazzled, Luke saw; her shirt was tucked in funny and one of her collar points was askew, her hair sticking out on one side as if she'd just climbed out of bed. But her light brown eyes had fixed on his like lasers.

"Is there anything new?" he said. "With the case."

"Well. Yeah. Joey Sanders is dead, for one thing. Down in Virginia. You know who he was?"

"Sure," Luke said, surprised. "Nick Champlain's assistant. His bodyguard. What happened?"

"Don't know yet. Local PD thinks suicide. I can tell you more after our meeting. It's—" Her eyes widened briefly with an unfamiliar impatience. "What've you got?"

Luke opened his left hand to show her the pendant. "Something Charlotte found," he said. "In the surf at Widow's Point this morning. I thought you might find it interesting."

Hunter carefully took the pendant between her fingers. She placed it delicately in the palm of her own left hand, and wobbled it side to side. Luke was struck by the intense interest that suddenly shone in her eyes.

"I—we—thought maybe it was possible that this goes with the necklace you found."

She was nodding vaguely, studying the pendant, the jewels glinting in the dull lobby light. "Tell me where you found it."

Hunter's impatience had evaporated; her fascination with the pendant seemed all-consuming. Luke watched her as she studied it, holding it inches from her face.

LUKE DROVE HOME with a new curiosity, as if Hunter's interest had been contagious. The pendant went with the necklace Hunter had found in the sand the night Susan Champlain died, yes. But there was something else about it. Hunter had seen something that he hadn't. He was fairly certain about that. He glanced several times at the dash clock, wondering how long she'd be in her meeting.

Chapter Thirty-two

There were two theories Amy Hunter had been playing with that morning, each exclusive of the other; each leading to a different explanation for Susan Champlain's death. One was what Gerry Tanner had suggested the night before: that Joseph Sanders had killed Susan Champlain in an alcohol-fueled crime of passion; and that, for whatever reason, his own death two days later had been a consequence. This seemed the less likely of the two, but the easier to explain.

Pastor Luke had just nudged her toward the other one: that the perpetrator was someone nobody had considered.

One of the files that Sonny Fischer had sent to her yesterday contained thirty still images from security tapes turned over by four Tidewater businesses. Sixteen new images were in her e-mail this morning. Each corresponded to a digital file, which Fisch or another homicide investigator had looked through. For now, with the meeting minutes away, Hunter needed only a single image. She scrolled through the sixteen new ones, and found it—among the pictures of Elena Rodgers, not those of Susan Champlain. Time-stamped last Monday morning at 8:23:

Rodgers walking through the lobby at the Old Shore Inn, where she'd been renting a room for the past six weeks. A fit-looking, nicely postured woman wearing a light-colored sleeveless dress, a thin valise under one arm. Headed over to Nick Champlain's house, probably, where she worked for several hours three days a week, answering mail, keeping his appointments calendar. Cool but hard. Her dark eyes turned to the security camera in one of the images; wide shoulders, arms slightly buffed, thick swoops of light brown hair, hard facial features.

Hunter enlarged the image, to just the shoulders and head; the pixels blurred, but it was clear enough. Hunter compared the shape, the texture, the number of diamonds. There was no question: On Monday morning, Elena Rodgers had been wearing the same pendant that was now sitting on Hunter's desk in Homicide.

It was 9:24. She made a printout of the image and saved it to her desktop. Then she got up and walked to the conference room two doors down.

Hank Moore was at the head of the table, studying a single-page report, something unrelated to the case. His transistor radio was on top of a pile of folders, turned off. He wasn't big on greetings. Tanner was there with his leather notebook opened to blank facing pages, his right hand wrapped around a coffee mug. His dark eyes glistened, watching her as she came in. Hunter sat across from him and nodded hello.

Finally, Moore looked up.

"Morning, Hunter," he said. "Want to get the door?"

"Sorry," she said, standing. "Where's Fisch?"

"Sonny's working on something at home," he said, "for you."

"Okay." Hunter closed the door and sat. She'd hoped the peace pipe might be passed between Fisch and Tanner this morning. But it would have to wait.

"We've got the footage, Hunter," Moore said. His eyes narrowed and he nodded grimly at his computer. "Your crank caller."

"Crank" was an interesting word choice, Hunter thought. "You know who it is?"

His eyes nodded. "Not what we expected. It's probably going to flip your wig a little when you see it."

Tanner lowered his eyes; she could see that he didn't know yet. Hunter had begun to think the caller might just be a disturbed prankster, nothing to do with the Champlain killing; she kept thinking of Marc Devlin, the art gallery manager, whom she liked; or John Linden, the uptight ex of Susan Champlain, whom she didn't. Or the sheriff's deputy, Barry Stilfork, who always reminded her of a cat under a chair, thinking that if he couldn't see you, you couldn't see him. At this point, though, she realized that she no longer particularly cared *who* it was.

"I've got something, too," she said.

"Okay."

"Let me go first?"

Moore squinted his eyes. He shifted in his chair so his left shoulder was more prominent. He coughed once, then he nodded.

NICHOLAS CHAMPLAIN GOT on the road at 8:30 that morning, driving the white Chevy van he'd purchased a month earlier and kept stored in a garage seven blocks from his downtown office. He followed Vincent Rosa's instructions on the cell phone that Rosa had delivered to his mailbox that morning. The directions took him on a convoluted route that threaded through the Philadelphia suburbs, looped way out toward Amish country and returned through the suburbs to downtown Philly.

The first stage was an elaborate series of detours, meant to reassure Rosa that Champlain wasn't setting him up, or being followed. There was no rulebook for this sort of thing; Champlain and Kepler had to abide by whatever Vincent Rosa gave them.

When Rosa was satisfied that Champlain wasn't being followed, he directed him to a metered parking lot near Torresdale Station. Nick parked, leaving his keys under the passenger seat, and fed the meter for two hours. Minutes later, Vincent Rosa pulled up, in a Lexus SUV. Champlain stepped out of the van and got into Rosa's passenger seat.

Rosa drove another circuitous route, the radio playing classical music. Kepler, listening in, was amused to hear that it was Mozart's final symphony, of all things. He doubted that Champlain had any idea what he was hearing. Twice, Rosa stopped in a parking lot and waited; each time, nothing happened.

He eventually pulled into a small parking lane above the Schuylkill River, two slots from the other parked vehicle, a white van. It was the same van that Champlain had left in the city two hours earlier. Frank Rosa, Vincent's younger brother, was sitting behind the steering wheel.

The masterpiece was now in the back of Champlain's van. Nick had five minutes to go inside, close the door and examine it. It was unlikely the Rosas would try to sell him a forgery; but it was possible they wouldn't know the difference.

Five minutes later, Champlain emerged out the front passen-

ger door and returned to Vincent Rosa's car. Vincent waited for
the van to pull out, Frank driving, and followed behind at a reasonable distance. Then Vincent handed Nick Champlain a phone.

Jacob Weber, sitting with Kepler at his condo in Delaware,
took Champlain's call.

"I'm clear," Champlain said.

"All right."

Kepler's attorney digitally authorized the payment transfer,
four million dollars to the account Rosa had set up in Bermuda.
They all waited again, monitoring the transmission by computer. Ten minutes later, the money had been drained. Five
million dollars gone now, with the down payment.

Kepler listened to the thin droning of the car engine. This
was the unnerving part, the part where the Rosas could take the
money and make the painting disappear, if they wanted; where
Kepler could lose the whole deal. Five million dollars *and* the
painting.

But he didn't.

Maybe it was the shared knowledge that there was an even
bigger deal waiting after this one. Maybe it was Nick Champlain.
Or maybe it was just the principle of honor among thieves.

Vincent Rosa called ahead to signal Frank in the van. Kepler
listened. Twenty minutes later, Frank pulled the van into a remote
bend of a public park and stopped. The Lexus followed, parking
beside it. Doors opened and closed: Frank Rosa and Champlain
trading places, Nick back behind the wheel of his van.

"Be safe," Kepler heard Vincent Rosa say.

The Chevy van was still running. Kepler heard Nick shift and back up. He listened as the van's engine accelerated. Another several unnerving minutes. But nothing happened. "All right," he heard Nick Champlain say, cheering himself. "All right."

He was on his own now, driving away toward the Delaware Expressway with Rembrandt's 1633 masterpiece in the back. It was 2:37. Champlain was headed toward a farmhouse in the Pennsylvania countryside. The painting now belonged to him. Three hours later, it would be Kepler's.

Chapter Thirty-three

You know who killed her," Tanner said.

"I think I do."

"I thought so when we talked last night."

Tanner turned his eyes to their boss, Hank Moore. Moore's left hand was bouncing absently above the table, as if his transistor radio were playing. Tanner always lost a little of his self-assurance around Moore.

"I didn't know it then," Hunter said. "I have evidence now."

She showed them the printout of Elena Rodgers, Champlain's personal assistant, walking through the lobby of the Old Shore Inn Monday morning. Then she opened her left hand to display the diamond pendant. They all stared, expectantly. Tanner's mouth was open like a coin slot.

"Pastor Luke's wife discovered it in the surf this morning," she said. "Twenty-five yards from where Susan Champlain died.

"I didn't realize for sure until a half hour ago what the necklace was," Hunter continued. "I'd been assuming the necklace had been worn by Susan Champlain."

"We all had," Moore said.

"This makes it clear it wasn't."

Tanner pulled the image of Elena Rodgers to the center of the table and they all looked at it—Elena walking with a confident air through the lobby at the Old Shore Inn, her head turned to one side, the diamond heart pendant visible on top of her dress.

"So you're saying Elena Rodgers did this," Moore said.

"I think so."

"She killed Susan Champlain?" Tanner said. Both men trying to put it together.

"I think they must've struggled on the bluff," Hunter said. "Susan grabbed at Elena, she tore off her necklace. The pendant fell from the necklace on the way down. It would also explain the cuts on Susan's right arm."

She glanced up at Moore.

"There were skin flakes under Susan's fingernails. Right?" Moore asked.

"Yes. And you remember Elena Rodgers wore a windbreaker jacket Wednesday night when she came in for her interview. May have been to cover scratches Susan made on *her* arms."

"That's right," Tanner said.

Funny how things fit together when you have the correct solution, Hunter thought.

"There were also bare footprints in the sand below the point, which, from the length of the stride and the size of the foot, forensics believe were a woman's. It's probable those were Elena Rodgers'."

"Meaning what?" Moore said, watching her. "That she'd gone down there looking for the necklace? And couldn't find it?"

"We'll need to find her to prove that. But, yeah."

"Why would *she* have done it, though?" Tanner said. "Jealousy? I guess that would go to the idea that she was having an affair with Champlain."

"That's one idea," Hunter said. "Although I think the case might be more complicated than that. I think that Susan Champlain may have been killed because of what she may have known about a stolen painting," she said, speaking to Tanner. "I don't know that for sure, but that's what I think. Which means it would have been premeditated, as we were discussing last night."

"*Painting?*" Tanner said.

Hunter brought him in, then. She gave Tanner a summary of the case in five minutes—the photo of the stolen Rembrandt on Susan Champlain's phone, the Gardner theft, the call from Scott Randall, Walter Kepler—feeling a surprising relief to finally unload these details. She left out only Pastor Luke's role in the case.

Tanner listened, as still as a mannequin, surprised no doubt, maybe resentful that Hunter hadn't brought him in earlier. He raised a finger at one point, as if to ask a question, but then lowered it without asking.

"Susan Champlain was involved because her husband was involved," Hunter said. "*Is* involved. She heard odds and ends about this deal and probably didn't know what they added up to, but she'd talked about it with a few people. She may have been considered a liability and was killed because of it."

"By Elena Rodgers."

"Yes."

Moore nodded periodically, tracking with her.

"So you're saying Elena Rodgers did this on someone's *orders*?" Tanner said. "To keep her quiet?"

"I don't know, something like that," Hunter said. "Motive's still an open question."

"Never would have imagined," Moore said, shaking his head. "I had a conversation with Miss Rodgers just a couple weeks ago over at the Inn. Kind of a chilly fish, but she had some style. Never would have imagined."

"That was her leverage," Hunter said. "No one suspected her."

"So you're saying Elena Rodgers was working for this Kepler," Tanner said.

"I don't know," Hunter said. She really didn't. There was still a big part of the case—the motive—that felt murky. "It may be that Elena Rodgers is a watcher for Kepler, and that's the reason she was here in Tidewater."

"Watching Nick Champlain, you mean," Moore said.

"Yes. Maybe Kepler made him hire her as a personal assistant and he never realized who she was," Hunter said. "I've also heard, several times now, that Kepler has a partner. And that the partner is the one who does the dirty work for him."

"But you said the partner's name was Belasco," Moore said.

"I know," Hunter said. "I did. That's the name I heard."

Moore scratched absently at his left hand. "So, what—? Are you saying Elena Rodgers *is* Belasco?"

"It's possible," Hunter said. "There's no reason Belasco couldn't be a woman. Is there?"

Tanner raised his eyebrows, and kept them raised, not getting it.

"The thing that worries me—" Hunter went on. "There's a term that Kepler supposedly uses: collateral damage. I'm concerned there may be more collateral damage as this thing unfolds.

"This deal for the painting, I mean," she said. She glanced at Moore. "Although, on the other hand, that's not our case, is it?"

"Our case is finding the person who killed Susan Champlain," he said.

"Yes. And I think we just have." She nodded at the pendant. "I think we've solved the case."

Moore allowed a smile on the right side of his mouth.

Tanner said, "Do we have any leads on where Elena Rodgers is right now?"

"Not yet. As you told me last night, she seems to have disappeared. But there may be an electronic trail that we can trace. I'm sure she's in touch with Kepler, and maybe with Champlain. Computer forensics is running phone and e-mail. Fisch is monitoring that. In the meantime, maybe we can do some more datamining on her background."

They sat silently looking at the diamond pendant that Elena Rodgers had been wearing the night of Susan Champlain's death, now resting near the center of the conference table.

"What was it you wanted to show *me*?" she said finally. "My caller."

"Oh. Yeah." Moore sat up straight and cleared his throat. "I don't know if I want to show you anymore."

"Go ahead." Hunter braced, lacing her fingers on the table. It surprised her all of a sudden how much she hoped it *wasn't* Marc Devlin, the gallery manager. She liked him, she'd decided; if it turned out he'd been stalking her, it would only further Hunter's idea that she was a terrible judge of men.

"Fischer brought this in," Moore said.

"You ID'd the cell phone."

"ID'd the cell phone, that's right. The woman is from Records. She had her phone at Kent's. A bunch of folks from the cop shop were out, doing crabs and pitchers on Friday night. She left her phone sitting on a chair, someone picked it up. We have video."

"This was before the call came to me."

"Six minutes before, uh-huh."

"Okay."

"I don't know how you're going to feel about this," Moore said.

Just play it, she thought.

Moore exhaled. He turned his laptop to her. Tanner leaned over, extending his elbows on the table, to see. It was a short sequence, dark and fuzzy: bulky man in a cloth jacket, walking around a table full of crab shells and beer pitchers, his arm swooping down, lifting the phone from a chair, walking with it cupped behind his hand. The high contrast blurred his features, and he was out of the picture in a second. But Hunter could see from the halting walk who it was. Not Devlin, who moved with a light, distinctive rhythm. Or Deputy Stilfork, whose legs chopped like stilts.

None of them said anything the first time through. Then Moore ran it again.

Nothing the second time, either.

"Holy crap," Hunter said.

Tanner said, "Who is it?"

"Are we sure he made the call, though?"

"Here we go, look at this." Moore called up a second sequence and played it. This one showed the man walking past the table again, front-on now.

"That looks like the sheriff," Tanner said.

Moore closed his eyes briefly. The emotions it stirred in Hunter were slow: surprise, sadness and worry, in approximately that order. She could imagine how ugly things would get confronting the sheriff, even with this evidence. Calvert was a stubborn, prideful man who held fast to Tidewater's traditions; but this showed him as someone else—angry, resentful, petty, probably in the deep end of a drinking problem. "At least we know the calls weren't connected with Susan's death," she said.

"Yep."

"What are we going to do about it?" she asked Moore.

"What do you think?"

"Can we do nothing?"

Tanner's eyes were back with the pendant.

"I can't really do *nothing*."

"For now, I mean. Until we're on the other side of this case," she said. "I don't think it matters for now. Does it? Now that we know?"

Moore fidgeted; he tilted his head, meaning *Maybe. I don't know.* Then he gave Hunter his agreeable, squinty-eyed look, and leaned back. "For now," he said.

"I THINK A little Bowers will go a long way," Charlotte told Luke when he returned home.

"I do, too." He smiled at her. "Did you just think of that?"

"A minute ago. Yeah. Are you back home to work on our project or—?"

"I left my sermon notebook, actually. Although, now that you mention it . . ."

Sneakers lifted his head from the Indian rug below Charlotte, his tail thumping three times, stopping, and then thumping again. Confused: Luke hadn't been gone long enough to warrant a full-press greeting; but it wasn't like he'd just gone to the other room, either. Sneakers lowered his chin to the floor and closed his eyes. A moment later, his tail thumped once more.

"So?" she asked, turning her chair from the computer. "What did Hunter say?"

"She wasn't able to talk. She was going into a meeting and seemed quite harried."

"I worry about her a little."

"You told me," he said. "She seemed very interested in the pendant, though, but didn't have time to get into it."

"I don't think it belongs to Susan," Charlotte said.

"You don't. Why?"

"Because she didn't wear necklaces. And I don't think she'd wear a heart-shaped diamond one if she did."

"So you think it's unrelated?"

"Yes. Unless Susan was fighting with someone on the bluff, and in the process the necklace was torn off—but it was the *other* person who was wearing it."

"Well, that's an idea I hadn't thought of," Luke said. "Although I doubt if Joseph Sanders would've been wearing a heart-shaped diamond necklace."

She gave him her contrarian's frown. "A woman."

"Oh, okay. Any suggestions?"

"I don't know," she said. "Elena Rodgers?"

"Really?"

She shrugged. "Probably not. Except: I almost think I saw her wearing that necklace once. Or else heart-shaped earrings. I've been sitting here trying to remember. She's a strange, very detached woman. Not right for the job of Nick Champlain's assistant at all."

"I didn't think you knew her."

"I don't, of course. But I observed her. I spoke with her once, at the Shore Inn. She was sitting on the porch, reading John Hersey's book on *Hiroshima*, of all things."

"Huh."

"I *tried* to talk with her, rather. It wasn't easy . . . Anyway."

"Hmm," Luke said. He was thinking again about the sermon he had to write, on the puzzle of faith: the assurance of things hoped for, the conviction of things not yet known. "And what's the deal with *that*?" he said, nodding toward the two coffee-table art books on her desk; one opened to a self-portrait he recognized. "You're reading about Rembrandt now?"

"Yeah." Charlotte smiled, the parentheses showing on either side of her mouth. "I went by the library. This whole thing has made me sort of curious, I guess. I always wonder why one artist stays so prominent for hundreds of years, while others are forgotten."

"Any theories?"

"One or two. Rembrandt painted these dark and superficially unattractive scenes," she said, turning pages in the book to show him. "But there was always this mysterious thing going on underneath, as if they were lit up from within. It's like he dipped his paintbrush in sunlight, someone said. And that relationship between light and dark—it gets at something that you don't quite find in any other artist."

"Something in human nature."

"Well, yes. I can see why people become obsessed with Rembrandt."

"Like Walter Kepler."

"I guess so." Charlotte gave him an expectant look, saying Your Turn.

"I guess I better get my notebook . . . unless . . ."

"Unless?"

"You wanted to work on our project."

"You're a devil," Charlotte said.

"No, I'm not. Unless you want me to be . . ."

"Figure of speech. Okay," she said. "Actually, that's an interesting idea. Except you're supposed to be at work, aren't you?"

"It's been a while since I've played hooky, though."

"Let's play hooky, then."

Charlotte stood and they kissed, and then walked into the bedroom holding hands. "I do want this," she said.

They'd just gotten started when Luke's cell phone rang. He didn't have to look to see who was calling, but he did.

"Aren't you going to answer?" Charlotte asked.

"No," he said. "I'll let it ring."

Chapter Thirty-four

Fischer came into Hunter's office that afternoon with a vinyl zip-satchel full of papers. He had what he promised would be "all kinds" of new information. Moore had authorized the department to gather ISP records, and Fischer, acting as an intermediary with the state police computer forensics lab, had collected and evaluated all they'd turned over so far and produced a two-page summary.

The original access points had been Sally Markos's and Beth Sanders's cell phones, from which the state computer forensics lab had produced records of hundreds of phone calls and e-mail exchanges. More was coming. The most relevant information so far, according to Fischer's summary, was an exchange of eight e-mails back and forth between erbela@gmail, who had also e-mailed with Markos once, and someone using the handle vanrijn1633@gmail. They were the only e-mails that had turned up on the vanrijn account.

"E-R Bela," Hunter said, getting it right away. "ER as in Elena Rodgers. Bela as in Belasco."

Fischer's face seemed to tighten. He didn't yet know that Elena

Rodgers and Belasco might be the same person. This seemed a pretty strong corroboration.

"There's also an old number for Kepler that still works," Fischer said, just as Hunter was about to gently scold him for missing the morning meeting. Administration didn't come to her naturally.

"It 'still works.' Meaning—you called it?"

He nodded.

"Left a message?"

"Just called, to see if it worked."

"And hung up?"

"It's there," he said, pointing at a line on the summary.

Hunter read through the whole summary as he sat there. Then she filled him in on what had happened at the meeting. If he'd attended, he would have written a different memo, she said. He would have known that Elena Rodgers was now the prime suspect in Susan Champlain's murder. Fischer's face held a blank look.

"The last message is interesting," he said, interrupting her.

The last e-mail from erbela to vanrijn1633, he meant.

Sent yesterday at 3:37 in the afternoon. Fisch had bolded it in the memo: *Onward, then. Thursday end of day, at Half Past Three. B.*

vanrijn1633 had written back a one-word response: *Yes.*

vanrijn had to be Kepler, Hunter thought. As in Rembrandt van Rijn.

"This is good," she said, wanting some time alone with the raw data. "Great work."

Fischer's face darkened slightly. Hunter knew him well enough to know that he appreciated compliments but that, like many people, he wasn't good at accepting them.

"We're all meeting this afternoon at two thirty, by the way," she said, as he began to leave. "I need you to attend."

"M'kay."

"Okay?"

He nodded once; he wasn't going to say it again. Hunter stayed at her desk until the meeting, going through the e-mail and phone records, feeling a rising excitement for a while, followed by a sense of letdown: most of the intercepted information was unrevealing. The phone records contained a few interesting patterns—several calls back and forth between Sally Markos and Joe Sanders, for instance—but not much that was actionable, and nothing offering valuable information about Sanders's or Susan's last hours. Joey Sanders's only calls, besides those to Sally Markos, had been to his wife, Beth, in Pennsylvania.

Hunter called the number Fisch had given her for Kepler, which Delaware police had traced to a cell phone registered to a Jacob Weber almost five years earlier. She got a robotlike automated voice.

Shortly before the afternoon meeting, she sent her own messages—to erbela and vanrijn1633. The same message to each: "This is Amy Hunter of the Maryland State Police. I'd like to talk with you ASAP regarding a case I'm investigating." With the subject line: "Request from Amy Hunter, Maryland State Police." She left both her cell phone and office numbers.

erbela.

Hunter stared at the last of the e-mails from Elena Rodgers's account. If there was anything here that offered a good clue, this seemed to be it: *Onward, then. Thursday end of day, at Half Past Three. B.* It seemed like an invitation. Did it mean the deal was going to happen on Thursday, tomorrow? Was it unrelated? Or was it a bluff?

She decided to forward the e-mail to Pastor Luke. And, though her instincts were telling her not to, she also forwarded a copy to Scott Randall at the FBI.

At 2:30, Hunter sat down in the conference room and shared the phone and e-mail evidence with Moore and Tanner. Fischer was there, his eyes lowered, eight fingertips on the edge of the table, as if he were playing piano.

"Vanrijn1633," Moore said, getting it right away. "Kepler?"

"Yes, I think so." Tanner frowned. "Sixteen thirty-three was the year that Rembrandt painted *Storm on the Sea of Galilee*. We're still sifting through the rest of it," Hunter said, nodding at Fischer, who didn't look up. "So we should have some other connections later."

Moore read through Fischer's summary carefully, even though she'd made it available to him a half hour ago. Unlike some people, he was comfortable processing information with others in the room. Not surprisingly, he zeroed in on the last e-mail from erbela.

"What's this mean?"

Hunter shook her head. "No idea. The time frame is very specific, though. Thursday being tomorrow, we could construe it as meaning that whatever's happening will happen within the next day."

"We're talking about the painting?" Tanner said.

"That's what I'm thinking," Hunter said. "Which, if so, is a lot sooner than the FBI thinks."

Moore glanced at Fischer, who was fidgeting, his fingertips

still touching the table, his eyes lowered. "I suppose we're obligated to pass this along to the FBI?"

"Already have," Hunter said. "Although they may have it, anyway. As we discussed earlier, this isn't our case. Our case is Susan Champlain. And I think we've wrapped that up."

Hunter's phone chirped. She glanced at the screen, then up at Henry Moore. It was not what she expected.

"That was quick," she said.

"What is it?"

The message was from the erbela address.

Belasco, evidently, had replied to her e-mail.

ELENA WAS DRIVING west through the Pennsylvania countryside when the incoming e-mail dinged her phone. Her thoughts, though, were in a different country. Belasco was an idea again at that point, separate from the person who was driving this white van; who took 23,000 breaths every day. The *idea* was what she breathed now: The idea that would carry her to another life in just 24 hours.

Belasco pulled over on the shoulder-less road and read the message on her phone:

> This is Amy Hunter of the Maryland State Police. I'd like to talk with you ASAP regarding a case I'm investigating.

It was the ASAP that was a little concerning. *Why ASAP?* Threat or obstacle? How had she acquired this e-mail address?

She lowered her window and let her thoughts run out for a

while. Insects hummed in the still summer air. She thought of Salvador Dali's fascinatingly grotesque dual figure, fighting with itself.

What case?

she keyed on her phone.

Why me?

Two minutes ticked by, the warm air causing her eyes to water and her throat to itch; ragweed.

Finally, a reply:

Routine investigation—death of S. Champlain last Wed.

She had not answered the second question.

Elena looked out at the rolling Pennsylvania country and re-called the rush she had felt after killing Susan Champlain, the certainty that she had gotten away with it. She recalled the taste of the cooling air that night, as she'd sat on the porch at the Old Shore Inn, smiling at the well-dressed guests, watching the wind play in those great oak leaves.

Why me? Why ASAP?

Hunter came right back this time. Again ignoring her second question.

You worked for her husband.
So?
I'm talking with thse who knew her or husband.
Didn't know her.
You knew the husband, tho.
So?
Can we talk briefly?

Her nose was beginning to run. She didn't like any of this. Eleventh hour is what Kepler called this. And then she suddenly imagined a way of heading it off. Of dealing with Hunter before the sun went down, without bringing Walter into it—unless he wanted to be brought in.

After a minute of soul-searching, she e-mailed back:

This evening?
Yes. Where are you?

Hunter typed.

In Pa. Come here?
Yes. Where and when?
Will call you. I have your #.

She cut it off there, and felt a tingle of adrenaline. She'd be seeing Kepler in another hour and a half. Which meant Elena had that much drive time to think, to figure out the details of what she wanted to do about this Amy Hunter. She hadn't thought there would need to be any more collateral damage. You send out bait, false stories, and see who takes it. Randall had bitten down hard. Not Hunter, though. Hunter was smart. Too smart evidently to survive.

BY THE TIME she arrived at Kepler's farm property, Elena had worked out Amy Hunter's fate in her head: a way to make her disappear, a place to take her, follow-up contingencies. Killing is an art form when you don't see the artist's hand. She was that kind of artist.

Weber and Champlain were already there, waiting for her. The sun was still bright over the western countryside.

She parked in the barn next to Champlain: two white vans side by side. Walter would be arriving in a third. *Three-card monte*, he had called it. Just in case.

Elena watched Nick Champlain pretending not to be surprised by her presence. He gave her a hug and a quick awkward kiss on the cheek. He was a primitive man, in most ways. She'd grown up with men like that, in Philly and in New Jersey. Her brothers had been that way; Joey Sanders had been like that. Champlain had flirted with Elena ineffectually all summer, trying to break through her defenses. So he'd probably see this as just another chance. He'd be ecstatic when he learned they were going to drive off together; that Elena was going to literally drive him away from all this.

Weber nodded an obligatory hello and then turned his narrow shoulders back to the job at hand. Strange little man. The Ant Man, she called him in her head.

Elena led Champlain to the duffel bag on the floor of her van.

She unzipped it to flash a taste: five hundred thousand dollars in cash; five thousand Ben Franklins, eleven pounds of paper currency. The rest to come. He nodded at her nonchalantly, knowing not to smile, but almost doing it anyway. His eyes sweeping over her, coming back to her neck and chest.

Together, they carried the five-foot by four-foot painting from the back of Champlain's van to the sturdy wooden easel that Walter Kepler had set up there for its afternoon showing. Then Elena and Champlain began to uncrate it as the attorney watched. She couldn't help but be entranced by what lay beneath the protective crating and wrapping paper—the stunning, layered, glazelike effects of the paint, the under-glows, the transparent darks and opaque lights dancing with one another. The elemental contrasts. No one knew exactly how Rembrandt had achieved those startling optical effects; they were not something that could ever be duplicated.

Champlain pretended to be interested, too, although his eyes traveled up and down her body again, not just over the painting.

"That's amazing," he said as she told him how Rembrandt had built his paintings, how he may have even mixed chalk and ground glass to achieve the glaze effects. Weber had walked off to the entrance of the barn where he was waiting now, rubbing at his neck, occasionally watching them. He *knew* what was going on. He was too smart not to, even if he didn't approve of her.

The possible number of things that could go wrong had diminished by several orders now, with the Rosas' part of the deal complete. If there'd been a sabotage at that level, it would be known by now.

"So where are we going after here?" Champlain asked her, making his voice whispery.

"Where do you want to go?"

Nick Champlain shrugged. "Celebrate." He said it half as a question.

"Yeah, all right," she said, knowing that saying it without emotion would only stir him further.

Elena eventually walked to the barn entrance, Champlain falling in step beside her.

The third white van had appeared, snaking over the late afternoon hillsides. Kepler. After months of planning, working out the minutiae of the negotiations, it was going to happen overnight. A week ago, they'd gone over all the possible ways this could fail, all the things that could go wrong, and addressed them one at a time. None of those things could stop them now. Of course, Amy Hunter hadn't been on that list. She'd barely existed then.

Kepler parked outside the barn. He walked toward the painting. Seeing nothing else until Elena touched his hand and stopped him. He kissed her cheek and then she told him. He listened, nodding distractedly, his eyes with the painting.

"Do what you need to do, then. It's late in the game to be dealing with this."

"I know it is."

"Do what you have to do."

Champlain was watching her as Elena walked back to the van. She shrugged instead of explaining, like a ditzy woman might shrug. Champlain let it go, a version of chivalry, perhaps. Elena understood that.

Several minutes later, they were driving back through the rolling countryside, Elena at the wheel, a half million dollars right behind them, on the floor in the backseat. Traveling, eventually, to Philadelphia, but with a promised "celebration" somewhere in between. It would be a circuitous ride.

Chapter Thirty-five

Sometimes, competition brings out the best in people. But it depends on the people, Hunter had found. Gerry Tanner and Sonny Fischer had been in competition ever since Tanner started working for the Maryland State Police in late May—it's just that Fisch wasn't aware of it. Fischer was a self-motivator; he seemed to work better without competition.

After reading Fischer's report at the afternoon meeting, Tanner had retreated a few paces, Hunter noticed; then he'd disappeared for a couple hours.

When he showed up in Hunter's office at half past four, his voice reminded her of a nervous teenager's. "I think I may finally have it," he said, sitting on the front edge of the chair.

"Okay."

"Elena Rodgers?"

"All right."

"That's who we're looking at, right? That's who you believe did this."

"Right."

"Well, I think I've got her real name. And a little more on who she is. Background, etcetera." He paused, flipping pages in his notebook, then turning back the other way. "Okay. Her name, I'm told, is Linda Elena Fiorille."

"How'd you get that?" Hunter said.

"I worked some police sources. There's a detective with PA State Police who knows about her. He didn't really want to talk, but he's one of these guys who fills in silences."

"Okay," Hunter said, not sure what he was saying.

"If this is her—and I'm pretty sure it is—she evidently comes by it honestly."

"Okay. How so?"

"Her father and her uncle, for starters. Both were quote un-quote goombahs—that's the detective's term. In Philadelphia."

"What's goombah? Mobster?"

"Mobster. Her brother, Donald Fiorille, has done time for drugs and extortion. Pennsylvania on the drugs, Florida on the extortion. Five years total. There are still some missing links, but Fiorille—Elena—definitely knows Kepler."

"How?"

"Common interests, I'm told. Meaning art, stolen art. Elena was involved in an attempt two or three years ago to fence a long-lost Picasso painting for about a million dollars. She comes by the art honestly, too. She never finished college, but most of the classes she took, I'm told—this was at University of Delaware—were art history." Tanner's voice kept shifting to a higher register, lifted by the excitement of what he was saying; but his face remained virtually expressionless.

"Why do you say she knows Kepler, though?"

"This detective thinks they were romantically involved. *Are* romantically involved."

"Really."

"Yeah." He tilted his head to one side, a shrug.

So partner means *romantic* partner. *Why hadn't I thought of that before?*

"Did this deal with the Picasso involve Kepler, then?"

"That's what he said. This was in Upstate New York but involved PA tangentially." Tanner flipped a page. "Kepler was an interested party for a while, evidently, and then backed out. The painting in question turned out to be a forgery. The wife of an art dealer was killed not long afterward, in what this detective tells me was an execution-style hit. Quote unquote. For a while, she was considered a suspect."

"*Elena* was considered a suspect?"

"That's right."

"Wow. Too bad we didn't know any of this before."

Tanner sighed. "We probably should have," he said, closing his notebook, possibly a shot at Fischer. "We didn't go deep enough into it, I guess. This guy—my source—was reluctant to say *any*thing at first. But me mentioning Kepler and then the name Elena—anyway, there's probably a lot more there."

No doubt, Hunter thought. "Okay." So this *was* something that Fischer had missed, focused as he was on the electronic traffic. "Anything else?"

"Kind of, yeah. There was one other thing he told me—about an incident from eight or ten years ago. Before she met Kepler, presumably. This was in Trenton, New Jersey. A woman walked out of a bar one night and opened fire on the street, getting off six or seven shots. No rhyme or reason. A nutcase, police thought, or else she was high on something. No one was hurt, just some property damage. Broken windows. But they never made an arrest. I understand Elena was under investigation for that, too. This detective, who says he knows her, believes she did it and that her family covered for her and protected her."

"Wow," Hunter said. "This all puts the Susan Champlain case in a different light."

"I know."

"Any idea why she might've been using the name Belasco? What that's about?"

"No," Tanner said. "Not yet. I asked."

"Does he have any idea where we might find her? Any suggestions?"

"No." His eyes turned to her wall clock. "I'm still working on that."

Tanner tucked the book under his arm and sat up straighter. "That's pretty strange about the sheriff," he said.

"I know. Trying not to think about it much."

The receptionist buzzed her. Hunter waved to Tanner and mouthed the word "Thanks" as he stood. "Great work, Gerry."

"I'll catch up with you later," he said. Hunter liked this version of Gerry Tanner a lot.

She picked up her desk phone. "Hunter."

"Sergeant Hunter, there's a Scott Randall here to see you," the receptionist said.

What? "Here?" she said. "Or on the phone?"

"He's here." She lowered her voice: "Right here. I'm looking at him."

"Oh, my," Hunter muttered. She nonsensically began to straighten her desk. What would Randall be doing coming here to Tidewater County unannounced? She thought of Eddie Charles's daughter, the deep hurt in her eyes, as she told Hunter about "the FBI man." "Okay," she said, "I'll be right out."

She stopped at Tanner's doorway first. "This is a little crazy," she said, "but that guy I mentioned yesterday, Scott Randall? FBI? He's here. Have a good look at him if you'd like, but don't interrupt us."

"Ten–four. Sorry, I haven't had time to look into it yet."

"No, it's fine. That's great work on Elena Rodgers," Hunter said. "Thank you."

His face brightened. Hunter made a leisurely stop in the restroom before going out to meet Randall. It was okay to make him wait a few minutes when he'd shown up without warning, she decided.

"Sorry, Amy, for coming unannounced," he told her, extending his hand. He was dressed in crisp khakis and a dark polo shirt, sunglasses hanging from a neck strap. "I'm headed up to Philly," he said. "Just wanted to see what you were finding. Anything more on Nick Champlain?"

He sounded short of breath, she thought, as they walked to her office.

"No. He hasn't returned my call."

"How about his business manager?"

"No, we're not getting anywhere there, either."

"'kay."

Once he was seated in front of her desk, his crooked eyes took a quick inventory of the office. Hunter had no idea what he was up to or why he'd come here.

"Is that Susan Champlain?"

Hunter turned: the photo on her corkboard. "That's her," she said.

"So. Nothing more on her husband?"

"Nothing. As I said: I've left messages."

"Can you try him now?"

He nodded at her phone.

"He's out at the funeral, isn't he?" Hunter said.

"I don't know, is he? I don't think he is."

He tilted his head, as if trying to see more clearly what she was thinking.

"You still think this is a buyer with terrorist interests, right?" Hunter said. "Or was that just a story concocted to draw more attention to Kepler? Something like that happened before, didn't it? In Miami?"

He pulled his head back in mock surprise.

"What?"

Hunter said nothing, and he began to smile. She felt her dislike for him growing.

"Listen," he said, "there's a lot about this case that you don't know, Amy. Okay? And a lot that I can't get into."

Oh, come off it, Hunter wanted to say.

Instead, she said, "Why are you here, then?"

"With all due respect?" Hunter smiled. "I need you to let this alone for a while. We've got a track on Kepler now and—" He breathed out. "I've also spoken to the state police commander, Hamilton. And to your boss. Moore."

Oh. Hunter felt her face flush. She hadn't expected that. In other words, he'd come out to shut her down. For whatever reason.

"You're the one who said your case was just a local homicide."

"Not *just*."

"Okay, whatever. My concern is that we end up tripping over each other. And frankly, we can't afford that at this point, I'm sorry. I'm here as a courtesy," he said. Hunter looked away, letting him go on: "We have some new information on Kepler that's sensitive, and I'd like to ask that you stay on the sidelines for the next couple of days. *If* you hear from Nick Champlain, though, I'd like to know about it. Otherwise, we need you to step back."

"How soon is this deal going to happen?" she said, looking at him again.

"I can't get into it, Amy, I'm sorry."

"Solving one case will solve the other," she said, quoting him.

"Yeah, I know. I don't think that pertains anymore."

"Why not?"

"Because I don't."

They stared at each other, his weak eye drooping more than normal, it seemed, as if not able to hold up under his fakery any longer; Hunter felt his hidden agendas, his obsession with Walter Kepler, taking over the room.

"What *is* the status of your investigation?" he added. "Is there anything you haven't shared?"

"Well . . ." Hunter said nothing for a while. "Let's see: I think I know who killed Susan Champlain."

Randall licked his lips once, as if he could taste something he wanted.

"You do."

Hunter gestured affirmatively. "Someone named Belasco, maybe?"

"Belasco," he replied.

"Yeah."

He began to blink. There was no mistaking it, the name made him nervous. She'd noticed it before, too.

"You know the name Belasco," Hunter said. "I can see by your reaction."

"I know the name, yeah. I do. And I think it's another one of Kepler's diversions."

"Maybe so. But here's the rest of it, since you asked," Hunter said, deciding to go for it, to see his reaction: "I think Kepler's partner is a woman, who's been using the name Elena Rodgers. She was living here in Tidewater County for much of the summer, laying low. I understand her real name may be Linda Elena Fiorille, but I think she may also go by the name Belasco. Does any of that ring a bell?"

First he shrugged, then he shook his head. Then he cleared his throat.

"She's the one I think killed Susan Champlain."

"Who did?"

Gerry Tanner suddenly stepped into her office, as if to ask a question. "Oh, sorry," he said, "I didn't realize you had someone with you." He gave Randall a good look, more obvious than she'd have liked, and turned away.

"No comment?" Hunter said.

"No, no comment," he said.

"I was also talking with the family of someone named Eddie Charles," Hunter went on. "Up in Philadelphia. He was involved in Kepler's last deal, evidently. The one that fell apart, in Miami. I've learned some details about what happened—"

He showed his boy's smile and turned it into a laugh, cutting her off. "What, did you talk to that crazy cop up in Philly?"

"I talked with Calvin Walters."

"My God." He was shaking his head and grinning, but the color stayed on his skin and his eyes were blinking. He got up and closed the door. "You know what?" he said, scooting toward her. "I think you're being set up, Amy. I really do. I think you're being set up." Then his voice turned harder: "I've been through this a few times with Kepler now. Three, four times. I know how the man operates. He's trying to draw your eye away from what's happening. It's the most basic trick in the book, but he still manages to get away with it. That's what he does. He has us looking at four or five different things and none of them are the thing that *he's* looking at. You see? I'm just giving you a heads-up. A polite heads-up. That's why I'm here."

"I don't follow," Hunter said. "What would Kepler's connection be to Calvin Walters?"

"I told you before, the first time we talked: Kepler's a bridge to both worlds. Okay? It's not just organized crime. This is blood money. The man who's purchasing this painting is funding Sunni terrorist groups in the Middle East. And who's to say they won't be funding terrorism closer to home."

"I still don't follow," Hunter said.

He made an exasperated sigh and tried again. "*He* was the cause of what happened to Eddie Charles. Okay? Kepler, not me."

"But I didn't say you were."

"No, but I'm sure that cop was set up to tell you that. Who else did you talk with up there?"

"Charles's children."

His head pulled back again. "His son, you mean. What's his name, Cyril?"

"Children," Hunter said. "Son and a daughter."

"He had no daughter. Not that I know of."

"Okay." Scott Randall lowered his head over her desk, then, as if he was suddenly worn out from all this. Was he telling bigger lies to confuse her? Was this simply argument as a means of self-assertion? The man might actually be mentally ill, Hunter thought for the first time, observing the deep frown on his brow as he lifted his eyes again.

"Solving one crime will solve the other," she said.

"That's right, I said that." He smiled, and stood, tucked his hand in his waist and sucked in his stomach. He looked out the window, at the pinewoods. "And nothing's changed. Okay? But I'm just asking—just give us a couple of days. I appreciate what you've done, talking with Champlain. If you want to try Champlain again, be my guest."

He looked at her desk phone. Champlain was why he was here. They'd lost track of Nick Champlain and he was worried about that, despite the "new information" they'd received.

"Sorry," she told him, offering no explanation.

"All right." He started to extend his hand but then didn't.

"Give it a few days, then, Amy. We'll touch base again. We may have news by the end of the week."

"You're not concerned there'll be more collateral damage in the meantime?"

"No," he said. "That's what I'm trying to contain. Frankly, I'm concerned about *you*. I don't want *you* hurt."

"Okay," she said. He opened the door and looked out at the Homicide lobby. They parted without shaking hands.

LUKE HAD BEEN drafting his sermon about the puzzle of faith when Amy's message came through that afternoon. It contained a new puzzle:

Onward, then. Thursday end of day, at Half Past Three. B.

He forwarded it to Charlotte, hoping that it wouldn't interfere with her work, that it was something they could reserve for discussion after work over a glass of wine. But the chances of that weren't so good, he knew. No better than the odds of him getting his sermon done before 5 o'clock.

There was a built-in principle of temptation in the design of puzzles, Luke had decided. They were designed in ways to trip up lazy thinkers—most people, in other words. Puzzles offered the easy solutions first, the barely hidden Easter eggs, to coerce us into being satisfied too quickly, thinking we'd found what we were looking for long before we really had.

But this theory of puzzles, which he had worked into his sermon, didn't seem to apply to the new one that Hunter had sent over. He tried searching for references in the Bible to "Thursday," to "half past three," "end of day." A few ideas rose up, but they weren't even Easter eggs. He became moderately obsessed as the afternoon wore on, and then desperately so, forgetting his sermon entirely. And then, just as Aggie was turning off the copy and coffee machines and he realized almost an hour had slipped by unnoticed, Luke accidently hit on the solution.

"You've been mighty quiet in here this afternoon," Aggie announced, as she stood in the doorway to say good night. Her gaze moved over his desk. "Must've gotten a lot of work done."

"Oh." Luke smiled, feeling a wave of guilt. "Yes," he said. "Not as much as I would have liked. But it's getting there."

"Good."

"Yes."

"Tomorrow, then."

"Yes," Luke said. "Tomorrow, then."

He wasn't surprised when he got home to see that Charlotte had printed out the puzzle in twenty four-point type and tacked it to her bulletin board. She, too, was running searches.

"Any ideas?" he said, giving her a kiss.

"Not really. Was three thirty the time that Jesus died?"

"Mark gives the time as three o'clock," Luke said. "But that's Friday, not Thursday."

"I know."

"I'm sorry I pulled you away from your work."

"It's all right." Sneakers jumped on him, then, feeling neglected. Luke got down and gave him a serious belly rub. "I spoke with Claire, by the way," she said.

"And? Did she tell you the whole story about Susan Champlain?"

"No. She denied that she ever said it."

"No surprise."

"No."

"You have an idea, don't you?" Charlotte said, as he was finishing with Sneakers.

"How'd you know?"

She sighed. It wasn't a question that needed an answer. Anyway, it wasn't going to get one. Luke must've just had that look.

"Can I sit at your computer for a minute?" he said.

Charlotte stood. Luke sat and typed three words into a Google search page.

"The fact that it was in capital letters made me think this might be it," Luke said. "Of course, I might be completely off base. It may be one of the easy Easter eggs."

"The what?"

"Never mind."

"You mean the Half Past Three was in capital letters. Upper lower."

"Yeah." They both stared at what filled her screen: Marc Chagall's colorful abstract painting *Half Past Three*, which resided on the first floor of the Philadelphia Museum of Art.

"Possible?" Luke asked.

"Possible. What's it mean, though? The message?"

"I don't know," he said. "That's the part I don't get. Maybe Hunter will know."

Chapter Thirty-six

The Rembrandt, propped on a giant wooden easel in the Pennsylvania countryside, glowed in warm shafts of sunlight through the barn rafters. The natural light accentuated the wrath of the storm, the explosive waves smashing the ship's bow and port side, the hard green rain, the conflicted sky. The dramatic power of Rembrandt's subject—light battling dark, the allegory of nature's power and man's limits—and the artist's distinctive, otherworldly interpretation made this the perfect painting, Walter Kepler had often thought; and the real thing was infinitely more riveting than the reproductions. He felt a profound love for what he was seeing, a sensation beyond words.

Kepler used a jeweler's loupe to examine the paint, the mysterious layered amalgam of substances and colors that Rembrandt used to conjure his magic, pleased to see that it was still in moderately good shape. He noted each of the identifying characteristics, although all Kepler needed to see was Rembrandt's paint, the mixture of oil and impasto and various pigments that created effects never found in the work of any other artist.

"It's still a magnificent painting, isn't it?" he said, as he stepped back. *And it's ours.* He didn't say this.

"Rembrandt painted himself into it, did you know that?" he asked Jacob Weber. "See that fellow there, holding his hat?" He pointed to one of the fourteen men, whose other hand held onto the rigging. It actually reminded him for a moment of Jacob Weber. "That's Rembrandt," he said. "He often painted himself into his paintings. He was the precursor to Alfred Hitchcock, in that respect."

Weber seemed to appreciate this, although he was nervous, his eyes going to the doorway of the barn, to the glare of light on the rolling countryside. "But he was really making a point," Kepler continued. "We're all in that boat together. Aren't we?"

"Yes," Weber said. Kepler took several minutes more to drink in the painting, imagining as he did the sounds of the sea crashing the bow, the sting of the slanting rain, the looks of desperation, fear and supplication in the other men's faces. He stood slightly to the right, entering the scene from the safest position on the boat, and took another, final, minute, to live inside the parable.

Then he helped Weber crate the nearly four-hundred-year-old canvas and load it into the back of Weber's van, a custom-designed compartment set at 70 degrees, 50 percent humidity.

The painting's destination was six and a half hours to the northeast, meaning it would arrive around midnight, although the transfer—part three of his plan—wasn't scheduled to begin until 2:30 in the morning. That was Jacob Weber's part of the deal.

"Let's proceed, then."

HUNTER DID A short, fast run around the harbor, and then she showered, fed Winston and drove back in to the office. People were still leaving the PSC as Hunter walked in; Tanner and Fischer were both gone, although Tanner had e-mailed her some more information on Linda Elena Fiorille.

She called Hank Moore on his cell, relaying the details of her conversation with Scott Randall. He was at the fish market, he said, picking up some fillets for dinner. He sounded distracted.

Hunter read through what Gerry Tanner had sent her, then stared at Susan Champlain's picture for a while. Hunter was still missing something, she knew: something that was very close, probably sitting right in front of her. Something to do with Elena. With "Belasco." With Scott Randall's reaction to that name. Something she should have been able to recognize by now.

Her office phone rang, startling her. She hoped that it was Tanner, wanting to trade opinions. But what came up was "Unknown Caller." Maybe it was her heavy breather. Sheriff Calvert.

"Hunter," she said.

"Ms. Hunter?"

"Yes."

"This is Walter Kepler. I understand you were trying to reach me? You left a message?"

"Yes," she said. Hunter scrambled to open her notebook, paging back for an open space. "I was. I am. I'd like to talk with you, yes, sir. I would."

"This is in regards—"

"An ongoing investigation."

He waited, much calmer than she was. "You're Homicide."

"Yes."

"Uh-huh." He made a throat-clearing sound. "Unfortunately, I'm preparing to go out of town at the moment. But if it could wait a week—"

"Are you free to talk now?"

"Well, I could talk for a few minutes, I suppose. You mean by phone. Although, naturally, I prefer to see who it is I'm talking with."

"I do, too," Hunter said. "Where are you now, sir?"

"Where am I now? I'm in Pennsylvania." There was a crisp precision to his diction, and a cultured quality that made him sound like a stage actor. "I imagine I'm about an hour north of you, or an hour and a half. Unfortunately, I'm waiting on a delivery right now, so . . ."

"How about if I drive up there?"

"Tonight?"

"Yes. Right now."

"Ah," he said. "You mean, in an hour and a half, then?"

"Yes, whatever it takes."

His pause felt so dramatic it was almost as if he'd spoken it. "Well, all right," he said. "Let me give you directions."

Hunter looked at the clock: 6:42.

She turned out the light and walked back down the corridor. *He hadn't asked what it was about.* He hadn't asked *why* she wanted to talk with him. He hadn't asked anything. *He knew.*

She called Henry Moore as she neared the Delaware line to tell him what she was doing and give him the address where she was going. Moore answered her first with silence; then, much as she'd expected, he said, "I don't want you going alone, Hunter. Can you take Tanner with you?"

"Tanner's out. Fischer is, too. I'm already on the road."

Moore went silent again. It was a concerned and disapproving silence, probably an angry silence. Hunter heard easy listening music in the background.

"It's just a routine interview," Hunter said. "Which I'm doing on my own time," she added.

Moore didn't approve, but he wasn't going to push it. "Call me when you get there," he said.

"I will."

Hunter returned Pastor Luke's call as she drove into Delaware. He told her about an interesting theory he'd come up with: that the reference to "Half Past Three" in Elena Rodgers's e-mail may have had to do with a painting by Marc Chagall, which was at the Philadelphia Museum of Art.

"It's an idea, anyway," he said.

Considering some of the other ideas that Luke, and Charlotte, had given her over the past several days, she filed this one away under "to take seriously." It was something else she could ask Walter Kepler, perhaps. Hunter told Luke about the call from Kepler. She told him where she was going and promised to call him later. Then she tried Tanner and Fischer, leaving messages with both.

The sun turned a warm orange-yellow as it began to fall into the countryside. For a while, she listened to music, but that quickly became a distraction. Hunter wanted to be mentally clear and focused for this, to prepare herself as best as she could for Walter Kepler. Because it *wasn't* a routine interview. She'd been disingenuous saying that. It was anything but routine. It was the big part of the Susan Champlain case she didn't understand, she sensed. It was the entry to Belasco and the Rembrandt painting and Susan's fears and everything else that she didn't yet know. So why was this coming so easily? Why hadn't he asked her what she wanted to talk about?

Her GPS took her across the rolling country to the address that Kepler had provided, which was a small brick farmhouse, tucked into a hillside. There was a mailbox at the top of the drive and then a long gravel road to the house, with an opened garage beside it. A Bentley was parked inside, with Delaware plates. Darkness was settling but there were no lights on in the house.

Hunter parked. She called Moore to tell him she'd arrived and to give him the address once again; this time, she knew he was writing it down.

"Be careful," he said.

"I will. I've got my phone and my gun."

"Call me as soon as you're out."

"I will."

Before Moore hung up, Hunter heard his wife say "Who is it?" her voice sounding like a rusty hinge. Hunter smiled and clicked off.

She was surprised as she got out to see that a man was standing on the stoop to the house, waiting for her, dressed in a tailored khaki suit with a white dress shirt. He opened his hands cordially as she approached.

"You're Amy Hunter."

"Yes."

He extended his hand.

"Come in, please."

Chapter Thirty-seven

I'm not as hard to find as people think, am I?"

Hunter shrugged. "I didn't know people thought that," she said.

Walter Kepler led her into the wooden-floored living room. He gestured for her to sit, in a French-looking antique armchair. The windows were open, a pleasant breeze pushing out the curtains.

"Are you renting this house?" was the first question that came from her mouth.

"That's right, yes," he answered, giving her a warm smile. Kepler was an interesting-looking man, with prominent cheek-bones, light-colored eyes, graying hair that wisped over his fore-head. He looked to her like a museum director or an art teacher. "I'm doing some business on an estate collection in the area. My client's attorney found me this rental. Just for a couple of weeks.

"I understand you've been talking with Scott Randall," he added quickly, as Hunter was about to ask a follow-up. They were seated now, facing each other. "I'm sure he's told you some stories about me."

"Why do you say that?"

"Well, I mean, why else would you be here?" He laughed easily at this, a way of saying that he wasn't going to elaborate. It was a surprising laugh, which became a high giggle.

There were no lights on in the room. The furniture was antique, but seemed mismatched and placed incongruously. Something wasn't right about this, Hunter could see.

Outside, lightning bugs blinked against the trees. It reminded Hunter of her mother's living room at dusk. As her eyes adjusted, she noticed the paintings on the walls—three dark European-looking landscapes, along with one that seemed more familiar, a famous impressionist: Degas or Renoir, maybe.

"Can we turn on a light?" she said, standing. Kepler said nothing at first. He watched as she walked to a table lamp and clicked the switch, one notch and then two. Nothing happened. She lifted the switch on the wall.

"I'm afraid the power is still out," Kepler said, speaking with that clear diction she'd heard over the phone. "I'm terribly sorry."

Hunter sat in a straight-backed chair by the front door, feeling the .22 holstered under her jacket. She glanced out at the farmland behind her, the sky still losing its color.

"You're a *homi*cide investigator, you said. Isn't that correct?"

"Yes."

"So, naturally, I'm surprised that you would want to talk with me. You're investigating a homicide?"

"I am. Susan Champlain. She died in a fall from a bluff in Tidewater County last Wednesday night. There's evidence now indicating that her death may have been a homicide."

Kepler lifted his eyebrows attentively. "And so—how would that involve me?"

"Because there's some evidence tying her death to a business deal her husband was in," Hunter said. "A deal that may have also involved you."

"I see." He waited a moment, and smiled, a wide smile that seemed to have no emotion behind it.

"No comment?"

"No."

"You aren't doing business with her husband?"

"Is that what Mr. Randall told you?"

Hunter said nothing.

"Collateral damages," he said. "Did he use that term, too?"

"He did," she replied. "Although he said that was *your* phrase."

"God, no." Kepler laughed. "Really? No, that's *his* phrase. You can check the script. I cut it out, actually. That's from *his* draft, not mine."

Hunter shifted in the hard chair, feeling the grip of her gun.

"Script?"

"Yes. He still has all the drafts, I'm sure. *I* don't even have the damn thing. Did you ask him? Did he tell you about that?"

"No," Hunter said. She looked behind her, seeing something moving in the yard. Then not sure. "What do you mean, the script?"

"That's what this is. That's where all this comes from. He didn't mention it?"

"No."

Kepler displayed a reflective frown before explaining. "Many years ago," he began, "Scott Randall and I took an art class together. At Columbia. We got to know each other and even became friends. Of a sort. And, for a while, we got it in our heads that we'd write a screenplay together. And so, before the semester was over, we went to work on it, full of high hopes.

"Our story was about a man who makes a fortune in the art world by flipping masterpieces. We could never quite agree on the ending, and for that reason, and others, mostly pertaining to motivation—his, not mine—we never finished. I eventually moved on. Which I think bothered him. At any rate, we haven't spoken since."

"This was thirty-some years ago."

"Thereabouts," he said. "We were just two men in our early twenties, you understand, both with large but somewhat impractical ambitions. The world was our oyster. But only one of us figured out how to get the damn thing opened properly." He laughed at his characterization. "Some people grow beyond their youthful ideals, others don't. That's what high school reunions are for, I suppose. I wouldn't be surprised if he's been back to all of his."

Hunter studied him, still trying to figure what Walter Kepler was up to.

"We came from very different worlds, of course. He loved art but never could make it work for him. Which, I think, bothered him enormously. He was studying criminal justice at the same time. So it's kind of fitting, isn't it, that he ended up in the art crimes division?"

"You weren't friends for long."

"About a year. When we took the class together and then that summer and fall."

"His first wife worked in your gallery, too, I understand."

"Catherine, that's right. Not for long. You've done your homework, I see."

"You had a relationship with her, too?"

"Well." He smiled. "Yes, and I think that's the only reason he wooed Catherine, to be candid. I'm sure he didn't love her. I think marrying her represented some sort of early victory in Scott's life. I probably brought out the worst in him, I hate to say. Not surprisingly, the marriage was short-lived. I *am* told he married again and that they have a fairly well-adjusted daughter, grown now. I've never met them, of course. I barely thought of him *at all*, in fact, until several years ago, when I found out—purely by happenstance—how insanely *jealous* he was of me. Which was quite stunning, really, after so many years. And that he'd somehow gotten it into his head that I was involved with organized crime and terrorism. Did he tell you all that?"

"Some of it."

"Well." He showed the wide grin, but was regarding her more carefully now. "It's not true, of course, I hope you realize that."

Hunter shrugged. "He also thinks you're a dealer of stolen art," she said. "The *New York Times* seemed to imply the same thing several years ago."

"Well, yes."

"Why do people think that?"

"Because I haven't bothered to correct them, I suppose," he said. "I'm a private art dealer. I trade in rare, high-end work. People in the field know who I am—it's a very small field—people on the outside don't."

"*My* interest," Hunter said, "is a Rembrandt painting called *The Storm on the Sea of Galilee*. It's been suggested that you're trying to purchase it."

"*Really.*" He smiled, holding it longer than seemed natural. "And why would that interest you?"

"Because Susan Champlain made reference to it before she died," Hunter said. "She had a picture of it."

"A picture of it."

"Yes. Which the police have now. I'm investigating the death of Susan Champlain, as I said. That's why I contacted you."

"Yes, I know that," he said brusquely. He stood and stepped to a side window, looked out at the dark countryside surrounding them. "Well, I can't help you there, I'm afraid," he said. "I didn't know Miss Champlain. Never met her."

"But you know her husband."

"No."

"You're not doing business with him?"

This time he didn't answer.

"And Elena Rodgers?" Hunter said. "Or Elena Fiorille?"

He turned to face her. She could tell she had surprised him, although it was too dark to read his expression. "Why do you ask that?"

"Because the police have some evidence now linking her with Susan's death," Hunter said, using "the police" as an entity separate from herself. Her hand was inside her jacket, touching the grip of the .22.

When he didn't respond, she asked, "How do you know her?"

"How I know her isn't your business. Is it? What sort of evidence do they have?"

"Something she left at the scene. DNA."

Kepler turned back to the window. And then, as if on cue, a cell phone rang, several notes of classical music that Hunter recognized but couldn't identify. Kepler pulled a phone from his pants pocket. He walked into a back room, talking in a low voice. Hunter stood and tried to glance into the other rooms, but it was too dark to see anything.

She heard Kepler say "uh-huh" and "yes that's right" and "uh-huh" again. Hunter walked to the front door.

"Listen," he said, coming out. He showed his wide smile. "I'm going to have to cut this short, I'm afraid. I'd be glad to talk with you tomorrow, though. Any other conversations, I'd like to do on the record. I'm sorry you had to come all the way up here."

"Okay," Hunter said. "What time tomorrow?"

"Ten? Ten thirty? I can drive down to see you."

They watched each other across the room, Hunter's hand on the front doorknob. She hadn't gotten to the question she'd come here to ask him.

"All right."

"Ten thirty, then," he said.

Hunter handed him her business card as they stepped outside. Kepler locked the door. He took a deep breath of the cooling air.

"Supposed to get foggy tonight," he told her. "Be careful driving back."

"I will."

They began to crunch along the gravel path to the garage.

"One other question," Hunter said. "Can you tell me anything about someone named Belasco?"

"Named who?"

"Belasco," Hunter said. "I'm told Belasco was, or is, your partner."

He stopped walking. She expected him to deny it or to feign surprise, but he didn't do either. "Well, yes, in a sense," he said.

And then he laughed, expansively. "No, actually, Belasco was a character in our screenplay. Belasco was the villain, you understand. That's all he was."

"The villain."

"Yes. Our screenplay raised a simple philosophical question: Could you have an honest art thief, a Robin Hood, if you will. Or would the nature of the enterprise—unsavory human appetites, and all that—dictate that you also needed a villain who was willing to do some brutal things in order to succeed?

"It's an interesting question, I suppose." He began to walk again. "Or it was. An extension of a rather naïve philosophical conversation we used to have over drinks. If you could see tapes of us from back then, talking about it, I'm sure we'd sound absolutely ludicrous."

Kepler stopped behind the Bentley. "As for stolen art: I think if you were to search *his* home, or storage facilities, or whatever he keeps, you'd find that he has some fairly substantial treasures stashed away himself." He lifted his eyebrows for emphasis. "You'd be surprised."

"What are you talking about now?" Hunter said.

"Randall," he said. "Knowing him as I did, I'm sure he's taken advantage of his position over the years. I'm quite certain of it. You just need to find the hidey-hole.

"But we'll get to that tomorrow, won't we? For now, I need to go." He had his key out. The car lights flashed as he unlocked the Bentley. "But I'll come by your office tomorrow. Ten thirty, right?"

"Ten thirty," Hunter said.

Chapter Thirty-eight

H unter tried to turn on her phone as the Bentley pulled out of the garage and Walter Kepler drove past. But the signal was dead. She backed around and began to follow him up the long drive, trying again. Nothing. It was as if the phone's batteries had run down while she was in the house. But that couldn't be. She fiddled with the charger in the glove compartment, as Kepler's high-beams briefly lit up the fields.

Hunter braked and set the car in Park. She lowered her windows. It was dark now over the rolling country. She was supposed to call Hank Moore, and Pastor Luke, as soon as she finished talking with Walter Kepler. But she couldn't get a signal. There was a cool current in the air, a scent of cut grass. She listened, heard the sound of the wind sweeping high in the trees again; a sound she'd been hearing for days, which resembled human breathing.

Kepler turned left at the top of the drive. His taillights dipped out of sight, then appeared again, moving much faster.

Hunter felt a tug on the seat-back. She felt something moving against her shoulder. Then fingers touching her face.

She whirled around, trying to grab her gun. But too late. Her head slammed hard into the side window.

"Put your hands out! Now! Now!"

She smelled the woman's body, a sulfurous animal scent, as she reached over the seat and pulled Hunter's .22 from the holster.

"Now! Get out of the car. Now!"

Hunter felt the woman's breath, saw the .45-caliber handgun inches from her face. She opened the door and stepped out, keeping her hands up.

The other woman came out the back, pointing the .45 at Hunter with both hands. She was dressed in black jeans and a dark oversized windbreaker, her hair cut short, down to her scalp. But Hunter recognized the flat, sullen mouth and hard eyes of the woman she had known as Elena Rodgers. And she realized what she must have done: she'd used a jamming device to knock out Hunter's cell phone. This whole meeting with Kepler had been a setup.

Crap! Hunter thought. She'd been a fool, doing it like this. Coming up here alone. She'd walked right into a trap.

Hunter spread her arms against the back of the car and let Elena frisk her, Elena breathing heavily, running her hands down her body and her thighs, Hunter's phone and wallet quickly going into the pockets of Elena's windbreaker.

"Now step back," she said, signaling with the .45 for Hunter to stand by the door and get in. Elena took several long steps to the passenger side.

"Okay, let's go," she said. "You're going to be my driver now."

The seat belt warning began to bing as Hunter started forward. "Buckle," Elena said, holding the gun on Hunter's shoulder. "Buckle!"

She left her own belt unbuckled, and the binging sound continued until they came to the main road.

"Turn right here," she said. Hunter looked left, the way Kepler had turned; his lights were gone now.

Hunter drove. The road dipped and then folded into a dark patchwork of fields, which was spotted in the distance with occasional window lights.

"You don't need to do this," she said. "We can figure something out—"

"We're not going to talk," Elena said. "We're just going to drive. Okay?"

Hunter sighed. She watched the road, trying to pick out landmarks—fence poles, ruts in the fields, a large tree and a tractor on a hillside reflecting the faint light of the sky. Each time the breeze stopped, she smelled the woman's clothes and the heavy sulfurous scent of her skin.

They drove in silence down the two-lane road, Hunter entertaining all kinds of thoughts. Should she tell her what she knew? Should she mention Belasco? Should she try to disarm her? Try to strike a deal? Her instincts kept telling her to do nothing.

The country became even more rural and darker, a thin mist beginning to cling to the farm fields, stealing her frames of reference. She let the speedometer tick up a little and Elena told her to slow down. At a four-way intersection, she braked too late, missing it, and ended up running the stop. Elena jammed the gun barrel into the side of her head.

"Pay attention. Stay at the speed limit. Make this easy for yourself," she said.

Hunter drove on, feeling a lingering throb of pain now below her right ear. For another mile, then two miles, two and a half. And then Elena instructed her to slow down and take a turn. The landscape flattened out, into what seemed like miles of empty fields, Hunter feeling increasingly disconnected from anything or anyone that could help her. She pressed her brakes several times, a kind of SOS tattoo into the darkness, although she suspected there was no one out there to pick it up. She felt the inner tug of war—wanting to do something, needing to cooperate; knowing that her life was narrowing down to a few choices, like the closing moves in a chess game; how she'd gotten here didn't matter.

Then, suddenly, she realized that another vehicle was behind them. A pair of headlights had swung out from a drive and was following, a quarter to a half mile back. Elena turned around to look, keeping the gun barrel against Hunter's neck.

"Just stay at the speed limit," she said. "Stop braking."

They came to another intersection. Elena instructed Hunter to put on her signal and go left, onto an unmarked road. Hunter watched the mirror, saw that the other car had its signal on, too. They rode like that for three-tenths of a mile, four-tenths, Hunter watching the odometer and the mirror. And then, surprisingly, the other vehicle began to pick up speed, as if making a move to pass.

"Slow down!" Elena said. Hunter felt the gun barrel pushing against her skull, where she'd just hit her. "Let him get by you. Slow down!"

The road undulated and the center lines became solid. Elena

was leaning between the seats, looking back. Waiting for the other car.

Then the road leveled again and a stitch of broken center lines appeared.

"All right," Elena said, "now just let him get by you."

Hunter braked. The other car slowed, too. Hunter coasted, playing dumb.

"Goddamn it!" Elena said. "Go on and pick up speed. Get up to the speed limit and stay with it."

Hunter picked up speed, having no idea what the speed limit was. And then the night fields lit up with revolving blue and red lights.

It was a police car, its light bar and grill flashing behind them.

"Shit!" she heard Elena Rodgers mutter. Hunter's heart was pounding. This could be good or this could be bad. She kept driving slowly, waiting for instruction. Knowing what Elena's options were. If they sped away and led a chase, it wouldn't end well; if she pulled over, they'd probably have a record of it on the patrol car's dash cam.

"All right, pull over, ease into a stop," she said with sudden decisiveness. "Don't make any waves."

Elena told Hunter what to say. She talked her through how this had to go, her voice rising with authority as they waited for the officer to emerge from the cop car. Hunter glanced back in the rearview mirror each time Elena turned her head.

"You do anything stupid, I kill you both. You understand?"

"I do." Hunter took a deep breath, believing her; if she felt cornered, Elena probably would kill a police officer. Especially if there was only one.

The mist had grown thicker and cooled the night air. Hunter couldn't see the trooper clearly until he was right up behind the driver's window. An older man, heavy, walking a little bow-legged; receding gray hair and wire-framed glasses.

Only one.

"How you doing tonight, ma'am?"

"Fine," Hunter said, holding her license and registration. He shone his light in on Elena Rodgers and ducked his head down momentarily to look at her.

"Driver's license and registration?"

Hunter handed them to him, letting her left hand dangle for a moment; pointing her forefinger at the ground, like a gun.

"You're a state police officer?"

"Yes, sir."

Hunter opened her badge next, as Elena had instructed. The officer—Trooper Cavanaugh, his tag said—studied her picture, his eyes comparing it with the woman in front of them. He handed it back. "Where are you headed?"

"Back to Maryland."

"Where're you coming from?"

"Visiting with family. Just a couple miles down the road. We're going to Route 321, then down to Maryland."

It was what Elena had instructed her to say. She tried again signaling with the fingers of her left hand as she closed her police ID.

"All right," he said. "The reason I stopped you, the speed limit in here is thirty-five, you were doing forty-four. Sit tight a couple minutes."

He walked back to his car to run her license. Elena went silent.

Hunter could hear an impatience in her breathing that hadn't been there before.

"You do anything when he comes back, and I'll take out both of you. You understand? Just get back your license and we go. No one gets hurt."

"All right."

Elena was nervous now and that made her more dangerous, Hunter realized. There was a feral look in her eyes as she gazed back at the police car. Hunter didn't want to do anything that would cause her to hurt this man.

They sat silently, waiting, the police lights arcing through the mist, the night quiet, nothing but the police car's engine shifting and a chirping of crickets.

Finally, the officer came back, her license clipped to a ticket pad.

"Nice evening, isn't it?" he said.

"Yes, sir, it is."

It'd begun to feel like early autumn, the mist making the air wet. He handed Hunter her license and registration. "I'm going to let you go with a verbal warning tonight."

"Thank you."

"Just be careful with all this fog out here," he said.

"I will."

Hunter put the license and registration back in her wallet, and handed it to Elena, as the officer walked back to his car. She waited for him to pull out first. But then she sensed that he was waiting for her. "Go on!" Elena said. "Drive!"

Hunter pulled out and began to pick up speed. She saw the trooper's car in her rearview mirror, starting forward, stopping and reversing, turning around. So much for her hand signals.

"They're going to have a record of that stop," Hunter said after a minute or two. "We can figure out a way for this to end where no one gets—"

"We're not talking! Do you *understand* me? We're not figuring anything," Elena said. She pushed the gun barrel against the base of her skull. "Understand me?"

"Yes."

"You hear me?"

Hunter almost grabbed at her then, but managed to control herself. She drove on, through dark patches of country, big farm plots, horse farms, cornfields. Elena knew this country. She knew where they were going. She told her where to turn, when to speed up and slow down. "Turn in here," she said, and Hunter had to stop before she could see the turn. It was a gravel drive, barely a single lane, which ran into some thick, scratchy woods.

"All right, lights off, pull to the right and put the car in Park."

Just before clicking her headlights, Hunter saw a glint of glass ahead in the darkness. Another vehicle was parked in the clearing, facing them.

"Now turn off the car, hand me the keys."

Hunter did.

"Get out . . ."

Elena got out, too, right with her. Hunter felt the gun nudging her into the woods, smelled Elena, breathing right behind her.

Elena had worked all this out. She was going to leave Hunter's car here, as she had left Joey Sanders's truck in a remote wooded area of Virginia. She'd parked another car, which she would use to get away or maybe to transport Hunter someplace where her body would be found. Staged to look like an accident. Or maybe she *wouldn't* be found. Maybe Elena had a hole dug somewhere that she was going to cover and Hunter would become a permanent missing person. It was probably Kepler who had driven her here, she realized. Meaning Kepler was involved in whatever was going to happen. And had happened.

They walked toward the second car, which was a midsized Toyota, Hunter breathing the damp earth and tree bark, Elena guiding her from behind with the .45. The trunk popped, startling her; but no trunk light came on. Hunter stopped and faced Elena as her left hand came from the pocket of her windbreaker; she saw that she was gripping something; saw it for a moment, reflected in the light from the sky—small and cylindrical, a syringe, maybe. Hunter turned her head, scanned the landscape through the trees, her breath coming faster: miles of nothing. No one was coming, not in any kind of time frame that would matter.

"Get down now, to your knees! Get down!" Elena said, waving the gun emphatically.

That was when Hunter decided that she had to take the only option that made any sense anymore. The only option she had: she needed to attack Elena Rodgers.

"Down on your knees," Elena said.

Hunter said, "All right," feeling buoyed suddenly by a gathering of adrenaline.

Elena stepped toward her, raising the gun like a club. Hunter began to comply, lowering her shoulders, going into a crouch. But then she lifted up and charged forward, hammering her right fist into Elena's face. Elena staggered for a moment and got off a shot, missing. Hunter jumped her and took Elena down; then she was all over her, pummeling her face, jamming an elbow into her neck, Elena grappling desperately at her arms, scratching her, tearing the sleeve of her jacket, Hunter not even knowing where the gun was anymore.

Elena rolled them over, her fingernails cutting into the flesh of Hunter's forearms, slicing down her right arm, and then Hunter felt the .45 under her back. She kneed upward into Elena's groin and pushed off, getting to her feet, with the gun in her right hand now. Elena rose, too, crouching, looking at Hunter, breathing hard: the feral look. Then Hunter saw what she was doing: the other gun, Hunter's Glock, was coming out of Elena's windbreaker; it was in her right hand.

Hunter stepped forward and shot her twice, in the arm and then in the leg. For a moment, Elena kept coming, no longer holding the gun. Then she went down to a knee. And Hunter heard Elena groan and fall to the side.

Hunter waited, her legs trembling with adrenaline. She could hear her own heart beating now, hear herself panting. She watched, not wanting to kill her; not wanting to lose what Elena Rodgers could give her. She stepped sideways, preparing for Elena to stand up. But then she saw the side of her face: Elena lying there like a store dummy, her eyes closed, no longer moving. Barely breathing. What had happened? Hunter moved closer and kneeled down, holding the gun to her face, felt her pulse. Elena was alive but no longer conscious. She went in the windbreaker pockets and found her phone, her wallet. Felt the syringe. She lifted her Glock .22 from the dirt and stuck it in her holster.

Hunter stood and looked out at the country. Turning, searching for a reference point. Her breath was shaky, her heart thumping. She began to walk down the gravel lane, her right arm stinging a little where she'd been cut by Elena's nails. She reached the road and tried her phone. This time, it worked. She pressed 911, taking several long breaths of the wet air. The trooper had been right. It *was* a nice evening. Hunter didn't think she'd ever felt so grateful to be alive as she did right then. She walked back to check on Elena, knowing what she'd find.

IT WAS 9:43 when Luke received the first call from Henry Moore. He hadn't heard from Hunter since she'd gone into the house with Kepler, he said. That was 8:15.

"I just thought you might have heard something."

"Nothing," Luke said. "Has someone gone by the house?"

"A trooper stopped by, found that it was locked up, no one home, no lights on. Anyway, just let me know if you hear anything."

Half an hour later, Moore called again. He'd just gotten the call about the traffic stop.

"Another woman was in the car with her," he said. "Any idea who that might be?"

"No," Luke said. "Unless it was her. Elena Rodgers. The partner."

Luke knew that they were both thinking the same thing: Hunter shouldn't have gone up there alone. But it didn't do any good now to state the obvious.

"Call if you hear anything," Moore said.

"I will."

"And please, say a prayer."

"Yes," Luke replied. "I already have."

HUNTER STOOD ON the two-lane country road, listening to the crickets. Then, to fill the time, she began to walk in the direction she knew they'd be coming from. It wasn't long before she heard sirens, then saw the glow of revolving blue and red lights, dipping into a valley and over a crest. Hunter was in the center of the road waving her arms when they arrived.

The first responder was the same state trooper who'd stopped her earlier. Trooper Cavanaugh.

His eyes looked startled as he came toward her with a bow-legged urgency. Hunter saw why: the right sleeve of her jacket was torn off and her arm was streaked with blood.

"You okay?" he said.

"Fine. It's not as bad as it looks," Hunter said. Mostly she felt numb.

They stood beside the patrol car, Cavanaugh shifting his weight from one hip to the other as Hunter explained what had happened. He said nothing, absorbing her story. Afterward, they drove up the road to Linda Elena Fiorille. In the distance, the flashing lights of backup patrol cars moved silently over the hillsides.

Elena hadn't moved. She wasn't going to, not of her own volition. Hunter knew that. She had hit her twice. The arm wound wasn't serious. But she must've hit the femoral artery in her left leg. She'd probably bled out in ten minutes, maybe while Hunter was doing the 911 call.

Hunter hadn't intended it to end this way. Not in a million years. She'd wanted Elena Rodgers to tell them the whole story: what she'd done to Joe Sanders, where they'd find Nicholas Champlain, all about her obsession with Walter Kepler, if that's what it was. Hunter had wanted to see her in a courtroom, accused of pushing Susan Champlain over the bluff-edge. She'd wanted to see her sitting at the defense table, her stubborn face gone slack, as an attorney tried to defend her. She'd wanted to watch her in a prison jumpsuit at the sentencing when the judge gave her life without parole and the guards steered her away in leg shackles.

But none of that was going to happen.

Hunter was standing out there an hour and a half later when Henry Moore arrived in his unmarked MSP car. The EMS had bandaged her right arm by then and were gone. But the coroner was still waiting, as were half a dozen deputies, who were doing nothing but casting long shadows in the cooling air as police techs finished photographing the scene.

Moore gave her a quick hug and then stood beside her, looking at Elena's body.

"When she woke this morning, I'll bet she never thought her day would end like this," he said. It was a typical Henry Moore observation, hard and ironic, without a trace of humor.

"I wish I knew *what* she'd been thinking," Hunter said.

He waited a moment, then said, "No, you don't."

Hunter gave her statement to the investigating officer. Her unmarked police car stayed behind, impounded as evidence. She rode back to Tidewater County with Moore.

The fog came in drifting patches through Delaware and down into Maryland. It was a long drive home and Moore didn't say much. But Hunter understood the inflections of his silence. He listened as she told him about Kepler, and about the kidnap. And as she told him that she was sorry. "I shouldn't have gone in there alone," she said. "I know it wasn't smart. I'm very lucky."

Moore said nothing at first, his eyes scanning the road.

Then he said, "You once told me that you didn't really work for the state police, you worked for the homicide victims."

"Yeah. I know," she said.

Moore went silent again.

"I probably shouldn't have said that."

She'd thought he was going to say something like, *Just to be clear, for the future: You do work for the state police.* But he didn't. He said, "I like that you think that way. But I don't like the chance you took. I'm just glad you're okay."

That was all he had to say, in both senses of the phrase, for a long time. They were nearly back to Tidewater County before he spoke again. By then, Hunter had retreated into her own thoughts, trying to make sense of what Kepler had told her about Scott Randall. *The screenplay. The hidey-hole.* The funny part was that she kind of liked Kepler. Even if he'd set her up to be killed. She'd need to make sense of that, too.

As they came back into more familiar scenery, Hunter got an idea. A way of intercepting and confronting Walter Kepler. What if the e-mail message from erbela was real? What if Kepler was planning to meet Elena in front of Chagall's painting *Half Past Three* at the end of the day tomorrow?

They were ten minutes from home when Hunter decided to share her idea with Moore.

"Could we find a way not to release any information about what happened to Elena Fiorille tonight?" she asked him. "I mean, at least not before the end of day tomorrow."

"Out of our hands," Moore said. Most of the tension was gone between them by now. He was into his own thoughts, too. "Local media's probably gotten it already."

"I know. But can we keep her *name* out of it? For twenty-four hours."

He looked at her, and let her tell him why. It was a chance, maybe, to head off Walter Kepler. Not a great one. But a chance.

NORMALLY, KEPLER FELT comfortable driving at night, alone with the muted glow of the dashboard—bound for familiar places, the world at a safe distance but still within view. But there was nothing normal about tonight, of course. There was too much open space right now, it seemed, too much uncertainty.

Weber called twice: when he crossed the border into Massachusetts. And then, again, as he arrived in the city. There was no news from Elena, though. And by the time Kepler reached his condo on the Delaware coast, he'd begun to sense that she hadn't made it. It was one of the two possible outcomes he'd prepared for and, really, the one he had expected.

Kepler parked in the garage. He walked up the steps. It was 12:43 when he sat at his desk in the Italian Room and gazed out at the Atlantic Ocean. He would watch the miracle unfold from here in the morning. And then he would be gone, with Elena or without.

Either way, it would be a sad parting. Particularly so if he had to say two goodbyes—to the life he'd lived and to the life he'd imagined, with Elena . . . Elena, who had such strong feelings for art but not for people. Sort of like him, although her feelings were of a different variety. Kepler had thought at first that her complicated passion for art maybe reflected a world view. But it didn't; that was as far as it went, really.

He already knew what Weber would tell him: *It's probably better this way.*

Yes. Probably he was right.

LUKE AND SNEAKERS watched lightning illuminate the Bay, Luke thinking about unanswered prayers, which he'd decided he was going to talk about on Sunday, a piece in the puzzle of faith.

The door squeaked behind him and Charlotte was standing there, holding up his phone. The last time he'd gone in to get a beer—was it his fourth, or fifth?—he must've left it on the counter.

Charlotte handed it to him, making a face at the beer can. She thought he'd been drinking too much lately, but wasn't comfortable telling him. She stood aside as Luke answered.

"Hello?"

"It's me," Amy Hunter said.

"Hi," he said. "*Hi.* Are you all right?"

"I'm all right, I'm on my way back."

Luke looked at Charlotte and gave her a thumbs-up.

"We've been worried."

"I was, too, kinda," Hunter said.

"What happened?"

"Well. I got into a situation," she said. "It's over now."

"You're okay."

"I'm okay."

Luke was about to say, "What sort of situation?" But Hunter went ahead and told him:

"I found Kepler. I talked with him. And then Elena Rodgers found me. It's a long story. But the situation's over," she said.

"Oh."

"Yeah. Look, I just wanted to let you know. I'm all right. I'm uh—" He heard a quiver in her voice. "I think you're right about that Chagall painting, by the way."

"Really?"

"Between us."

"Why do you—?"

"I'll call in the morning." She hung up.

"What happened?" Charlotte asked. Luke was staring at the phone.

"She got into a situation," he said.

"And—?"

"She got out of it. That's about all I know."

Charlotte reached for his hand and sat on the chair arm. She lifted up the beer can as if it were a dirty sock and moved it out of the way. "Let's go inside," she said.

Chapter Thirty-nine

The first reports about what happened in Boston overnight began to trickle onto the Internet at a few minutes past 9 A.M., as Tweets and blog postings, although most of the early posters took it as a hoax, or, at best, a misunderstanding.

But by a quarter past ten, someone internally at the Isabella Stewart Gardner Museum had confirmed the story and it was out as a bulletin on the *Boston Globe* website. Several minutes later it was running on AP and CNN. From there, it was interesting to watch the dominoes fall.

Which was what Charlotte was doing. She called Luke at church just after 10:30 to tell him: "Go online."

Luke did. MIRACLE IN BOSTON? was the boxed lead by then on CNN, with the subhead, REMBRANDT MASTERPIECE RE-PORTEDLY RETURNED.

He read:

Reports are circulating this morning that Rembrandt's famous painting The Storm on the Sea of Galilee, *stolen from Boston's Isabella Stewart Gardner Museum in 1990 as part of the biggest art heist in American history, was anony-mously returned to the museum overnight.*

The Gardner has not officially responded to the story, but a museum source has confirmed to CNN that the painting found hanging on a wall in the museum's second-floor Dutch Room this morning was in fact the Rembrandt masterpiece.

"It's like a miracle," said the source. "It's back home, in the original frame, as if it had never left."

The painting's empty frame, along with those from several other stolen masterworks, has hung empty on the museum's walls for the past 25 years, in accordance with a provision in the will of museum founder Isabella Stewart Gardner. Thirteen works were stolen in the brazen late-night theft on the night of St. Patrick's Day 1990, including three Rem-brandts, a Vermeer and a Manet.

Painted in 1633, The Storm on the Sea of Galilee *is considered one of Rembrandt's most dramatic narrative paint-ings, depicting Jesus calming the sea, a parable of nature versus human frailty, from the Gospels of Mark, Matthew, and Luke. The painting was purchased by Gardner in 1898 and was on display to the public from 1903, when the museum opened, until 1990.*

Rembrandt Harmenszoon van Rijn is generally considered among the greatest painters in European art and the most important artist of Holland's "Golden Age." The Storm on the Sea of Galilee *is his only seascape.*

Several reports say the museum's security systems failed overnight, and that a guard discovered the work hanging in the Dutch Room at about 7 A.M.

*"I'm at a loss for words," said the museum source, who
spoke on condition of anonymity, "other than to say it has the
appearance of a miracle."*

AMY HUNTER MISSED all that. After saying goodbye to Henry
Moore, she went to her apartment, spent some time visiting with
Winston and then crashed at around 4 A.M. with her phones
turned off. Moore had agreed to monitor messages. When she
woke, she popped open a Diet Coke and called Luke Bowers. She
wanted to tell him her idea about *Half Past Three*.

Luke, as he was prone to do, listened patiently, waiting until
she had finished talking before sharing *his* news. "Did you hear
about our friend?"

"No. Which friend?"

"Mr. Rembrandt."

"How do you mean?"

"Go online."

So Hunter read about it first on the *Washington Post* website.
Then clicked on the *New York Times*, BBC, Reuters, Al Jazeera,
RT, Fox, MSNBC. Rembrandt was the lead everywhere.

"Son of a bitch," she said, a few times—recognizing, first,
that "son of a bitch" was not something that she ever said; and,
second, that she was actually saying it with a small degree of admiration. *Kepler.* He must have made a deal with the museum, to
return the painting anonymously, on condition that law enforcement not be notified, and that the story unfold to the public a
certain way. Why *wouldn't* they deal with him? If he was offering
to return Rembrandt's masterpiece free of charge, he probably
had enormous negotiating leverage.

But so why had Kepler met with her at all? Why had he told her about Randall and the screenplay? Had he known that Elena Fiorille was going to fail? Or was he simply covering himself, just in case the outcome wasn't as he had planned? What Hunter felt that morning was a new tug of war: a grudging admiration for Kepler and what he had done with the painting, against the knowledge that he had also set her up to be killed. What Kepler had done *did* have a sprinkle of the miraculous, it seemed. But could those two events be somehow separated, the one making the other not count? *Was* Kepler a bad man?

Hunter showered, dressed and finally headed in to work, pumped up with adrenaline and caffeine. It was a typical latesummer day, the air steamy with heat, already smelling of seafood and suntan oil, the roads through town snarled with summer traffic.

Tanner was standing inside the doorway to Fischer's office when she arrived. The two of them seemed to be talking cordially, something she'd never witnessed before. Hunter did a quick double-take at first, just to make sure it was actually them. Then she slipped into her office and pushed the door three-quarters closed.

She was officially on administrative leave now, as she had been after the Psalmist case, an awkward and inconvenient transition period. But there were several phone calls to return, she saw: Dave Crowe. Scott Randall. Nancy Adams. Someone named Thelma Williams.

She Google-searched a little more about the Rembrandt painting, and stolen art, before calling any of them, wanting to better understand Walter Kepler and his obsessions; more than wanting to catch him, she wanted to understand him.

Tanner interrupted her, his tall, stationary head peering around her door. "Hey!" he said when she noticed him. Then he knocked twice on the door. "You all right?"

"I think so."

He came in and hugged her, the last thing she'd have imagined Gerry Tanner ever doing, squeezing her hurt arm.

"Guess we were all caught napping," he said, stepping back, his dark eyes looking at her arm as Hunter held it.

"We were."

"What *happened*?"

"Well . . ." *So Moore hadn't told him*. Fisch drifted in to listen as Hunter told him about the events of the night before. She didn't get far in her story before her phone rang. Henry Moore was in the conference room; he must've heard her voice.

"Moore's calling," she said.

HENRY MOORE WAS at the end of the conference table, papers spread out, his transistor radio playing softly, a song she recognized as "Moon River."

"How's your wing?" he said, shutting off the music.

"I'm fine."

"Pull up a chair."

Hunter closed the door and took a seat. He nodded at his computer: Fox News was streaming, with the sound off. A self-portrait of Rembrandt came on the screen, the same one all the cable news networks seemed to be using.

"So?" Moore said. "What the hell's this about?"

Hunter shrugged. "I'm as surprised as everyone, sir."

He rocked back and to the side, giving her an appraising look. The news from Boston had added a strange filter to everything that'd happened the night before.

"Is this Walter Kepler?"

"I think so, yeah."

"And we didn't know about it? We didn't see it coming?"

"*I* didn't, no."

"The FBI?"

"I don't think so. Kepler caught us napping, as Gerry just told me. I suspect the FBI's thinking the same thing this morning."

Moore drew a deep breath.

"Thanks for last night," she said. He nodded, simultaneously backhanding away the sentiment. He wanted to talk about Kepler.

"The museum must've been complicit in this. Right?"

"I'm assuming," Hunter said. "Although it'll make a better story, of course, if they don't comment."

Moore shifted forward in his chair; he smiled with just the right side of his mouth. "My job, meanwhile, is solving homicides."

"I know."

"And so . . . I'm sitting here, asking myself: are there two or three homicides we're going to need to address here, or just one?"

"Two or three?"

"Susan Champlain. Joseph Sanders. And now I'm told Susan's husband has gone missing."

"Oh."

"Are they all connected?" he said. "Is this all Elena Fiorille?"

Hunter sighed. "Probably," she said. In effect, Hunter had inadvertently closed all three cases in one night, she recognized, even if two of them hadn't officially been opened yet. But Moore was talking about something else: perception and public opinion; and about how these killings were going to be prosecuted.

"The other two cases—if there are two—aren't ours," Hunter told him. "Sanders is Virginia, not in our jurisdiction. Nick Champlain, I don't know, it's too early to say."

Moore kept looking at her. "And you don't think we're going to get pulled in? You don't think they're going to be linked up?"

"I don't know."

"What bothers me," he said, "is motive. Did she kill Susan Champlain to help Kepler? Isn't that what you think?"

"Probably."

"So . . . aren't we going to have to explain Kepler?"

Hunter saw what was bothering him: what would happen if the Susan Champlain case became about Kepler. "Not really," she said. "Maybe the motive was that Elena Rodgers just didn't like Susan Champlain. We do have some evidence of that."

"Do we?"

"Claire French at the Humane Society told Pastor Luke that." Hunter added, "But that case isn't going to need a lot of motive, because we'll have evidence. Beginning with Elena's necklace. And I'm sure they're going to find Elena Fiorille's skin under her fingernails."

Moore nodded, not quite convinced. "And the other two?"

"Maybe they were personal, too. Maybe Sanders and Champlain were harassing her. I think the physical evidence will prove the cases. And the more evidence there is, the more motive will take care of itself," Hunter said. "Right?"

Moore slowly gave her his half smile.

"I mean, we don't have to prove a grand conspiracy," she added. "That's the FBI's domain."

"I was talking with the captain up there," Moore said. "He's not anxious to make this more involved than it needs to be. But we still have to tell them why this woman kidnapped you."

"Because I'd found her out," Hunter said. "I knew what she'd done to Susan Champlain."

"Is that our story?"

"That's our story."

He sighed, but there was a glint in his right eye.

"What was the thing they found on her?" Hunter asked. "Do they know yet?" She felt a rush of adrenaline, recalling the hard tone of Elena Fiorille's voice, ordering her to get to her knees.

"Yeah." He tugged a sheet of paper closer. "Preliminary says it was a compound called succinylcholine." Hunter said nothing. "You know what that is?"

"Sure," she said. "It's an anesthetic. Similar to one of the ingredients used in lethal injections."

"That's right. It causes paralysis. Very hard to detect on autopsies."

"Wow."

"Yeah. But the fact that we know about it means we can look for traces in Sanders, too. And Susan Champlain."

He exhaled thoughtfully, pulling his papers together.

Hunter said, "I just wish I could keep working the case."

"Well. We'll have to see about that," he said. "Maybe we can work out something quietly." He winked.

But then he saw she had something specific in mind and said, "Why? What do you want to do?"

"I'm thinking I'd like Tanner to work on a little side project," she said. "For you. Involving Scott Randall. It wouldn't take long. Maybe a couple of days."

The corners of his mouth turned down this time. "Go on," he said. "Tell me about it. I'll listen, anyway."

TANNER AND FISCHER had together created a preliminary background report on Elena Fiorille, with Fischer writing the summary. A copy was on Hunter's desk when she returned to her office. That must have been what they were discussing so cordially when she first came in.

Hunter closed her door and read through it for the next twenty minutes, absorbing the details of her life story: Linda Elena Fiorille had been raised in South Philadelphia by working-class parents, the fourth of four children and the only girl. Her father had been a hardware store owner who'd also worked for the Bruno crime family. When Elena was fourteen, he went away to prison for a year on racketeering and bookmaking charges. Elena was in trouble frequently as a girl, for drug and alcohol possession, and for theft and assault. The assault charge came after she beat up another girl in high school so bad that the girl spent a night in the hospital. Elena had shown a talent for painting and sculpture in high school, but it was evidently an "undisciplined and ultimately unrealized" talent, Sonny Fischer wrote in his summary.

Fiorille had been arrested four times as an adult: for aggravated assault, drug possession, attempted murder, and petty larceny. All of the charges but one were dropped. In 2002, she was convicted of misdemeanor marijuana possession. Someone who knew Elena in the 1990s and early 2000s told Tanner that she never lost her love of art; that she'd spend days sometimes in the galleries at the Philadelphia Museum of Art, alone with the paintings. She'd also taken college art classes, he recalled; she talked about becoming an artist herself, but never pursued it.

Along with the sketch of Fiorille's life were five photos taken of her over about fifteen years, four of them mug shots. She was smiling in all but one of them. But it wasn't a happy smile. It was a flattened, surly smile. In the earliest mug shot, it seemed to be trying to become a smirk. A dare: Don't come too close.

At 2 P.M., Tanner rapped on Hunter's door again. "It's official," he said. The museum had just sent out a statement confirming that the painting that had appeared in the Dutch Room overnight was in fact Rembrandt's *The Storm on the Sea of Galilee.*

Hunter switched her computer to cable news to watch. There was, by then, a uniformity to how the story was being covered: *A Miracle in Boston.* "The so-called miracle in Boston," some broadcasters were saying, already reporting on the reporting.

Surely, it had been planned that way, Hunter figured. Kepler must have made the use of the word "miracle" one of his conditions.

She was interrupted again by a call: Thelma Williams, a name Hunter didn't recognize until the woman identified herself: she was Eddie Charles's daughter. Her voice sounded unfamiliar, deeper and more assured than before. Had their meeting at the Philadelphia Museum of Art happened just two days ago?

Thelma had seen the news about the Rembrandt, and decided she needed to talk with Hunter again. Walters had given her the number.

"This was why my father died, wasn't it? This was the deal."

"Maybe," Hunter said. "There may have been some connection, anyway."

"I'm almost tempted to go to the media and tell them about it."

"No, I don't think that would be the best course of action at this point," Hunter said.

"Is there something I can do? Something that would help clear my father's name?" she asked.

"I think there is," Hunter said. "But not right away. Give me a little time to work on it first. I promise I'll get back with you."

"He died because of this, didn't he?"

"Give me some time," Hunter said. "I promise I'll work on it and get back with you."

Hunter stared out at the pinewoods after hanging up. Thelma represented the part of the case that Helen Bradbury had called the "moral tale." It was thornier than solving a murder, and not in Amy Hunter's job description; but it wasn't something that she wanted to ignore, either. She'd work on it with Calvin Walters, she decided, during her "administrative leave." Maybe go up and visit with him and have lunch with Thelma Williams. See if they could find a way to redefine Eddie Charles's death, to remove the stigma of "drug related"—although in real life, of course, it wasn't so easy to tie bows around crime stories.

Hunter still wondered if Eddie Charles *had* played a role in this case, which would make his death even more complicated. He'd been in the photo, after all, on Susan's phone, in the same frame with the stolen Rembrandt. But maybe he'd just been in the house that day to wire it for electricity.

Just as she was thinking this, and as if to provide dramatic relief, Marc Devlin called her desk phone. With his slow Southern inflection, he said, "Miss Hunter? Marc Devlin here. I saw the news from Boston and just wondered—I mean, if this had anything to do with what we were talking about?"

"What we were talking about?"

"Yes, about Miss Champlain."

"Oh, I can't say a lot about that," she said. "But, between us, yeah, it may have."

"Did you know this was going to happen? With the painting?"

"I didn't."

He cleared his throat; she thought about his unearthly blue eyes, the way he'd been walking behind Susan Champlain weeks earlier on an afternoon when the air seemed to be drugged with heat. "I was thinking," he said. "Maybe we could go out for a drink sometime. Just to talk."

"Okay," Hunter said.

"Really?"

"Sure."

Hunter smiled. He hadn't expected that. She hadn't, either.

"Okay, well. Tomorrow?"

"Tomorrow," Hunter said, feeling a tingle of gratitude again. She needed to loosen up. "I can meet you over at Kent's, if you'd like. Six o'clock?"

"Really? Okay. Great."

Hunter smiled and went back to the file that Moore had given her, although her mind kept taking her on tangents. Wondering how Kepler had managed to pull this off, and where he was now. At three o'clock, she turned on CNN just to see if there was any new Rembrandt coverage and was stunned to see Scott Randall's face on the screen. He was playing FBI spokesman, talking in a measured, annunciated voice: ". . . the culmination of a years-long investigation. I couldn't comment on any particulars at this point other than to say that it was a team effort, involving the assistance of several agencies."

Hunter tried calling him right away, her heart racing; but naturally she couldn't get him. She was a little too angry to leave a message. She tried Dave Crowe again, reaching him on his cell phone.

"It's been running since noon," Crowe told her, amused at Hunter's urgent tone. "You're just seeing it now?"

"It's like he's doing a victory lap."

"Oh, he is. Like I told you before, he's justifying the Kepler investigation, that's all." Then his voice fell to a more sober register: "Did you have any idea this was going to happen?"

"None. You?"

"No."

"Got to give Kepler some credit, I guess," Hunter said.

"Some. I just wonder where the money came from. I don't think it came from the government."

"No, I'm sure it didn't," Hunter said.

"Maybe a philanthropist or wealthy art patron. Or maybe the museum."

"Or maybe him," Hunter said.

Crowe said nothing at first. "Kepler?"

"Yeah."

"That wouldn't be his M.O.," he said. "Or make a lot of sense."

"That's right. And maybe that's why it worked." Hunter gazed at the familiar picture of Susan Champlain on her corkboard. "I was thinking about the *Mona Lisa* earlier," she told him. "I've been reading about her, how she came to be such an iconic painting."

"What are you talking about?"

"We thought the point of this deal was to make money," she said. "That's the logical assumption. But it couldn't have been. Despite what the Stolen Art Division might have thought. That's why this worked."

Crowe answered with silence. Then: "You're saying, what, that Kepler's only objective was to return the painting?"

"And to create this story. This so-called miracle. The idea that a great painting can come back and tell a story." Hunter waited a beat. "It's a theory."

"Okay." More silence. "But what do you mean, the *Mona Lisa*?"

"When the *Mona Lisa* was stolen from the Louvre a hundred years ago, it wasn't a widely known painting. It wasn't even the most popular painting in the museum. Scholars said it was great, but the public didn't know it."

"I didn't even remember it was stolen," Crowe said.

"Well, no, you probably wouldn't; this was in nineteen eleven. The point is, the theft helped *make* it an iconic painting. If it hadn't been recovered eighteen months later, and returned to the Louvre, it would be completely unknown today."

"Oh. I see," Crowe said. After a moment, Hunter sensed he

really *did* see. "And so you're saying he spent his own money to tell this story, for the sake of the *painting*?"

"Something like that. With a little subsidy from the U.S. government, maybe," she said. "I keep hearing that he cares more about art than he does about people or anything else. That would give a funny kind of logic to this whole thing."

"Does Scott Randall know this?"

"No. I don't think he's supposed to." Just hearing Randall's name gave her a prickly sensation. "Listen," she said, "I need to talk with you about Randall. You and Bradbury. The whole thing about when he disappears on weekends to see his mother. And the way he goes out West sometimes and no one hears from him for a while. Where does he go, exactly?"

"He owns property in Wyoming. Retirement property."

"And you said you thought he'd retire after this case."

"I think he will. Why?"

"Something Kepler said to me. I think there's something wrong about the whole setup."

"What—with Kepler?" Crowe wasn't following.

"No," she said. "I'm becoming less concerned about Kepler getting away than about Randall getting away," she said.

"Oh."

"You and Bradbury have all sorts of reservations about Randall, anyway, right?"

"Some."

"I think you need to find a way to take them to the Justice Department."

"What?" Crowe's confusion was becoming anger. "Why?"

"To help them find out if there's a hidey-hole."

"A *what*?"

"That's what Kepler called it."

Even Crowe's breathing seemed confused now. Hunter told him the rest of what Walter Kepler had said to her and then she let him know what she was thinking. "These are just suggestions," she said, afterward. "I'm on administrative leave now and not supposed to be involved. But we have an investigator here named Gerry Tanner who . . ." Then Hunter broke it off. She recognized the number calling in on her office phone. "Speaking of Scott Randall."

"What, is he there?" Crowe asked.

"Let me call you back."

Hunter cleared her throat and sat up straighter before answering.

"Hunter," she said.

"Amy? Scott Randall. Are you all right? I heard you were in a shooting."

"I'm fine, yes, thank you," she said. "I saw you on television earlier."

"Yeah, I know, I didn't want to do that." Hunter was surprised that her heart was racing again; a reaction to Randall's voice.

"You made it sound like this was some kind of victory for the Bureau," she said. "But you didn't have any idea that Kepler was *returning* the painting. Did you?"

"I couldn't really comment on that."

Hunter worked at keeping her composure. "You told me that you thought Kepler was selling it to a Middle East terrorist."

"Not a terrorist."

"A terrorist sympathizer."

"Yeah, slight difference." Hunter exhaled. He was right, although that wasn't the issue. "The bottom line, Amy? Is we got it back, okay? My job is heading up the Stolen Art Division. And we just brought in one of the art world's great masterpieces. The art's home, it's a happy occasion. We won. Okay? What are you griping about?" There was an edge to how he said the word *griping*.

"You didn't get the guy you wanted."

"No," he said. "But we will."

"I'm told you wanted to get the government to fund this operation," she said, "to set up a straw man as the buyer. That's how you did it the last time, right?"

Randall chuckled uneasily. "*Amy*," he said, scolding her.

She decided not to press him on that. It wasn't something he would talk about, anyway. Instead, she told him, "I think I understand about Belasco now. About your reluctance to pursue him. He told me all about it."

"Who did?"

"Kepler. He told me about your screenplay."

"Oh?"

"I didn't realize how well you knew Walter Kepler. The two of you were college pals at one time."

"Not pals," he said. "Acquaintances. That was thirty-five years ago, Amy. I told you that. Hey, I gotta go. Take it easy, okay? Talk with you later."

Hunter held the phone out and took a deep breath, then put it back to her ear. He was gone. "Yes, very nice talking with you," she said. She set the phone in its cradle and then went outside, where she took a walk around the perimeter of the parking lot; the slow warm breeze through the pinewoods made her feel better.

We won: Is that what Scott Randall really thought? Hunter didn't think so. It would be a while before this story was told properly, but she was pretty sure Scott Randall wouldn't be the one telling it. If the winners write the history, as they say, it was possible that Kepler had already written this one. He was probably doing a secret victory dance right now, wherever he was, watching this play out across the media. Maybe it was like being in the spy business for him, where recognition came away from public view, the satisfactions cultivated privately or not at all. Maybe winning wasn't about other people, anyway; maybe it was just about getting the art back.

Rather than return to her office, Hunter drove over to the church to see Pastor Luke. Aggie made her wait in the lobby first, while Luke finished a call. She sat and watched Aggie type at her computer for several minutes, her posture impossibly erect, her eyes moving maddeningly back and forth across the screen. Hunter wondered what she was typing.

Finally, without saying anything, Hunter stood and walked into Luke's office.

He looked up from his desk. His blue eyes seemed to smile. He hadn't been on a call, he'd been watching cable news on his computer: an art historian talking about Rembrandt; it was one of the clips the network kept repeating.

"Hi," she said. "Just wanted to stop by and say hello."

"Come on in." They gave each other a hug. Luke felt like an

anchor again. Sometimes, Hunter felt closer to her life's purpose, even if she didn't know what it was, when she was around him; this was one of those times.

"Sorry I didn't call back earlier," she said, having a seat. "Hectic day."

"I can imagine. I'm glad you're okay."

"Still sorting through last night," she said. "I didn't expect to wake to this."

On Luke's desk, she saw, was a color printout of Rembrandt's painting *The Storm on the Sea of Galilee.*

"Sermon topic," he explained. "Not this Sunday, but next, once the painting has gone back on public view."

"Appropriate."

"Yes," Luke said. There was a sadness in his eyes, she thought. She wondered if he'd been thinking much about Susan Champlain today.

"What do *you* think?" she said, nodding at the news coverage.

"About that? I keep wondering when, or *if*, the real story will come out."

"*If* is what I'm wondering."

"Won't people want to know that: where the painting's been, how it came back?"

"They will," she said. "I just have a feeling there'll be a lot of stories told about it. The truth may be among them, but it might get lost in the mix. Maybe by design. Particularly since the government may have played a role in this." She added, "It's fertile ground for conspiracy theories."

"But won't the media want to go after the so-called real story?"

"I don't know," Hunter said. "They don't do that so much anymore. Do they?"

Luke shrugged.

"Or, they might see it as a carefully crafted publicity stunt and not want to get involved."

Hunter glanced at her watch, then out the window. It was twenty-five minutes before the "end of day" in Philadelphia.

"I think you were right about *Half Past Three*," she said. "I think Kepler *was* planning to meet Elena Fiorille this afternoon. Before the end of the day."

"In Philadelphia."

"Yeah. It's possible he may still try to keep his appointment."

"You think?"

"No," she said. "Not anymore." Hank Moore *had* managed to withhold Elena Fiorille's name from the news today, as she had requested. So it was possible, but not likely, that Walter Kepler thought she was still alive; that he would show up at the Philadelphia Museum of Art as they'd planned, expecting to rendezvous with her. The Pennsylvania State Police had sent an undercover man in with a description to watch for him. To be ready to detain Walter Kepler for questioning about Elena Fiorille, if he happened to walk into Gallery 172 on the first floor of the museum. The home of Chagall's painting *Half Past Three*.

But it didn't happen. She waited with Luke until well after the "end of day" and there was no phone call. She told him at length about what had happened the night before as they waited; about Elena Fiorille and Walter Kepler and the peculiar partnership they must have forged over the past several years. Then Hunter got up to go home and feed Winston, feeling better than she had all day.

She was driving along the harbor when her phone finally did ring. It wasn't Moore, with news about Kepler. It was *Unknown Caller*. She pulled over and took it anyway, sensing who it might be.

"Hunter," she said.

She heard the splintery breathing, in and out, several times.

"*Huun*-ter," he said, sounding like a character from a horror movie.

"Sheriff?"

The breathing stopped.

Hunter waited. Then she said, "Tuck in your shirt!"

It was the sheriff who hung up first.

GIVEN THE OPPORTUNITY to prove himself, Gerry Tanner could become a force of nature. He filed his report on Scott Randall four days later, on Monday morning, setting the stage for Dave Crowe and Helen Bradbury to go to the Justice Department. The report was addressed to Henry Moore and State Police commander Justin Hamilton, although he'd left a copy on Hunter's desk.

Tanner had learned of several alleged building code violations at a property in central Virginia owned by an 87-year-old woman named Beverly Peters. For more than a year, Peters had been in an assisted living facility fifty miles away, suffering from Alzheimer's disease. It was her son, Scotty, who'd occasionally stayed at the house, often arriving late at night, neighbors said.

Peters's house sat on a large, sloping property with several stands of beech and maple trees providing privacy. But the neighbors saw things; at least two of them harbored suspicions about "the son," as they called him. One, an elderly woman named Betsy Stiles, said she thought that Scotty might be "trafficking in stolen property"; she also expressed concerns over the "unauthorized alterations" he'd made to the basement and back of the house. She pointed Tanner to an adjoining landowner, Mrs. Wilson, who claimed she'd seen "the son" several times "unloading merchandise after dark from a truck." Her guess was that he was a drug dealer, although it might've been anything. "He could be transporting bodies for all I know."

Crowe and Bradbury came into the Public Safety Complex the next day to visit Hunter, Bradbury wearing the same muumuu-style dress she'd worn when Hunter had called on her at the old house near Easton.

"Calvin Walters enjoyed meeting you," she said. "He said you're working on Eddie Charles now?"

"We're talking about it," she said.

Crowe explained that they were talking with a local Virginia prosecutor, gathering evidence to justify a probable-cause entry to the Peters's home. They wanted Hunter to bolster their case by providing a statement about what Kepler had told her.

Hunter shook her head, declining for several reasons. She didn't particularly want to get involved in a stolen art case or, more to the point, a Dave Crowe investigation. Her parameters were homicide, and Tidewater County. But, more important, she didn't think her testimony would be necessary. She also didn't believe it was a good idea bringing Walter Kepler into the mix, when the outcome seemed assured without him. What Randall had done didn't involve Kepler—at least not in ways that were visible.

"I can leave an anonymous tip," Hunter offered, seeing the frustration that was furrowing Crowe's forehead. "Anyone can do that, right?"

She shifted her gaze to Helen Bradbury, who secretly smiled her agreement.

"Or any two," Bradbury said.

"Or three," Hunter added.

IT WENT QUICKLY from there. Four days later, the story had become national news, although nothing on the order of the Rembrandt story, which was still playing out daily in anticipation of the painting's public unveiling on Sunday.

Local police, working with federal investigators, had executed a search warrant and raided Beverly Peters's home in central Virginia the day before. In a fortified, temperature- and humidity-controlled basement room, they discovered eight stolen paintings, hung on the walls of a private art gallery. Included were lost paintings by Pablo Picasso and Lucien Freud, along with works by five lesser-known artists. The value of the stolen art was given as in the "tens of millions" of dollars, according to news accounts (none of which gave attribution for the figure).

Less than five minutes after the raid, Justice Department agents showed up at Scott Randall's office on Fourth Street in Northwest D.C., to question and then arrest him.

Crowe called Hunter at work to give her the news on Friday, his voice hopped up as if he had instigated the whole thing. This was one "hidey-hole," he told her; he suspected there was another, probably larger one, out West, at his retirement property in Wyoming.

"I'm glad you figured all this out," Hunter said.

"I am, too."

Crowe was acting officious again, and a little smug. He offered to tell her the whole thing over dinner on Saturday. Hunter turned him down, wanting to focus on her own case. She *wasn't* just working for the victims now, she was also working for the victims' families: in this instance, the brother, sister, and parents of Susan Champlain and the daughter of Eddie Charles. They would keep her busy for a while.

"There were some interesting papers, too, in a desk," Crowe told her, when she thought the call was ending. "Including an old screenplay."

Hunter felt her pulse tick up. "Screenplay? What do you mean? Something *he* wrote?"

"Evidently, yeah."

"Huh."

"It's called *The Tempest*."

"Huh," Hunter said again. "I'd like to have a look at some point."

"I could probably slip you a copy."

"Okay—who knows, there might be some clues there," she said.

"To your case or to ours?"

She could see him smiling at her, sitting in his office on Fourth Street downtown, while Hunter watched the sun going down in the Chesapeake Bay.

"Either one."

"I'll slip you a copy," he said, "once it's been processed."

"Please."

The night of Scott Randall's arrest, Amy Hunter went out on a long run to Widow's Point, pushing herself up the winding incline to the bluff. Coming back, she ran three wind sprints on the open stretch of blacktop beside the harbor and then cooled down in twilight along the marina road, sweating pleasantly, watching the restaurant lights on the water, the stars brightening above the farmland. She was looking forward to going home and fixing dinner, spending the night with Winston.

She stopped in the shadows past the Johnson Seafood company, hearing the familiar sound of wind high in the trees, sweeping very slowly back and forth in waves; the sound that she associated now with this summer: with Susan Champlain's death and with Elena Rodgers's deceptions. With the evil that had seemed to quietly infiltrate Tidewater County, a sound that had come to feel like the ghosts of her own past, breathing in the night. She listened now and didn't hear any of that, though. It was just wind again, rustling the leaves on a late-summer evening.

Chapter Forty

Sunday

Rembrandt's *The Storm on the Sea of Galilee* was projected on side screens in the old sanctuary at Tidewater Methodist Church. The air was dusty and the wooden church creaked eccentrically with strong winds from over the Bay.

In Boston, Luke told the congregation, Rembrandt's *The Storm on the Sea of Galilee* was going back on public display this afternoon for six weeks before it was removed for a year of conservation. People had begun lining up overnight to get in, according to the news reports.

Luke wasn't going to talk about the painting this morning, though; he was going to talk about its subject and its message.

"The sea of Galilee," he said, "as many of you know, is actually a freshwater lake, the largest lake in Israel and one of the most beautiful you'll find anywhere. Charlotte and I had the privilege of visiting there a couple years ago. It lies about seven hundred feet below sea level, making it the lowest freshwater lake on earth. On its eastern side . . ." Hunter smiled, knowing that people seemed to like his sermons best when he threw in some facts and figures like this. ". . . are the mountains of the Golan Heights, which drop sharply down to the lake. This disparity in height between the mountains and the lake surface causes temperature and pressure changes that often result in violent storms, like the one shown here." Luke paused and briefly scanned the congregation, seeming to raise his eyebrows to acknowledge Hunter, who was seated in a back row.

"The storm shown here is not a historical event, though, it's a Biblical parable, told in Mark 4 and in Matthew 8. It's a parable about faith and fear—about how we can sometimes still the storms in our lives through our faith.

"There are fourteen men in the boat, and you can see that each is responding to the situation a little differently. Some are panicking." He used a laser pointer to encircle four of the figures in the center of the boat. "This one here seems to be sick over the back of the boat. Some are panicking in a practical way—this man at the front is trying to fix the mainsail even as the waves crash over the bow of the ship.

"But in the back of the boat, where Jesus is seated, there is a great calm. In the parable, in fact, Jesus is described as sleeping through the storm. And his disciples, fearing for their lives, wake him up. Jesus stands and rebukes the wind. He says to the waves 'Quiet! Be still!' And the wind dies down and the lake becomes calm. But then he says to his disciples, 'Why are you so afraid? Do you still have no faith?'"

Luke again scanned the congregation, his eyes stopping for a moment on the fourth pew, where Susan Champlain had often sat on Sundays—or perhaps Hunter was imagining that.

"The parable is telling us that we need to have faith, even when there are great storms in our lives. It's telling us that there are many things we can't control and many things we aren't supposed to understand. But with faith, we can make ourselves ready for whatever comes. We can recognize what is expected of us and what we need to do. We can't control the storms that come into our lives. But we can control how we respond to them."

Hunter waited after the service to talk with Luke. She took a place at the very end of the line, enjoying the feeling of camaraderie that filled this venerable old building as the congregants inched forward to shake Luke Bowers's hand. Hunter didn't often come to church, but she felt uplifted nearly every time she did.

She wanted to tell Luke that she'd enjoyed his sermon. But also to pass on to him what Henry Moore had told her the night before—that the medical examiner's autopsy report, coming on Tuesday, would show that the DNA found under Susan Champlain's fingernails did in fact belong to Elena Fiorille. The report would also confirm that the foot impressions found on the beach matched Fiorille's.

Evidencewise, it was an open-shut case now: Elena Fiorille had struggled with Susan Champlain on the bluff and pushed her over. Her necklace had fallen to the sand and she'd gone down to look for it, not successfully. But there was a complicating factor: Nicholas Champlain still hadn't been found. His daughter Carlotta had given several tearful interviews with the Philadelphia media, pleading for anyone with information on his whereabouts to come forward. The fact that Champlain's wife had died days before his own disappearance had cast a small spotlight on Tidewater County. But it wouldn't last, Hunter suspected. Police were already associating Nick Champlain's disappearance with Philadelphia organized crime; with figures like Vincent Rosa, John Luigi, and Dante and Anthony Patello.

Hunter saw peace and patience in Luke's face as he greeted and listened to each of the congregants, his head bowed slightly. She recognized in that look something she yearned for in her own life; something like the calm depicted in that painting, on the back of the boat.

When it was Hunter's turn, Charlotte Bowers suddenly came up behind them and linked her arm with Luke's. She stood there while they talked as if she were the chaperone, pulling her husband closer to her at one point. It was strange: They'd been acting a little different lately, Hunter had noticed, as if something was going on in their personal life. Maybe they were having problems at home.

"So you'll be able to close the case, then, once this autopsy comes through," Charlotte said.

"It looks like."

"And Kepler?" Luke said. "He gets away?"

Hunter shrugged. "That we don't know."

Charlotte glanced at Luke, then at Hunter. "Somehow, I don't think the story's over yet," she said.

"No, I'm sure it isn't," Hunter said.

She looked out at the Bay, the three of them standing side by side, Luke in the middle.

"What story ever is?" he asked.

Epilogue

Walter Kepler was five or six years old when he first became aware of the effects that great art could have on other people. He would study the expressions of strangers in museums, standing entranced before the world's masterpieces, and wonder: What were they seeing, exactly? What were they thinking, and feeling? What hold did these mysterious old paintings have over them? There was no way of knowing, of course, because those moments were impenetrable, as utterly private as prayer, it had seemed. Even now, there were times when Kepler found himself more interested in the looks on people's faces than in the paintings they were viewing—although what really intrigued him weren't their outward appearances so much as what was going on inside, what he *couldn't* see.

It had been the incongruities in Elena Fiorille's face—serene from one angle, remote from another, and that sly sullen curve of the mouth pulling it all together—that had drawn him to her that first day. She'd been admiring Chagall's tumultuous *Half Past Three*, on the first floor at the Philadelphia Museum of Art, a painting Kepler knew well although he had never seen anyone study it at such length, or with such apparent reverence. And so, he'd followed her out of the galleries into the hallway and struck up a conversation.

The terms of the miracle had been born then, in the first weeks of their relationship, when they would talk for hours into the night, telling each other stories about themselves, some probably true, inventing realities and then setting them free, as a painter does a painting. Eventually, Elena had become his loyal partner, with all the strangeness that would entail, and their story had become a love story, more for her than for him; she had even come to accept his pet name for her, "Belasco," odd as it was. It was Elena who had led him to Champlain, and Champlain to the Rembrandt.

Now, Elena was gone. Kepler had found out about it through Weber the morning after it happened. He had mixed feelings about that, including a heavy burden of guilt, a feeling he'd have to work through for a while. He'd known all along that Elena was a troubled soul, though, and a sociopath; and he'd known that he could not long afford those things in his life.

He was at a different museum today, the Musee Marc Chagall, on Avenue Docteur Menard, several kilometers from his apartment, waiting in the café for Jacob Weber again. It was an apt meeting spot, this small but grand museum built around the Biblical paintings of the artist who'd been responsible, in a sense, for their miracle. Now Elena was gone, and it was becoming easier for Kepler to separate the imagined from the remembered. And the real.

On Sunday, Rembrandt's *Storm* was back on display to the public, and people had lined up around the block to get in, just as he'd imagined. It would be shown for six weeks and then be taken away for a year of conservation and heightened security measures. No one would ever steal it again.

"People like this story," Jacob Weber told him, settling with his coffee.

"So I gather," Kepler said.

Weber looked especially small today, Kepler observed, dressed in an oversized striped boy's sweater. It was the first time he had seen Weber since Pennsylvania, when they'd stood together in the barn for their private audience with Rembrandt.

He had brought with him the American newspapers and magazines, to show Kepler how the event was being covered, as if he hadn't been following online.

There, on the cover of *Time*: MIRACLE IN BOSTON

On *USA Today*: THE REMBRANDT 'MIRACLE'

Even front-page stories in the *New York Times* and the *Washington Post* had picked up the word *miracle*.

"So far, the angels are with us, aren't they?"

Jacob Weber didn't know how to answer, so he didn't.

"But what are the serious people saying?" Kepler asked.

"The serious people," Weber repeated. "Some are calling it a publicity stunt."

Of course. "And is the museum feeling any pressure to push back on that? To explain?"

"No, none. Per the agreement." Weber's face showed a rare flicker of amusement. "We're going to be fine, I think."

Kepler nodded. Yes, the world was awakening to Rembrandt and to *The Storm*, this magnificent painting that otherwise would have been lost to obscurity. Now, it had a mystique to go with its greatness. People were seeing it in ways they never would have if it hadn't been stolen. The painting had layers of meaning now that even Rembrandt couldn't have imagined.

"And what will our liability be? Will they try to make a case against me?"

"I don't think so. Scott Randall's been arrested, you know."

Kepler tried not to smile. "Yes, I saw that. He'll attempt to make a deal, of course."

"He's going to have a credibility problem, though," Weber said. "He's taken advantage of the federal government for years. They're not going to trust him now."

"No. Will the media tie him to our miracle?"

"They may," Weber said.

"Which might just add another level to the mystery."

"Yes."

The two men drank their coffees, eyes lowered. Kepler changed the subject: "But they will blame Elena."

"The local police will, yes. Her DNA came back on the woman, Susan Champlain. I'm afraid that's inevitable now."

Weber had predicted this would happen. More than just predicted: he'd *wanted* this to happen. In a way, it *was* cleaner. A case against a dead person was no case at all. Still, Kepler felt a yearning whenever he thought of Elena, remembering how they had met at the museum in Philadelphia and talked so easily for hours at a time, at her home and at his. The remembrances conjured up a version of himself that Kepler didn't like—a man who couldn't return the love Elena had for him, whose own greatest love affairs had always been with paintings.

Weber went over his financial accounts, then, as Kepler had

requested. And, in the way that a doctor shares the result of a patient's annual physical, Weber gave him a clean bill of health.

He was in good shape—legally, financially, and imaginatively.

But Kepler felt lonely when Weber walked away. It would be a while, he suspected, before he would see him again. Kepler would stay at his apartment in France for several months, until things settled down with Scott Randall. That hadn't been the plan. The plan had been to spend time with Belasco, visiting the great art museums of the world.

But it probably *was* better this way. The plan now was to wait, and then to visit the great museums by himself. Eventually, he would find another Belasco. That would take some time. And some looking. But Walter Kepler didn't mind. He was hopeful. It was something to live for.

Author's Note and Acknowledgments

The events and people in this book are fictitious (with the exception of those that aren't). The Stolen Art Division of the FBI does not actually exist, although it may bear some passing resemblance to the Art Crime Team, which does. The FBI's Art Crime Team, founded in 2004, has to date recovered more than 11,500 works of stolen art (but not, yet, the Gardner art).

Much has been written about the Isabella Stewart Gardner Museum theft of 1990. Some of those articles and books served as valuable reference materials during the writing of this book, in particular Stephen Kurkjian's investigative reporting for the *Boston Globe* (his book on the subject, *Master Thieves: The Boston Gangsters Who Pulled Off the World's Biggest Art Heist*, was due out as this novel was going to press). Books on stolen art and the Gardner theft that were particularly helpful included *Stealing Rembrandts: The Untold Stories of Notorious Art Heists* by Anthony M. Amore and Tom Mashberg (Palgrave Macmillan, 2011), *Priceless: How I Went Undercover To Recover the World's Stolen Treasures* by Robert K. Wittman with John Shiffman (Crown, 2010), and

The Gardner Heist: The True Story of the World's Largest Unsolved Art Theft by Ulrich Boser (Smithsonian, 2009).

Many books and online sources provided information and insights about Rembrandt's remarkable life and career, among them *Rembrandt's Eyes* by Simon Schama (Knopf, 1999), *Rembrandt: The Painter at Work* by Ernst van de Wetering (University of California Press, Revised Edition, 2009), *The Rembrandt Book* by Gary Schwartz (Harry N. Abrams, 2006), and *Rembrandt and the Face of Jesus* (Yale University Press, 2011).

A special thank you to my agent, Laura Gross. And thanks to Emily Krump, for her editorial guidance on *The Tempest* and *The Psalmist*, and the staff at Witness, who, among other things, came up with two great covers. Thanks also to Elizabeth Reluga, collections administrator at the Isabella Stewart Gardner Museum, and Joseph Gamble, retired commander of the Homicide Unit of the Maryland State Police. And finally, I thank J, T & C for staying calm through the storms.